MW01139013

The Planter's Daughter

by

Michelle Shocklee

SMITTEN
HISTORICAL ROMANCE
LIGHTHOUSE PUBLISHING OF THE CAROLINAS

THE PLANTER'S DAUGHTER BY MICHELLE SHOCKLEE
Published by Smitten Historical Romance
an imprint of Lighthouse Publishing of the Carolinas
2333 Barton Oaks Dr., Raleigh, NC, 27614

ISBN: 978-1-946016-09-6
Copyright © 2017 by Michelle Shocklee
Cover design by Elaina Lee
Interior design by Karthick Srinivasan

Available in print from your local bookstore, online, or from the publisher at:
lpcbooks.com

For more information on this book and the author, visit: www.MichelleShocklee.com

All rights reserved. Noncommercial interests may reproduce portions of this
book without the express written permission of Lighthouse Publishing of the
Carolinas, provided the text does not exceed 500 words. When reproducing text
from this book, include the following credit line: "*The Planter's Daughter* by
Michelle Shocklee published by Lighthouse Publishing of the Carolinas. Used by
permission."

Commercial interests: No part of this publication may be reproduced in any form,
stored in a retrieval system, or transmitted in any form by any means—electronic,
photocopy, recording, or otherwise—without prior written permission of the
publisher, except as provided by the United States of America copyright law.

This is a work of fiction. Names, characters, and incidents are all products of the
author's imagination or are used for fictional purposes. Any mentioned brand names,
places, and trademarks remain the property of their respective owners, bear no
association with the author or the publisher, and are used for fictional purposes only.

All scripture quotations, unless otherwise indicated, are taken from the King James
Version (KJV).

Brought to you by the creative team at Lighthouse Publishing of the Carolinas:
Eddie Jones, Kathryn Davis, Shonda Savage, Payton Lechner, Brian Cross,
Lucie Winborne

Library of Congress Cataloging-in-Publication Data
Shocklee, Michelle
The Planter's Daughter / Michelle Shocklee 1st ed.

Printed in the United States of America

PRAISE FOR *THE PLANTER'S DAUGHTER*

Shocklee's novel carried me to a past time and a unique culture, and held me captive. Its realistic setting, believable characters, and gripping storyline—told honestly yet never wallowing in ugliness—came together in a beautiful tale about following one's conscience regardless of the cost. Kudos to Michelle on a lovely, heart-stirring debut.

~ **Kim Vogel Sawyer, Award-winning Author**
My Heart Remembers

Set on an antebellum Texas plantation, *The Planter's Daughter* is an inspiring story of love and courage. Readers will revel in the historical detail as they follow Seth and Adella Rose on an eventful journey toward their own happily ever after.

~ **Dorothy Love, Author**
Mrs. Lee and Mrs. Gray

The Planter's Daughter captivated me from chapter one. I didn't just read this story, the author put me in the middle of the setting and I watched the story unfold around me. Michelle Shocklee has done a masterful job of allowing her three-dimensional characters to perform the story on a sensory-rich stage. One of the best books I've read this year. BRAVO!

~ **Connie Stevens, Author**
Brides of Georgia and Hope's Dwelling Place

"*The Planter's Daughter* will move you. The romance is there, and it's wonderful, but Michelle Shocklee's debut novel is so much more than a romance. It's a real and redemptive look at slavery on a Texas plantation. Brave and honest, sweet and true, this pre-Civil War love story will stir your heart and your conscience. Above all, you will find yourself rooting for freedom, not just for the slaves of Rose Hill, but for Adella and Seth, two people struggling to escape their own bonds of enslavement and accept love and redemption from each other and their heavenly Father."

~ **Paula Scott, Author**
Until the Day Breaks

Dedication

To my beloved Brian.
Forever and ever. Amen.

Go down Moses
Way down in Egypt land.
Tell ole Pharaoh
To let my people go.
When Israel was in Egypt land.
Let my people go.
Oppressed so hard they could not stand.
Let my people go.
"Thus spoke the Lord," bold Moses said.
"If not, I'll smite your first born dead."
Let my people go.
No more in bondage shall they toil.
Let my people go.
Let them come out with Egypt's spoil.
Let my people go.
~Slave Song, 1800s

CHAPTER ONE

Williamson County, Texas
May 1859

Adella cringed at the sound of shattering glass. *What now?*

Exasperation pushed her taut nerves to the edge. Two vases and a china teacup had already met their demise as house servants feverishly prepared for Natalie Langford's arrival on the morrow. That her brother's fiancée sparked such anxiety did not bode well, considering the wedding was still two weeks away. Would things only worsen after the blonde beauty became mistress of Rose Hill Manor—a role Adella herself had filled since Mama took ill three summers ago?

A small shadow appeared in the open doorway to her bedroom. Adella Rose Ellis waited from her perch on the window seat, her bare feet tucked beneath a wide bell skirt, for the guilty servant to emerge. A warm afternoon breeze teased her loose hair. A moment later, Carolina's fuzzy braids poked around, followed by wide, fearful eyes.

"Missy Ellis?" The little girl's timid voice squeaked. Perspiration glistened on her dark skin, and her bottom lip trembled when she stepped around the corner. "I sorry, Missy. I didn't mean to break it. It just tumbled outta my hand." A tear slid down an ebony cheek before she tucked her chin into the too-large homespun dress, which hung off of thin shoulders.

"Come in, Carolina." Adella softened her voice the way Mama always had when dealing with the servants. "Tell me what happened."

Carolina moved into the room, head down. A shuddering breath shook her small frame. "Aunt Lu sent me to fetch the lamp from Miss Natalie's bedroom so's she could fill it with kerosene." Eyes shiny with tears peered up at Adella. "I real careful to hold it with both hands like she tol' me, but"—her voice quivered—"my toe done caught the carpet in the hall."

Adella closed her eyes. She knew which lamp Carolina meant. It had been a favorite of Mama's made of white glass, with painted roses on its chimney. At Papa's request, Adella had begrudgingly placed it in Natalie's room, just down the hall from her own. Although everything in the house would ultimately belong to Natalie after she and George married, Adella harbored a strong desire to protect the things Mama once treasured.

But she couldn't be angry with Carolina—not when the girl should have been playing with cornhusk dolls instead of working twelve-hour days in the big house, as the slaves called the manor.

"It was an accident." Adella offered a sympathetic smile, hoping to ease the girl's worry. Mr. Haley, their former overseer, had whipped slaves for lesser offenses, so Carolina's fear was not unfounded. Mercifully, that horrid man was no longer an issue. He'd passed in his sleep a fortnight ago, and Papa wouldn't hire a replacement until he returned from purchasing new field workers in Galveston. "Help Aunt Lu clean up the mess, and we will keep this to ourselves."

Carolina's brow shot up. "You ain't gonna tell Massa Ellis?"

"There is no need to tell Papa. He is in charge of the plantation, but I am in charge of the house." *At least for two more weeks.* "Go on, now. Tell Aunt Lu we need another lamp for Miss Natalie's room—and be very careful if she asks you to carry it upstairs."

"Yes'm, Missy." Carolina disappeared down the hall, but not before she glanced back to Adella with a look of pure relief on her round face.

With a cat-like stretch, Adella unfolded her legs and wiggled her toes, which were blessedly free of the pinching slippers that matched her pale blue gown. Even at twenty years of age, she still preferred to go shoeless, much to Aunt Lu's dismay. The head house servant scolded and grumbled whenever she caught Adella barefoot. *"Young women soon ta be betrothed don't gallivant 'round without shoes."*

Moving to her dressing table, Adella ran a brush sprinkled with fragrant rose water through her hair. The headache that drove her to her room had thankfully abated, but the thought of bundling her thick, dark tresses back into the velvet hairnet with a much-too-tight silk headband did not appeal. Perhaps she would have Hulda simply tie it with a ribbon since Papa was not due back from Galveston until noon tomorrow, and it would only be George and herself at supper.

Thinking of George naturally led back to thoughts of Natalie and her impending visit. As a wedding gift, Papa gave Natalie permission to redecorate the parlor as well as order new furnishings for the suite of rooms she and George would occupy. Adella was to help with the undertaking. Natalie had declared it their first sisterly endeavor, but Adella found it far more difficult than anyone knew. Watching Mama's house being prepared for another woman served as a stark reminder that her beloved mother was gone forever. Taken from earth a little more than a year past, the loneliness still felt fresh and raw in Adella's heart. Yet Papa and George carried on as though the void Mama left was easily filled with plantation busyness and wedding plans.

Not so for Adella. She studied her blue gown in the reflection of the mirror, noting the delicate lace on the collar and cloth-covered buttons running down the bodice, and was reminded of the plain black gowns wrapped in paper and folded neatly away in a trunk in the attic. Her year of mourning had come to an end in March, but she would have continued wearing black if Papa had not protested. It was no secret he hoped to secure a marriage proposal for her soon. She was long past the age when most girls married, but her priority the last few years had been seeing to

Mama's needs. Suitors that dared seek courtship were turned away, much to Papa's consternation. Now, with Mama gone and Adella's time of grieving over, Papa had wasted no time announcing his plans for her to marry within the year.

Finished with her toilette, she padded across thick, warm carpet to the canopy-covered bed. The boards holding the goose-down mattress protested when she sat on the edge, drowning out her own discouraged sigh. If only Papa would listen when she tried to discuss her future. While marrying one day did interest her, her real desire was to stay on as Rose Hill's mistress. It didn't seem quite fair that George should inherit the plantation when he stood to gain the Langford property as well. As an only child, Natalie was heir to the large cotton plantation that bordered Rose Hill. Surely she and George could just as easily live with the Langfords and leave the Ellis manor in Adella's care. Perhaps she should broach her idea with George at supper tonight and—

A disturbance in the yard interrupted her plotting. Excited voices drifted upward, and by the time she peeked out her window, a number of slaves had gathered below. They faced south, toward the long, poplar-lined drive that led to the main house. Vast cotton fields stretched on either side, reminding her of an emerald ocean, with gentle waves carrying knee-high plants down one rolling hill, only to reappear on the next rise. Moving shapes speckled the neat rows, where dozens of workers took hoes to ever-present weeds or inspected plants for worms and other crawling things that could devastate a crop in a matter of days.

"They's comin'! They's here!" Aunt Lu's rich voice echoed from the foyer. The plump woman appeared in the bedroom doorway a few moments later, out of breath from her sprint up the stairs. "Missy Ellis, your pappy done come home a day early!"

With a gasp, Adella turned again to the scene outside. Two riders and a wagon emerged from the shadows of the trees and headed toward the house. Indeed, she recognized Papa's white gelding as he nudged his mount on ahead of the others. She couldn't make out the second rider, who was still some distance away, though he sat taller in the saddle than her father. Old Joseph drove the plantation wagon, which had departed empty the week before but was now crowded with a number of dark-skinned men and at least one woman.

"It *is* Papa. What a happy surprise!" She hurried across the room and into the hall.

Aunt Lu harrumphed. "Missy, your hair be undone."

"Papa won't mind," Adella said over her shoulder as she practically flew down the stairs, the hem of her full skirt held high so as not to trip her in her haste. "I'll miss welcoming him home if I wait for you to put it up."

Bare feet slapped against the cool marble floor of the foyer as Adella swept through the airy space to the open front door. The travelers were just dismounting when she reached the porch.

"Papa! We didn't expect you home until tomorrow."

Papa glanced up after handing the reins to one of the servants. "Adella Rose, you are a sight for these tired eyes of mine." With a groan, he lumbered forward as Adella descended the dozen whitewashed steps to the ground. "I am too old for these long journeys anymore."

Adella stood on tiptoe to kiss Papa's cheek, her lips grazing his whiskered jaw before she slid her arm into the crook of his elbow. "You should have sent word of your arrival. I fear the house is in an upheaval preparing for Natalie's visit."

"Stop your fretting, daughter." Papa patted her arm as they mounted the steps. "A bath and my own bed are my only concerns. I could not bear another night on one of those flea-infested straw ticks innkeepers call mattresses. We were up before the sun so we would make home today." Gaining the shade of the porch, Papa's gaze skimmed over the servants who'd lined up to welcome him home. "Where is George?"

Aunt Lu, who had arrived on the porch a bit breathless, possessed the uncanny ability of knowing everyone's whereabouts on the plantation. But she stared straight ahead as though she hadn't heard Papa's question.

"I haven't seen him since the noon meal," Adella said, just now noticing her brother's absence.

"Never mind." Impatience brought a frown to his face. "Brantley, come meet my daughter. Then you can see to the stock."

Adella had been so surprised by Papa's unexpected return that she had completely forgotten the other man. She now noted that he walked with a distinct limp, favoring his left leg. Perhaps he was saddle-weary, like Papa, but her instincts told her the limp frequently plagued him. Though his face remained shadowed by the brim of his dusty hat, she noted his physique was that of a strong, youthful man, quite in contrast to his hitching gait.

"Adella Rose, this is Seth Brantley, son of my good friend Daniel Brantley."

At Papa's introduction, the stranger mounted the porch and lifted his face. Removing his hat revealed dark hair plastered against his head, and he gave a polite nod. "Miss Ellis, it is a pleasure to make your acquaintance … again."

She gaped at the stranger. Ruggedly handsome, with hazel eyes and generous lips that twitched with humor, Adella was certain she'd never seen the man before.

"Mr. Brantley." Her back stiffened at his improper insinuation. "I do not believe we have had the pleasure of meeting prior to today."

"No need for a fuss, my dear," Papa said. "He is referring to when you met as children. When was that, Brantley? Eighteen forty-two? Forty-three?"

"I believe it was forty-two, sir. I was eleven years old." An easy smile lifted the corner of his mouth. "Pa was called to Austin, even though he was no longer a congressman. Wasn't that when Sam Houston feared a Mexican invasion and had the government documents moved from the capitol?"

Papa laughed. "Ol' Sam wanted to move them all right, but

the folks down in Austin wouldn't have it. They worried he would declare Houston the capitol if the archives reached that city, so they put up a resistance and eventually won. I tried to stay out of the whole affair, but your father wanted the Austin folks to know he stood with them."

"I had tagged along to keep him company. We stopped for the night at Rose Hill." Seth turned his smile to Adella, warming her to her bare toes. "So you see, Miss Ellis, we have indeed had the pleasure of meeting prior to today." His eyes boldly roamed her face. "I must say, though, you have certainly changed since that long-ago day."

Rendered speechless, her insides quivered as a sudden thought burst into her consciousness. Had Papa brought Seth Brantley home as a possible suitor? He was dressed more like a cowboy than a gentleman farmer—perhaps he took a more active role in running his plantation than Papa. While the men conversed, a warm flush filled her cheeks at the thought of being courted by the handsome man. Admittedly, she found the idea rather appealing.

"We will keep the new stock in the barn tonight," Papa was saying to Seth, motioning down the hill from the main house toward several large structures. "Monroe can find room for them in the quarter tomorrow."

"Yes, sir." Seth donned his hat, politely nodding to Adella before he made his way back down the steps to confer with Old Joseph.

Confusion swirled through Adella's mind. "Papa." She trailed him as he made his way into the house, the crinoline beneath her full skirt swishing against her legs in her haste. One last look toward the yard revealed Seth mounting his horse to follow the wagon to the barn. "Why is your guest tending to the slaves? Shouldn't we invite him in for refreshments after your long journey?"

Servants who'd gathered to welcome home their master scurried away like mice after the cat awoke from its nap.

"Brantley is not my guest, Adella Rose." Papa chuckled as though her question was the silliest thing he'd heard all day. He handed his wide-brimmed hat to Anderson, his waiting manservant, and then faced Adella.

"Seth Brantley is the new overseer of Rose Hill."

CHAPTER TWO

*O*verseer.

It wasn't a title Seth ever thought he'd wear. It certainly wasn't one he'd sought. He didn't associate with many plantation overseers, who were often known for their cruelty and brutish ways. But when a man has few choices in front of him, Providence may step in and force his hand. At least that's what Pa called it when he met up with his old friend, Luther Ellis, in San Antonio and learned Luther's overseer had died unexpectedly.

With his shoulder propped against the doorpost of his small cottage and his lungs full of fresh morning air, sweetened by a light overnight rain, Seth stifled a yawn. He'd been up long before the mockingbird began its mixed-up melody, mentally preparing for his first day. What exactly it would entail, he wasn't certain. But he knew Luther Ellis expected him to maintain control over the workers from the very beginning. Seth hoped they wouldn't test him since he'd never been an overseer before. He'd rather earn their respect than their fear, yet he couldn't afford for even one slave to believe he didn't hold things firmly in his command.

A frown tugged his brow. Pa owned a dozen slaves to help work the farm, so Seth had some knowledge of how to handle them. But Pa didn't whip his slaves into submission and wouldn't allow Seth's older brother, Stephen, who'd taken over running the farm a few years ago, to beat them either. Luther already let Seth know that Monroe, an enormous black man who served as the plantation driver, took care of the "rough treatment" of the slaves. As overseer, Luther explained, one of Seth's duties was to make certain the driver didn't overstep his authority and injure the stock beyond what could heal.

Stock.

That was another word Seth didn't much care for, at least not when talking about people. Luther referred to all his slaves as stock, as though they were some of the famed Texas Longhorn cattle. The newspapers said northern abolitionists believed the black man was the white man's equal. Until recently, Seth hadn't given it much thought, considering most of his dealings with Negroes took place on his family's farm, where they seemed content. He'd known of landowners who experienced trouble with their slaves, which was why most dealt harsh punishment for even the smallest infraction. But for Seth, people with dark skin had been a benign part of his world.

That is, until the night a black man shot him.

Rubbing his sore thigh, Seth battled threads of all-too-familiar anger that snaked into his thoughts as memories flashed across his mind. He wouldn't be working for Luther Ellis if it wasn't for the runaway slave he'd tracked down to the Mexican border. The look of pity in Captain Clark's eyes when he informed Seth he could no longer serve as a Texas Ranger still ignited a smoldering hatred for the slave months later. It left little room for sympathetic thoughts toward the dead runaway or his kind.

The smell of fried bacon wafted down the hill from the main house. Seth's empty stomach rumbled in answer. Before turning in last night, Luther unexpectedly invited him to join the family at table in the morning, despite Seth's lowly position as overseer. It seemed Pa's longstanding friendship with Luther superseded tradition. Grinning, he had to admit he was looking forward to the meal. Not only would he eat well, but it would give him the opportunity to see the planter's pretty daughter again.

Stepping off the cottage's narrow porch, he ambled up a well-worn path toward the two-story mansion, his leg stiff from too many days in the saddle. The big house sat at the end of a long expanse of lawn, gleaming white in the bright morning sunshine.

Impressive was the only word adequate to describe it. Four grand columns held up the second-floor balcony, while a wide wraparound porch surrounded the lower level. The house was far larger than he remembered from his visit as a boy, with several wings jutting off the sides and back. During the ride from Galveston, Luther boasted of adding land and slaves over the years, too. Clearly, the Ellis plantation was doing well.

Still a bit early for the meal, Seth stopped under the branches of a large oak tree and took in his surroundings with the practiced eye of a Ranger. The modest cottage he now called home sat between the main house and the slave quarter. Anyone coming or going from the quarter had to pass his house—no doubt the location was planned for that very reason. Beyond the two rows of small log cabins were several oversized barns and various outbuildings, including a pigpen and a sizeable hen house. Worn footpaths and roads led here and there, disappearing behind a building or into a clump of trees where he could hear a gurgling creek. The vast cotton fields surrounded the main house and extended far beyond Seth's view. Already groups of slaves made their way to the fields, carrying hoes and lunch buckets, with Monroe leading the way on horseback. After the meal, Seth would follow on his own mount.

He formed a mental list of what he'd need to accomplish in these early days. Learning the lay o' the land was a priority. The slaves held an advantage over him with their familiarity with the extensive plantation. The sheer size of the property meant he would be on his horse much of each day. Becoming acquainted with every inch of dirt, every tree, and every road coming in and out was vital if he had any hope of keeping track of the ninety-seven Negroes Luther Ellis owned. The task seemed more daunting today, after waking up on the plantation, than it had two weeks ago when Pa met Luther in San Antonio where Seth had recuperated after the shooting.

It still puzzled him why Luther offered him the job. Farm work and a few months behind the counter of Uncle Earl's mercantile, after the captain's discouraging visit, was all the experience he possessed beyond the four years he'd spent with the Texas Rangers. Yet Luther told Pa he felt sure Seth could handle any type of trouble that might arise, which, if Seth were honest, produced a measure of confidence he'd lacked since being told he couldn't ranger anymore. *However*, Luther had stated with his unmistakable Virginia accent and a cool look in his piercing blue eyes, he would withhold Seth's wages the first few months, until Seth proved himself.

Footfalls slapped the dirt behind him, drawing his attention. A slave girl of no more than eight or nine years ran in his direction, apparently coming from the house, with braids flapping against her ears. When she saw him in the shade of the tree, she skidded to a stop.

"Mistah Brantley, suh," she squeaked, her dark eyes wide and fearful. "Aunt Lu says breakfast ready shortly."

Before he could reply or even ask her name, the child turned and bolted back up the hill, reminding him of the time he had a rabid coyote on his tail. He couldn't fault the girl for being afraid of the new overseer. The passage of time, he hoped, would teach her and the others they could trust him to be fair. If they tended their business without trouble, he'd have no cause to seek Monroe's whip.

Seth started up the slight incline, recalling the ledgers he'd found in his cabin last night. The name, gender, and age of each slave, along with notations regarding punishments, illnesses, and births, were recorded on lined pages of the thin books. They also contained a column for a purchase date and a column for a sale date. He hoped Mr. Haley, the former overseer, had kept current records. When he had more time, Seth planned to go through the ledgers to learn more about the slaves and the practices at Rose Hill regarding buying and selling.

A baby's hungry wail sounded from the quarter.

A memory surfaced.

He'd never seen a slave auction before the one in Galveston. Screaming children ripped from their mothers' arms. Men and women stripped bare, only to be poked and prodded like animals. The experience would not be easily forgotten. Watching the little girl ahead of him, whose hurried run had turned to skipping the closer she drew to the house, he hoped he wouldn't be asked to attend another auction. Overseeing slaves on the plantation was one thing—taking part in the sale of humans was another entirely.

When he reached the yard in front of the house, Seth glanced up to the front door. Should he use the main entry? His employee status left him uncertain. He'd resolved not to take advantage of the friendship between Luther and his pa. He would do his work as best he could, proving himself to Luther and earning his wages fairly. It might take some time, but he'd slowly add to the meager amount in his bank account. Once he had enough saved—he grinned—he'd head for Oregon, where a man could forget the past and start over.

"Good morning, Mr. Brantley."

The soft voice came from his right. He'd thought himself alone and was surprised to find Adella Rose seated in a wicker chair on the porch. A large potted palm partially hid her from view, and if she hadn't spoken, Seth would have walked right past her.

"Good morning, Miss Ellis. It is a beautiful day." He moved to where he had a clear view of her. Her long, dark curls were properly tamed this morning with combs and pins, instead of flowing loosely down her back as they'd done the day before. A chuckle threatened as he recalled seeing pink toes beneath the hem of her skirt when she'd greeted her father. As becoming as she looked in her pale yellow day gown and neat appearance, he secretly preferred the less genteel woman he'd met the previous day.

"It is a lovely morning, yes. I always enjoy watching the sun rise." A little frown tugged her smooth brow. "However, I hope the afternoon won't be quite as warm as the past few days have been."

Seth nodded at her polite banter and mounted the steps. "We did receive a bit of rain during the night, though. I suppose we must be grateful for that." He planted his booted foot on the top step to relieve the pressure on his injured leg. Doc Harding had given him some tips to keep his leg from aching so, and one was to keep his weight off it when standing. But Doc had also been perfectly blunt in his prognosis of Seth's injury: *"You'll have pain in that leg the rest of your life. Might as well get used to it."* The sage advice was easier said than done.

"Indeed, we are always grateful for any amount of rain, unless it's harvest time. Then Papa rails at the sky if it even hints of rain." She glanced at him, then quickly looked away.

Seth found her shyness charming. "I have been admiring the plantation grounds this morning," he said, hoping to lengthen their conversation. "I'm sure it was enjoyable growing up here."

Her blue eyes found him again. A slight smile touched her pink lips. "It was. I found more mischief to get into than my poor mother ever imagined." At his chuckle, she sighed and looked out on the property. "I do love it here. Those roses"—she indicated the dozens of manicured bushes that surrounded the house, bursting with fragrant, colorful blossoms—"were my mother's pride and joy. She brought the plants all the way from Virginia as a new bride. Papa named the plantation Rose Hill in her honor. I hope to follow in her footsteps and tend to them as well as she did."

A stout female servant appeared in the screened doorway. The bright red kerchief tied around her head contrasted sharply with her dull gray dress. "Missy Ellis, it be time for breakfast." Her dark eyes grazed Seth. "Mistah Brantley, suh."

Adella Rose stood. Seth hurried to meet her at the door. He extended his elbow. "May I?"

Surprise lit her eyes. She looked at his arm, then met his gaze. "Why, thank you, Mr. Brantley. It is refreshing to find our new overseer is also a gentleman."

Satisfaction slanted Seth's grin as he escorted his new employer's beautiful daughter to breakfast. Perhaps this job wouldn't be quite as dismal as he'd imagined.

CHAPTER THREE

"They look like a fine batch of Negroes, Father. I would say you got your money's worth."

George stuffed a large bite of buttered toast into his mouth. He chose to forgo the napkin in his lap and instead used the back of his hand to wipe errant crumbs from his chin. Adella, who was seated across from him, wondered if Natalie knew what an ill-mannered creature her brother was at the table. Despite years of Mama tutoring to the point of nagging, George was almost as bad as a pig at trough when it came to mealtime.

"They may be fine, but I doubt I will ever get my money's worth from them," Papa said, dabbing the corners of his mouth with his linen napkin. Did he hope George would take notice and follow suit? "The markets in Galveston are just as overpriced as New O'leans. The six we brought back are good stock, but we will need several more if we want to plant the new acreage we bought from Dobbs."

Not really hungry, but not wanting to draw her father's attention, Adella took a small bite of fried potato. Her normal morning appetite had disappeared the moment she sat down across from their new overseer, seated to her brother's right. Throughout the meal, while George peppered Seth with questions about his life as a Texas Ranger, her gaze repeatedly drifted to the new man. And more than once she found him studying her with those rich hazel eyes framed by dark lashes.

"Brantley, I want you to take charge of the new stock the next few days. George can show you where to put them to work."

Papa pushed his plate away. Young Carolina stepped from her

place in the corner of the room and quickly removed the dish from the table. The girl made eye contact with Adella, seeking approval. When Adella gave a slight nod, Carolina grinned and disappeared into the hallway leading to the kitchen wing, carefully holding the china plate with both hands. Adella made a mental note to convey her satisfaction in Carolina's training with Aunt Lu, particularly after the lamp fiasco. Aunt Lu, she knew, could be hard on the younger girls, especially if they made mistakes.

Seth Brantley's deep voice drew her attention back to the table conversation. "Pa understands why I couldn't come back to the farm. Stephen has always been more of a farmer than I will ever be. I look forward to meeting the challenges this new job will present."

"Good." Papa nodded. "Monroe will see to the field workers, making sure they get to the fields on time and such. You can make your presence known from time to time throughout the day, but I want the new group put on the south fields, closest to the house. I'd like to see how they perform before we put them out with the others."

With his concentration on Papa, asking questions about the plantation to which both Papa and George answered in turn, Adella took the opportunity to sneak long looks at their new employee. He hadn't shaved this morning, and the same week-old whiskers he'd arrived with yesterday lent him a roguish look. To his credit, his long hair was neatly combed, though he desperately needed a trim. His cotton shirt bore the telltale wrinkles of being stuffed into a pack for many days, but it appeared clean and fairly new.

Seth lifted his coffee cup to his lips, listening intently to something Papa was saying about a wild mustang stallion he'd acquired. Adella watched the movement, remembering the strength she'd felt in his arm when he escorted her to breakfast. For a fleeting moment, she wondered what it would feel like to have his strong arms wrapped around her.

Embarrassed by her own silly thoughts, she quickly looked away, lest he find her staring. She knew little about the man beyond that he was the son of her father's longtime friend. That he'd been a Texas Ranger spoke well of him, yet why wasn't he with his company? This morning, rampant gossip among the servants reached Adella through Hulda as she helped Adella prepare for the day, with the consensus being Mr. Brantley must have done something mighty terrible and could no longer be a Ranger. She'd firmly put the tall tale to rest before breakfast, reminding two housemaids in particular who were known to spread tittle-tattle that it was not permitted.

But one simple fact learned through the years could not be ignored, neither by her nor by the slaves. Overseers—even those with captivating hazel eyes—were of the same breed. And former Texas Ranger or not, an overseer was not the type of man Adella should have been daydreaming about.

"I think you should know," George said around a mouthful of food, pointing the tines of his fork at Seth. "I was not in agreement with Father's decision to hire you, but he convinced me your years as a Ranger would be beneficial to us. I hope you will prove him right."

"I will do my best," Seth said.

George set his fork down on his plate with a loud clatter. When Carolina, who'd quietly returned to her station in the corner of the room, moved to take the plate, he gave her hand a stinging slap. "I am not finished, girl. Can't you see I am still eating?"

Carolina's eyes grew round, and she sprang back. Her chin quivered when she looked to Adella before her gaze sought the floor. A tear slid down her smooth cheek.

Mindful of the new man at the table, Adella couldn't remain quiet. "George, you needn't speak so harshly. Carolina is doing a fine job. She has only worked in the kitchen a few weeks. She will learn." She smiled at the young servant, but Carolina continued to stare at the floor.

George blew out a sigh full of impatience. "The girl won't learn if she's not shown her mistakes. Natalie won't tolerate servants who cannot perform their jobs correctly. We will be entertaining quite a bit after we're married. I won't have my new wife distraught over servants who are incapable of carrying out a simple task."

Adella bit back a tart reply, knowing Papa disliked it when she argued in favor of the slaves. Mama had always shown patience with the house servants, and she taught Adella to do the same. A kind word, she'd said, was a far better teacher than chastisement. Sadly, neither her father nor her brother subscribed to this way of thinking.

"I don't condone brutality toward the slaves as a general rule, Brantley," Papa said, as though reading her thoughts, "but discipline must be fast and firm with the darkies, or they won't learn. We keep a shed behind the quarter you can make use of as you see fit. If the bullwhip is needed, Monroe will handle it." Papa eyed Seth. "Unless, of course, you prefer to administer it yourself."

Adella held her breath, waiting for his response.

The mantel clock ticked off several seconds. "If it is all the same to you, sir," Seth said, seeming to measure his words. "I'm not partial to the bullwhip. Pa believes there are better ways to punish a slave who misbehaves than to ruin him with the whip."

For reasons she couldn't pin down, Adella nearly wilted with relief at his bold answer. But what would Papa think? She sneaked a glance to find his narrowed eyes studying Seth before his lips slowly turned upward in a smirk.

"Daniel and I never did see eye to eye on things," Papa said, chuckling. The tension in the room dissipated with the sound. "We came to Texas together in thirty-five. I was bound and determined to create the largest cotton plantation this side of the Mississippi, but all Daniel wanted was a plot of ground to grow a few acres of corn. He won't listen even now when I tell him he would make far more profit growing cotton."

Seth nodded. "Pa has always said he prefers a simple life. Stephen is anxious to expand the farm, though. He is looking into growing sugar cane."

"He will need to purchase more stock if he goes into cane. The dozen Negroes your Pa keeps won't be sufficient for work in the cane fields," Papa said, rubbing his bare chin where his long side-whiskers ended. "I would be happy to accompany him down to Galveston when he's ready. I am always in the market for a strong specimen or two."

Seth's smile ebbed. "I will be sure to mention that to Stephen."

George pushed his plate away, apparently finished with the meal after all. Carolina sought Adella with terror-filled eyes—she responded with a nod and an encouraging smile. As she watched Carolina execute her task and practically run from the room, she came to a decision. If Natalie didn't show any more kindness to the girl than her brother had just demonstrated, Adella would speak to Papa about taking charge of Carolina. Her own maid, Hulda, was getting on in years. Carolina was a sweet girl and eager to please. Adella would enjoy having her around.

Papa stood. Seth and George followed suit. "We'd best get the day started, gentlemen."

Adella waited for Papa to step behind her chair and pull it out so she could rise.

"And what do you have planned today, Adella Rose?" he said as she stood. "I am sure there is still much to do to prepare for Natalie's arrival, what with the wedding in less than two weeks."

Feeling little excitement regarding her brother's upcoming nuptials and the changes it would bring, she forced some cheerfulness into her words. "Yes, work in the east wing is right on schedule. While Natalie is here visiting, we will choose fabric for the sitting room curtains and pillows. I have samples ready for her to look over."

Papa's attention had already moved on. "Brantley, come to my study to discuss a few matters before you head to the fields."

Seth nodded and fell into step beside her father and George. The three men headed into the foyer and down the hall toward Papa's private office, leaving Adella feeling forgotten and useless.

"There have been five runaways in the area lately," Luther said as soon as the three men were seated in the masculine room, with Luther behind a massive mahogany desk and George and Seth facing him in matching horsehair chairs. Floor-to-ceiling bookshelves lined the chamber and held more books than Seth had ever seen in one place.

"Two darkies ran from a plantation further east of us, but one escaped from Langford's and two from Carter's. The patrol caught Carter's, but Langford's man is still missing." A hard line formed on Luther's mouth. "I have invested too much in these Negroes to allow them to simply vanish. If there is an uprising in the making, I do not want any Rose Hill slaves to take part in it. Do I make myself clear?"

Seth's jaw clenched at the mention of escaped slaves. "It was a runaway who shot me near the Mexican border last year. Believe me when I say I have no sympathy for them."

Luther nodded, his eyes scrutinizing. "I believe you. I would hold a grudge too if I were in your shoes. It's bad enough your leg is forever damaged, but that you had to give up your position with the Rangers because of a no-good Negro wouldn't sit well, I imagine."

Seth's gut twisted at the memory of the night he was shot. He hadn't known the black man hiding in the brush had a gun. "No sir, it doesn't sit well at all."

Nodding with approval, Luther continued. "When new slaves are integrated, we keep a watchful eye on things to be sure the new stock doesn't infect the existing slaves with ideas of escape. The right word from the overseer, especially one who's seen the dead body of a runaway, can go a long way in cases like this." He leaned back in his chair, folding his hands across the mound of belly fat overlapping his trousers. "Those young bucks I brought back from

Galveston will bear some watching."

"What about the new yellow gal you bought?" George asked, a glint in his eyes. "She's too fine for field work."

"I have plans for that gal, so leave her be," Luther said, lowering his voice even though the heavy door was closed. An unmistakable warning edged his tone.

Seth glanced between father and son. It wasn't uncommon for white slave owners to freely use their female slaves, but Pa frowned on such behavior. Seth had a feeling, however, that the Ellis men held no such convictions.

"What kind of plans?" A petulant look filled George's face, reminding Seth of his visit to Rose Hill as a boy. He recalled how he and George were sent outside to play, but each time Seth won a game or a race, George would pout.

Luther ignored his son. "I believe it is high time I breed my own slaves instead of buying them at the markets. Galveston. New O'leans. They are all the same. The slave traders charge far more than any Negro is worth, yet what can us planters do but pay the exorbitant prices."

It took a moment for Seth to comprehend what the older man meant. "You are going to breed slaves?"

A look of giddy pleasure crossed Luther's face. "Yes. It is brilliant, don't you think? I have the perfect man for her, too— Jeptha. I bought him years ago with his mother when he was just a baby. Now he's a strapping man, bulging with muscles, so I suspect his father was a large Negro. I have kept him out of the fields, saving him for something special. That gal"—he pointed out the partially curtained window that looked out to the cotton fields— "and Jeptha will make some mighty fine children. Who knows? I might go into the slave trade myself. However, it is a shame it takes nine months for a Negro gal to drop a young'un."

While George congratulated his father on his new enterprise, Seth sat mute, stunned by the revelation. His mind recalled Luther's interest in the young slave woman at the Galveston market. With golden skin and pale eyes, she'd been highly sought after. Luther outbid several men, gloating when he won the prize despite the outrageous price of three thousand dollars.

"'Course, that is privileged information, you understand," Luther continued, apparently unaware that his admission shocked his new overseer. "Don't mention it to Adella Rose. She would have a fit if she knew. She is just like her mother, God rest her soul. Doesn't have the least understanding of the business of runnin' a plantation."

The sound George made revealed his disgust. "My sister coddles the darkies. If it were up to Adella, she would probably give them their freedom papers, never minding it would be the demise of the plantation."

"My dear wife allowed Adella Rose to play with the slave children when she was growing up because George never had the patience for his sister." Luther gave George an unhappy glare. "I am afraid it caused my daughter to become much too sympathetic when it comes to the Negroes. George and I don't discuss plantation business in front of her for that reason. She would not approve of my plans for Jeptha, though I daresay Jeptha won't mind." He chuckled.

"But we won't have to worry about Adella's hurt feelings much longer," Luther continued, exchanging a satisfied look with George. "I have consented to her marriage to Marshall Brevard. He owns a large plantation in Rusk County. The engagement will be announced as soon as George and Natalie are wed."

❧ ❧

"Missy Ellis, what you doing sneakin' around this here barn?"

Adella jumped, startled by the male voice that came from the shadowed horse stall she'd just tiptoed past. Tucking the apple she snuck from the kitchen into the deep pocket of her skirt, she turned to see Jeptha in the dim light of the barn, hammer in hand.

"Jeptha, you scared me." She gave a mock scowl. "You should give a body more warning of your presence." Biting her lip for a brief moment, Adella searched her mind for a valid excuse for being in the barn. "I thought to check on Clementine since her foal is due any day now." She grinned, satisfied with her ploy.

"You can't fool me." The young man shook his head. Beads of sweat dotted his dark skin, and he used his rolled-up shirtsleeve to mop his brow. "Since when you check on a hoss what's due to foal? You gonna get us both in trouble if Massa Ellis hear you been down yonder. It ain't ladylike for you to hang around a smelly ol' barn now that you all growed up."

A smile tickled Adella's lips, knowing her secret was safe with him. "Papa is far too busy with the new overseer to notice my absence. Besides, with Natalie arriving this afternoon, I won't have a minute to call my own." She glanced down the straw-covered aisle. "Now tell me, where are you keeping him?"

Jeptha shook his head again and set his hammer on the ledge of the empty stall. The nails and freshly cut planks on the ground around him spoke of the job assigned to him this morning. When his black eyes met hers, Adella saw the mischievous twinkle she'd come to know when they were children. "Who you talkin' about?"

She laughed. "Now who is trying to fool who? I know there is a wild stallion somewhere in this barn. I heard Papa talking about it, and I am determined to see him."

"Massa Ellis have my hide if he find out I took you anywhere near that devil hoss." Jeptha glanced toward the door, worry tugging his brow. "Monroe sure to tell him, too, just to get me in trouble."

"I saw Monroe ride out to the fields. He won't be back for hours." She hoped so anyway. The beefy plantation driver unsettled her. His beady eyes took far more liberty than they should when she happened to be nearby.

Jeptha shrugged. "I know you ain't gonna give up 'til you see him. Come on, then."

They set off to the far end of the horse barn. The smell of fresh hay mingled with the musty odor of manure and horseflesh, though all the barns on Rose Hill were meticulously maintained. Papa wouldn't have it any other way.

An angry nicker came from the last stall when they approached, followed by what sounded like wood splintering. Their steps slowed, and Jeptha reached a hand to still Adella.

"You got to go real slow now," he whispered. "He's tied tight, but that don't mean he ain't a'workin' on getting loose."

With a nod of understanding, Adella took a small step forward and peeked around the corner of the stall. Her breath caught at the sight of the magnificent creature. "He's beautiful," she breathed, taking in the matted black coat and powerful muscles of the stallion. His long mane and flowing tail held burrs and tangles, but Adella could well imagine what the horse would look like fully groomed. The beast's large eyes stared at her while his nostrils flared. He snorted angrily and lunged forward, causing Adella to back into Jeptha, though the sturdy ropes tied to either side of the horse's neck kept him in place.

"Whoo-wee, that one's a devil, I tell ya. I don't 'spect no one will ever tame him."

Jeptha backed away from the stall, but Adella stood watching the beast, its breath coming out in hard blows. She wished she could stroke his neck, reassuring him she wouldn't hurt him, but she dared not get any closer. "I suppose I would be mad too if some strange men came and took me away from my home and family, then kept me tied up."

"Mm-hmm," Jeptha said with a wry nod.

His tone made Adella wonder if he felt a kinship with the animal. They didn't speak of it often, mainly because it was too dangerous to do so, but on more than one occasion—usually at Adella's prodding—Jeptha confessed his longing for freedom. It was especially keen after her mother's sister had arrived from Boston for the funeral with two free black servants in tow. Word of the free blacks spread through the quarter like flames in a dry cornfield, convincing Papa an uprising would soon follow. He hadn't been at all pleased when Aunt Beth announced her involvement in the abolitionist movement up north, but Adella secretly tucked away everything her aunt revealed, wondering if there would ever come a day when slaves were truly free. Papa scoffed at the idea, declaring the South would never allow such a thing, but something about the determined gleam in her aunt's eye convinced Adella the possibility wasn't so far-fetched.

She returned her attention to the horse. "Can I give him the apple I brought?"

Jeptha chuckled. "Since when do you ask permission to do anything? Just keep your distance."

Reaching into her pocket, Adella pulled out the piece of fruit. The horse's ears perked, and his eyes followed her movement. His nostrils twitched at the scent. "I brought this for you," she said, hoping her soothing tone would calm him. Holding it on the palm of her flattened hand, she inched forward with her arm outstretched, though she wasn't near enough for the animal to snatch the apple away even if he'd tried. "I would like to be your friend. I will bring you one of these every day—"

A loud snort interrupted her speech. "Your pappy ain't gonna let you come down yonder every day to give that devil hoss an apple."

She tossed a glare over her shoulder. "Hush, Jeptha. I am having a conversation with … with …" Her longstanding habit of giving the animals names made her grin. "Freedom. Yes, that's it. Freedom and I are getting acquainted."

Jeptha rolled his eyes heavenward and went back to cleaning harnesses.

"As I was saying, Freedom"—she edged closer to the stall, keeping an eye on the horse's powerful body. It wouldn't do well to spook him, thus causing him to injure himself. "I would like to be your friend."

Ever so slowly she sank to her knees, unconcerned that her yellow silk gown could get dirty. With a practiced aim from years of playing marbles with Jeptha, Adella rolled the apple beneath the stall door, directly in front of the horse. Freedom glanced down, then looked at her. She held her breath. After a long moment, the horse turned his head away from the apple and from Adella.

Her shoulders fell. She'd been snubbed. By a horse.

"Don't look like he aims to be your friend, Missy. Best you get on back to the big house before someone starts a'wonderin' where you at."

Disappointed but not defeated, Adella turned to follow Jeptha back up the aisle. Her thoughts on the horse, she nearly collided with Jeptha when he skidded to a stop. Before she could ask why, a tall figure moved out of the shadows ahead of them.

Fearing Monroe was upon them, Adella's heart thrummed a nervous beat before Seth Brantley emerged into the dim light. Her relief at seeing him was short-lived, however, when his gaze traveled between Jeptha and herself, his scowl growing darker by the second.

CHAPTER FOUR

"Well?" Aunt Lu's brow tugged into a worried frown beneath the red kerchief tied around her short-cropped hair. Her ample bosom stilled while she waited for Adella's reply.

From her perch at the long kitchen worktable, Adella took a second taste of creamy cake batter dripping from her finger. "Maybe a bit more cinnamon."

Aunt Lu's shoulders sagged. She heaved a sigh while adding more of the spice to the bowl. "Who the Prince a' Wales anyhow? And why he got to have such a fancy cake named after him? I tells ya, I ain't never gonna get this here recipe right, Missy Ellis. We gonna be in all kinds a trouble if Miss Langford get here an' this here cake ain't right. Why cain't we just make a nice honey cake? I do them real good."

"Because," Adella said, dipping her finger into the delicious batter one last time. "According to George, Prince of Wales cake is Natalie's favorite. He wants to surprise her."

Aunt Lu's frown deepened. "My Zina done her best to get the recipe from ol' Harriet over to the Langford place, but that ol' gal don't cotton to me learnin' her secrets. I 'spect she left out somethin' important, and that's why we cain't get it right."

Secretly, Adella worried Aunt Lu wasn't too far off the mark. Zina, Aunt Lu's sixteen-year-old daughter who served as Natalie's maid, sent instructions that made no sense, at least to someone who possessed little knowledge regarding baking and cooking. The recipe evidently called for two separate batters that were combined into one pan, using a knife to cut and swirl them together. Muttering under her breath about the Prince and his high and mighty ways, Aunt Lu puttered around the kitchen, adding a few more ingredients of her own device—for good measure, Adella supposed.

With a glance out the window to the cotton fields, she chewed her bottom lip. Prince of Wales cake was the least of her concerns. Her earlier encounter with Seth in the barn wouldn't leave her mind. An unmistakable question had shone from his hazel eyes as he stood in front of her and Jeptha. He hadn't voiced it, much to Adella's relief. She had no good reason to be there with Jeptha, keeping him from his work. And the last thing she wanted was to bring Jeptha trouble with the new overseer.

"Miss Ellis," Seth had finally said, his deep voice polite yet more authoritative than she cared for. He sounded very much like Papa when he thought she needed reprimanding. "I believe this man has work to do. Are you in need of something here in the barn? I would be happy to assist you."

The nerve of the man! As though she needed his help. But without knowing if he'd mention their encounter to Papa or not, she decided it best to keep her thoughts to herself and simply told him the same story she'd told Jeptha. She'd come to check on her favorite horse, who was due to foal any day, and she was now on her way back to the big house. Whether or not he believed her, she couldn't say. After a lengthy pause, Seth merely nodded, tipped his chin, and continued on to the stall where his own horse stood peering over the rail. Jeptha, as skittish around the new overseer as Freedom had been around her minutes before, made quick work of getting back to his repairs. Adella, too, had scooted from the barn as fast as she could, stealing a quick peek at Clementine on her way out so her story was not a blatant lie. She decided as she stomped up the path to the house that she would need to be more cautious with Seth Brantley around. Having yet another man spying on her and telling her what to do did not sit well.

"What you think, Missy? Should I follow the 'structions? They seem strange to me." Aunt Lu's voice drew Adella back to the issue at hand.

"Go ahead and pour it in the pan the way Zina said."

With a look of skepticism in her eyes, Aunt Lu obeyed and dumped the first batter, creamy and yellow, into an awaiting cake pan. She eyed the bowl with the second mixture. "It shore do look darker than this other, Missy. You sure we s'posed to put 'em together in one pan? Makes more sense to cook 'em sep'rate like."

"That's what Zina said. Since this bowl has the molasses and spices, it doesn't look like the first one. I suppose that is why it is important to mix them together a bit with a knife."

With hesitant movements, Aunt Lu poured the second batter into the pan, the two mixtures melding together. She picked up a butter knife and began to carefully swirl the batters together, her elbow high in the air as though she were an artist creating a masterpiece. After several moments, she stood back with a critical eye.

"Well, I s'pose it do look kinda purty like, with them curly lines runnin' through it. I guess we'll know soon 'nough iffen we done it right." Taking a thick cloth in hand, Aunt Lu opened the big oven door, slid the pan in, and gently closed it.

Adella reached for the nearly empty bowl of light-colored batter. "I imagine things will be different around here once George and Natalie are married," she said, using a spoon to get the last of the creamy mixture. She popped it into her mouth, licking every bit off in a very unladylike manner.

"Lawsy, Missy. You said it." Aunt Lu heaved a sigh before plunging the second bowl into a tub of soapy water. "I missin' your mama somethin' fierce lately. She was such a fine woman, that Miz Martha." Her misty eyes found Adella. "You's just like her and don't you let no one tell you different."

Adella gave a sad smile, wishing her mother were there with them. Mama'd always enjoyed being in the kitchen with Aunt Lu, planning menus and tasting new recipes. Natalie's coming to live at Rose Hill wouldn't be so hard to accept if Mama were still alive and mistress of the manor. "I remember how much she loved your rice pudding. I think she requested it more than any other dessert."

A deep chuckle rumbled in Aunt Lu's throat. "She once tol' me that her mama weren't much of a cook, but one thing she made real good was rice puddin'. Said they had it nigh every week when she was a chil', so it reminded her of her mama when I made it."

"I didn't know that," Adella said, happy to tuck the new information about her mother into the special place in her heart where Mama still lived. "Grandmother Sterling only visited us once that I know of. She didn't approve of Papa moving Mama to Texas, or so Mama said."

"It's hard to be sep'rated from yer chillens, that fo' shore." Aunt Lu took the bowl Adella had scraped clean and dunked it into the soapy water. "I gots three I don't know where they is, iffen they alive, or nothin'. But," she said matter-of-factly, gazing out the window to the tree-covered eastern horizon, "I pray for them ever'day and trust the good Lawd to watch over them. That's 'bout all any mama can do fo' her chillens, I 'spect."

Adella watched the older woman work, wondering why God created people so different that one race would determine their superiority over another. Many times she'd wondered why God allowed slavery in the first place. She'd asked Mama about it after Papa sold Zina, who was barely nine years old at the time, to the Langfords, nearly breaking Aunt Lu's heart. The look of regret that washed over Mama's beautiful face resurfaced in Adella's memory.

"Man makes his own decisions, Adella Rose," she'd said, her Virginia accent softened with a sad tone. "Slavery is as old as sin itself. We aren't puppets in God's hands, doing His bidding. He lets us make our own choices and our own mistakes. No matter what lot in life we have been handed, whether rich or poor, slave or master, one day we will all have to stand before the Lord and give an accounting of the choices we made. I often fear what the Lord will say to me, knowing that I have been party to owning other human beings."

Years ago, when Adella asked Papa why he owned slaves, he'd laughed at her childish naivety. "If we had no slaves, who would plant and pick the cotton and corn? Who would care for the livestock and cook our meals? Negroes are born to work, Adella Rose. Don't feel sorry for them when they are fulfilling their purpose." She'd accepted his words at face value, but somewhere in the depths of her being she wondered if Mama was right and God would hold them all accountable for keeping Jeptha and the others in slavery.

"I'm happy you will have Zina here again," she said, hoping to cheer Aunt Lu after such sad thoughts. Natalie would bring Zina and several other servants with her.

The older woman's face brightened. "I is too, Missy. Don't you know I is. Will be so good to have that chil' nearby again."

"It will be strange having Natalie as mistress of Rose Hill, though," she said, a feeling of despair washing over her at the very thought.

"Yas'sum, it will." Aunt Lu opened the oven door just enough to peek inside. Apparently satisfied with what she saw, she closed it gently. "But we's happy Massa George is gettin' hissef a wife. There'll be little uns running through the house in no time, I 'spect." She chuckled. "My, how I used to have to chase you chillens outta the kitchen when I was baking sugar cookies."

Adella smiled at the memory. "George would dare me to sneak in and snitch a handful of dough when you weren't looking. I was smaller, so he figured I could get in and out of the kitchen without you seeing me."

The two women laughed over several more happy memories before a knock sounded at the back door, although it stood open to let the heat from the stove escape. Adella glanced up and found the new overseer in the doorway, his hat in hand. Startled, she straightened her slouching shoulders.

"Miss Ellis." Seth greeted her with a nod. His eyes lingered on her face for a moment before he turned his attention to Aunt Lu. "Monroe said I should speak to you about preparing me a midday meal. I would be much obliged. I hope to lay in some supplies at some point, but until then …"

After a momentary look of surprise, Aunt Lu bustled about the kitchen. "'Course, 'course. It no trouble a'tall. Come in an' sit a spell while ya wait. I'll have you a pail packed right quick like."

Seth hesitated in the doorway, his glance shifting to Adella before he moved inside. His large frame took up considerable space in the overly warm room. "Something sure smells good," he said, taking a long whiff.

When Aunt Lu didn't respond, apparently not hearing him while she poked around in the pantry, Adella felt obligated to answer. "It's a cake in honor of George's fiancée's arrival."

"Ah, yes," he said. "I recall your father mentioning Miss Langford's visit. I am sure you will enjoy having another woman around once they're married."

Though she understood he simply made idle conversation while he waited, his comment struck a nerve. He, like her father and brother, had no care or understanding of the difficulty a woman experienced when forced to allow another woman to take over her home—Mama's home.

Her mouth stiffened. "There are plenty of women at Rose Hill Manor as it is," she said, rising from the chair she'd occupied for the past hour. "I should think adding another will only complicate things." Before he could respond, she turned to Aunt Lu. "I'll be back to check on the cake in a little while."

Without another word to the overseer, she swept from the room.

CHAPTER FIVE

Row after row of knee-high green plants filled the north fields. The occasional clump of live oak trees had been left standing when the land was cleared, but otherwise, it was an unending sea of young, healthy cotton plants. Clearly, the drought of the past two years had ended. Though he had little practical knowledge of how much cotton Luther needed to turn a profit, from what Seth saw, things were on schedule to do just that.

Riding farther into the field, he observed groups of workers resting in the shade of the trees on their midday break, with some sitting back to back for support, while others lay on the ground. A small boy wearing a floppy hat carried a bucket among them, offering drinks of water from his dipper. It was the same boy Seth had seen in the south fields, where he'd spent time watching the new arrivals.

With a gentle tug on the reins, he drew his mount in a few feet from where Monroe lounged in the shade, some distance from the others. The driver's horse was tethered to a low-hanging branch nearby, and an empty gunnysack lay beside him. Seth expected the slave to rise, but the big man remained in the same horizontal position, his eyes just visible beneath the brim of his hat. Unlike the other slaves, who meekly dropped their gazes when Seth spoke to them, Monroe eyed the overseer without a shred of fear. Whether this was due to his position at Rose Hill or was simply his nature, the huge man bore watching. Not even Luther's favored driver should feel he was above showing Seth the respect his position as overseer warranted.

"I would like to get your report on the morning's work." Seth kept his voice even despite his irritation with the man.

Monroe waved an insect away. "They's lazy, like usual. Had ta box da ears on some a dem boys who weren't doin' they job. One gal done sat down to rest when da others still workin'. I yanked her up to her feet an' tol' her she best get to work or I puttin' her in the shed."

With a clenched jaw, Seth bit out his displeasure. "When I speak to you, you need to rise. The same as you would for Master Luther or Master George."

Several moments ticked by. Seth's eyes never wavered as they bore into Monroe. He had to make certain the driver understood his position of authority now, or he would pay for it later. There was no doubt in his mind the other man could best him if it ever came to physical blows. Monroe's arms were thick and muscled, and he outweighed Seth. As a Ranger, he'd been in one or two fistfights and could hold his own, but he'd never gone up against a man Monroe's size. Best to have the driver under control now than live—or die—to regret it.

Finally, the man rolled onto his side and slowly worked his way to his feet. His angry glare challenged Seth. "This bettah?" His upper lip curled with the words.

"Yes." After a moment, Seth decided it best to say his piece and get it over with. "I am not a hard man to work with, but I will demand your respect. Now," he said, looking toward the group of slaves nearby then back to Monroe. "Show me which men you had to reprimand, as well as the woman."

Uncertainty flashed across Monroe's face for a split second. "You's don't need to bother yo'seff with dem folks. I handle dem fine." He paused, his eyes narrowing. "Mistah Haley nev'ah question me."

The last words held a shadow of defiance.

"That may be," Seth said, keeping his tone low and even, "but I am not Mr. Haley. I am in charge of the workers on this plantation, and I will be the judge if someone needs punishment. Now, let's go see what the men and woman have to say for themselves." With that, he nudged his mount toward the slaves, expecting the other man to follow. He didn't want to have it out with the driver in front of the workers.

The group of thirty or so slaves rose as Seth neared, their wary eyes clouding with distrust. He couldn't blame them, especially after hearing that the previous overseer allowed Monroe unquestioned authority. There was no telling what kind of treatment they'd experienced over the years.

Sitting atop his horse, Seth gave a quick nod, his glance encompassing the entire group. "As I am sure you already know, I am the new overseer of Rose Hill. My name is Seth Brantley. You will find me to be a fair man, but I won't tolerate laziness or disobedience." He looked back to Monroe, who had indeed followed behind. "Monroe tells me he had trouble with some of you this morning."

The big man hesitated a moment before striding toward the group. "You's." He pointed with a beefy finger to two teenage boys on the fringe. "Come heah an' tell Mistah Brantley you's bein' lazy is why I had ta box you's."

Fear shone in the boys' rounded eyes as they shuffled forward, bare feet dragging in the dust. A streak of dried blood ran along the side of the smaller boy's head.

"Well? What have you to say for yourselves?" Seth asked, looking down on them from atop his horse. His dealings with the slaves on his father's farm didn't go much beyond passing along instruction or having easy conversation with them. Discipline belonged to his father and brother. This new position of authority over Rose Hill's slaves felt as comfortable as a boot two sizes too small.

The accused pair looked at each other before the taller of the boys spoke up, his eyes focused on the ground. "Mistah Brantley, suh, we's just doin' what we tol' to do is all. Work them rows, hoe them weeds." With a cautious glance toward Monroe, he swallowed hard. "We do a bettah job from now on. We promise, ain't that right, Henry?"

The other boy gave a silent nod.

Satisfied, Seth waved them away. If being called out by the new overseer didn't provide the motivation they needed, a stint in the shed would. "See that you do." He looked at Monroe. "And the woman?"

The big man glanced over the crowd until he pointed out a young woman standing near the back, wearing a dress far too big for her. "That un."

Seth motioned her forward.

The silent group parted to allow the woman through. Stopping a few feet from him, she kept her eyes downcast, though Seth saw a tear trail down her light brown cheek and roll off her chin.

"Monroe says you took a break when it wasn't time for one," he said, feeling the ogre, yet knowing he couldn't let even the smallest misdeed slip by without acknowledgment. A precedent had to be established from the very beginning if Seth were to succeed as an overseer.

Without looking up, the woman gave a slight nod. "Yassuh, I did," she said, her voice barely audible.

Surprised by her honesty, Seth wasn't entirely certain what to say. "Would you like to tell me why?"

Brown eyes drifted up to meet his for a brief moment before she quickly looked down again. "I gots dizzy an' thought I might fall, so I sat a minute ta clear my head."

A stout older woman stepped forward. "Mistah Brantley, suh, if I might be sayin' somethin'."

Indicating she could, the woman continued. "Lucy heah be in the family way, suh. Pardon me fo' sayin' sech out in public like, but carryin' a young'un is mighty hard on a little gal like her."

"We ain't heah to listen to them pitiful excuses fo' not doin' yo' jobs," Monroe bellowed. Lucy jumped and took a step back. "Ever' other gal be sittin' down iffen we 'llow that foolishness."

Seth tossed a glare at the man. He'd enjoy taking him down a notch with a well-placed word, but Luther clearly favored Monroe. It wouldn't do any of them any good if Seth disrupted the line of authority already established at Rose Hill.

He returned his attention to Lucy, who waited with trembling lips for him to dole out her punishment. His gaze traveled to her rounded belly hidden in the folds of the baggy dress. The memory of Mr. Haley's plantation ledger he'd read just last night flashed across his mind. It mentioned miscarriages, stillbirths, and women dying in childbirth over the past few years. The previous overseer, too, noted the same troubling news.

Rubbing his jaw, Seth recalled his own mother feeling exhausted and dizzy when she carried his younger sisters. Though his hat kept the sun from his eyes, its heat beat down on his back. He could only imagine how miserable a pregnant woman would be toiling in the sun all day, even a slave woman. Though some people—Luther included—believed Negroes were born to perform hard labor, it only took a pair of good eyes to know they weren't all that different from white people. A stroke of ill-fated luck colored their skin and their futures.

For some reason, Seth suddenly wondered how Adella Rose would handle the situation with the pregnant woman. Her father and brother declared she mollycoddled the slaves, but so far he'd only seen her treat them with respect—even Jeptha. He'd come upon the two of them in the dim light of the barn, and though he hadn't meant to eavesdrop, he'd overheard part of their conversation. It was clear she thought of him as a friend rather than a slave.

Seth eyed the young woman in front of him.

He made his decision.

"Women in a family way will be allowed two extra rest periods. One in the morning and one in the afternoon."

Lucy's eyes widened with surprise, as did those of the woman who'd stepped forward. When Monroe's head jerked in his direction, his mouth open for argument, Seth met his angry gaze. "If anyone has a complaint against this new rule, he can take it up with me later. Now, get back to work, all of you."

The crowd dispersed, with several people casting curious glances toward Seth as they went.

"Massa Luther ain't gonna like this when he hears," Monroe sneered.

Seth heard the unspoken threat. "As overseer, I will take it up with him when I see him next. Until then, I expect you to follow my instructions."

The two men glared at one another for a long moment before Monroe turned his back and stalked to his horse. Seth watched him gallop off in the direction of the field workers, barking orders as he went.

Heaving a sigh, Seth took off his hat and rubbed the back of his sweaty neck. If these first few days were any indication of what the future held for him as Rose Hill's overseer, he knew he'd have his work cut out for him. Last night he'd fallen into bed, exhausted from trying to learn his job while having to act as though he knew what he was doing. Monroe's surly attitude didn't help. Luther expected Seth to have things under control from the beginning, and that's the image he was trying to portray to everyone.

Except he knew the truth. He wasn't cut out to be an overseer on a large cotton plantation. The fact was, he wouldn't be there if it weren't for his injury. He longed to be in the saddle, riding the open range, never knowing what danger or excitement might find him that day. That's the life he'd dreamed of since he was boy and saw his first Texas Ranger. When a Comanche raiding party terrorized settlers near his father's farm, they sent for help. Seth would never forget the day a group of riders galloped into the yard, sitting high in their saddles with long rifles across their laps. Young Seth stared in awe and wonder, gaping at the rough, rugged men. Days later, when they returned with tales of their success fast on their tongues, Seth knew farming was not the life he wanted.

"Mistah Brantley, suh?"

The small voice startled Seth from his memories. He looked

down to find the boy with the floppy hat a few paces away, staring up at him with inquisitive eyes.

"Yes?"

Suddenly shy, the boy ducked his head. "I jest wonderin', suh, iffen you'd like a drink, suh."

Seth's brow rose in surprise. "Well, that is very thoughtful of you to offer." The boy lifted his head a notch to peek up at him. Seth tapped the canteen hanging from his saddle. "I have my own water, though."

Disappointment drooped the child's shoulders. "Oh."

"But I'm sure my horse would like some water." Seth dismounted with the boy watching. "I'll cup my hands, and you pour water into them. We'll give Chester a nice drink."

The boy hurried to obey. After they'd watered the animal, Seth eyed the child. "What's your name?"

"Oliver, suh. Oliver Ellis," he said, using the last name of his master the way most slaves did.

Seth looked him over, from his baggy overalls to his dirty bare feet. "How old are you, Oliver?"

"Mammy says I seven last month." He beamed with pride. "Says I old 'nough to tote water now, like my brother done toted 'fore he went to work in dem fields."

"Well, you are doing a fine job, Oliver."

The boy's grin grew. "Thank'ee, Mistah Brantley. Mammy be right pleased to hear such. Says I gots to learn how to be val'able to Massa Luther so he don't up an' sells me to some other white man."

The honest words hit Seth in the gut. He stared at the child, wondering if Oliver simply repeated unfounded fears he'd overheard grownups talking about. Then he remembered the slave auction in Galveston and knew the fears were real. Children younger than Oliver had been ripped from their mother's arms and sold to the highest bidder.

He looked into Oliver's happy face, who was smiling because

he was being valuable to his white Massa. No seven-year-old boy should have to worry he might be sold away from his family. Seth knew his father would never think of selling off the children of his slaves, splitting up families the way other plantation owners—including, apparently, Luther Ellis—had no qualms doing.

"No," he finally said. "We wouldn't want that. You keep doing a good job, and I will be sure Master Luther hears about it."

Oliver tilted his head to the side, studying Seth in a way no grown slave would ever do. "You shore is diff'ernt from Mistah Haley." With a shrug of his bony shoulders, he lifted the bucket by its wooden handle. "I best gets back ta work or Monroe come a'lookin' for me an' box my ears."

Seth watched the rail-thin boy head out to the cotton fields, his spindly arms weighted by the heavy bucket. How many miles did the child travel each day, toting his pail back and forth from the creek or well out to the fields? A flash of his own carefree childhood, running and playing as children should, reminded him what an impossibly different life Oliver and the other slaves lived.

CHAPTER SIX

Dusk settled over the plantation, bringing with it a quiet that Adella craved. Natalie's arrival that afternoon had the entire household in an upheaval. Aunt Lu was in a foul mood, and even Papa had retired to his study with the door closed, leaving George and Natalie in the parlor, oblivious to everyone but each other.

Taking a chance no one would notice her absence, Adella hurried down the path that led to the horse barn. Warm night air scented with the sweet fragrance coming off Mama's rose bushes along the porch caressed her skin, while a sliver of moon in the cloudless night sky lit the way. She wanted to see Freedom again since it was unlikely she'd have another opportunity while Natalie visited. With a pat on the round bulge in her pocket, she glanced about, making certain she was alone.

The heavy barn door gave a loud screech upon opening. Adella stilled, her hand on the latch, listening for voices from within. But with the sun long settled below the horizon, the stable hands were most likely back in their cabins for the night. A glance in the direction of the quarter revealed cooking fires ablaze with shadowy forms moving back and forth in the glow. Bits of conversation floated on the evening breeze. A laugh. A baby's cry. It seemed everyone was in for the night.

With that knowledge, Adella crept inside the cavernous building on silent feet. Once the door closed behind her, blocking out the pale moonlight, she realized a lantern was required to find her way down the aisles without tripping. Recalling that one usually hung on the post near the door, she felt in front of her with outstretched hands. Carefully inching her fingers up the wood, she met the cool metal of the lantern along with a bundle of matches wedged between the handle and chimney.

Warm yellow light spilled into the gloomy darkness once the wick flamed. Horses shifted in their stalls, disturbed from their rest. Some poked their heads out to see who was stirring. Speaking in hushed tones, she moved down the row with unhurried steps, reassuring them all was well. The last thing she wanted was a stable full of spooked animals.

Rounding the corner to the second row of stalls, Adella slowed. Freedom's was at the end, far away from any of the other horses. She hoped the stable hands were taking good care of him and not starving him out, as she'd once overheard some of her father's guests describe. Wild horses, they'd claimed, could be brought to submission much easier if they were weak from lack of nourishment. One of the other guests had laughed, saying he found the same to be true of his Negroes.

Closing the distance with cautious steps, Adella held her breath when he came into view. His huge eyes glowed in the lantern light, giving him an even wilder look than usual. In the shadows of the stable, she couldn't tell if he was still tethered on each side of his powerful neck.

"I imagine you thought I wouldn't come back," she said, her voice soft and low. With her free hand, she slowly reached into her pocket and pulled out the apple. "But I made you a promise, and I intend to keep it."

The horse didn't move but continued to watch her. The fact that he didn't shy away as he'd done that morning was a good sign. It meant he was getting used to human contact, which would make taming him that much easier.

Locating a nail on a nearby post, Adella hung the lantern then stepped back into the pool of light it cast. "See," she said, the apple flat on the palm of her hand where the horse could see it. "This is for you." She crept closer. "Now, be a good horse, and I will give it to you."

When she'd come as close as she dared and the horse hadn't moved, Adella relaxed her tense muscles. "There, I knew we could be friends."

Her teeth clamped on her bottom lip. She leaned toward the animal, but a strong hand reached through the darkness and grabbed her arm. The apple dropped to the ground.

"I wouldn't do that," a deep voice said at the same moment she let out a shriek. Freedom backed deeper into his stall at the ruckus.

Adella whirled to find Seth Brantley holding her. Her heart pounded so hard she was certain he could hear it. For one frightening moment, she'd thought Monroe had found her alone in the barn. "You scared me nearly to death," she said, wrenching her arm from his grasp. "What do you think you're doing, sneaking up behind me like that?"

"Possibly saving your hand from a nasty bite, or worse," he replied, a hint of a smile on his lips.

His audacity fueled her annoyance. "I sincerely doubt that, Mr. Brantley. I have been around horses from the time I could walk. I was simply giving Freedom a treat. Not exactly a threat to my well-being, wouldn't you agree?"

His brow raised. "Freedom?"

Too late, she realized she'd used the pet name she'd given the wild horse. Embarrassment quickly cooled her irritation, and she looked away, hating that she had to explain herself to this stranger. "Just a silly habit, I suppose. I have always given names to the animals on the plantation."

She braced herself for his laughter. It didn't come.

After a moment, he glanced to the horse and nodded. "It fits him. A big beast like that should run free, not be confined to a stall."

Surprised he understood, Adella relaxed a bit. "I hope you won't mention this to my father. He doesn't think it is proper for me to be down here in the barn."

"I would have to agree with him. It is not a place for a lady. Not in the daylight hours—" one dark brow arched, assuring Adella of his disapproval at finding her here with Jeptha earlier "—but especially alone at night. Any number of things could happen, the least of which is you being injured by a wild mustang."

The censure in his voice rankled. "Mr. Brantley, Rose Hill has been my home my entire life. I have no reason to fear for my safety."

His gaze boldly swept her from head to toe. "Then you underestimate the temptation you present, Miss Ellis."

Her eyes widened at his improper insinuation.

"While I don't think most slaves would abuse a white woman and risk a hanging, I understand there are runaway slaves in the area." His hand brushed over his thigh in what seemed an unconscious move. "A man in a desperate situation will do just about anything."

Adella frowned. She'd heard Papa and George speaking of the runaways, but it never entered her mind they might pose a danger to her or anyone else on Rose Hill land.

"My intention is not to frighten you, Miss Ellis," he said, retrieving the apple and handing it to her. "Your father has entrusted me with a great responsibility on his plantation, although I realize you are not necessarily part of that responsibility. Nevertheless, I will do my utmost to ensure the safety of *everyone* at Rose Hill, should I believe they are in danger."

Taken aback by this show of gallantry, Adella accepted the apple hesitantly. "I … I appreciate that, Mr. Brantley. Quite honestly, it never occurred to me the runaways could cause harm, but I suppose, as you say, desperation could lead one to do something he would not attempt otherwise."

Their eyes met in the dim light. Warmth spread across Adella's belly and up her neck, realizing how completely alone they were. A nicker from behind her thankfully drew the handsome man's attention away.

"I think Freedom would like his apple now."

Glad for the distraction, she looked at the apple in her hand and back to the horse. "I suppose I will just roll it to him as I did before since you don't think it wise for me to get too close."

"I didn't say that." He leaned his shoulder against a post and crossed his arms over his chest.

"You most certainly did." She waved the apple in his direction. "I was about to give this to Freedom when you nearly scared me witless."

He had the nerve to chuckle. "I simply said I wouldn't do that if I were you. Freedom's restraints have been loosened, and you hadn't given him enough time to become familiar with your presence before getting close. I have no doubt he would have bitten your hand." He nodded to the animal. "We've been here long enough now that he understands we aren't going to hurt him."

His words made sense, much to her chagrin. Presenting her back to the vexing man, Adella flattened her palm to balance the fruit. Freedom's nostrils twitched at the scent, and his big eyes followed her every move. "This is for you, Freedom. Now, take it nicely and show Mr. Brantley that you and I are friends." With cautious steps, she neared the big animal. When she'd come as close to the stall door as she dared, she leaned forward as she'd done before Seth grabbed her arm.

"Take it," she whispered, her hand shaking slightly, more from excitement than fear of being bitten by the horse.

Freedom stared at her for several long seconds. Finally, he took a step closer, his ears alert and tail swishing. Ever so slowly, he stretched his neck over the stall door, and in a quick movement, snatched the apple off Adella's palm without touching her.

A munching sound was her reward.

With a laugh, she turned to Seth, triumphant. "See? All ten fingers still intact."

"I see." He grinned. "But now I think you best get back to the big house before someone comes looking for you."

Adella knew he was right. If George or her father found her in the barn—alone with a man, no less—there was no telling what kind of restrictions they would place on her.

Seth took the lantern from the nail and led the way down the aisles toward the door. Just before they reached the opening, a chestnut-colored horse poked his nose from his stall, nickering and showing his teeth.

"Chester, boy." Seth stopped to rub the animal's nose. "Sorry, I don't have a treat for you. Freedom is the only lucky one tonight." He tossed a grin at Adella.

Smiling, she joined him, the horse nosing her cupped hand in a friendly manner. "Is he yours?"

"Yep." He rubbed the animal's sleek, powerful neck. "Chester, this is Miss Ellis. Maybe if you smile real big, she'll bring you an apple too."

He tickled the horse under the jaw, causing the animal to bare his teeth.

Adella laughed. "I don't think I have ever seen a horse smile like that before."

With a good night pat on the horse's neck, Seth continued to the barn door. "I've had Chester nearly five years now. He's carried me halfway across Texas and back. We've been through a lot together."

Stepping into the faint moonlight, a dozen questions tumbled across Adella's mind about their new overseer. She cast a curious glance at him as he secured the door. "I imagine being a Texas Ranger was quite exciting."

He didn't look at her but motioned with his hand up the path toward the house. "It was. It was all I ever wanted to do."

His quiet admission touched her. Papa had cleared up the mystery of why Seth had to leave the Rangers, stating it was because of an injury, although he didn't go into detail. The limp indicated that Seth's leg still hadn't fully healed, if it ever would.

"I hope to see Galveston and the ocean someday," she said, hoping to change the subject. She hadn't meant to pry by bringing up his time with the Rangers. "Papa does his best to describe it, but

I am sure one has to see it for oneself to fully appreciate it."

"It is something, all right. All gray and powerful. The sound of waves crashing onto shore is like nothing I have ever heard." He glanced at her, then away. "But Galveston isn't a place for a lady like yourself."

She harrumphed. "There you go again. First, I am not allowed in a barn, and now I can't go to Galveston. Where *can* a lady such as myself go? The parlor? The kitchen?"

A look of surprised humor filled his face. "Now, don't get all riled because I think a lady should be protected and sheltered. Some unsavory business takes place in Galveston, which in turn draws in disreputable people. It isn't a place I would take my daughter, should I ever have one."

The image of the slaves Papa recently bought came to mind. Shackled together in the back of the plantation wagon, looking sad and lost. She could only imagine what the slave markets must be like, knowing even babies and children were often sold there.

A shudder went through her. "Perhaps you are right. But I would still like to see the ocean."

He gave her a thoughtful look. "I have never told this to anyone before, but someday I plan to see the Pacific Ocean."

"Gracious, but that is so far away," she said, his declaration taking her by surprise. "I have heard tales about California, but I have never known anyone who traveled there."

"Actually, I'm thinking I would like to go to Oregon now that it has become a state in the Union."

She came to an abrupt stop, the big house directly in front of them. "Oregon? Forevermore, why?"

He chuckled at the astonished look on her face. "For the adventure. To be the first to settle a new land, like our fathers did when they came to Texas." He shrugged and extinguished the lantern.

They walked the short distance to the bottom of the steps in silence. Reaching them, Adella proceeded to ascend when his soft touch to her arm stopped her. "I am sure it is only a fanciful dream, my going to the Oregon Territory someday," he said, his voice low so only she could hear. "But as I intend to keep your visit to Freedom a secret, Miss Ellis, I hope you will return the favor."

She glanced at the house, knowing windows were open to allow the cool night breeze in. Meeting his gaze, she nodded. "Of course, Mr. Brantley. I am not one to divulge confidences bestowed upon me."

He bowed politely. "Good night then, Miss Ellis."

She watched him disappear into the darkness, oddly satisfied at sharing a secret with the handsome man.

CHAPTER SEVEN

As soon as the horizon hinted at morning, with threads of pink and purple edging out the darkness and dimming the multitude of stars, Seth made his way to the kitchen wing at the back of the main house. He'd lain awake far longer than he should have after escorting Adella Rose back to the house last night and was in desperate need of a strong cup of coffee. Their encounter in the barn had filled his head with thoughts that refused to rest, and he'd pay for that lack of sleep today.

"Mornin', Mistah Brantley, suh," Aunt Lu said when he arrived at the door. She stood at the large stove, pouring steaming black liquid into a mug from a shiny blue coffee pot.

When she held it out to him, he laughed. "How did you know?" He came forward and accepted it with a nod of thanks.

"I seen you comin' 'cross the yard, draggin' yo' feet like. I says, that man needs hisse'f a good cup o' coffee is what he needs." She gave a self-satisfied nod. "Guess I's right."

"Yes, you were right." He took a sip of the hot liquid, letting the pungent aroma rouse his senses. "I didn't sleep too well last night."

"Well, you just sit yo'seff down an' take a minute a'fore you go runnin' off to start the day. A man cain't get much done iffen he's asleep in his saddle."

He settled onto a stool to sip the strong drink. Though he'd come to the kitchen the previous day to pick up lunch, he hadn't stayed more than a few minutes. Now he leisurely took in his surroundings while Aunt Lu and two other servants went about preparing breakfast for the family.

The room was spacious and well laid out. An enormous stove occupied the wall directly across from the door, and its surface contained several deep, steaming pots emanating delicious smells. Cabinets with plenty of workspace lined the other walls, with a big sink and hand pump beneath a window. A narrow door stood slightly ajar, and Seth saw stairs leading down, presumably to the cellar and cold pit. He made a mental note to investigate the area one day soon. Runaway slaves were good at hiding just about anywhere, and he certainly couldn't afford to have one right under his nose.

Aunt Lu hummed a low tune as she stirred a thick batter. After a bit, she began to sing.

"They is a balm in Gilead to make the wounded whole.

They is a balm in Gilead to heal the sin-sick soul.

One o' these mornin's bright an' fair,

I gonna lay down my heavy load.

Gonna kick my wings an' cleave the air,

I gonna lay down my heavy load."

While Seth mulled over the words, a pretty young servant woman entered the room, dressed in clothes more fitting for a white woman than a slave. Her black hair was neatly combed and caught up in a thick crocheted net instead of the colorful kerchief most Negro women wore. Her caramel-colored eyes widened when she saw him, and she came to an abrupt halt.

Aunt Lu stopped humming and glanced up. A warm smile filled her wide face. "Mistah Brantley, suh, this here is my daughter, Zina. She Miss Natalie's maid." Pride rang in the woman's voice.

Seth acknowledged the girl, curious that she was so much lighter skinned than her mother. He guessed her to be about the same age as Celia, the young woman Luther had bought in Galveston. *The one he has plans for*, Seth recalled with distaste.

"Mr. Brantley, sir," Zina nodded, her voice soft and respectful. Turning to her mother, she said, "Miss Natalie prefers to take her breakfast in her room this morning, Mama."

Seth noticed her speech didn't hold the usual diction of most slaves. Clearly, she'd been a house servant the majority of her life and had learned proper English and manners. Glancing at Aunt Lu, he wondered how old Zina had been when she went to work for the Langfords.

"I'll make up a tray for her right quick an' you can take it on up." Aunt Lu bustled about the kitchen. "Zina, get that china teapot from the cupboard. No, not that un. The one with the pink flowers painted on it. An' the matchin' cup an' saucer."

Celia arrived in the midst of this scene. Seth hadn't seen her since the day they returned from Galveston. She paused a moment when she saw him, before hurrying to the washtub where a stack of dirty pots and pans awaited cleaning. She plunged her hands into the soapy water and set to work. A look passed between Aunt Lu and Zina he couldn't quite discern.

With one last gulp, Seth downed the remainder of the liquid in his mug and stood. "Thank you for the coffee," he said, taking in the women with one glance.

Aunt Lu tossed him a distracted nod. "Yassuh, you's welcome. I have your lunch packed in a jiffy."

He exited the kitchen and headed to the front of the house, having suddenly felt out of place with the women. He'd wait outside until breakfast was served. A busy day spread out before him, and he needed his mind cleared of the cobwebs his lack of sleep produced.

Planting himself on the bottom step, he ticked off the mental list of all he had to get done that day: assign the new slaves to a section of land now that they'd proven themselves capable workers; see that a crew was sent to repair a leaking roof on the grain barn; check the crop in the southern fields for black beetles. Workers reported seeing large quantities of the insects, which could mean the entire infested area might need to be burned to prevent further spreading. Luther, ever suspicious, thought it might be a ploy to lay a smoke screen in order to help a slave escape.

He heaved a sigh. Exhaustion nearly overwhelmed him simply thinking about it all. Work and worries never ceased on Rose Hill. He wondered if that was the reason Pa had never desired an operation as big. His father was perfectly satisfied with his five hundred acres and dozen slaves.

The blast of an antelope horn sounded in the quarter. From where he sat, Seth saw Monroe atop his horse, blowing the thing, calling the slaves to work. Because it wasn't harvest time, they were allowed to sleep a little later. But come August, when the cotton plants were high and prime for picking, Monroe's horn would sound long before the sun made its appearance on the horizon.

With a tired groan, Seth shifted his position to better view the workers heading out. Some walked, and some climbed into a wagon that would take them to the fields farther away. A group of women went in the direction of the sewing shack where wool from Rose Hill's sheep was carded, spun, and woven into material for their clothes. Others headed toward the livestock pens, chicken coops, mills, and barns.

Thinking of the barns reminded him of his encounter with Adella last night.

After dinner, he'd retired to his own cabin to continue reading through the ledgers Mr. Haley and the previous overseers kept, but the warmth from the day still lingered in the small space, so instead he'd chosen to sit outside until bedtime. His proximity to the main house afforded him a clear view of any comings and goings, and when he spied a lone figure wearing a wide bell-shaped skirt slip through the front door and disappear into the night, he'd followed her.

Seth chuckled, recalling his surprise when he saw her sneak into the horse barn again. Curious, he'd used a separate entrance, one where the hinges didn't announce one's arrival. It had been easy to shadow her once she lit the lantern. For a brief moment, he'd wondered if she were meeting a lover, and the pang of jealousy that rolled over him still confused Seth. The memory of finding her with Jeptha slid across his mind, but he immediately shoved it away. He'd overheard their friendly banter and found no reason to believe their relationship was untoward.

When she went directly to the wild stallion's stall, he'd been relieved—and fascinated. His impression of Adella Rose Ellis was that of a spoiled rich man's daughter. To find her in a dirty barn, sneaking an apple to a wild horse ... well, his esteem of her grew immensely. He'd be willing to wager that's what she was doing the first time he found her down there.

But the memory of their conversation quickly turned his fascination to one of dismay. Why had he revealed his dream of going to Oregon to her? It was pure recklessness to tell the boss's daughter he had plans that didn't include staying at Rose Hill indefinitely. Yet their discussion of the ocean and the comfort of being in her presence led him to talk of things better left unsaid. At least he hadn't told her the details of his plan. That he would stay on as Rose Hill's overseer only until he'd saved enough money to travel and buy land, where he hoped to raise horses. Though he'd never make a good farmer, he'd always had a natural knack with horses. Perhaps becoming a horse breeder would somehow fill the void losing his position with the Rangers had left.

Voices came from the foyer through the screen door and brought Seth to his feet. A moment later, Luther stepped onto the wide porch.

"Brantley," he said, his voice and demeanor cool.

"Good morning, sir."

"I had hoped to speak with you before we go inside."

The serious tone in the older man's voice didn't bode well for the conversation ahead. Seth wondered if he'd done something wrong already.

"Monroe came to see me late last night." Luther's eyes narrowed, studying Seth.

Understanding quickly dawned. "Yes, sir, I imagine he did, although I gave him specific instructions that I would speak to you regarding the matter myself."

It infuriated him that the slave had disobeyed his orders. How he would deal with that infraction, he didn't know. Clearly, he'd underestimated the closeness between Luther and his driver.

"So it is true?" Luther's tone hardened. "You have instituted an additional rest period for female workers without asking my permission to do so?"

"Not female workers, sir," Seth said, refusing to back down under Luther's intimidating glare, though he kept his tone respectful. "Pregnant female workers."

"And what makes you believe they need more rest than any other Negro? I have been in this business thirty years now, and I have never heard such foolishness from an overseer." He shook his head, looking off to the fields where workers had already begun to swing their hoes. "I fear it was a mistake to hire you. I should have listened to George. The son of a corn farmer knows nothing of how a cotton plantation operates."

Seth felt the position and the salary he'd hoped to save slipping through his fingers. As much as he hated to admit it, he needed this job. At least for a while.

"If I might explain, sir," he said, keeping emotion out of his voice.

Luther glanced at him and then inclined his head. "Please. I cannot wait to hear this."

Ignoring the sarcasm in his employer's words, Seth said, "Mr. Haley, as well as the overseer before him, kept fairly accurate records over the years. I found the ledgers in my cabin, and I've been going over them at night."

"Yes, I am aware of the records. What does that have to do with your being soft on the Negroes?"

"The records over the past several years indicate that quite a large number of female slaves miscarried or went into early labor, resulting in stillborn babies. Some even died in childbirth." Luther's expression didn't change. "You have invested quite a lot of money into the purchase of these slaves, as you yourself have said. It only makes sense that you would want your investment well cared for, especially if it results in a healthy baby that will grow up to work in your fields without your spending any additional funds."

A heavy silence followed his speech. Seth wondered if he should go pack his bags.

"And you think letting them have extra rest periods will solve these problems?" Skepticism coated Luther's words.

"I don't know if it will help, sir, but I remember my own ma needing to rest during the day when she was carrying each of my sisters. A Negro woman may be of a stronger constitution than a white woman, but in the end, they are all just women."

Luther rubbed his whiskered jaw while staring at Seth. After a long minute, the man gave a humorless laugh. "You are a strange one, Brantley, just like your father. I never could make heads nor tails of some of the things that man said. Heaven help me now, but what you just explained actually makes sense."

Relief washed through Seth. He wasn't fired. Yet.

"I will allow this new rule to stand, but from now on see that you discuss your ideas for changes with me before instituting them. Rose Hill is, after all, my plantation."

"Yes, sir," Seth said, realizing for the first time how presumptuous his actions in the field had been. No longer was he the owner's son, as he'd been on his father's farm, nor was he a Ranger, independent and in charge of his own destiny for the most part. Here he was simply an employee under the rule of Luther and, for that matter, George.

Trailing his employer into the house, the call of the Oregon Territory seemed that much louder.

❦

"Adella Rose, I simply despise the blue wallpaper in my new sitting room."

Adella looked up from the embroidery hoop in her lap to see Natalie sweep into the parlor with Zina trailing behind. Natalie's mass of golden curls gleamed in the morning light streaming through the tall windows, and the sky-blue day gown she wore perfectly matched her eyes. Ironically, it was nearly the same hue of blue as the paper she apparently did not like.

"Why, Natalie, dear," Adella chose her words carefully. She'd already learned her soon-to-be-sister-in-law had a bit of a temper. Just yesterday she'd thrown a fit when one of the Rose Hill servants straightened her room without asking permission. "Isn't that the paper you chose when you were here last? I specifically had all the papers ordered from the samples you selected."

With an overly drawn-out sigh, Natalie settled in a chair across from Adella. "Yes, I know I chose it myself," she said, a faint Southern drawl coloring her words. "But I didn't realize how overpowering it would be once the entire room was covered with it." She motioned for Zina to pour her a cup of tea from the service on a low table near the door.

Fighting to hide her annoyance, Adella laid her needlework aside. "What do you propose we do about it? Choose another pattern? I don't know that it will arrive before the wedding, but with you and George taking a wedding trip to Louisiana, I don't suppose it matters."

Zina handed a brimming cup to Natalie and turned to Adella. "May I pour you some tea as well, Missy Ellis?"

"No, but thank you, Zina." She smiled at the servant. It was good to have Zina back. The girl had a sweet disposition and seeing Aunt Lu happy was worth putting up with Natalie and her never-ending demands.

After a dainty sip of the liquid, Natalie's brow puckered. "I have never understood why the servants still call you Missy Ellis. It may have been appropriate for a child, but it seems rather odd to call a woman that, don't you think?"

Adella's mouth dropped at the rudeness of the remark. "No, I don't. Miss Adella Rose is a mouthful. I have always been Missy Ellis to our people, and I always will be."

A snide little smile settled on Natalie's lips. "I am sure that will change after you're married. I doubt your future husband would appreciate servants using your former name."

"Perhaps." She shrugged nonchalantly, refusing to let Natalie's disagreeable attitude spoil her day. "I suppose it will depend upon the man's name. Preston Van Middlesworth, for instance, asked Papa's permission to court me some months back. Imagine if I were to marry him. I would be Mrs. Adella Rose Van Middlesworth. Why, it would take half the day for the servants to simply get my attention with a name that long."

Zina giggled, and Adella threw her a wink despite Natalie's scowl.

"Such nonsense. You know perfectly well your papa is not going to allow that Van Middlesworth boy to come calling." She looked aghast at the very idea. "He is a second son, for mercy's sake."

"Gracious, Natalie," Adella said, weary of the young woman's condescending manner. Though merely two years older than Natalie, Adella often felt like a mature matron schooling a youngster during discussions with her. "You needn't say it as though he had a contagious disease simply because he is second born. Preston is a nice young man. I have no interest in pursuing more than friendship with him, but had I felt differently, it would not be such a terrible thing to marry a second son. I have every confidence he will make something of himself."

Smoothing nonexistent wrinkles from her voluminous skirt, Natalie raised her brow. "Well, thankfully your papa has more sense than to let you decide for yourself."

Adella frowned. Natalie's tone hinted she knew more on the subject than she revealed. "What are you speaking of?"

Natalie's big blue eyes met hers, a look of pure innocence on her rosebud face. "Why, nothing, Adella, dear. I have simply come to know your father as a man of purpose. I have no doubt he will make a good match for you when the time comes."

To argue further would be pointless. Natalie's engagement to George had been orchestrated by their parents, for the most part, their adjoining plantations playing a large role in the union. The couple did seem fond of one another from what Adella had observed, which hopefully opened the door for a lifetime of happiness. But she wanted more than fondness when she married. She wanted love and passion. The kind demonstrated in the Book of Solomon. Adella didn't see how marriage to a man her father chose could possibly produce that.

"What do you want to do about the wallpaper?" she asked, closing the door on the subject.

For the next hour she half-listened to Natalie expound on the merits of more than two-dozen swatches of wallpaper—all the while, Adella dreamed about the mystery man who would one day capture her heart.

Oddly enough, she pictured him with hazel eyes and unruly dark hair.

CHAPTER EIGHT

A dinner gala in honor of Natalie and George's upcoming nuptials was planned for the end of the week. Guests from all across the county, as well as from Austin and as far away as San Antonio were invited. Servants came from the Langford plantation to help, throwing Aunt Lu into a tizzy with so many strangers in her kitchen. Enormous amounts of food were bought, hogs were butchered, and tables were constructed on the lawn to accommodate the crowd. A group of female slaves had been put to work sewing more linens and napkins while others cleaned and polished every square inch of the big house, inside and out.

It would be the first social event to take place at Rose Hill Manor since Mama died. Adella wasn't at all certain how to feel as she orchestrated the activity, knowing the bulk of the decisions fell on her now. Though the black crepe and mourning clothes had been put away for several months, she still hadn't come to terms with the fact that Mama was gone. Papa missed his wife, but he'd thrown himself into the business of the plantation with gusto and had little time for grieving and memories. George, too, had easily moved through the loss of their mother with his eyes firmly planted on his future with Natalie. Neither of them would understand her inner struggle and longings. Neither of them seemed as alone without Martha Jane Ellis as Adella felt.

With no one to confide in and the house in an uproar of preparations, Adella escaped the commotion and wandered down to the quarter. She hadn't seen Jeptha in several days and wondered if he'd perhaps been moved to field work, although he'd never spent much time hoeing the cotton plants and was usually assigned tasks that took place in the barns or mill. When harvest came, however, he and many of the "petted" slaves, as household staff and those who didn't work the fields were called, joined the others to pick cotton long before the sun came up, ending when it slid out of sight beyond the horizon. Harvest took many weeks and required every able-bodied servant that could be spared, even children.

The day had already grown overly warm and humid as Adella walked down the well-traveled path. The oppressive heat of summer would quickly be upon them, something she'd grown to dread now that she was too old for swimming in the creek with Jeptha. She much preferred early springtime, when bluebonnets and Indian paintbrush filled the meadows, or autumn when cool breezes and rainy days vanquished all reminders of the summer's heat.

The happy sound of childish voices greeted her when she neared the double row of small cabins. There she found Mammy, the ancient black woman charged with looking after the babies while their mothers worked. The woman seemed to have her hands full. Seven half-naked children, all around three years or younger, sat in the dirt in a cluster in front of Mammy, who sat on a stump, holding a bowl of what looked like corn mush. Taking turns, she popped a spoonful of the meal into the small open mouths. It reminded Adella of a mother bird feeding her fledglings. A group of children a few years older played nearby.

"Well, lookie who came ta see you, chillens," Mammy said when she spied Adella coming toward the group. She offered a toothless grin as a few of the little ones who could walk jumped up and toddled to greet their visitor. "Don't touch Missy Ellis's purty dress, now," she admonished, still spooning mush into hungry mouths.

Adella reached out to tousle the soft heads of the youngsters around her, wishing she had a treat for them like the apples she took to Freedom. But Papa forbade the practice years ago when he caught her raiding the pantry for cookies and candied fruit to take to the Negro children. He'd reminded her the slaves received a weekly ration of meat, cornmeal, flour, sugar and coffee. When surplus allowed, they also received eggs and milk. Between that and the vegetable gardens they raised behind the quarter, he'd said, they had plenty and didn't need her spoiling them.

The youngsters returned to Mammy, babbling about Missy Ellis and her purty dress. Adella settled on a nearby stump to watch.

"Guess there be lotsa goin's on up to the house, getting things ready for the big shindig." Mammy used her thumb to clean mush from the corner of one child's mouth. She wiped it on her soiled apron and continued with the feeding.

"Yes." Adella sighed. "I am sure it will be a grand party."

Mammy's eyes found hers. "Don't sound like you is too 'cited 'bout it."

With a shrug, Adella sought for the right words to describe her feelings: selfish, cranky, and sad all mixed together. "It's not that I'm not happy for George. I am, truly. I want all the best for him and Natalie. But …" She sighed again. "I wish Mama were here, that's all."

Understanding came to the wrinkled face. Mammy poked the last bite into an awaiting mouth then shooed the children to go play with the others. Setting the bowl on the ground, she reached to pat Adella's knee. "I knows you misses yo' mama. Wouldn' be right if ya didn'. Miz Ma'tha was da finest lady I evah met. No one finer than her, 'cept maybe you."

The praise caught Adella off guard. "I will never be as good as Mama. She loved everyone and had the patience of Job. I have already lost my temper a dozen times since all the commotion at the house began. And if I have to listen to Natalie prattle on one minute longer about her plans to redecorate Mama's house, I think I will scream."

Instead of being shocked at Adella's scandalous admission, the old woman chuckled. "Change ain't nevah easy, chile. Don't mattah how old we uns get. It's hard to 'cept things when change is in da air."

She bent to scoop up a tiny girl who had crawled over to lick traces from the mush bowl. The child giggled then laid her head on Mammy's shoulder while Mammy rubbed her back.

"It seems as though everyone has forgotten Mama except me." Adella watched the little one's eyes drift closed.

"Dey ain't forgot, Missy. Some folks—'specially da men—have a easier time tuckin' away da pain an' movin' on."

Adella supposed Mammy was right. Papa, and even George, had loved Mama. They'd all been happy before Mama got sick. In the long months Adella nursed Mama, the two women had grown closer than ever. Maybe that was why she felt the loss so much more keenly than the men.

Mammy closed her eyes and hummed a low tune, rocking from side to side. The baby was soon fast asleep. "I gonna lay dis sweet thang down, then get you a cup o' Mammy's special tea. It perk you right on up an' he'p you's feel more like yo'sef." She stood and looked at the cluster of filthy children nearby, some playing with crude stick-and-rope toys while others dug in the dirt. "You chillens stay put. Mammy be right back."

The old woman and baby disappeared into the open door of the nearest cabin. Although Adella had lived within yards of the quarter all her life, she'd never been invited into one of the small homes. There were simply some lines that weren't crossed on the plantation, and that was one of them. Mama had ventured into the slave homes a few times when a servant became ill or when a baby was born, but even then it was for a brief visit to check on the patient. Papa was never happy when she did and reminded her the slaves had Mammy to doctor them with her herbs and poultices. It wasn't seemly, he'd said, for the mistress of the manor to step foot in a quarter house.

Mammy returned with a chipped teacup and handed it to Adella. "That Mammy's special tea. You feels right good after you done drink it all."

Adella wrinkled her nose at the peculiar odor wafting up. "I don't think I will ask what you put in it."

Mammy chuckled. "Lotsa this 'n' that. Da Good Lawd make all kindsa plants 'n' trees with healing power in dem leaves and roots. He done tol' Mammy how to use 'em to make folks bettah." She grew thoughtful. "Sometime, though, not even Mammy's doctorin' is mo' pow'ful than God's plan."

With a sad nod, Adella guessed Mammy was thinking of Mama. After the doctor Papa brought in from Austin declared that Mama wouldn't recover, he'd consented out of desperation to allow Mammy to try her homemade remedies. That was the moment Adella knew her mother was dying.

While Adella sipped on the bitter brew, Mammy washed the bowl and spoon in a bucket of water near the door. "Dat new ovahseeah shore is diff'rent," she said, wiping the bowl dry on her apron. "We uns still cain't believe he gonna let Lucy an' dem other gals in da family way rest some durin' the day."

That drew Adella's attention. She'd wondered how Seth was faring with the slaves. "What do you mean?"

Mammy's brow rose. "Why, he done tol' Monroe to 'llow pregnant gals an extra rest time. Got da massa to 'gree, he did. No siree, he ain't like dem others, like that ol' Mistah Haley. That man meaner than dirt. Didn't care one bit if we uns dropped dead right there on da ground."

Adella blinked in surprise. "I hadn't heard about this. You are sure it was Mr. Brantley's idea and not Papa's?"

"I sure." Mammy appeared to want to say more then shook her head. "Dem out in da fields tells me how it happen." She talked about Lucy nearly fainting and Seth's ultimate proclamation. "Monroe fit to be tied, dey said, but he has to obey 'cause Massa Luther say so."

Admiration for their new overseer swept through Adella. Not only had he shown himself a caring human being, but he'd stood up to her father and put Monroe in his place.

She smiled.

Perhaps she wasn't the only white person on Rose Hill who had a soft spot for the slaves.

❧ ❦

"Leave me be, woman!"

Seth heard the angry voice while currying Chester after a long day in the fields. He'd neglected the animal since coming to Rose Hill and determined he'd do his four-legged friend right tonight, despite his own exhaustion. He'd thought himself alone in the barn.

"Why won't you's come home?" a female voice whined. "I make it real nice, but heah you is in da barn with da critters. Massa ain't gonna be happy when he heahs."

The voices came from the other side of the building, where a second row of stalls was located, but in the stillness of the musty space, Seth heard them loud and clear. Setting the stiff-bristled brush on the ledge, he quietly made his way toward them.

"Don't you tell no one, you hear? We both be in trouble then."

The words were said through gritted teeth just as Seth came around the corner. There he found an angry looking Jeptha facing Celia in the middle of the aisle, very near where he and Adella had met the other night. Freedom stood in his stall at the end of the row, watching them.

"What's going on here?" Seth glanced first at Jeptha then at Celia, whose eyes had grown round. Maybe it was paranoia brought on by Luther's constant warnings, but Seth hoped the two weren't planning some kind of escape.

Jeptha lowered his gaze to the ground, but the firm set of his jaw spoke of his agitation. "Nothin', Mr. Brantley, suh. We's just talkin'."

Celia peeked at Jeptha before dropping her gaze as well.

"It sounded more like arguing than talking to me." Seth

watched the two closely. He knew George had informed Jeptha the day before that he was to take up with Celia. Luther ordered one of the small cabins in the quarter cleared of its residents so the young couple could set up house and begin producing offspring in private.

The muscular slave remained silent.

"Well?"

Celia raised her head. "I jest tryin' to get my man home, is all."

"I ain't your man," Jeptha ground out. His gaze flitted to Seth before he stared at the floor again. His fists were clenched tightly at his sides.

Understanding dawned on Seth. Jeptha was not as pleased to have Celia paired with him as Luther had expected, which was clearly a problem. Luther expected a child from the couple nine months from now. Seth wasn't sure how to handle the situation. Perhaps a talk with the young Negro man would help.

"Celia, go on back to the quarter."

She looked up. "By myse'f?"

Jeptha stilled, waiting.

"Yes," Seth said. Whatever discussion the men had didn't need to be overheard by the young woman.

With defeat in her eyes, Celia cast one last longing glance at Jeptha before making her way down the long straw-covered aisle. Seth didn't think she would disobey him and hide in the barn listening, but he waited until the squeal of the hinges told him she'd exited.

The interior of the building was growing dim, with the last remnants of daylight filtering through random gaps in the plank wall. The day had been long and hot, and Seth was ready to be done with it. He knew the sooner he dealt with this, the sooner he could stretch out on the lumpy tick mattress in his cabin.

He studied Jeptha, who remained unmoved, staring at the ground, his muscles tense. There wasn't a tactful way to get to the bottom of the problem. Despite his disapproval of the plans

Luther had for the two Negroes, he had to abide by his employer's wishes. The slaves were, after all, Luther's property.

"I understand Master Luther wants you to pair up with Celia."

After a moment, the black man gave a brief nod. "Yassuh."

"And that doesn't please you?"

Another long pause. "No suh, it don't."

The answer confused Seth. "Why not? There is nothing wrong with Celia. She is young, healthy, attractive." He didn't continue.

"Ain't nothing wrong with Celia, suh. I just don't want to pair up with her, is all. She deserves someone who care for her."

Seth's brow rose in surprise. He'd always heard Negroes didn't have feelings the way white people did, especially when it came to intimate relationships. A neighbor once told young Seth slaves were like animals, mating with each other without the need for marriage or love.

Now a healthy young slave stood in front of him exposing that fact as myth. Jeptha had been offered a woman for his own pleasure, and yet he wasn't happy about it.

"Is there a gal you care about?" The question was out before Seth could stop it.

Jeptha's head came up. If a black man could blush, Jeptha's guilty face is what it would look like. "There is, suh."

The quiet admission put Seth in a difficult position. If Jeptha ignored Celia and pursued a relationship with this other woman, Luther would be livid. "Who is she?"

The slave hesitated.

"I give you my word this information will be kept between us." Seth sensed Jeptha's distrust. "It is important I know. You will save us both a lot of trouble if you're honest about this whole affair."

After a long moment, Jeptha took a deep breath. "Zina, suh. I been sweet on her since we's chillen. With her over to the Langfords, weren't no way to court, like you white folks. Now with her moving back to Rose Hill, I hoped …" His shoulders drooped as his words faded. Much like his hope to pair up with

Zina must have faded when Luther made it clear he wanted Jeptha and Celia together.

Seth looked up to the barn rafters. He understood Jeptha's attraction to Aunt Lu's daughter, yet what could Seth do about it? Luther wanted Jeptha and Celia to produce offspring. In order to do that, they had to live together and sleep together. At least temporarily, until Celia became pregnant.

His gut twisted with disgust. The whole thing felt wrong, yet he had no choice but to go along with it and make certain Jeptha obeyed. An overseer didn't express his opinions of what is right or wrong where the master's wishes were concerned.

"Whether you care for Celia or not, Master Luther wants you with her." Seth steeled himself to finish Luther's sordid edict. "Once Celia is with child, you don't have to sleep with her again until after the baby is born."

Jeptha's eyes lifted then and met Seth's straight on. In that brief moment, Seth saw anger, hopelessness, and something else he couldn't quite define before Jeptha looked away.

"Yassuh."

The quiet submission rang in Seth's mind for hours afterward.

CHAPTER NINE

The delicious aroma of roasting pig filled the cool night air while laughter, music, and happy voices echoed throughout the house and yard. The gala was starting to wind down, with many of the nearly one hundred guests slowly beginning to head home, although those who'd traveled quite a distance would spend the night in Rose Hill's guest rooms or at a nearby inn.

Adella let out a satisfied sigh from her place outside, at the edge of the gathering. The evening had been a success, and even Natalie's cheeks flushed with happiness as she and George bid good-bye to the departing guests. Most would return the following week for the wedding at the Langford plantation, which promised to be an even bigger affair. Aunt Lu and many of the Rose Hill servants would be dispatched to help, sharing the workload as the Langford servants had done tonight. Celebrations like this didn't take place often, so everyone looked forward to the festivities with great anticipation.

Glancing about to make certain no one noticed, Adella slipped off her shoes, relishing the feel of the cool grass on her tired, stocking-clad feet. Acting as hostess was far more exhausting than she'd expected, and she wondered how Mama had done it so effortlessly for so many years. Greeting guests with her father, trying to remember names and faces, and making sure the food and drink never ran low proved to be an arduous task. To make matters worse, Marshall Brevard, her father's friend from Rusk County, hardly left her side after arriving ahead of the other guests. She supposed he thought himself useful, but she found his constant attention annoying at best. Thankfully, Papa had him occupied in the library now, giving Adella a rare opportunity to be alone.

"It appears the merrymaking has come to an end."

Startled by the male voice so close to her ear, Adella whirled to find Seth Brantley behind her, his face darkened by the shadows of night.

She gave a nervous laugh. "You are forever sneaking up on me, Mr. Brantley." Quickly, she slid her feet back into her shoes.

He chuckled and moved into the lantern light. "I will try to announce myself from now on."

Her eyes roamed over him involuntarily. She hadn't seen him all night—she had to admit, she'd looked—and now took in his neatly trimmed hair and freshly shaven face. Though his clothes were not as new and stylish as some of the men in attendance, Seth looked incredibly handsome in his jacket and string tie.

Realizing she stared at him, Adella turned to watch the thinning crowd. "It does appear everyone is taking their leave. I am not even certain of the hour, but it must be quite late." She glanced up and found his eyes on her. Her cheeks filled with heat.

"You should be proud of yourself." The tender way he spoke sent her heart racing. "You were the perfect hostess."

Surprised, she smiled. "Thank you. That means a great deal to me. I admit I was quite nervous. Mama always made it look so easy."

"So did you."

She gave a slight laugh. "You must not have been watching very carefully then."

"Oh, but I was."

Adella swallowed, pleased and yet panicked to learn she had been the object of his observations the entire evening.

"Back home we don't have too many parties." He glanced around the lantern-lit yard. "But we have a corn shucking every year after harvest. Pa will roast a hog or a side of beef. Sometimes neighbors will join in. It's a lot of fun."

She smiled. "I have been going to the corn shucking our people hold every harvest for years. It is one of my favorite times here on the plantation."

"The planter's daughter attends the slaves' corn shucking? You are certainly full of surprises, Miss Ellis." He grinned, a teasing note in his voice.

They stood in awkward silence for several minutes, pretending to watch the activity around them. But in truth, Adella racked her mind for something clever to say. He had been on her mind since Mammy told her about the new rule he'd instituted—even before that if she were honest. Ever since their encounter in the horse barn, she hadn't been able to stop thinking about him.

The musicians Papa hired struck up a waltz. Several couples not ready to end the evening twirled around the outdoor dance floor, which the servants had constructed that morning.

"I had hoped I would have the pleasure of dancing with you before the night is over."

The deep timbre of his voice sent a chill racing down her spine.

When her eyes met his, he smiled. "May I have this dance, Miss Ellis?" He offered his arm.

With a quiver in her belly, Adella nodded. "Thank you, Mr. Brantley."

Together, they made their way to the dance floor, his limp barely noticeable. Just as they reached the edge of the wooden planks, Papa and Marshall Brevard approached.

"Here you are, Adella Rose." Papa's gaze briefly took in Seth. "This is the last song of the night. I promised Marshall you would dance it with him. You understand, Brantley."

The muscle in Seth's jaw ticked before he gave a slight bow. "Of course."

When his eyes met hers, she thought she saw regret before Marshall whisked her away.

❧ ❧

Long after the last guest departed, the slaves continued the celebration in the quarter. As he did at Christmas and harvest time, Papa had provided a pig for roasting in a pit as well as extra rations for their own merrymaking. It wasn't every week the future master of the plantation got married, and Papa felt more benevolent than usual. With all the house servants, as well as others who'd been enlisted to help, working during the gala, the slaves held off their own shindig until the white folks were finished with theirs.

Declaring herself exhausted, Adella bid everyone goodnight and pretended to go to bed. But once the big house was quiet, she slipped from her room to the kitchen wing. Aunt Lu had already gone to the quarter, but she had done as Adella instructed and left out the platters of uneaten cakes and cookies on the counter. There had been far more than they and their guests could ever consume, and Adella intended to take as much as she could carry for the children in the quarter.

With arms loaded, she hurried as fast as she dared in the dark, carefully picking her way along the path. Muted voices, laughter, and fiddle music rose from the campfires ahead. As she tiptoed past Seth's cabin, she paused, thinking she heard a sound from the open window. How she wished they'd been able to enjoy a dance together. Just the thought of being held in his strong arms sent a shiver racing up her neck.

Supposing he was sound asleep—and feeling rather disappointed with that knowledge—Adella continued on.

"I am announcing myself, Miss Ellis," he said a few moments later, causing a thrill in her heart. "I am coming up behind you, so promise not to scream."

Their private joke made her smile. She turned, though it was difficult to make out his features in the starlight. "If you promise to help me carry these things to the quarter." Her stomach gave a little leap when he drew close.

"What is all this?" He reached to take the gunnysack and napkin-wrapped items from her. Their hands brushed in the exchange, and the warmth from his fingers seemed to invade her entire body.

"Um …" She blinked. What had he asked? Oh, he wanted to know about the items. "It is some of the leftover food from the gala. We will never be able to eat it all, and there will be more next week at the wedding. My mother was always generous with the slaves when we had an abundance. I am determined to carry on the tradition."

Seth's steps slowed, and he turned to her. "I am sure she would be pleased."

Aided by the glow of the campfires, she could see his face clearly now. The sincerity shining in his eyes warmed her almost as much as his touch.

"Missy Ellis!"

Oliver broke away from the gathering and ran toward them. When he reached them, he skidded to a stop as if remembering who they were and who he was. He ducked his head. "Mistah Brantley, suh."

Adella watched, pleased to see an easy smile settle on Seth's face. "Oliver, you're up mighty late.

Oliver peeked up and grinned. "Yassuh, I is. We's cel'brat'in'." He eyed the items they held. "You gots somethin' good to eat in them wrappin's?"

Adella and Seth both laughed.

For the next half hour, they distributed the sweets. Adella couldn't help but notice how respectful the slaves were to Seth—as well as surprisingly relaxed in his presence. Even the older ones who'd been on the plantation long enough to experience the wrath of numerous overseers were fairly at ease. The few times she'd helped Mr. Haley dole out extra rations, the slaves had kept their eyes downcast and said nary a word except to mumble thank you. The laughter and conversation tonight set a vastly different scene.

Perhaps it was the celebratory mood in the air. The wedding of the future master brought a sense of newness and expectation, she supposed.

However, glancing over to where Seth knelt on one knee to

speak to Oliver, she wondered if it were perhaps something more.

❧ ❦

Seth observed Adella speaking to Mammy, a slave woman older than Methuselah, he guessed. The two women laughed, then Adella gave Mammy a hug before moving on to the next person. Each of the slaves seemed to want to speak with "Missy Ellis," despite their shyness in her presence. Even the big, rough men who worked the fields bashfully dipped their heads and grinned at whatever she said. Adella was a patient and attentive listener, and Seth couldn't help but feel a sense of pride as he watched her gracefully fulfill her role as the owner's daughter. Here was a woman who practiced what she preached.

It amazed him how much she occupied his thoughts these days. He'd looked forward to the gala, daydreaming about holding her in his arms for just one dance. Hopefully more. After taking an inordinate amount of time to clean up and dress for the affair, he'd arrived only to find Marshall Brevard following Adella around like a puppy on a leash. For the rest of the evening, he watched Marshall position himself as Adella's escort, although Seth got the distinct feeling she found his presence more of a bother than anything else. Not once did she flirt with the older man or appear overly friendly the way women sometimes do when interested in a man. That Luther had already consented to Brevard's request for Adella's hand in marriage should have kept Seth from seeking out that dance with her, but it hadn't. Marshall won again, however, when Luther sent Seth packing.

Soon a man on a fiddle began to play a lively tune. Another strummed a washboard, while someone else tapped on a leather-covered drum. The tune was nothing like Seth had ever heard, but he liked it. Couples, young and old, broke into dance, skirts and bare feet flying. Children joined in, giggling and wiggling.

Adella came to stand near him, a relaxed smile on her face. "I'm glad we came," she said, looking up at him with shining eyes.

"I am too." He watched the slaves enjoying themselves. "I guess I sometimes forget they like to have fun just as much as anyone."

Adella's smile grew. She turned away, leaving him to wonder what the big grin was about.

"It's strange," she said after a while. "I feel so much happier here with the slaves than I did all evening. Perhaps it's because I was trying to fill Mama's role as hostess and didn't do a very good job."

"On the contrary," Seth said, taking in how soft her skin looked in the fire's glow. "You were amazing tonight." She looked up, and he had the strongest urge to kiss her upturned mouth. Instead, he cleared his throat. "Every time I saw you, you were making someone feel welcome. Everyone had a wonderful time due to your hard work. Your mother would be proud of her daughter, Miss Ellis. Of that, I am quite certain."

Their eyes held for a long moment. "Thank you, Mr. Brantley," she said softly, her warm voice washing over him like a sunrise. "Your kind words mean more to me than you know."

After several more spirited tunes, the musicians slowed the music to a soulful ballad. The mood instantly changed, and couples swayed gently in the cool night air to the soothing melody.

Seth swallowed his nerves. It was now or never. With a deep breath, he leaned toward Adella. "I believe you owe me a dance, Miss Ellis."

Her wide, beautiful eyes met his. She glanced at the slaves then toward the main house. For a moment, he thought he'd made a terrible mistake. Perhaps the daughter of the plantation owner would rather not dance with a lowly overseer. Or perhaps she thought him incapable of dancing because of his limp.

Then her smile melted his fears. "I believe you are correct, sir."

Taking her hand, he led her a short distance from the others, but still within sight for propriety's sake. Some of the slaves cast curious glances at them while others, like Mammy and Aunt Lu, simply grinned and nodded their approval.

With her small hand tucked in his, and his arm carefully around her waist, they stepped into a slow waltz. The eerily hypnotic music filled the air, circling, wrapping, and finally making everything besides the two of them seem to fade away. Even the ever-present pain in his leg disappeared with her nearness.

"Thank you," he said barely above a whisper.

She looked up, her face so close he felt her warm breath. "For what?"

"Saving a dance for me."

Her smile began in her eyes before it reached her lips. "You're welcome."

Tightening his hold on her, Seth hoped the music would last forever.

CHAPTER TEN

Floating.

That seemed the perfect word to describe how Adella felt the next morning as she descended the stairs, dressed in her favorite rose-colored day gown. Floating on a cloud of happiness and contentment. She couldn't remember the last time she greeted the dawn with such lightness of heart and anticipation for what the day held. The secret smile she'd seen in her dressing mirror remained firmly in place when she entered the dining room, set there by the memories of being held in Seth's strong arms, dancing into the wee hours of the morning.

The men in the room stood to greet her.

"Well, don't you look lovely and fresh this morning, Adella Rose? Just like a spring flower."

Papa smiled from his place at the head of the table. An enormous breakfast buffet lined the sideboard to his right, filling the room with delicious aromas and allowing family and guests to help themselves whenever they chose to rise after the late night. Marshall Brevard and two other men whose names she couldn't recall—plantation owners from a neighboring county—joined him at the table. Their wives must still have been abed.

"Good morning, Papa." She hurried to kiss his cheek. "Gentlemen."

"Good morning, Miss Ellis." Marshall left his place and hastened to her side. "I trust you slept well after such a wonderful night."

A giddy giggle nearly escaped her at his choice of words, but she held it in check. "I did indeed, thank you. And I must agree. It truly was a wonderful night."

Her answer seemed to bring him great pleasure. "I too enjoyed our time together. I hope we can continue getting to know one another in the coming days."

The comment struck her as odd, but before she could sort it out, George noisily entered the room, greeted by the men as though he were a conquering hero. Slaps on the back and congratulations regarding his upcoming nuptials abounded. Being the lone female surrounded by boisterous men held little appeal, so Adella slipped from the room and headed to the kitchen. She hadn't seen Jeptha at the slaves' celebration last night and hoped Aunt Lu knew his whereabouts.

The kitchen bustled with activity when she arrived. Despite catching little sleep, the Langford servants worked along with Aunt Lu, Carolina, and the new serving girl, Celia, a pretty thing about Zina's age and with the same light-colored skin. Preparations for the lunch menu Adella and Aunt Lu decided upon last week were already underway, with half a dozen chickens lined up on the counter, plucked and ready to cook. Jars of canned vegetables, fruits, and other meats crammed every available surface.

"Mornin', Missy," Aunt Lu called from her place near the stove, where she stirred a saucepan containing a bubbling brew. Steam rose from several other large containers crowding the hot surface. Though the morning air coming from the open door still held the coolness of night, sweat dripped down the sides of Aunt Lu's face.

"Good morning." Adella drew near the stove, hoping to find the coffee pot hidden among the containers. Spying the bright blue enamel tucked in the back, she waved off Aunt Lu's offer to pour her a cup and instead filled her own mug.

Locating a spot where she hoped she wouldn't be in the way, she settled on a stool and watched the activity around her. She had no desire to return to the dining room and listen to the men discuss cotton and slave prices. Nor did she wish to have Marshall Brevard follow her every move, making his strange comments. Honestly, she didn't know why Papa had invited the man to stay for the wedding, requiring that he remain at Rose Hill the entire week. He wasn't a close friend of either family.

"That sho' was some shindig last night," Aunt Lu said, peeking into the oven where three loaves of bread were just beginning to brown.

Adella smiled, taking a sip from the mug of hot, black liquid. "Which one?"

Aunt Lu chuckled. "Both, I 'spose."

"Natalie was pleased, and that is what matters." Watching the servants scurry around the room and knowing they must have been exhausted, she added, "Thank you, all, for your hard work. I truly appreciate it."

Tired smiles and nods answered her, but the work never slowed. Aunt Lu yanked a chicken off the counter, inspected it for any remaining feathers, and plunked it into a pot of boiling water.

"I didn't see Jeptha last night," Adella said to Aunt Lu. "Do you know why he wasn't at the party?"

The room grew still as all eyes turned to her, then to Celia. After a moment, everyone went back to their duties, but a strange tension filled the air.

"He weren't feelin' too good, is all," Aunt Lu said without meeting her gaze.

Concern immediately gripped Adella. Jeptha hadn't been sick a day in his life. "Is he ill? Does Mammy know what is wrong with him?"

Aunt Lu cast a brief glance across the room to where Celia stood at the washtub, her hands deep in the sudsy water, listening. "He fine, Missy. No need ta worry yo' pretty se'f."

A frown tugged Adella's brow. Aunt Lu wasn't telling her something. And if she guessed correctly, it involved Celia. Her gaze wandered to the window as she wondered why Jeptha would miss the festivities. He, like everyone else, enjoyed letting loose and having fun for a change. If he wasn't sick, then why hadn't she seen him the past few days? Something was wrong, but how could she find out what with so many guests crowding the house?

"Mornin', Mistah Brantley, suh," Aunt Lu said.

Adella's heart tumbled over itself when she turned and saw Seth filling the doorway. Their eyes met, and his smile sent tingles all the way to her toes. "Good morning."

Aunt Lu came forward and handed him a mug of coffee. "I knows you need this, after dancin' nearly 'til the sun come up." A telling grin filled her face when she looked at Adella. "I guess you like our Negro music."

An intense heat rose to Adella's cheeks, the memory of Seth's arms around her still vivid. That every slave on the plantation bore witness to their dancing should have concerned her, but surprisingly it didn't.

"I guess we do." Seth's face crinkled with humor.

Aunt Lu chuckled and went back to work.

Seth moved closer, his eyes bright despite a lack of sleep. "How are you this morning, Miss Ellis?"

She couldn't help but smile. "I am well. And you?"

He inclined his head. "Very well, indeed. In fact, I am so well that I had hoped to tour the entire property today. With it being Saturday, the workers won't be in the fields, so I'd like to take the opportunity to get the lay o' the land, so to speak. Learn where the creeks are, nooks and crannies. That sort of thing. I can't think of a better guide than yourself since I imagine you covered the entirety of the plantation in your youthful curiosity."

Keenly aware that the servants in the room listened to the exchange, Adella held her answer in check. But inside she leaped at the chance to spend more time alone with Seth. "I am sure that can be arranged. Perhaps later this afternoon, after our midday meal."

"Do you ride? I think it would be best done on horseback rather than a carriage."

She didn't have an opportunity to answer. Papa arrived in the kitchen at that moment with an uncomfortable-looking Marshall Brevard trailing behind. The surprise she felt seeing the men surely mirrored Aunt Lu's open-mouthed expression. Papa rarely, if ever, came to the kitchen.

"There you are, Adella Rose," he said, a touch of annoyance in his voice. "We wondered where you'd disappeared to. You should be in the house entertaining our guests, not hiding out in the kitchen with the Negroes."

Astonished he would say such a thing in front of others, Adella felt the sting of embarrassment. "I am not hiding, Papa," she said, although that wasn't entirely true. "I had something to discuss with Aunt Lu."

Papa scowled and then looked at Seth. "Brantley, what are you doing here?"

"I thought it best if I took my breakfast in the kitchen this morning rather than disturb you and your guests in the main house."

"Am I to understand you allow your overseer to dine with the family?" Marshall asked, clearly shocked. He looked at Seth as though he were a thief bent on stealing Rose Hill's good silver.

"You recall me saying Brantley is the son of a good friend. It is a bit different than having someone like Haley join us for a meal." Turning to Adella, Papa held out his hand. "Come along."

With little choice, she set her mug on the counter and allowed her father to escort her from the kitchen like a wayward child. She dared not look back, but she knew Seth's eyes followed her.

❧ ❧

Seth checked his timepiece again. Nearly two o'clock. Surely the midday meal had come and gone in the main house. Where was she?

Frustrated, he yanked on the saddle cinch, causing Chester to nicker. Patting the gelding's neck, he apologized. "Sorry, old boy. I shouldn't take it out on you."

A mare stood nearby, saddled and ready for Adella. He hoped

she rode astride because he hadn't been able to locate a sidesaddle.

He looked at his pocket watch again and heaved a sigh. It might not matter if she rode astride or not. It appeared as though she wasn't coming. No doubt her father and Marshall Brevard managed to occupy her time.

Feeling defeated, Seth moved to the mare. No sense in letting the animal stand around all afternoon wearing a saddle. Just as he began loosening the straps, he heard hurried footsteps. A moment later, Adella appeared in the barn doorway, breathless.

"I'm sorry," she said, panting and laughing at the same time, her cheeks bright pink. "I had to sneak out the back. Papa and the men are holed up in his library, and the women are taking naps."

Seth grinned, his eyes drinking her in. She looked beautiful in an emerald green riding habit, her dark hair tied loosely with a black ribbon that matched the one tied around her hatband.

"I wasn't sure you were coming." He led the mare toward her. "Are you certain you should go? I wouldn't want to bring your father's displeasure down on you."

A frown replaced her smile. "Papa needs to accept that I am a twenty-year-old woman and not a little girl. I can certainly make my own decisions about where to go and whom to go with."

This from a woman who'd snuck out of the house, he thought with a grin.

With her determination in place, Seth tightened the saddle straps again and helped her up. "I didn't find a sidesaddle, so I hope this one is all right."

High on her mount, Adella chuckled. "Much to Papa's dismay, I've been riding astride ever since I learned to sit a horse."

In one swing, he was on Chester, and they headed out of the barn. After a short canter through the yard, Adella kicked her mount into a gallop, her long hair and the horse's tail flying out behind them. Seth laughed and gave Chester the lead since the horse clearly wanted to catch up with the girls.

They rode down paths Seth had never seen before, with Adella giving a grand tour as they went. She pointed out the places where she and Jeptha played hide-and-seek when they were children, where they fished, and where George broke his arm when he fell into a gully chasing her with a bull snake he'd found. They skirted the vast fields, finally arriving in a wooded area about two miles from the house. A creek tinkled nearby. Here they stopped and dismounted, letting the horses drink their fill of the cool, clear water.

"This is one of my favorite places on the plantation," she said. Her voice was soft, almost reverent. "It is so peaceful and serene. Mama would have had a fit to know I was so far from the house, but I used to come here often just to soak in the stillness."

"It reminds me of a place near our farm. With so many younger sisters nagging me and an older brother bossing me, I would sneak off with my pole the first chance I'd get."

She smiled. "I always wanted a sister. George thought I was a pest."

He shrugged. "I guess I thought my sisters were pests, too."

After a moment, she wandered over to the stream. "Jeptha came with me sometimes. We would sit for hours without saying a word. Just listening to the silence."

"It sounds like you spent a lot of time with Jeptha," he said, remembering her father's disapproving tone when he spoke of his daughter's friendship with the slaves.

"Jeptha was my best friend." She bent to pluck a wild daisy and twirled it in her fingers. "In some ways, he still is, although we don't go on adventures together anymore." She gave a mock scowl. "It wouldn't be proper, Adella Rose," she said, making her voice low and stern like her father's. With a slight shrug, she studied the dainty flower. "There weren't any white children to play with, and George never wanted me around. I had no choice but to play with the slaves."

Seth agreed with her father, but he didn't voice that opinion. He certainly wouldn't want a daughter of his playing with a slave boy. "I would have thought you'd be happier playing with the little girls."

Tossing the flower into the stream, she watched it bob and swirl away. "By the time I was old enough to play outside without my mammy or Mama watching over me, the slave girls my age were already working in the kitchen or the weaving house or somewhere else on the plantation. Jeptha always seemed to be around, though. He helped in the barns, but Papa never made him go out to the fields unless it was harvest."

Luther's confession that he'd *saved* Jeptha for something special resurfaced in Seth's mind. Knowing how Adella felt about the slave convinced him she would be furious to learn what exactly her father had saved him for.

"Does your family own slaves?"

Seth met her curious gaze. "Yes, we have a dozen or so. Pa treats them well and has never had any problems."

She seemed to contemplate his statement. "Treating slaves well is certainly commendable, but wouldn't you agree that simply claiming ownership of another human being is the opposite of fair and good treatment?"

Surprised to hear the daughter of a large plantation owner say such a thing, Seth responded, "My father—and any slave owner, for that matter—are well within their rights according to the law. I realize many people disagree with slavery, but if the slaves are well taken care of, with plenty of food and shelter, then who's to say they would be better off free."

"I imagine they would!"

Her indignant reply made his brow raise. "Are you telling me you are an abolitionist, Miss Ellis?"

She bit her bottom lip and huffed out a sigh. "I honestly don't know what I am. I know Papa needs the slaves to work the land and crops. He has often said he would go bankrupt if he ever had to pay the slaves a wage. But I simply can't reconcile the ownership of another human being in my head. Or my heart."

Her vulnerability made Seth want to take her in his arms.

"Slavery has been in existence through the ages," he said, hoping to soothe her fretting. "Our families aren't doing anything wrong by following the laws and traditions of our nation."

"Not everyone agrees with slavery," she countered, her brow furrowed. "The northern states have banned it, as have other countries. And simply because something is lawful doesn't mean it is something worthy of engaging in."

Seth grinned despite the gravity of the conversation.

"What are you smiling about?" she asked.

"I find it rather fascinating that a woman of your genteel breeding is so passionate on the subject of slavery. In my experience, most daughters of wealthy plantation owners take pleasure in the benefits of having someone answer to their beck and call. Are you so against slavery that you would willingly give that up in order for them to be free?"

She sighed. "I would be lying if I said I didn't enjoy having maids to help me dress and do my hair and cook my meals. Not one day of my entire life has passed without the assistance of many servants. But lately, I find that their lack of freedom to choose bothers me a great deal. Shouldn't they be free to choose the life they wish to live rather than being told they must obey a master?"

The answer to her question rang true somewhere in Seth's mind, but he couldn't bring himself to believe slavery should be abolished. "Some people believe that Negroes aren't capable of living on their own. That they need to be governed by a master for their own survival."

She scoffed. "That is ridiculous. Negroes are every bit as intelligent as a white person. Why, I taught Jeptha how to speak correctly and—" Her eyes widened, and she clamped her mouth shut.

"You taught Jeptha how to what?" He had a suspicion he knew the answer. It was illegal to teach a slave to read and write, but it wouldn't surprise him to learn that was precisely what Adella had done.

"Oh, nothing." She moved away so he couldn't see her face. "I simply believe a slave can learn anything they put their mind to, same as us."

Seth followed her. He didn't care if she'd taught Jeptha his letters. In fact, it made him a little jealous to know she'd spent so much time with the slave. Jeptha probably knew Adella better than anyone.

They walked along the creek in silence for a time before she stopped. "I'm glad we came here today," she said, casting a shy smile at him. "With all the commotion in the house, preparing for Natalie to move in, I needed the peace and quiet of this place."

"I would be happy to escort you here anytime you'd like."

She closed her eyes; her face tilted upwards to catch the filtered sunrays, looking so beautiful she took his breath away. Drawn to her, he took an involuntary step closer, dry leaves rustling under his feet. When she opened her eyes, her steady gaze held his expectantly. Before he could stop himself, he took her face between his hands. When she didn't protest, he lowered his mouth to hers. A small sigh escaped her, and she leaned into his chest. Heartened, he deepened the kiss.

With reluctance, Seth pulled away, his body tense with desire. "Like I told you in the barn the other night, you pose a great temptation, Missy Ellis."

She smiled at his use of the name the servants called her, but her eyes continued to burn with passion, making him want to take her in his arms again. As much as he hated to, he turned away. "I think we had better get back to the house before someone misses you."

Touching her lips with her fingers, she nodded, although he sensed her reluctance. "I suppose you're right. Papa has an evening of music and recitations planned for the guests. He'll no doubt come looking for me soon."

They mounted and leisurely rode back to the house, saying little but exchanging happy smiles every so often. Once in the horse barn, Seth helped her dismount, keeping his hands on her small waist far longer than necessary, hoping to steal one more kiss. When a noise from the back of the barn sounded, they stepped away from one another.

"Join us tonight," she said as they walked toward the house, keeping a proper distance between them. "Dinner will be served at seven o'clock, followed by an evening of grand entertainment."

He chuckled at the exaggeration in her voice. But her invitation made him uneasy. "I don't think your father would appreciate me barging in on his guests. You recall Mr. Brevard's reaction to learning that I sometimes take meals with the family."

Adella turned a pretty scowl to him. "I don't give one whit what Mr. Brevard or anyone else thinks. I am mistress of this plantation for five more days. I will invite whomever I choose to dine with us, and I choose to invite you, Mr. Brantley."

Desperate to kiss her pert mouth, but knowing this was not the time or place, he conceded. Perhaps attending the evening's festivities would afford them some time alone. "Your wish is my command, Miss Ellis." He gave a gallant bow, making her giggle.

"That's better."

He watched her enter the house, giving him one last secret wave before she disappeared. Seth made his way back to the barn to unsaddle the horses, wondering how in the world he'd allowed himself to fall in love with Adella Rose Ellis.

CHAPTER ELEVEN

"I don't understand why you invited the overseer to join us this evening, Adella Rose."

Natalie stood behind Adella where she sat at her dressing table, putting the finishing touches to her hair. Hulda had expertly piled her curls on her head, leaving a few wavy strands loose to soften her face. A ribbon the same cobalt blue as her dress threaded through the mass, and she turned her head from side to side to make certain it hadn't puckered. She wanted to look perfect for Seth.

Seth.

His very name sent a shiver pulsating through her. She put a finger to her lips, remembering their kiss. The passion it elicited should have shocked her, but it didn't. Instead, it ignited something deep inside. Something that told her she'd never tire of kissing Seth Brantley even if she spent a lifetime doing so.

"Well?" Natalie asked.

With more than a little annoyance, Adella met Natalie's frown in the mirror. "I invited him because he was a friend of the family long before he was our overseer. If Papa hadn't hired him, he would have been here as a guest. His own father is invited to your wedding. I don't see what difference it makes now that he works for us. Besides, I think it would be rude to leave him out, considering Papa has allowed him to take his meals with us since he came."

Lifting the wide hooped skirt of her lavender evening gown, Natalie settled on the edge of Adella's bed. A long golden curl lay across her bare white shoulder, accentuating a pearl drop necklace at her throat that Adella instantly recognized as Mama's. George must have given it to Natalie as a wedding present. Though she didn't begrudge the young woman the jewels, since she herself had a sapphire and diamond necklace that once belonged to Mama, it served as yet another reminder of all the changes taking place.

"I may have to address that once I'm mistress of Rose Hill." Natalie ran her fingers across the smooth beads when she noticed Adella's interest in the necklace. "It doesn't seem proper to have an employee dining with the family."

Adella nearly growled. Natalie sounded just like Marshall Brevard. "Remember, Natalie. Even after you and George marry, this is still Papa's plantation. You will abide by his rules in the same way I do."

Natalie cocked one perfectly shaped eyebrow. "I imagine I will abide by them better than you, Adella, dear."

"What is that supposed to mean?" She turned to face Natalie.

With a humorless chuckle, Natalie stood and sashayed to the open window. The slaves' cabins lay in the distance. "What would your father say if he knew you'd been in the quarter last night?"

At Adella's gasp, Natalie laughed. "Oh, yes, dear sister. I know all about it. How you took the leftover sweets from the gala and distributed them among the slave children. You can't hide anything from me."

Heart pounding, Adella waited for Natalie to spill the rest of the story. About how she and Seth danced for hours unending, gazing into each other's eyes until nothing else existed.

But her brother's fiancée simply looked at her, waiting for a response.

Relief washed over Adella after a long minute, supposing Natalie's informant left out that part of the story. Why, she didn't know, but she was grateful. "Very well. You have caught me. But Mama would have done the same thing. She always treated our people with kindness and taught me to do the same. If you intend to wear her jewelry and live in her house, then I expect you to continue her legacy once you step into her role as mistress of Rose Hill Manor."

Natalie's mouth dropped open, apparently taken aback by Adella's little speech. The two stared at one another, facing off in what Adella hoped would not be an ongoing battle. But Mama's memory and all she stood for were part of Rose Hill, and Adella would not have Natalie or anyone else destroy that with selfish, unkind motives.

After several tense moments, a thoughtful expression erased Natalie's outrage. "I ... I hadn't thought of it like that." She appeared more contrite than Adella had ever seen her. "Your mother was always kind to me, and ... and ... I hope she would be pleased that George and I will marry."

Feeling a bit contrite herself, Adella moved to the young woman's side. "Mama would be overjoyed that George chose you for his wife, Natalie. Your family has always been good friends to the Ellises." She chuckled. "I am sure my parents' greatest disappointment is you didn't have a brother for me to marry."

Natalie didn't smile at Adella's joke. "I did have a brother," she said quietly, moving to sit on the bed again. "His name was Samuel. He died before his second birthday. I think Papa has always been disappointed I wasn't a boy to replace him. Mama never became pregnant again after I was born."

"Oh, Natalie, I am so sorry." Adella felt like the biggest clod for making a joke of it. "I had no idea."

The young woman nodded and forced a smile. "Papa is thrilled he'll have George for a son-in-law, though. He can't stop talking about how the two plantations will someday be one, and how his grandson will run it."

This rare look into Natalie's life reminded Adella not to judge someone by their outward appearances. Natalie had obviously suffered deep pain over her father's unfulfilled desire for a son. Who knew how many times he'd made that known, consciously or not, to his daughter. Even as she prepared for what should have been the happiest day of her life, her father seemed only to think of the benefits her marriage would bring to him, including a grandson to carry on the Langford legacy.

How sad for Natalie, Adella thought later, on her way down the staircase toward their guests. How thankful she was Papa wasn't anything like Mr. Langford.

❧ ☙

"I am not sure I understand why you thought your experience with the Texas Rangers would qualify you to be the overseer of a large cotton plantation, Brantley."

Seth faced Marshall Brevard in the well-appointed parlor of Rose Hill Manor. The eyes of everyone in the room were on him, and not even Luther Ellis appeared willing to come to his rescue. It was obvious Luther's friend baited him, hoping for a verbal spar, he supposed. He would need to answer carefully, lest he appear the fool or exhibit too much bravado.

"The life of a Ranger isn't that different from an overseer as far as I can tell," Seth said, appearing far more confident in his words than he felt. "I would actually go so far as to say the overseer has it easier than the Ranger."

"How so?" Marshall asked, his tone giving ample evidence he didn't agree.

"Rangers deal with unruly lawbreakers just as an overseer does. They both must dole out discipline and make sure everyone is abiding by the laws of the land. But a Ranger has the entire state of Texas to patrol, with her thousands upon thousands of residents. The overseer has only the land and slaves his employer owns to keep track of." Seth shrugged nonchalantly. "It seems rather obvious to me who has the advantage."

A murmur of agreement swept the room, much to Seth's relief. Marshall, however, was not finished.

"Wouldn't it seem logical that the same injury that kept you from returning to your post with the Rangers would hinder you as an overseer?" He took a sip of the amber liquid in the glass he held, then turned to Calvin Langford, Natalie's father, who stood beside him. "I mean, I would think that a man whom the State of Texas didn't have enough confidence in to get the job done would seek something less challenging. Like, say, a storekeeper, for instance."

Langford chuckled while Brevard smirked.

Seth's fists clenched into tight balls, and it took everything he had to keep himself from laying the dandy out on the floor right then and there.

"I have full confidence in Brantley," Luther said, effectively putting an end to Marshall's examination. "His father and I go back many years. I for one believe the State of Texas made a mistake when they didn't offer Seth his position. Their loss is my gain."

To say he appreciated Luther's vote of confidence would be an understatement. Though he would have enjoyed putting his fist to Marshall Brevard's jaw, the man was a guest at Rose Hill. It wouldn't do to come to fisticuffs over something as unimportant as his pride.

As the other guests continued their conversations, Seth made his way toward the door. It was a mistake to come. It was one thing to enjoy a meal with the family of his father's friend, but to try to fit in with rich Texas planters was foolish. He wasn't like them, nor did he wish to be.

When he arrived at the door, he stopped.

Adella stood just outside in the foyer.

"Good evening, Mr. Brantley." Her soft voice barely reached him, but her beauty nearly knocked him off his feet.

"Good evening, Miss Ellis." He inclined his head politely, but what he really wanted to do was sweep her into his arms and take her away from here. Especially knowing Brevard stood in the parlor waiting for her. "May I say you look exquisite tonight?"

A pretty blush brightened her cheeks. "You may."

Looking into her shining eyes, nearly the same deep hue as her gown, he knew he would disappoint her if he left. But to stay would force him to be cordial to Brevard, and the last thing he wanted to do was be nice to that man. That the dandy had already gained Luther's approval to marry Adella nearly drove Seth mad. Yet until the engagement was officially announced, he still had a chance. The fact that Adella had kissed him this afternoon proved she hadn't given her heart to the man. To leave now would only give Brevard the upper hand. And he wasn't about to do that.

The dinner bell rang in the candlelit dining room across the hall.

"May I escort you to dinner tonight, mademoiselle?" He imitated an old gentleman he once overheard in a restaurant in San Antonio. From the corner of his eye, he saw Marshall coming toward them.

With a laugh, Adella linked her arm with his. "Why, Mr. Brantley, I didn't know you spoke French."

"Miss Ellis," Marshall said when he approached a moment later, his lips pressed into a tight smile. "I had hoped to secure the honor of escorting you to dinner myself so we might have the pleasure of conversing over the meal." He glared at Seth. "I'm sure Mr. Brantley understands."

Adella offered a pleasant smile to the man, though she didn't relinquish her hold on Seth's arm. "Thank you, Mr. Brevard, but I am confident Mr. Brantley can see me safely across the hall. And we have name place cards tonight," she said loud enough for all the guests to hear. "This way we have new dinner companions to liven things up."

A tense moment ticked by. The muscle in Brevard's jaw tightened when his eyes met Seth's, but he finally bowed out without another word.

As they moved toward the dining room, Seth was certain of two things.

He loved Adella even more for choosing him over Brevard.

And he had just made an enemy.

Seth watched Luther Ellis and Marshall Brevard disappear into the library, the door closing behind them. The other guests, including Natalie and her parents, remained in the parlor, where George entertained them with his grand plans for the future of Rose Hill Manor. Mr. Langford especially appeared captivated by every word.

With everyone happily occupied, Seth knew this might be his only opportunity to get Adella's attention and beg a private moment with her. Even though they'd sat beside one another at dinner, thanks to her arrangement of place cards, they couldn't speak freely with so many people around. Brevard had kept a watchful eye on them from his place at the opposite end of the table, biding his time no doubt. A sense of urgency struck Seth during the last course of the meal, knowing he had to speak to Adella alone tonight. But how?

"Seth, is something wrong?"

He turned and found her coming toward him, a worried frown marring her beautiful face. He breathed a prayer of thanks. This was the chance he'd been waiting for all evening. That she'd used his Christian name encouraged him further. "No, nothing is wrong." He offered his arm. "Would you care to sit on the veranda? The air has cooled now that the sun is set."

A smile quickly replaced her frown. "That sounds lovely."

Rose Hill's wide porches wrapped around nearly the entire first floor of the house, with cozy seating areas here and there. Seth led Adella to the farthest one he could find, hoping no one would disturb them. His feelings were a jumbled mess, but he couldn't leave without letting her know he loved her. Brevard's proposal might come any day. Seth couldn't offer her a grand home, acres of land, and servants to wait on her, but he would work hard and love her more than Brevard ever could.

"I'm glad you came tonight." She settled her voluminous hooped skirt across the small wicker sofa. Light from a nearby lantern cast a soft glow while crickets and toads began their nightly song.

Seth leaned against the porch rail and chuckled. "You would be the only one."

She gave him a sympathetic look. "I don't know why some people have suddenly become such snobs. You were a friend of the family long before you became our overseer. Why, you even visited here when you were a boy."

"I was thinking about that visit last night. Or, should I say, this morning after we left the quarter." He grinned, recalling her from all those years ago. As adorable then as she was now. "I remember George wouldn't let you play a game with us, and you ran away crying. You were barefoot, as I recall." He nodded toward her feet. "Some things never change."

"Oh, you scoundrel." She feigned offense. Laughing, she poked the tips of her slippers out from beneath the hem of her skirt. "See. I have my shoes on." After a long moment, her creamy shoulders lifted in a slight shrug. "I suppose it's because Jeptha and the other children didn't wear shoes when it was warm outside. Of course, I didn't know at the time they didn't own any beyond the hard leather ones they use in the winter. I thought it was wonderful that they didn't have to wear shoes that pinched their feet. It probably drove my mother to exasperation the way I would kick them off the moment she turned her back."

"It sounds as though you weren't exactly an easy child to raise, running around the plantation barefoot with the slave children. One day, you will probably have a little girl as wild." *And beautiful,* he thought, the strange new desire to be that child's father taking him by surprise. He'd never thought of being a father, yet somehow it felt right with Adella.

"Jeptha said the same thing once. Oh"—she frowned—"I have been meaning to ask you about Jeptha. I haven't seen him in several days, and he wasn't at the party. I asked Aunt Lu about it, but I got the feeling she wasn't telling me something. She said he hadn't felt well, but she kept looking at Celia, the new girl. It was very strange. Do you know anything about it?"

"I haven't moved him to the fields, if that is what you're asking," Seth answered, hedging her question. As far as he knew, the young man had followed Luther's instructions and moved into the cabin with Celia despite his reluctance. Perhaps that was the reason Adella hadn't seen him.

"Have you noticed anything different about him? If he isn't feeling well, perhaps I should talk to Mammy." Concern filled her eyes.

Seth hated being deceptive with her, but it wasn't his place to inform her of Jeptha's new living arrangement. "I am sure he's fine. I will make a point to speak with him tomorrow if that would make you feel better."

She relaxed against the sofa cushion. "Yes, it would. Thank you, Seth."

The sound of his name on her soft lips stirred something deep. Boldly, he sat beside her and took her warm hand.

For a long moment, they stared at one another. Seth's heart hammered. Never before had he told a woman he loved her, and he felt as nervous as a schoolboy now that the moment to do just that had arrived.

"Adella, there is something I—"

"Missy Ellis? Are you out here?"

Adella removed her hand from his grip and turned toward the sound of Zina's voice. The young woman appeared from around the corner. Her gaze traveled from Adella to Seth and back. "Your father is looking for you, Missy. He thought you were in your room."

Adella stood, and Seth followed. "Thank you, Zina. I will be right in."

With an apologetic look, she turned to Seth. "I'm sorry. Papa will be angry if I don't come now."

He nodded, disappointed but not defeated. "Perhaps we will

have another opportunity to talk."

Her smile warmed him. "I would like that."

Together they made their way to the parlor. When they entered the room, Marshall Brevard frowned and exchanged a look with Luther. Luther nodded and walked toward them.

"Adella Rose, we have been waiting for you," he said, ignoring Seth altogether. Taking her by the arm, he led her to the front of the room near the marble fireplace. Marshall moved to Luther's other side, looking highly pleased.

An uneasy feeling washed over Seth.

"Friends, I have an announcement," Luther said, gaining the attention of the occupants in the room. Adella stared at him. Her brow puckered, and confusion shone in her eyes. "While we look forward to George and Natalie's wedding in just a few days, I want you all to be the first to know we will have another wedding very soon." Placing one arm around Adella's shoulders and the other around Marshall's, Luther smiled. "I would like to announce the engagement of my daughter, Adella Rose, to Marshall Brevard."

CHAPTER TWELVE

Dazed, Adella stared at her father. Surely he jested. Before her mind could sort out his ridiculous announcement, however, Natalie swept her into a sisterly hug.

"I am so happy for you, Adella Rose. We will both be brides now."

Mrs. Langford and the other women in the room also came forward to congratulate her, even as their men shook hands with Marshall Brevard.

Marshall Brevard? The man was at least twenty years her senior and lived on a plantation in faraway Rusk County. If she recalled correctly, he and his wife had never had children before she passed away several years ago. He was a snob and a bore, and she'd never once looked at him as a suitor. Oh, what had Papa done?

As the chatter in the room began once again, now with a new topic, she turned her back to the guests and faced her father. Yet before she could utter the angry words swirling through her mind, Papa held up his hand.

"Hear me out, Adella Rose." His voice lowered so only the three of them could hear. Marshall remained near, but she refused to even acknowledge him.

"This is for the best. Marshall is a fine man with lands that rival Rose Hill's. You will be well taken care of, which is no small comfort to me."

Fighting for composure, for she did not want to make a scene in front of their guests, she met his gaze with an unflinching stare. "I should have been consulted before you made such an announcement." She shot a look at Marshall then back to Papa. "I am not a piece of property to be given away to the highest bidder. Mr. Brevard and I are barely acquainted."

"Miss Ellis, I have the highest—" Marshall began, but she cut him off.

"Please, Mr. Brevard. I don't mean to be rude, but this does not concern you."

"He is your fiancé, Adella Rose." Papa's hushed words were stern. "I have given my consent to the marriage. Marshall and I have an agreement, and I expect you to abide by it."

Adella couldn't believe what she heard. "*You* have an agreement? And what of my wishes? Do they matter at all?"

The room suddenly grew quiet. Adella realized she'd raised her voice in a most unladylike and highly disrespectful manner.

Ignoring the guests' curious glances, Papa stood firm in his judgment. "No, Adella Rose. Your wishes do not matter in this decision. As your father, it is my duty to see that your future is secure. You will thank me someday that I did not allow you to make a grave mistake." His eyes looked past her to the foyer.

Adella turned to follow his gaze.

Seth stood in the doorway.

✤ ✤

Bright morning sunshine shone through the small window in Seth's bedroom, but he remained stretched out on his bed covers, fully clothed, where he'd been all night. Sleep had eluded him, with memories of the evening past tormenting his mind throughout the wee hours.

Adella is engaged, resounded, again and again, nearly driving him mad.

He closed his eyes and moaned.

He'd never forget the look on her face when she turned and saw him standing in the doorway. It was the look of one who'd found a treasure only to have it slip through her fingers. He'd also never forget the triumph fixed on Brevard's face. Seth hadn't waited around to offer congratulations to the couple—instead, he practically bolted from the house.

With a heavy sigh, he forced himself into a sitting position on the edge of the lumpy mattress. He hung his head in his hands, feeling as though he'd spent the night drinking whiskey rather than lying awake trying to figure out an impossible situation. Despite the many hours of wrestling with one idea after another, he'd come up empty-handed. He'd known about the engagement before last night's inevitable announcement—long before Seth became overseer, Luther and Brevard had concocted their plan. That he and Adella kissed made no difference to them. That he loved Adella mattered even less.

Just before the sun poked over the horizon, Seth had come to a painful conclusion. He couldn't stay on as Rose Hill's overseer. He couldn't bear to watch Brevard strut around like a peacock, putting his hands on Adella and claiming her as his own. No, Seth had to leave. Now. Though he'd told Luther he would stay on for a year, things had changed. He didn't have nearly enough money saved to get him to Oregon, but he'd figure something out. All he knew was he couldn't stay here and watch Adella marry Marshall Brevard.

Glancing out the window, he remembered it was Sunday. No field work would take place, allowing the slaves time to rest. Luther allowed them to have services in the small chapel Martha Ellis insisted on having built down by the creek, as Seth was told. One of the Langford slaves, Moses, would lead it today, and the Rose Hill slaves all seemed eager to hear what the big man had to say. At least, that's what he gathered from the bits of conversation he'd overheard the past few days.

A knock on his door drew his attention.

Seth stared at the wood, wondering if perhaps Adella had snuck away to talk to him. Hurrying to see who it was, his shoulders slumped when he saw the ancient Mammy standing on his porch.

"Mornin', Mistah Brantley, suh. I hopes I ain't 'stirbing you." She flashed him a toothless grin.

"Morning." He ran a hand through his unruly hair. His voice sounded gravelly even to his own ears. A stiff cup of coffee would help, but he was loathe to go anywhere near the big house until he'd figured out his next move.

"I won't keep you, it bein' yo' day off an' all. But I wanted ta bring you this ointment I has to he'p with yo' leg." She pointed to his injured thigh. "It real good fo' takin' da pain outta them muscles an' sech."

"An ointment?"

"Yassuh." She grinned again. "Da good Lawd done give me a gift for makin' healin' potions an' sech. I seen you rubbin' dat leg of yourn, and limpin' when da pain is bad. Dis here ointment soak in real good an' make that throbbin' go 'way."

She held out a small clay pot with a dark mixture inside. Seth accepted it, still confused by the unusual offering.

"Now, it made o' roots an' growin' things, so it might stain yo' trousers." She turned as though leaving. "Once you got it on yo' leg, jest put a bit o' cloth 'round it. Should be fine."

Seth stood staring at her retreating back, touched by the old woman's thoughtfulness. She'd noticed him limp and wanted to help. A slave had never done anything like that for him. No one had, in fact. He stepped onto the porch. "Thank you, Mammy."

She turned and nodded. "We all God's chillens, Mistah Brantley. I do for you same as I do fo' my own people." She started to leave then turned again. "You welcome ta come join us'n's service this mornin'. Goin' ta start soon 'nough over yonder in da chapel. I 'spect Missy Ellis be da on'y one dat come from da big house, what with all the doin's an' goin's on up der last night."

His ears perked up. "Miss Ellis comes to your services?"

Mammy smiled. "Shore 'nough, she do. Jest like her Mama done. Massa Ellis an' Massa George come time ta time, but ain't reg'lar like Missy."

The old woman couldn't know how her invitation poured hope into Seth's wounded heart. If he could just get Adella alone and tell her how he felt, then together they could go to her father and explain why she couldn't marry Brevard.

"I just might do that. Come to the service, I mean."

A sly grin creased her already wrinkled face. "I 'spect you will, Mistah Brantley. I 'spect you will."

A short time later, he trailed some distance behind the slaves as they made their way to the small log building tucked in the trees near the creek. Already a song had started among them.

"Children of the Heavenly King,
As we join and let us sing.
Sing our Savior, worthy of praise.
Glory in His work and ways,
We are traveling home to God
In the way our fathers trod.
Christ our advocate is made.
Christ our advocate is made."

The soulful sound echoed Seth's somber mood. He wasn't much of a churchgoer himself, but his ma and pa made certain their children were God-fearing. Bible reading took place each evening after the supper dishes were cleaned, and though Seth hadn't always paid attention to the words his father read aloud, he believed what he heard.

"*Christ our advocate is made.*"

He wondered if the slaves understood what they were singing. Since it was against the law to teach a Negro to read and write, he questioned how they held church services without Bible readings and preachers who'd been taught in seminary schools back East. Did they understand things like salvation and eternal life? Even he didn't grasp everything the Good Book said, so how could an uneducated person comprehend something so complicated?

Approaching the small building, he felt out of place and stood back while the others filed through the door. Some nodded a greeting to him. Most simply ignored him. A few minutes passed without any sign of Adella. He hoped Mammy knew what she was talking about in saying Adella never missed a service. He also hoped that if she did come, she'd come alone. Yet it wouldn't surprise him for Brevard to feel entitled to follow her everywhere she went, now that she was his fiancée.

The last of the slaves had entered the building, raising their voices in song, when he saw her hurrying across the lawn. Relief hit him. She was alone. He knew when she spotted him because her pace slowed and she glanced behind her, no doubt making certain no one from the house could see them.

He didn't move toward her but waited for her to approach. Her cheeks were pale, and dark circles rimmed her eyes. He guessed she hadn't slept much either.

"How are you?" He wished he could fold her into an embrace and let her know everything would be fine. Yet how could it be?

"I don't really know how to answer that." Her eyes searched his. "You understand I had no idea what my father planned last night."

He nodded. "I know." Glancing to the open door to the chapel, he said, "Perhaps after the service we can take a walk."

Surprise lit her eyes. "You're staying for the service?"

Seth couldn't help but grin. "Mammy invited me."

Together they entered the crowded building. A dozen benches were filled with slaves singing a lively song, leaving just enough room for an aisle down the middle. Conspicuously, two places remained open on the back row even though several men stood leaning against the wall.

Seth followed Adella to the empty seats. Already, Moses stood at the front of the room behind a crudely built pulpit, leading the singing with his deep, melodious voice.

When the singing subsided among shouts of "Hallelujah," Moses raised his hand to quiet the crowd. "We uns knows a thing about dat heavy load, don't we?" he asked, receiving more shouts and *uh-huh's*.

He looked over the crowd, his eyes grazing Seth and Adella as well. "Yassum, we know 'bout heavy loads. But we don't know nothin' compared to the heavy load our Lawd an' savior Jesus knowed."

"No, we shore don't," Mammy said from her place near the front.

"Our Lawd Jesus done carried the heaviest load there is when he took our sins 'pon his shoulders. He hung there on that cross holdin' that load. Ev'er sin there ever was. Yours. Mine. Ev'er person who ever been bo'n. Bible says he didn't mind carryin' that load for you an' me. He weren't forced ta carry it. No, siree. He wanted to." Moses shook his head as though he couldn't believe it. "He done it 'cuz he wanted to."

His eyes scanned the crowd again. "How many o' you uns be willin' to climb up that ol' cross an' hang for the sins o' others? For the sins o' yo' white masters?"

No one volunteered.

Seth squirmed uncomfortably, being the only white man in the silent room. Preaching about sins and such in an all-white church didn't seem so personal as it did here, surrounded by black men and women who'd been enslaved all their lives.

"That's what I thought," Moses continued. "But the Book o' John say God loved the world so much He let His Son die that'a way so's we don't have to. So's we can be free from sin. We uns be the ones that deserves punishment, but Lawd Jesus done stood in our place."

"Then why we still get lashes?" someone asked, followed by someone else's, "Yah, why?"

Moses shook his head. "It ain't da Lawd Jesus whooping us'n's. Them folks that doin' that sort o' thing ain't done the Lawd's work. They followin' they own will. Jesus said 'take my yoke 'cuz it be light.' But like them Israelites ol' Moses brung outta Egypt ... they had ta suffer some even if they was God's chosen folks. When you's sufferin', just remember that Jesus knowed sufferin' too."

The big man left the pulpit. Someone near the front broke into song, and other voices joined in. Adella motioned to Seth that it was time for them to leave, and he led the way back out into the sunshine.

When they'd gone a short distance away from the chapel, Seth shoved his hands into his pockets. "I've never been to a Negro service before." He shrugged. "I didn't know what to expect. Moses surprised me, I guess."

"Natalie said he used to belong to a preacher." Adella walked beside him, heading away from the big house and prying eyes. "The old gentleman died, and Moses ended up in the slave markets in New Orleans. Mr. Langford bought him from someone who'd brought him to Texas."

They grew silent after that. The only sound was birds chirping in the trees as the two made their way down the path along the creek. Seth knew they could ill afford to waste precious time, despite the awkwardness of the situation. It was best to plunge in the way one jumps into a creek of chilly spring water.

"Listen, Adella." He turned her to face him. "Last night, before Zina came to find you, I had something I wanted to say. Something important."

Her wide blue eyes gazed at him with an intensity that was almost tangible. "You did?"

With the long-awaited moment finally here, he suddenly felt tongue-tied. "Yes. When your father first hired me, I didn't expect to be captivated by his daughter."

She offered a shy smile.

Emboldened, Seth continued. "The fact is, when he said you were to be engaged to someone else, I didn't care. I hadn't gotten to know you yet. I hadn't grown to care about you the way I do now."

Expecting a joyous response to his admission, the deepening frown that creased her brow confused him.

"You knew?"

His confusion increased. "That I cared for you? No, not until—"

"I mean, you knew Papa planned to announce my engagement to Marshall Brevard?"

Seth froze, realizing he'd made a terrible mistake. "I … Yes. No. I didn't know he was going to announce it last night, no."

"But you knew about it." A hard tone edged her words.

"Yes," he admitted. Any hope he held of gaining Adella's love slipped away with the look of betrayal on her face. "Your father mentioned it the day after we returned from Galveston."

Her chin trembled with anger. "You kissed me knowing my father had already pledged me to another man."

Seth's sins seemed to multiply by the minute. "Yes."

She closed her eyes. "I am such a fool."

"Adella, please listen." Seth groped for words to remedy the situation if that was possible. She looked at him, but the damage he'd done shone on her face. "You were not engaged when we danced in the quarter, or when we rode down to the creek. I didn't expect to … to …" Could he say the words?

"To kiss me?" she wrongly guessed. Tears filled her eyes. "I thought you were different. I thought …" With a sob, she bolted past him, her skirts lifted high.

"Adella! Wait!" He ran after her, but she quickly reached the grassy clearing visible from the house. The last thing he needed to do was create a scene for everyone to see. Luther would surely send him packing if he didn't plan to already.

Frustrated, Seth ended the chase. He watched her disappear around the corner of the house, away from prying eyes. As much as he longed to follow her, he had to give her time to sort things out. With a heavy heart, he prayed he'd have another opportunity to make things right between them. She needed to know he loved her.

Turning to make his way back to his cabin, he stopped.

The slaves must have ended their service while he and Adella spoke, because every last one of them stood outside the chapel, staring at him.

CHAPTER THIRTEEN

Natalie and her parents departed early Monday morning to prepare for the wedding, which would take place on Saturday. A few guests remained at Rose Hill, businessmen mostly, and Papa put George in charge of their entertainment so Adella and Marshall could get better acquainted. Adella, however, refused to leave her room for two full days before Papa arrived at her door, his frustration barely contained.

"You will dress and come downstairs this instant, Adella Rose!" His loud voice caused Hulda to skitter from the room. "I have had enough of your childish nonsense. You are a grown woman with a fiancé waiting for you. You have obligations in this house, and I will not allow you to hide in your room another moment."

Listening to him now, it amazed Adella he'd ever been the father she adored. The man standing before her barking angry orders was a stranger. The same stranger who'd betrothed her to a man she didn't love. "Not that anyone has bothered to ask, but I have been ill with all that has transpired." Which was the truth. First her father's betrayal and then Seth's. It was all too much for her to bear, and she'd taken to her bed with a raging headache and a broken heart.

Papa heaved a sigh. "Spare me the melodramatics, daughter. You act as though something terrible has happened, when in fact, you have been incredibly blessed. Not many girls your age marry men with the kind of wealth Marshall possesses. You will want for nothing as his wife, and you will be the mistress of one of the largest plantations in Texas."

"When have I ever led you to believe those things are important to me?" She searched Papa's face. "Mama would have loved you if you had lived in a one-room cabin, and I want to love my husband in the same manner. Money and land are not what is important."

"So says the spoiled girl in her comfortable home, surrounded by luxuries most people never lay eyes on." Sarcasm dripped from each word. "I have worked hard to make this plantation what it is today. I am one of the most respected growers in the state. As my daughter, the least you can do is honor that by marrying the man I have chosen for you. A man who can further us both."

Hurt by his attitude, she hoped to reason with him. "Papa, I appreciate everything you and Mama have given me. I know how blessed I am. But what I am most thankful for has nothing to do with the big house or the vast lands. I'm thankful we were a happy family, full of love and goodness toward one another. Mama loved you. I can't imagine going through life with a husband I do not love and who does not love me."

"Brevard is quite fond of you, Adella Rose. He is looking forward to a future with you. Love can grow from that; I assure you."

The way he spoke put a shadow of doubt in her mind. "Are you saying you didn't love Mama when you married her?"

Impatience flicked across his features. "I am saying not every marriage begins with passion and silliness. Some are born from more important agreements but still manage to be happy."

Adella stared at him, wondering if her parents' marriage was perhaps not all it had seemed.

"Luckily," Papa continued, "Marshall is an understanding man and still wishes to marry you, despite this outrageous show of immaturity on your part."

"That is a shame." She lifted her chin in defiance. "Because I do not wish to marry him."

Apparently, her words were too much, for Papa's face grew red and his nostrils flared. He stalked over to her bed and yanked the covers off of her.

"You will dress and come downstairs now, or I will drag you there myself! Mark my words. Your marriage to Brevard will take place. There are more important things at stake than inane girlish dreams."

Stunned, Adella gaped at him. Never before had he spoken to her with such hostility, as though she were not his daughter but a mere servant. Several tense moments ticked by before he tossed the coverlet at her and stormed from the room.

Tears streamed down her cheeks once the door slammed behind him. Hurt beyond words, she buried her face in her hands, knowing nothing would ever be the same between them again.

❧ ❧

"I fear we have gotten off to a bad start, Adella Rose."

She and Marshall Brevard walked across the vast lawn, going nowhere in particular. She'd simply needed to get away from the house, and Marshall volunteered to accompany her. With Papa watching closely, she couldn't refuse, even though she longed to be alone.

"I, of course, feel responsible for the way things have come about," he continued, his hands clasped behind his back. He offered a small smile when she glanced at him. "My desire all along was to court you properly and allow our relationship to grow naturally before I proposed marriage."

"And why didn't you?" Adella asked, irritated by the man's assumption that she would have accepted him as a suitor in the first place.

He seemed taken aback by her question. "Well, because your father and I noticed Mr. Brantley's interest in you. He seems like the kind of man who might take advantage of a young woman's inexperience. We thought it best to announce our engagement in order to put an end to any ideas he might have regarding you and the inheritance you stand to receive in due time."

His presumptions ignited her fury. "You assume that a man would only be interested in me for my money?"

Marshall's face paled, and he scrambled for words. "No, no, of course not. That is not what I meant. Please, Adella Rose. I do not mean to insult you. You are a beautiful woman, and any man would be fortunate indeed to have you as his wife. Mr. Brantley is, as you know, without land or means. It would not be a far stretch for anyone to wonder at his motives, should he choose to seduce the plantation owner's daughter."

Had he said these words to her before she spoke with Seth after the service Sunday and learned he'd known all along she was to be engaged, she might have argued further. But now she wondered if what Marshall said held more truth than she wanted to admit. Had Seth seduced her? She thought back to the night they danced under the stars in the quarter, and then to their kiss under the trees. He'd been the one to instigate their meetings, although she'd been a willing participant.

"I see I have given you something to think about." A look of satisfaction crossed Marshall's features. "It is not my intent to malign Mr. Brantley. Rather, I humbly ask that you will at least give me a chance. Perhaps you would even consider visiting Le Beau, my plantation. It means 'the beautiful' in French, and it truly is. The trees, the marshes. I think you will like it."

Adella studied him, taking in his features for the first time. He wasn't a bad-looking man, although his receding hairline and graying sideburns spoke of his age. His elegant clothes fit his trim form well, and one could almost consider him dashing, with his height and courteous smile. But try as she might, she simply could not envision herself married to him or find any sense of the passion she'd known in Seth's arms. The mere thought of living as his wife for the rest of her life left her depressed.

"Your father has asked me to escort you to your brother's wedding Saturday." When she began to protest, he raised his hand. "I told him I would only do so if you gave your consent."

Adella narrowed her eyes. "Why would you do that? You and Papa seem to have everything regarding my future planned down to the minute."

"I am sorry you feel that way, Adella Rose. Truly, I meant no harm in moving forward with our engagement before you and I had a chance to properly court."

His apparent sincerity drained the last of her fight. Emotionally exhausted, she closed her eyes for a long moment. When she looked at him again, eager hope filled his countenance. "Very well. You may escort me to the wedding."

With a slight bow, he reached for her hand and placed an unexpected kiss on her knuckles.

From the barn, Seth watched Adella and Marshall as they stood on the lawn, talking. He couldn't hear what they said, but their conversation seemed intense. When Marshall kissed her hand, Seth turned away, a sick feeling in the pit of his stomach.

"Chester sho' did get him a nasty cut, Mistah Brantley, suh," Jeptha said, examining the horse's foreleg where trails of blood had already begun to dry. "But I fix him up real good with one o' Mammy's poultices. That do the trick."

Seth had to chuckle. "Mammy doctors the horses too?"

Jeptha grinned. "Mammy doctors ever'body."

While Jeptha went off to make the poultice, Seth ran a hand over Chester's strong neck. "I'm sorry, ol' boy," he said, feeling a world of guilt after taking the horse through a briar patch. He should have been paying closer attention to where they were going, but his mind could think of nothing but Adella. Maybe it was fate that brought him back to the barn in time to see her with Marshall.

Jeptha returned with a thick, smelly yellow mixture smeared onto a rag. "We tie this around his leg an' change it ever' few hours. That oughta keep infection from gettin' in."

Seth watched the slave clean the wounds before carefully tying the bandage on the horse. Thinking back on the day he and Adella rode through the plantation, he recalled the stories she told about her childhood with Jeptha as her playmate.

"Miss Ellis was worried about you." He kept a firm hold on Chester's bridle so the horse wouldn't spook at Jeptha's ministrations. "She wanted to know where you've been. You weren't at the party."

Jeptha glanced up. "Missy askin' 'bout me?"

Seth nodded. "She thought you might be sick."

Uneasiness crossed Jeptha's face. He resumed his treatment of the horse, but Seth got the distinct feeling he wanted to say more. When Chester's bandage was in place, the slave gathered his supplies and stood.

"Is something troubling you, Jeptha? Something about Miss Ellis?"

The slave's eyes stayed downcast, but he nodded. "Does Missy know 'bout Celia an' me?"

"No." Seth wondered why that was important. "I haven't told her, and I doubt Master Luther or George would mention it."

Jeptha visibly relaxed. "If it be all right wit' you, Mistah Brantley, suh, I'd 'ppreciate it if you didn't tell her. No need for Missy to know."

Although Seth had no intention of revealing Jeptha's situation to Adella and had successfully avoided it once before, he still wondered why it mattered to the slave. "Why don't you want her to know?"

For the first time since he'd entered the barn, Jeptha looked directly into Seth's eyes. "Because I ashamed of it, Mistah Brantley. I ashamed, and I don't want Missy to know. Please. Please don't tell her."

The sheer panic in the other man's eyes told Seth how important this was to him. "All right. I won't tell her. But I don't see what you have to be ashamed of. You are obeying what your master told you to do."

Jeptha shook his head slowly. "Don't matter none if it be what Massa Luther say. God say it wrong. Celia an' me don't jump the broom or nothin'. An' I has me a bad feelin' she ain't gonna be the only gal Massa want me to lie with."

Seth had never heard such honest words from a slave about the realities of living in bondage. Jeptha wasn't an animal looking to breed with every female he could find, as Luther assumed. The same uncomfortable twinge he'd felt Sunday in the service crept over Seth, knowing he was responsible in some way. He may not have owned Jeptha, nor was it his decision to force Jeptha and Celia together, but his role as overseer made him just as guilty as Luther and George.

"I could ask Master Luther to allow you to jump the broom with Celia." He knew the offer wasn't a solution, but it seemed better than nothing.

Jeptha shook his head. "No, sir. Wouldn't want you to do that."

"But isn't that what's bothering you? That you aren't married to her."

"I don't love Celia, Mistah Brantley. I don't want ta jump the broom with a gal I don't love."

Several moments ticked by with Seth sorting through the things he'd always believed about Negroes and what he'd learned the past few minutes. It forced him to see Jeptha not as a slave but as a man—a man not so different from himself, except for the color of his skin. How would Seth feel if he'd been forced to marry someone he didn't love? Adella and her engagement to Brevard came to mind. In some ways, Luther Ellis was doing to his daughter exactly what he'd done to Jeptha.

The realization made him sick.

Turning his back on the slave, he led Chester to his stall. When he returned, Jeptha had just finished putting the bucket and rags away.

"How is the mustang doing?" Seth almost referred to the horse as Freedom.

"Real good." Jeptha seemed relieved to talk about something else. "He takin' to the bridle an' rope. Won't be long 'fore he ready to break."

They walked down the aisle to where Freedom stood groomed and untethered in his stall. He looked like an entirely different horse than the one Seth and Adella had seen only the week before. The horse eagerly came forward, and Jeptha let him nuzzle his hand. Seth wondered if Adella had snuck down to the barn lately with an apple tucked in her skirt pocket. No doubt Brevard would put an end to such activities once they married. The thought made him sad.

"You ever break a horse?" Seth noted how the animal appeared to trust Jeptha as he stroked its powerful neck.

The slave shook his head. "No suh. Mistah Haley al'ays hired a man to come break 'em." He lifted his eyes to Seth. "But I be willin' to learn."

Seth grinned. "You may not be so willing after Freedom bucks you off a dozen times."

Jeptha's brow rose. "You know 'bout Missy namin' him Freedom?"

"She let it slip." Seth shrugged. "I guess I did too. Let's just keep the name between us, okay?"

Serious eyes met his. "Wouldn't ever say nothin' to nobody that might bring trouble for Missy."

For some reason, the slave's loyalty to Adella brought Seth a measure of comfort. He'd want to know she was taken care of when he left Rose Hill. Even if that meant marriage to Brevard.

"If you're serious about learning to break a horse, we have a lot of work to do."

Jeptha smiled. "I ready, suh."

"Fine." Seth moved back down the aisle with Jeptha trailing behind. "We'll start first thing in the morning. Monroe can keep watch on the field workers. It will take the better part of a day to get Freedom used to the saddle. Depending on how stubborn he is, it may take all week to get him used to a rider."

Later, as Seth rode back out to the fields on a new gelding, he grinned, thinking of the following day's events. He might not know much about overseeing a cotton plantation, but he knew about horses. Breaking a wild horse was second nature to him. He'd trained more than a dozen to heed his command and had a reputation back home for never being bucked off.

Glancing toward the big house in the distance, he blew out a breath. He wished women were as easy to manage as horses.

Near the end of the day, after Seth began his headcount of the slaves, a lone horseman came toward him. Squinting beneath the brim of his hat to see who it was, ire filled him when he recognized Marshall Brevard. What the dandy was doing in the fields, he didn't know, but it was safe to guess it couldn't be good.

His mount began to prance as Brevard's mare drew close, but Seth kept the animal under control as he waited for the man.

"I want a word with you in private, Brantley." Marshall's tone was as unfriendly as his eyes. He rode a short distance away, where the slaves returning to the quarter wouldn't hear the conversation.

Loathe to give the man any respect, Seth knew it wouldn't do well to have every word of their exchange circulate through the quarter, so he nudged his horse forward. When he came abreast Brevard's mount, Seth steadily met the man's gaze without speaking.

After a moment, Marshall smirked. "You think because your father is an old friend of Luther's you have some sort of legitimate place here on Rose Hill. An overseer who takes his meals with the family and escorts the owner's daughter to dinner."

Seth ignored the comments. "I would appreciate it if you would say your piece. I have work to do."

"Precisely my point." His gaze traveled over the acres of cotton then back to Seth. "I am a landowner, Brantley. I am a rich and important man with connections in Austin and Washington. The woman I marry will never want for anything, nor will our children. The reality is, I am everything you will never be. Why, even the State of Texas saw you for what you are."

Though the jab stung, Seth didn't let it show. "There are more important things in life than position and money."

"A laughable statement coming from a man who has neither. You have nothing to offer a woman. Certainly not a woman of Adella Rose's station." When Seth didn't reply, Brevard smiled. "I believe you think yourself in love with her."

Fighting to keep his face devoid of reaction, Seth wondered if everyone suspected his feelings for her.

"Hear this, Brantley." Marshall's face turned stony. "Your days on Rose Hill land are numbered. I have much influence over Luther. Once I am married to his daughter, I will make certain he understands your services are no longer necessary."

Seth leaned forward in the saddle. "Sounds like you want to get rid of me real bad. Almost as though you're afraid of something."

Brevard looked Seth up and down, disdain practically dripping from his nose. "What could I possibly be afraid of?"

"That she cares more for me than she does for you."

The gauntlet thrown, Seth waited for the reaction.

It came swiftly. Marshall's face turned scarlet and his fists clenched. "Consider this your one and only warning, Brantley," he said between gritted teeth. "Stay away from Adella Rose. If I so much as see you look in her direction, you will regret it."

Seth watched the man ride away, feeling dread in the pit of his stomach.

CHAPTER FOURTEEN

"Hold on, Jeptha!"

Seth's shout of encouragement brought Adella out from behind the barn where she lurked, desperate to watch the action in the corral, yet wanting to remain unseen. Seth stood a short distance away, leaning against the corral fence, his back to her and his eyes on Jeptha astride Freedom. If she stayed here, she could watch the excitement without attracting attention, which suited her just fine. She hadn't spoken to Seth since Sunday, and she had no idea what to say when she did come face to face with him again. Her emotions were so mixed up, she didn't think she could put together a coherent thought, let alone explain how much he'd hurt her.

"Whoo-ee, ride 'em, boy," Joseph called, her father's old carriage driver grinning as he watched Jeptha hang on for dear life. Freedom kicked and galloped around the corral, stirring up a cloud of thick dust. The wild mares brought in with Freedom, who were penned nearby, whinnied and snorted, watching their leader fight against the saddle and rider.

All morning, the shouts and wild bellows coming from the corral had tormented Adella. At first, she thought a horse was being tortured, its cries and screams traveling across the plantation grounds and up through her open bedroom window. But word soon swept through the servants that Jeptha and Mr. Brantley were breaking the mustang stallion. Feeling a kinship to both the horse and the slave, she hurried from the house at the first opportunity. Thankfully, after the midday meal, Papa and George took Marshall and the other guests target shooting on the east side of the property where the fields were fallow. They'd be gone for hours.

Filled with fascination and more than a little fear, Adella watched as Freedom bucked and jerked, trying to unseat Jeptha from his place in the saddle. The whites of Jeptha's wide eyes flashed by as the horse galloped around the corral, looking for all the world like the wild beast he was.

"Magnificent," she whispered. If she were a man, that is exactly where she'd want to be—astride that beautiful animal.

"That's it. Hold him steady," Seth called.

Suddenly, Freedom leaped off the ground, lifting all four hooves simultaneously. He arched his back, and then with a quick twist of his powerful body, spun around, causing Jeptha to lose his balance and his grip on the reins. Before he could right himself, Freedom's back legs beat the air, sending Jeptha flying.

Thud.

He landed hard in the dirt.

In one swift move, Seth was over the top rail and hurried to Jeptha's motionless body. Joseph and the other slaves, who'd been shouting encouragement only moments before, now stood silent, watching with worried expressions. Freedom darted to the opposite side of the corral, still bucking the now empty saddle and dragging his lead.

Adella ran to the fence. Lifting the hem of her skirt, she climbed onto the bottom rung and hoisted herself up so she could see. A breath of relief escaped when she saw Seth help Jeptha to a sitting position. "Is he hurt?"

Seth looked over at her, a flash of surprise in his eyes. "He's all right. Just got the wind knocked out of him."

She nodded. Their gaze held for a long moment before he turned back to the injured man. After another minute or so, Jeptha got to his feet, dusting himself off. Seth walked him over to the gate where she met them.

"You could have killed yourself," she said, making sure he was indeed all right. No blood or visible wounds were obvious, but a fall like that could have damaged something inside.

With dirt smudged across his face, Jeptha grinned. "Nah, Missy. I too ornery."

But she noticed he kept his arms wrapped protectively around his middle and winced when he leaned against the fence post.

Seth closed the gate behind Jeptha, remaining in the corral. "Take a rest while I get him calmed down. You stayed on longer that time. Next time will be better."

"Next time?" Adella looked from one man to the other. "He can't ride again. He's injured."

The men locked eyes, some silent message going between them before Seth's attention returned to her. "I am sure we appreciate your concern, Miss Ellis, but I know what I'm doing. Freedom needs to understand he can't buck off his rider and get away with it."

Adella frowned. "It is not the horse I am concerned with, Mr. Brantley. Jeptha's hurt." She turned to him for confirmation. "Aren't you?"

With indecision in his eyes, Jeptha glanced from her to Seth and back. "I shore I'll be fine, Missy Ellis. I wants to ride Free— uh, that mustang. Cain't let him get the best of me, now can I?"

His grin didn't fool her. She poked him in the ribs, causing him to recoil. Satisfied, she turned to Seth. "See? I think he has a broken rib. Maybe several."

Retracing his steps, Seth opened the gate, closed it behind him, and walked over to Jeptha. Appearing to know what he was doing, he placed his hands on the slave's rib cage, giving gentle pushes here and there. With each one, Jeptha grimaced, though he didn't cry out.

Heaving a sigh, he stepped back. "She might be right." His tone said he wished it weren't true.

"I fine, Mistah Brantley, suh." When he saw the stern look on Adella's face, Jeptha added, "Maybe just a bit bruised. Nothin' bad wrong."

Adella waited for Seth's reply. If she had to, she'd use her position as Luther Ellis' daughter to keep Jeptha from getting back on that wild animal.

Seth rubbed his jaw in thought. "I've had bruised and broken ribs before. The last place you need to be is on that horse." He shook his head. "But I don't like putting Free—" he briefly glanced at Adella, "*the horse* in his stall after he's bucked you off. He'll think he won."

"Then I reckon you need to finish the job, suh," Jeptha said with respect and admiration in his voice.

After a moment, Seth gave a half smile. "You did real good today. I would hate for all your hard work to go to waste."

Jeptha accepted the praise with a nod.

Without glancing at her, Seth returned to the corral, motioning for Joseph and the others. They climbed the fence, entered the arena, and spread out. Adella watched the four men slowly circle Freedom, who'd finally settled down and stood as far away from them as possible. As Seth drew close, the animal searched for an escape, trying to dart between the men. But Seth was too quick. He grabbed the reins and soon had the horse under control.

"He real good with hosses." Jeptha's voice was low and almost reverent as he watched Seth speak to the animal. "Knows things I ain't nevah heard."

Adella glanced at Jeptha, momentarily forgetting all about Freedom and Seth. "Where have you been? I haven't seen you in days. When you didn't come to the party, I thought you might be sick."

A guilty look swept across Jeptha's features. "Oh, I been around, Missy. Weren't feelin' so good the night of the party so I stay in bed." His eyes grew round. "I mean, I just …" He seemed to lose track of what he was going to say. Finally, he gave a nervous shrug. "I been around. Guess you just been busy with Miss Natalie and the others."

His answer seemed odd, and his behavior even odder. She and

Jeptha had never kept secrets from each other, but she had the feeling he wasn't telling her something. It was the same feeling she'd had when Aunt Lu wouldn't tell her why he hadn't been at the party.

"Well, I'm glad you're all right. Have Mammy look at your ribs. Do you think they're broken?"

He shrugged. "I'll have Mammy check 'em." The old Jeptha grinned. "It right nice to have you worryin' over me, Missy."

With a chuckle, they resumed watching the progress in the corral. Seth had backed Freedom into a corner, with the barn wall on one side and the men on the other. With slow, careful movements, Seth ran his hands along Freedom's neck and shoulders, gradually making his way to the saddle. Once there, he repositioned it and gave the stirrups a jerk then ran his hands back up the animal's trembling body, repeating the whole process several times.

"What is he doing?" Adella whispered, captivated by the patient way Seth worked with the horse. For a moment, she remembered how it felt to be in his strong arms, knowing the tenderness of his hands on her body.

A shiver ran up her spine.

"You cold?" Jeptha gave her a quizzical glance, the afternoon sun beating down their backs. When she shook her head, he whispered, "He gettin' Freedom used to the feel an' smell of him. Movin' the saddle reminds Freedom it ain't goin' nowhere."

After several more minutes of this, Seth spoke to Joseph. Joseph took hold of Freedom's lead rope, braced his legs, and seemingly prepared for a fight. The other men climbed onto the rail to watch.

With slow, deliberate movements, Seth stepped into the stirrup. Freedom turned his head to see what Seth was doing but otherwise didn't move. Sending Joseph a nod, Seth swung his other leg over the horse. The moment his full weight settled into the saddle, Freedom bolted, nearly knocking Joseph to the ground.

"Ride 'im, Mistah Brantley!" Jeptha hollered, followed by a grimace. He put a hand to his injured ribcage.

"Mm-hmm." Adella gave him a knowing look. "Just think how you would feel if you had climbed back on that horse."

He shrugged.

Seth and Freedom were a blur as they flew around the corral. When the bucking started, Adella held her breath, frightened Seth would become unseated like Jeptha. She had never witnessed a breaking before and found it more than a little unnerving, especially when the rider was someone she cared about.

Around and around they went, the air thick with dust. Then Freedom tried the same trick he'd used to throw Jeptha to the ground, arching his back as his hooves left the ground. But when he twisted his body, Seth was ready. He held on, his thighs tight against the horse's shoulders and his hands grasping the pommel.

"That'a way, Mistah Brantley!" Joseph yelled, grinning like it was his own boy out there.

Just when Adella thought this fight between man and beast might go on all afternoon, Freedom broke into a canter. Seth said something to the animal, rode him around the circle several more times, and finally brought him to a stop with a gentle tug on the reins.

"Whoa, boy."

As carefully as he'd mounted a few minutes earlier, Seth dismounted the same way.

"He don't want ta spook Freedom, so got to go real slow," Jeptha supplied. "Mistah Brantley done taught me mo' about handlin' hosses today than I evah learned from ol' Joseph."

When Seth stood on the ground again, he led Freedom around the corral to get the animal's breathing back to normal, then walked over to where she and Jeptha waited. Adella noticed his limp had worsened.

Jeptha grinned from ear to ear as he reached through the rail to pat the animal. "You shore 'nough did it, Mistah Brantley. You got this here hoss to ride wit'ch you sittin' proud on his back."

Seth chuckled. "Like I said before, Jeptha. You did all the hard work. He was already tuckered out by the time I got to him."

Jeptha moved to open the gate and took Freedom's lead. "I take him on in to his stall an' rub him down. Been a long day for this fella."

Adella watched Jeptha and the horse disappear into the barn, conscious of Seth standing just a few feet away. Joseph and the other men were already gone.

"That was incredible." She pretended her stomach wasn't suddenly filled with butterflies.

"Jeptha should have been the one to get him to walk. He'd worked hard all day." Dust covered Seth from head to toe, and he looked more ruggedly handsome than any man ought to.

The butterflies swirled faster.

She needed to explain why she ran off after the service. Maybe then they could sort out all that had transpired. She moistened her lips.

"Seth—" she said at the same moment he spoke her name. They smiled.

"Adella," he repeated, then blew out a breath. "You have every right to be mad at me. I did know what your father was planning, but he said he wouldn't announce your engagement until after George and Natalie's wedding. I didn't feel it was my right to repeat information he'd told me in confidence, even though I wanted to warn you. I hoped he might change his mind and not go through with it."

She knew he told the truth. Marshall himself admitted he'd encouraged Papa to move up the announcement because of her friendship with Seth.

"I feel like a horse who's gone to the highest bidder," she said, moving to the corral fence—away from the entrance to the barn, where someone might overhear their conversation. Seth joined her.

"Marshall and I have never courted. I have never spent more than a few hours in his presence, and that is only when he came to see Papa on business. They have known each other for many years. Marshall's wife took ill a few years ago and died without ever having children. I can't blame him for wanting to remarry, but he is much too old for me. I have never shown the slightest interest in him as a suitor."

"Why would your father consent to your marrying Brevard then?"

That was the troubling part of this whole mess. "I don't know, other than he wants to ensure I marry well. I suppose he doesn't trust me to make my own decision. George and Natalie's marriage was agreed upon ages ago by our parents. It seems Papa intends to continue his ways and arrange mine as well."

Seth ran a hand through his tousled hair. "I thought we would have more time before I spoke to him."

"Before you spoke to him?"

The intense look that came to his hazel eyes nearly took her breath away. "I have come to care for you, Adella. I hoped you felt the same way."

Marshall's words about Seth wanting her money echoed in her mind. Surely he was wrong. "So much has happened … I don't know what to think or feel."

He took a step closer. "If you believe you can love Marshall and want a life with him, I will abide by your word. I won't like it, but I won't interfere." He paused, his gaze caressing her face. "But if our kiss meant anything to you … made you feel something for me … then I beg you, don't marry him. Marry me. I can't offer you what he can, but we could make a good life. Maybe we would even go to Oregon and see the ocean."

A sob caught in her throat. He remembered her wish to see the ocean. This was not a man who cared only for her money. "I will never love Marshall," she whispered. "I love you, Seth."

He stared at her with disbelief written on his face. "You do?" When she nodded, his lopsided grin melted any lingering reservations. "I think I have loved you ever since you snuck that apple to Freedom."

She laughed, feeling happier than she'd ever known. Seth loved her. "What should we do now? Tell Papa?" The very thought sent a tremor of fear coursing through her. He would be furious.

Seth grew serious. "No. Not yet. We don't want to ruin George and Natalie's wedding."

Adella agreed. "But as soon as they are off to Louisiana on their honeymoon trip, we'll tell Papa. I don't want to spend another moment engaged to Marshall."

The look of love on his face sent a chill racing up her spine. "I thought I had lost you." His voice was low and tender.

How she wished they weren't standing in the middle of the barnyard. She wanted to fly into his strong embrace and feel the warmth of his lips on hers.

The sound of horse hooves on the road broke the spell. Papa and the others were returning.

"I best get to the house before Papa and Marshall discover me here with you." Regret filled every inch of her being. More than anything, she wanted to stay with Seth.

He nodded. "Soon," was all he said, as though reading her thoughts.

Adella hurried toward the house, her heart nearly overflowing with joy.

CHAPTER FIFTEEN

Aided by dim lantern light, Seth made his way through the quiet barn to Freedom's stall. After his wild ride that afternoon, he'd been so focused on Adella and how to break their news to Luther, he'd forgotten all about the stallion. Now, long after dark, Seth was still too wound up for sleep and decided to visit the horse.

He tossed the apple he carried into the air and caught it, wishing Adella were there with him. *Soon*, he'd told her. Soon they would be together. More than anything, he hoped he hadn't lied. They still had many obstacles to overcome, the most important being her father's disapproval. Seth played with the idea of enlisting his own father's help since Pa would be at George's wedding the day after tomorrow. Pa and Luther went back many years, to their childhood days in Virginia. Surely Luther would eventually see that Seth would make a good husband for Adella. The Brantleys weren't rich, but he'd do his best to provide everything she could ever need or want.

He lifted the lantern high when he came to the end stall—Freedom's eyes glowed as he watched Seth approach. "Hey there, fella," he said, keeping his voice low. "How are you doing after a long day?"

He hung the lantern on the same nail Adella had used, opened the stall door, and approached the horse. Freedom took a step back.

"I'm not going to hurt you, fella." He slowly reached to pat the horse's neck.

Freedom's big eyes kept careful watch, but he didn't shy away again. His nostrils flicked when he caught the scent of the apple in Seth's other hand.

Seth chuckled. "Yes, I brought you a treat. Adella isn't the only one who can sneak them out of Aunt Lu's cellar." He held the fruit flat on his palm. The horse took it easily, his big teeth chomping. Seth continued to pat the animal's neck while he ate. "I'm sorry we had to work you so hard today. It gets easier, I promise. I can't wait to take you out of the corral and let you run through the plantation. It may not be the same as running free across Texas, but you'll get used to it."

Jeptha came to mind. In a strange way, Freedom reminded Seth of the slave. Both were strong. Proud. Bound by rules not of their own making. Until recently, Seth had never given the plight of the slave more than a cursory thought. Some folks said they were born for bondage and weren't intelligent enough to take care of themselves without a master. He didn't necessarily agree with that kind of thinking, but having never lived anywhere but Texas, slavery was simply a way of life to him.

With the ache in his leg worse tonight after his ride on Freedom, Seth sank to the barn floor and sat with his back against the stall, his leg straight out. He massaged his thigh, remembering the day he was shot. When he'd followed the escaped slave into the brush a little over a year ago, Seth hadn't known the man was armed. Most slaves barely escaped with the clothes on their backs and rarely had a weapon beyond a club made from a tree branch. The gun had probably been stolen from his master, though Seth never learned who that was. The Mexican border lay a few miles south, and like most runaways, that's where he was headed. But he'd been spotted, and Seth and two other Rangers set after him when he ducked into thick brush. Seth figured it would be easy to flush him out and rode in behind the man. He'd never forget the shock that shook his body when the gun went off and a bullet tore through his thigh.

Familiar anger seeped in. That slave got what he deserved. The other Rangers fired dozens of shots into the brush, killing the man. When they dragged his body out, Seth, in a fog of pain, remembered seeing thick scars crisscrossing his back through his torn shirt. Evidence of previous escape attempts, no doubt.

His fellow Rangers apparently thought so too. "A scarred up Negro means a troublemaker," Roy Clemons had said. "This boy got what was coming to him this time."

Seth hadn't pondered it at the time, but now he wondered what would drive a slave to risk life and limb to run away, knowing the odds of making Mexico were slim? Was life at the plantation or farm where the slave came from really so awful?

Again, Jeptha came to mind. Forced to couple with a woman not of his own choosing, he had little choice but to obey. Slaves had no choice in anything. What the master wanted, the master got. Punishment came in the form of beatings, whippings, and starvation. Worse yet, the threat of being sold loomed heavy if they didn't measure up.

Was that why the man who shot Seth ran? Had he decided a chance at freedom was worth taking the ultimate risk? What if he'd made it to Mexico? What if Seth and the others had simply let him go? Would he have found the freedom he sought?

Seth stood. No sense dwelling on what ifs. The man sealed his fate when he pointed his gun at a white man.

Taking the lantern, he headed to the door, blew out the lantern flame, and left the lamp on the ground. There was just enough moon to allow him to find his way back to his cabin, where he hoped some of Mammy's ointment might help his leg. It hadn't hurt this bad in months. As he limped slowly toward his house, the light of a cabin in the quarter caught his eye. Shadows passed back and forth behind a cabin window, indicating someone was awake.

That's unusual. At this time of night, everyone was typically fast asleep after a long day of work, knowing morning would bring more of the same. A glance toward the last cabin on the first row, where Monroe lived, revealed darkened windows. The big man apparently wasn't aware someone else was stirring.

Moving on quiet feet, Seth drew near enough to see two people in the cabin, although there wasn't enough light to make out who they were. From his vantage point, several feet away, it appeared to be a man and a woman. Though he had no desire to watch a private moment, he stayed where he was, waiting. Something about the man piqued his curiosity. His build didn't match any of the Rose Hill slaves Seth had become familiar with over the past week.

When the door opened, light spilled into the dark night. The man stepped out, and Seth nearly stumbled backward as a wave of shock rolled through him.

George Ellis.

With his shirt unbuttoned and the tails hanging loosely about his hips, George strode from the cabin without a backward glance. Lucy appeared in the doorway, her protruding belly clearly outlined in the thin cotton gown she wore. Though he couldn't be certain, Seth thought he saw tears glistening on her cheeks when she backed into the room and closed the door.

George walked out of the quarter and then stopped to lean against a tree. The flicker of a lit match followed by the red glow of a cheroot revealed he wasn't in a hurry to get back to the house.

The way Seth saw it, he had two choices. He could wait out George, keeping hidden under the cover of darkness, and pretend he hadn't seen anything. That seemed the best choice if he wanted to keep his job, at least until he and Adella made their plans. Or, he could make his presence known.

His gut twisted. He knew what he had to do.

"Evening, George," he said, moving out from the shadow of the trees and into the moonlight. When he drew closer, he could make out George's startled expression.

"What are you doin' out so late, Brantley?"

"I was checking on the stallion. We worked him pretty hard today. I wanted to make sure he was settled for the night." Seth glanced back to the row of small cabins. "I could ask you the same question, but I'm pretty sure I already know the answer."

George gave a laugh. "Just having a little fun before I become a married man."

His humor sickened Seth. "I take it the child Lucy is carrying is yours."

George tossed the cheroot to the dirt and ground it out with the toe of his shoe. "I wouldn't have any idea. You know how these Negroes are. They breed with each other like animals."

"And I suppose what you were doing with Lucy is somehow different."

He knew he shouldn't have said it, but the other man's flippant attitude galled. Siring children with a slave just didn't sit well with him.

George pushed off the trunk of the tree. "I don't see how what I do is any of your business, Brantley. You may be the overseer here, but these are my slaves. I've been taking my pleasure with Negro gals since I was fifteen. If my father doesn't care, I don't see why you should."

So many responses flashed through Seth's mind, but none were appropriate to say to the son of his employer. Finally, he acquiesced. "You are right. What you do isn't any of my business."

Mollified, George chuckled. "If it's jealousy that has you riled, go ahead and help yourself to that gal. I won't need her anymore. I will have a beautiful wife to satisfy me."

Disgusted by the conversation, Seth watched the man walk toward the darkened main house without another word. When he was alone again, he looked back to the quarter, heavy with the knowledge that Lucy carried George's child.

❧ ❧

The day of the wedding dawned sunny and bright, without the slightest hint of rain in the azure sky. Inside the house, frenzied excitement had everyone scurrying to get ready for the short trip to the Langford plantation. The wedding was set for two o'clock in the afternoon, and Natalie had asked the family to arrive early to help complete the preparations.

A caravan of wagons carrying servants, boxes of baked hams, cakes, and dozens of other dishes soon left Rose Hill, with Aunt Lu supervising to ensure everything arrived safely. Family and guests followed behind in the new carriages Papa had purchased for the occasion. Adella had hoped she and Marshall would ride with Seth, but to her disappointment, Papa made certain they had a carriage all to themselves.

"I look forward to the day when you and I will be the happy couple celebrating our wedding," Marshall said, settling on the seat next to her.

Adella scooted away, pretending to arrange her skirt. How she wished she could peek over the driver's seat and wave to Seth in the wagon ahead of theirs. He hadn't looked happy when Marshall led her away.

The carriage lurched forward, passing through green cotton fields and groves of mesquite and live oaks. The remaining slaves lined up along the road, waving and shouting well-wishes to George as he went by.

"I wonder if you would care to visit Le Beau next week. Your father said he would be happy to bring you since he hasn't been there in several years and would like to see the improvements I have made." He smiled and reached for her hand. His palm felt warm and sweaty, and she wished she could remove her hand without appearing completely rude. "My family came from Louisiana when Stephen Austin gained Mexico's permission to bring settlers to Texas. Grandfather Brevard was French and enjoyed adventure. The tall pine trees are what made him settle on Le Beau land."

Knowing she had to keep up appearances until she and Seth gained Papa's approval, she offered a friendly smile. "I am sure it is lovely. However, I think it is too soon to consider a visit." She gently withdrew her hand.

Disappointment shone in his gray eyes. "I understand your wish to move slowly, Adella Rose. If the circumstances were different,

I might agree. Perhaps it is because I am older and know life can be uncertain that I am anxious. I have experienced the joys and sorrows this world offers, and I assure you, I much prefer the joys."

She knew he spoke of losing his wife. "I don't recall ever meeting Mrs. Brevard, but I am truly sorry for your loss."

"Thank you." He looked away. "Helen was always frail and sickly. Her greatest disappointment was that she never bore a child." After a pause, he added, "It is mine, too." He turned back to face Adella. "I want children, Adella Rose. I would like a son to carry on the Brevard name, and a daughter who looks just like her mother."

Uncomfortable with the intimate conversation, Adella sought in vain for an appropriate response. More than anything, she wished she could tell him she was not the woman for the job. The only children she hoped to bear were Seth's.

After several moments of silence, he chuckled. "I see I have done it again. Pushed too hard, I mean. I am sorry. I will make a concerted effort to simply be happy with escorting you today and leave our tomorrows to their own fate."

Relieved, she nodded. "Thank you, Marshall, for understanding."

The caravan arrived at the Langford plantation a short time later. Already swarms of servants hurried to and fro: cleaning, polishing, setting out tables and chairs. Adella noticed they all wore new black-and-white uniforms. An enormous canvas tent rose up in the middle of the expansive lawn where the ceremony would take place. Mr. Langford sent all the way to Boston for it, having seen one at a circus years before. He'd proudly stated that rain would not prevent the wedding from going on undisturbed.

With Marshall at her elbow, Adella mounted the steps. Papa and George followed while the other guests remained near the carriages. She noticed Seth moved to help unload the wagons despite wearing his good clothes, following Aunt Lu's directions as though he were just another servant.

Mrs. Langford stood on the porch, a strained smile on her face.

"Welcome. I am thankful you have all arrived." Taking Adella by the arm, she led her away from the others and bent near Adella's ear. "Natalie is beside herself with nerves, Adella Rose. Perhaps you can calm her." Her low voice and worried eyes spoke her unease.

"Of course." Leaving the men to fend for themselves, she hurried up the carpeted stairs. The Langford home wasn't as grand as Rose Hill, but it was well appointed and handsomely decorated with plush furnishings, marble floors, and portraits of Langford ancestors lining newly painted beige walls.

At Natalie's door, she knocked. "Natalie, it is Adella Rose. May I come in?"

Zina's face appeared in the open door a moment later. "Oh, Missy Ellis," she whispered, worry shadowing her amber eyes. "I'm so glad you've come. Miss Natalie …" She glanced over her shoulder quickly. "She's not well, Missy. She's not well at all."

Adella frowned. "What do you mean?" She moved into the room. Natalie was nowhere to be seen.

"She's in the bathing room, Missy, and won't come out. I tells her we need to fix her hair and get her ready for her big day, but she just hollers at me to leave her alone."

For a moment, Adella wondered if Natalie's dramatics were a ploy for attention. But it didn't make sense considering today was all about her. Something must have been terribly wrong.

"Zina, listen to me. Go make a pot of strong tea. Has Natalie eaten anything today?" At Zina's negative answer, she continued. "Have Aunt Lu make some dry toast. If anyone asks, say it's for me. Don't say a word about Natalie to anyone. Do you understand?"

"Yes, Missy." Relief filled Zina's voice. She hurried away.

Adella took stock of the room after Zina's departure. Natalie's wedding dress lay draped across the bed, yards of white organdy and lace obscuring the entire coverlet. A bouquet of white roses tied with a silk ribbon sat in a vase of water on the dressing table. All was ready, except for the bride.

Uncertain what she would find in the bathing room, she crossed the carpet and cautiously rapped on the door. "Natalie, dear. May I come in?"

A sniffling sound came through the crack under the door. "Go away, Adella Rose. Tell your brother I can't marry him."

It was worse than she'd feared. Testing the knob, she found it wasn't locked. Slowly, she peered into the small tiled room. There she found Natalie crumpled on the floor in front of a half-full bathtub, wearing her dressing gown. Her hair was a wild mess, and her face was splotchy from crying.

"Oh, Natalie." Though they'd never been friends, they were about to be sisters. She hated to see the young woman upset, especially on her wedding day. When a stream of fresh tears slid down Natalie's cheeks, Adella rushed in, her imagination running rampant. "What's wrong? Has something happened? Did George do something to hurt your feelings?"

A pitiful sob gushed forth from Natalie, and she flung herself into Adella's arms. "Nooooo." She hiccupped and gulped air. With her face buried in Adella's shoulder, she blubbered something unintelligible and then sobbed some more.

It seemed best to let the wave of misery play itself out. Adella patted Natalie's back and made soothing noises as one would with a tearful child, waiting, wondering. After Natalie had quieted, Adella pulled her away so she could see her face. The girl was a mess.

Leaving the bride on the floor, Adella took a soft cloth, dipped it in the basin of water on the washstand, and proceeded to wash Natalie's face. The cool water helped fade the red blotches, but the puffiness under her eyes would remain for some time.

"Now," Adella said, laying the cloth aside. She put out her hand. "Come. Let's sit on something more comfortable than a hard tile floor, and you can tell me what this is all about."

With one last sniffle, Natalie took Adella's hand and got to her feet. Another wave of tears came when Natalie saw her dress on the bed. "I can't go through with it. I just can't." She practically fell into a chair near the fireplace.

"You have to tell me what has you upset, Natalie. Why can't you marry George? You have been planning this for ages." Adella sat at her feet, imploring the other woman to explain.

Red-rimmed eyes met hers. "You will hate me if I tell you."

Adella couldn't possibly imagine having such an extreme reaction, no matter what the young woman might reveal. "I promise I won't."

The clock chimed on the mantel. Eleven o'clock. They had three hours to get Natalie ready for the ceremony, if indeed there was to be a ceremony.

"I don't love George," she finally whispered, then covered her face, sobbing.

The confession stunned Adella. Not so much that Natalie didn't love George, but that it suddenly mattered to the young woman. From the moment their engagement was announced, she'd talked of nothing but marrying George and becoming mistress of Rose Hill. Why had she chosen today, her wedding day, to decide love was important?

But with her own recent betrothal to a man she didn't love, Adella felt more compassion than she might have even a week ago. Although she planned to break her engagement to Marshall and marry the man she truly loved, she couldn't help but feel empathy for Natalie's situation.

"I don't hate you, Natalie."

Tear-stained eyes lifted to hers. "What am I going to do, Adella?"

Though she didn't want to pry, she wondered if Natalie might be in the same predicament she was in. "Is there someone else? Someone you are in love with?"

Natalie sadly shook her head. "No. There is no one. I have never been in love." She sniffled and mopped her nose with a soggy handkerchief she pulled from her pocket. "I thought I loved George. I truly did."

"What makes you think you don't?"

She shrugged thin shoulders. "He seems to care more about joining our plantations than he cares about marrying me."

While Adella would never admit that was true, even if she suspected as much, she knew some things about her brother that Natalie didn't. "Papa has groomed George to take over the plantation since he was a little boy. Everything is always about the plantation. It never crossed George's mind to look for a girl to marry if she couldn't benefit Rose Hill."

"Is that supposed to make me feel better? Because it doesn't."

Adella chuckled. "What I am saying is, you were his first and only choice. He has never looked at another girl, and I have never seen him happier."

Natalie sniffed. "I suppose that does make me feel special, in a strange sort of way."

That made Adella laugh, and Natalie laughed too.

"Do you think we'll be happy?" Natalie asked, growing serious again.

What would Mama say to an impossible question like that? "Mama once told me happiness is a state of mind. We can choose to be happy, or we can choose to be unhappy. But when we are surrounded by so many of God's blessings, choosing to be unhappy is selfish."

Although there was truth in the words, Adella wondered if she could find the happiness Mama spoke of if she were forced to marry Marshall. Fervently, she hoped she would never be in a position to find out.

Natalie sat quietly for several moments. What if she still felt she couldn't go through with the wedding? It would be left to Adella to break the bad news to the families.

Taking a deep breath, Natalie stood. She reached up to her messy hair. "I am sure I must look a fright. Poor Zina has her work cut out for her. And Mama ... oh, she must be so upset. I yelled at her."

"I am sure she understands." Adella stood and shook out the wrinkles in her dress. "All brides get nervous on their wedding day, or so I'm told."

"Thank you, Adella Rose."

Adella would never forget the sincerity shining in Natalie's blue eyes.

"You are welcome. Now, let's get you cleaned up. You are getting married in just a few hours!"

❧ ❧

"Miss Ellis, I would like you to meet my father, Daniel Brantley."

Seth couldn't keep the smile from his face nor the pleasure from his voice when he introduced Adella to Pa after the ceremony. Pa eyed him curiously before turning to Adella.

"It is a pleasure, Miss Ellis. My, but you have grown into a beautiful young woman since the last time I saw you."

"Thank you, Mr. Brantley. I'm happy you were able to come to the wedding, although I'm sorry Mrs. Brantley could not make it."

"Yes, Abigail took ill, though thankfully it is nothing serious. She insisted I come anyway, but I think it was mostly because she wanted me to check on how Seth here is doing. She has always been a little partial to him." He winked, causing Adella to smile.

"I hope you will stay several days with us at Rose Hill. I know Papa would enjoy a nice long visit with you," she said, performing her role as mistress of the plantation to perfection. Seth felt unspeakable pride well up inside him, knowing she would one day be the mistress of his home.

"I appreciate the offer, Miss Ellis. There is nothing more I would like to do than stay on a bit, but with Abigail unwell, I think it is best if I head back first thing in the morning."

Adella nodded. "You know you are always welcome, so I hope you will come back soon."

"I understand congratulations are in order," Pa said, smiling.

He glanced at Seth then back to Adella.

Her eyes widened, and she looked to Seth questioningly. "Congratulations?" she asked. Her tone indicated she thought he must have mentioned their secret plans to his father, which of course, he hadn't.

"Yes, on your engagement to Marshall Brevard. Your father is quite pleased, I gather."

Adella hesitated then forced a smile. "Yes, quite."

"I don't know Brevard personally, but I have heard of him over the years. The other planters in our area speak well of him. When is the wedding?"

Seth wished he could tell his father right then that Adella wasn't marrying Brevard, she was marrying him. But with so many people nearby, it didn't seem wise to discuss such a sensitive subject until they were somewhere private.

"A date has not been set," Adella said, appearing strained with the turn in the conversation. Seth needed to change the subject, fast.

"Pa, how are the girls?"

His father sent him a quizzical look. "They are fine like I told you earlier. Susanna is in her last year of schooling and hopes to get a teacher's certificate. Addie and Jessa are quickly becoming young ladies, though it is hard for me to admit. They will all be married and off on their own before long. I am sure your father will miss you after you are married," he said to Adella. "Brevard's plantation is in Rusk County, isn't that right?"

She nodded politely, though Seth saw discomfort in her eyes.

"We're breaking a new stallion here at Rose Hill, Pa," he said, attempting to gain his father's attention again. The older man looked at him with an odd expression. "A herd of wild mustangs was brought in a few weeks ago. One of the slaves has been working with him. Should have him saddle-broke in no time. Maybe you would like to go down to the barn to see him later."

"Don't be so modest, Mr. Brantley." Adella's eyes shone with pride before turning to his father. "While Jeptha most assuredly deserves commendation for his work with the horse, your son rode the wild beast until the fight drained out of him. It was amazing to watch."

Pa's brow rose. "Not many young women are interested in such things, Miss Ellis. But I agree with you. Seth has a way with horses. Always has. We have a number of fine animals he broke for us. In fact, some of our neighbors were asking just the other day if Seth was coming home anytime soon because they have some young horses that need a knowledgeable wrangler to get them saddle ready."

While the praise felt good, Seth knew his saddle-breaking days were over. His leg simply couldn't tolerate the strain of the rough ride. But after working with Jeptha, teaching the eager young man the correct techniques and seeing them put into action, an idea began to develop in Seth's mind. An idea for his and Adella's future.

Just then, Natalie called for Adella. Seemingly relieved, she excused herself and made her way across the yard to where the beaming bride stood with George. Seeing Natalie radiant and happy made him anxious to see his own bride in a beautiful gown, her smile all for him. He hoped it wouldn't be long before he and Adella could become man and wife.

When he returned his attention to Pa, his father's frown met him. "All right, son. What is going on between you and Luther's daughter?"

CHAPTER SIXTEEN

The morning after the wedding, Papa, Marshall, and the other guests slept later than usual. The house was quiet when Adella went downstairs and out the front door. She hoped for a chance to speak to Seth before the others rose. When they'd returned to the plantation late yesterday evening in time for a light supper, she found Seth's father's gaze on her so often she wondered if Seth had told him their news. And if so, she wondered, what did the elder Mr. Brantley have to say about it?

Tiptoeing across the porch, she paused to watch the sun peek over the eastern horizon. Birds greeted the day with happy songs, and bees already buzzed Mama's rosebushes. It promised to be a beautiful June day.

Lifting her skirt to start down the steps, she startled when someone cleared his throat nearby. Whirling to her right, she found Daniel Brantley sitting on one of the small wicker sofas, a cup of coffee in his hand.

"I have always enjoyed watching the sun rise," he said, his gaze fastened on the new morning.

Uncertainty crept through her, and she wished Seth would miraculously arrive to fill in the questions. Forced to handle the situation on her own, she put on a pleasant smile. "Yes, I do as well. When I was a little girl, I would sneak out of bed and come sit on the porch, barefoot and in my nightgown. Mama would scold me, but it didn't stop me from wanting to make sure the sun truly was going to appear that day."

Daniel chuckled. Setting his cup on a small table, he motioned to the seat next to him. "Please, join me. I believe we need to have a chat before the others rise."

Adella's heart pounded. Surely, Seth must have told his father their secret, but she had no way to know if he approved or disapproved. It seemed she was about to find out.

Once she'd settled on the cushion, he took a deep breath. "Seth tells me he is quite fond of you, Miss Ellis." He looked at her and smiled. "I am sure I can see why. You are a lovely young woman. You remind me very much of your mother when she was your age. And from what Seth tells me, you have inherited her generous heart and sweet disposition. Lord knows the world could use more people like Martha Ellis."

Nerves kept her silent, though she deeply appreciated the compliments. Perhaps it boded well for her that he thought so highly of her mother.

He gazed out beyond the house again, and they sat in quiet companionship for several minutes before he spoke again.

"I have known your father a long time. Once his mind is settled on something, it is near impossible to get him to budge. Many businessmen have felt the harsh reality of crossing Luther Ellis." With eyes so like Seth's, he studied her. "I fear he will be completely unmanageable should you break off your engagement to Marshall. Seth has nothing to offer you, Miss Ellis. His older brother will inherit my land. I have no doubt Seth will find his own way and will do well, but it will be a simple life." He waved his hand to indicate the house and plantation grounds. "You would be giving all this up. And more, if what I have heard about Le Beau is true. Brevard is a very wealthy man."

While he didn't sound disapproving of their plans to marry, he hadn't given his blessing either. "I understand your concern, Mr. Brantley. It is not my intention to hurt Papa or even Marshall. However, you should know that my betrothal was agreed upon without my consent."

"Yes, Seth said as much." He shook his head. "My girls would have my head if I ever tried that."

She smiled, hoping to find a champion for their cause in Seth's father. "I love your son. It doesn't matter to me that he isn't rich or that we won't have much starting out. Isn't that how my parents, as well as you and your wife, began life together when you moved to Texas? I am sure it won't be easy, but I would much rather lead a simple life with a man I love than have everything money can buy with a man I don't love."

Looking at her a long time, he finally nodded. "I believe you mean that, Miss Ellis. If you have half your mother's spirit and fortitude, you will do just fine. For what it is worth—and I told this to Seth last night—you have my blessing. I don't know how you will convince Luther, but if there is anything I can do, I will."

Overjoyed, she threw herself into his arms. With a fatherly hug and kiss on her cheek, he grinned. "I have to admit, it has always been my hope one of my boys would catch your eye."

"Seth did more than catch my eye, Mr. Brantley," she said, smiling at her future father-in-law. "He captured my heart."

After her conversation with Seth's father, Adella practically floated through breakfast. Not even Marshall's constant presence at her side spoiled the morning. Mr. Brantley soon took his leave to return to the farm, sending her a special smile and a wink on his way out the door. He would tell Seth good-bye at the overseer's cabin. The other guests also departed for their homes, leaving only Marshall, who planned to return to Le Beau on the morrow. The sooner he left, the better. She didn't dare broach the subject of ending their engagement until all the excitement from the wedding celebrations had died down and things were back to normal. Then she would carefully plan how to break the news in such a way that Papa would clearly see marrying Seth was for the best.

After the others were gone, Papa and Marshall retired to the parlor, the price of cotton ever on their tongues. Adella had no desire to sit and listen to them drone on about business all morning and announced she was going to the slaves' Sunday service in the chapel. She and Seth had already agreed to meet there, and she was anxious to see him and tell him about her conversation with his father.

But Marshall stood and smiled. "That sounds like a fine idea. Your father mentioned the traveling preacher who performed George and Natalie's ceremony would be there to bring the good word."

Disappointment swept over Adella when her father also stood. "Yes, I thought we would all attend, Adella Rose."

Recovering quickly, so as not to draw Papa's attention, she forced a pleasant smile. "It will be nice to have a formal preacher for a change. But I must say, Moses did a fine job last Sunday. I left the service truly uplifted."

Marshall scoffed. "I doubt an uneducated slave understands the complexities of the gospel message. They can't even read the Bible for themselves. Much of what is passed down among them is folklore and superstition. True religion escapes them, of that I am certain."

"They cannot read the Bible for themselves through no fault of their own." Adella tried to keep her voice even, but his comment riled her to the core. "Perhaps if we taught Negroes to read and write, they wouldn't have to rely on folklore and superstition. But let me assure you, Mr. Brevard, Moses fully grasped the meaning of salvation through Jesus Christ. Much better than many white people I have known who wear the name Christian yet have no compassion for their fellow man."

The air tingled with her words. Marshall seemed taken aback, and Papa's unsmiling face grew red. Adella knew he would reprimand her for her rudeness the moment they were alone, but she wasn't sorry she'd spoken the truth.

"I certainly meant no disrespect, Adella Rose," Marshall said. "I am sure you are correct about Moses. He had the benefit of being owned by a man of the cloth, as I now recall Langford mentioning. Perhaps I have been hasty in making such a broad judgment of the darkies."

His choice of crude words nullified any apology he might have intended. Turning her back, she strode to the door without a backward glance. If she remained in the foyer another moment, there was no telling what she might say, beginning with how she sincerely doubted Moses would consider it a "benefit" to be owned by anyone, clergy or otherwise.

Hurrying across the yard, with Papa and Marshall following more slowly, their heads together in deep conversation, Adella caught sight of Seth waiting near the entrance to the chapel. She knew the moment he realized she wasn't alone because he ducked into the building. When she arrived at the door, she waited for the men to catch up before entering. Already, lively singing ensued.

The three entered the crowded sanctuary, causing a bit of a stir among the slaves. Papa hadn't graced the place with his presence in months, and most of the slaves had never seen Marshall except at a distance. Though the singing continued, it was definitely more subdued.

Before settling into the last row, Adella spotted Seth partially hidden among several men standing along the back wall. Papa and Marshall hadn't noticed him, thankfully, as they took their seats. For a brief moment, she made eye contact with him. His encouraging smile sent a warm tremor through her. It was as though she heard him repeat his promise: *soon*. Soon they could attend the service as a couple.

When the singing subsided, Reverend Nelson, the short, older man who'd performed the wedding ceremony, stepped up to the crude pulpit, his Bible in his hand and a smile on his weathered face.

"God loves our praise, folks. It don't matter what color your skin is, how old your bones are, or if you sing like an old bear growlin' for his supper." Everyone chuckled, satisfying the preacher. "God loves our praise."

He paused a moment to let the statement sink in then flipped open his worn, black Bible.

"I was reading in the book of Philippians the other day," he began, looking out to the crowd, making sure he had their attention. "The Apostle Paul wrote this book, or letter as we know it was, when he was in prison." At the surprised murmur that rose, Reverend Nelson nodded with enthusiasm. "Oh yes, Paul, like me, was a traveling preacher, but he'd been arrested and thrown in prison. All because he preached the good news about Jesus Christ. The folks in charge back then didn't want anyone thinking Jesus was the Messiah, the one God promised to send to set them free. No, sir. The folks in charge said Jesus was a liar."

"Shame on dem," Mammy said, with others agreeing.

"Yes, Mammy." Reverend Nelson nodded. "Shame is right. They will be ashamed one day when they stand before Jesus; that's for certain. But on the day they threw Paul in prison, after beating him and no telling what else, they didn't feel shame. They felt pride. They felt they had done God's work by getting rid of a troublemaker. I don't rightly know how long Paul stayed locked away in chains. I don't rightly know what kind of mean things his guards did or if he had enough to eat. But I do know something about Paul's time in prison that surprises me."

"What that, Preacher?" someone called from the back.

"I know he rejoiced in his circumstances."

The room fell silent. People exchanged confused looks, as though they'd misunderstood.

A large man stood, glancing around him for support. Adella recognized him as one of the new slaves, although she didn't know his name. "What'chu mean, Preacher man? You sayin' that there Paul was happy bein' in prison?"

Others around him repeated the question, skepticism ringing in the joined voices.

Reverend Nelson waited for the man to take his seat then picked up his Bible. "Let me read Paul's own words, and you decide for yourself. This is from the book of Philippians, chapter four, verse four:

"Rejoice in the Lord always; and again I say, Rejoice."

He tapped the book with his finger. "I don't believe Paul would write words like that, from prison, no less, if he didn't live by them himself. A little farther down in verse eleven he says he has learned *'in whatsoever state I am, therewith to be content.'"*

Reverend Nelson looked at the text and nodded, as though confirming that was indeed what it said. "Paul doesn't tell us to rejoice only when things are going well. When you have plenty to eat or money in your pocket. He doesn't make mention of what color your skin is or whether you live in the big house or the slave quarter. He simply says rejoice ... *always*."

"Ain't easy to do, but we trys. We trys," Mammy said, wiping tears from her face.

"Yes, we must try, folks. Each of us. But remember what Paul said to rejoice in: *the Lord*. The Lord Jesus Christ and what he did for us on the cross. God doesn't expect us to feel joy for the hard times, or the empty stomachs, or the beatings."

Next to Adella, Marshall fidgeted in his seat. Papa too looked uncomfortable. Even she had a prick of conscience at the man's words. Was she content with the circumstances and blessings God had bestowed upon her? The life she lived held no hardships compared to the people around her, yet was she content? It warranted a deeper look when she next found herself alone.

"God doesn't expect us to rejoice because we are suffering," the reverend continued, his compassionate eyes searching the crowd. "We are called to rejoice *in spite of* those things. We rejoice because Jesus overcame all of the ugliness of the world when He died and rose again on the third day. We rejoice that through Jesus' own sufferings, his death and his resurrection, we too can overcome the hard things in this life, even unto death."

Mammy stood, clapping her hands. "Thank ya, Lawd!" Others

joined in with shouts of their own until everyone stood around them. A song broke out.

Papa and Marshall apparently had the same idea and, without looking at the other, headed for the door. With little choice, Adella followed. When she glanced to where Seth had stood at the back of the room, she found the spot vacant. He must have slipped out at some point, not wanting to be seen by the two men.

Exiting the noisy building, Papa and Marshall stood waiting for her.

"I don't know how you stand that ruckus each week, Adella Rose," Papa said, looking surly and out of sorts. "Martha insisted we allow the slaves their own church service, but I wonder now if it's such a good idea. You saw that new boy stand up, challenging a white preacher without the slightest fear, despite knowing his master was just a few feet away."

While Marshall appeared to agree, Adella shook her head. "He wasn't challenging Reverend Nelson, Papa. He simply asked the question that was probably on everyone's mind."

Papa and Marshall exchanged a brief look. She could guess what it meant, making her want to scream her frustrations. Instead, she turned back to the chapel.

"I am going to wait for the service to end. I would like to thank the reverend for coming and invite him to stay for dinner."

Marshall appeared indecisive, unsure whether to remain with her or go with her father.

"We will see you back at the house then," Papa said, solving his dilemma.

Relief washed over her. Watching them walk away, a saying her mother used at times flashed through her mind. "*Cut from the same cloth.*" Papa and Marshall definitely fit the saying.

"I thought they would never leave."

Smiling, she turned and saw Seth come out from behind the small building. "I wondered where you had gone. Papa insisted on coming to the service and then hated every minute."

He nodded, tucking her hand into the crook of his arm. "Let's walk to the creek where we can talk. When I noticed Brevard squirming, I figured it wasn't long before he'd duck out, so I left before he did. Reverend Nelson didn't mince words."

"No, he didn't. Papa wasn't at all pleased, especially when the new slave stood up." She frowned. "I tried to explain he asked a question most everyone there wanted answered, but Papa didn't agree."

Maneuvering through the brush lining the shallow creek, Seth led her to a grassy area. He took off his jacket and laid it down, bowing in a gallant manner. "Miss Ellis, I am at your service," he said, grinning.

Adella chuckled then sat, settling her wide skirt in a circle around her folded legs. "Thank you, kind sir." She sighed, enjoying the peace and quiet. The singing from the chapel had quieted, and she guessed Reverend Nelson had once again taken over the pulpit. The service could go on for quite some time.

"Rose Hill is one of the few plantations I know of that allows the slaves to meet together for a church service." He sat next to her and stretched out his injured leg, leaving his other knee bent.

"What harm can come from letting them have a church service?" The Langfords didn't allow their slaves a service, but she'd never pondered why. Instead, some of their trusted slaves, like Zina and Moses, were allowed to come to Rose Hill on Sunday if the weather held. "I can only think it would benefit a slave owner to teach their people about Jesus and the Bible. A person who loves God isn't going to cause trouble. Look at Mammy, and Aunt Lu, and Moses. You'd never meet anyone, white or black, more kindhearted than they."

Seth picked up a stone and tossed it into the sparkling water, sending ripples to the far edge and back. "They fear if they allow the slaves to meet in large groups, an uprising or some other plan might be hatched."

"If those plantation owners would join the slaves' services, they would see that simply isn't true," she said, the praises of the Rose Hill slaves fresh in her memory. "You saw yourself that our people truly want to worship and hear the Word. They aren't gathering to plot an escape."

"That may well be true here, but it isn't true on every plantation." Seth grew serious. "I know you care about your slaves, Adella. You treat Aunt Lu and Jeptha like family. But you need to remember they aren't at Rose Hill by choice. If the opportunity to escape ever came, they would take it."

Disappointment flooded her. "You sound just like Papa or Marshall. I know our slaves better than anyone, and I know none of them would ever run away." She paused a moment, thinking of the new slaves Papa brought the day Seth arrived. "Perhaps some of the newer ones might, but even then, it wouldn't be because they were mistreated."

A patient smile lifted his lips. "I hope you're right. Your father would have my hide if one escaped on my watch."

"Speaking of fathers." She remembered she hadn't yet told him about the conversation she'd had with the elder Mr. Brantley that morning. "I spoke to your father before he left."

"I know." He grinned. "We have his full blessing, Adella Rose."

She couldn't keep the smile from her face. "He said he had always hoped one of his sons caught my eye."

"Then I suppose I should be thankful he didn't bring my older brother here to sweep you off your feet years ago."

Adella laughed, then grew serious. "But what will we do about my father? He is so set on me marrying Marshall and becoming mistress of Le Beau. I don't know for certain, but I have a suspicion they have made some sort of business agreement that is tied to the betrothal."

Seth sobered. "Pa and I had a long talk about that last night. He, too, wondered if they might have an agreement that included you. Why else would your father force you into the marriage?"

The stark truth of the question hung in the air. "I sincerely hope we are wrong about Papa. It is impossible for me to believe he would use me in that manner." Yet hadn't she been suspicious of that very thing since the day he had stormed into her bedroom?

"I think it is best if we let things settle down and get back to normal. Then we will go to him together and tell him we want to be married." Seth took her hand and squeezed. "Soon."

"Soon," she repeated the promise.

But she couldn't quiet the feeling of foreboding that rose up in her. Papa would not give in easily. Of that she was certain.

CHAPTER SEVENTEEN

Early Monday morning, Moses and Zina arrived at Rose Hill with a wagonload of Natalie's belongings. Trunks and crates stacked several high filled the bed. Seth had just finished breakfasting in the kitchen and was on his way out when the wagon pulled up at the front door.

"Howdy, Mistah Brantley, suh," the big black man said once he had dismounted. He reached to help Zina down, and they both stood in front of Seth. "We's done brought Miss Natalie's things. Didn't know if I should go 'round back or come right on through the front like."

Seth considered the loaded wagon. When they returned from their honeymoon trip, the newlyweds would take up residence in the east wing of the big house, which had a private entrance at the back. It would be much easier to bring Natalie's belongings through that way.

"Take the wagon around to the back of the house. I'll send Jeptha to help you unload. I'm sure Zina can direct you where everything goes." Seth started to leave, but Moses' deep voice stopped him.

"Mistah Brantley, suh," he said, dipping his head slightly.

"Yes?"

"I just wanted ta say even though I belongs ta Miss Natalie, bein' her carriage driver an' all, I be livin' here at Rose Hill now. I 'spect there be times when I ain't so busy that I cain't he'p 'round here." When he smiled, Seth noticed several teeth missing. "I real good with the livestock an' sech. Be right happy ta work in them barns with the critters."

Seth accepted the offer with a nod. "I appreciate that. Of course, when Miss Natalie and Master George return in a few weeks, you'll need to make sure that is acceptable with her. Until then, I'll see that Monroe understands you are working with the animals upon my orders."

The slave seemed pleased. "We'll go on to the back now an' get the wagon unloaded."

Seth watched them go, wondering what other changes would take place once George and Natalie returned. Although both Moses and Zina legally belonged to Natalie, through marriage they now actually belonged to George. And that man had certainly proven himself an unscrupulous owner by his actions with Lucy. Seth hoped the attractive Zina would be safe from George's pleasure-seeking ways.

He made his way to the barn to locate Jeptha, finding the young man already at work mucking out stalls. Jeptha stopped what he was doing when he saw Seth.

"I would like you to go help Moses unload Miss Natalie's belongings," Seth said, drawing up to the chest-high wall of the enclosure.

"Yassuh." The slave leaned the shovel against a wheelbarrow half full of manure.

"Zina will tell you where to put the things." Seth turned to go but stopped when a strange expression flashed across Jeptha's face. "Is something wrong?"

The black man shook his head, but his eyes told another story.

"Out with it." Seth folded his arms across his chest and waited. Ever since the day they spent working with Freedom, Seth felt an odd kinship with the slave. Something he'd never experienced before in dealing with his father's slaves.

"It's just that I'd rather not be around Zina, suh." Jeptha wouldn't meet his eyes.

"Why not?"

Jeptha glanced up, a pained look on his face. "'Cuz I with Celia now."

Recalling Jeptha's admission to being sweet on Zina, Seth could understand his discomfort being around her. But they lived on the same plantation now. They were bound to see each other. Best to get it over and done with and move on.

"I understand," he said, "but I'm afraid I still need you to go help Moses. It won't take long."

Jeptha nodded. "Yassuh." He trudged out of the stall and exited the barn, leaving Seth weighed down with a load of guilt. Wasn't he in a similar position, with Adella engaged to Marshall? Seeing them together made his blood boil, but at least he knew he and Adella would be together soon. Jeptha had no such assurances.

Saddling Chester, he rode out to the fields, wondering if his views of slavery were as valid as he'd always believed. As far back as he could remember, his father had owned slaves. Most everyone they knew owned slaves. Granted, Luther Ellis owned more than anyone Seth had ever met, but then he owned more land than most. He needed more workers than Seth's father and their neighbors.

He'd never given slavery much thought until the day the runaway shot him. After that, he'd looked at every slave with suspicion, knowing they all weren't as easy to manage as his father's people. In fact, Seth had to admit he'd actually begun to hate Negroes. They represented the very reason he'd had to give up his career as a Texas Ranger and why he walked with a painful limp. He had never actually considered the plight of the man he was chasing until the other day. Even now, he wasn't entirely sure what to think about it. Had the slave not been armed and yet tried to run, Seth probably would have shot him. That the escapee shot him first in his attempt at freedom left Seth wondering which of them had more right to fire on the other.

Coming up on a group of slaves hoeing rows of cotton plants, Seth watched from a distance. The group was mostly women, although several younger boys and a few men were sprinkled throughout. The work was hard, with the day promising to grow blistering hot by afternoon. Yet these people had no choice in the matter. They had to work the fields, rain or shine, bitter cold or raging heat. Their lives were not their own. They were property, belonging to Luther Ellis, living at the mercy of the master's whims.

One woman stopped hoeing. She stood upright, arching her back, her big belly protruding from beneath her dress. Lucy. Carrying George's baby. Working the fields owned by her child's grandfather. The irony left Seth disgusted. He watched as she rubbed the small of her back, in obvious discomfort. When she spotted him astride his horse, however, she quickly returned to work.

What would Adella say when she learned about the baby? A secret like this couldn't stay hidden forever. She would be aunt to the child. Knowing how upset the situation would undoubtedly make her, Seth felt he should be the one to tell her. But the timing would be tricky. He'd rather wait until they were safely married and away from Rose Hill. That way any upset or confrontation she might demand with George would not stand in their way of marrying. Whether Luther was aware of the baby or not, Seth didn't know, but either way, he suspected the elder Ellis wouldn't care. He was, after all, the man who wanted to breed his own slaves.

As the afternoon sun began to make its lazy descent toward the western horizon, a strange hum reached Seth. Though it wasn't unusual for the slaves to sing while they worked, this low chant was something he'd never heard before. It seemed to drift from field to field until those slaves nearest him also repeated it.

"Patter the pat. Patter the pat."

Over and over. Never loud. Just a low murmur that seemed to take on a life of its own as it wove its way from one field to the next. No one looked up but continued hoeing and muttering the unusual phrase.

A few minutes later, Seth noticed riders coming up the long drive. Five horses yet only four men in the saddle. Two large dogs trailed them. Curious, he urged Chester into a gallop and met the group when they rounded the last bend before reaching the house.

"Hello," he called as he neared. It was then he noticed the body of a man lying face down across the saddle of the fifth horse.

A slave's body.

"Hello," the older man in front said drawing to a halt. He eyed Seth a moment. "You the new overseer?"

"I am."

Seth didn't need to be told these men were patrollers, or patterollers, as the slaves called them. They earned their living hunting down runaway slaves and keeping watch over the roads. Any slave unaccompanied by a white person without a pass faced the bullwhip if caught, although Seth knew such men often made trouble for slaves with passes just for the fun of it.

Now the low chant made sense. It warned of the presence of a patrol.

"Name's Bill Dunn." With his thumb, he motioned toward the body. "Got old man Langford's boy here. Thought I'd let Mr. Ellis know we found him."

Seth glanced at the body, shirtless and bloody. Flies buzzed around the open wounds on his back, arms, and legs. "Where did you catch him?"

"Halfway to ol' Mexico." Dunn laughed. "That boy might'a made it too if someone hadn't seen him holed up with one o' them *sympathizers*. Can't understand why anyone would help a no-good Negro runaway, but there are plenty of 'em that'll do that all the way to Mexico." He sent a stream of spittle to the ground.

Seth nodded. The information wasn't new to him. In his years with the Rangers, he'd heard of people who willingly harbored runaway slaves and helped get them across the border to freedom. Many were *Tejanos*—Mexicans living in Texas—but some were white. They faced fines and punishment if they were caught, but still hundreds of slaves were aided in escaping to Mexico every year.

"You couldn't bring him in alive?" Seth asked.

Dunn sneered. "Langford didn't care one way or the other. That boy wouldn't cooperate with us, would he?" He turned to his men, who laughed. "Had to set the dogs on him."

Looking back to the body, Seth's stomach churned. He didn't want Adella to see the grisly sight. "I would rather you fellows didn't go up to the house. There are womenfolk who don't need to be exposed to this."

Dunn spat again. "Ain't nothing but a dead Negro, but we'll head on to Langford's. Tell Mr. Ellis we'll stop by when we ride out again."

Watching the group depart, Seth couldn't help but feel sickened. Had he been as callous as those men when he'd hunted down the runaway?

The thought pierced him with shame.

Turning Chester back toward the fields, he stopped in his tracks. In front of him, every slave watched the horsemen.

❧ ❦

Adella moved out of the way as Jeptha and Moses brought in yet another large trunk, which was obviously heavy, judging by the way they struggled up the stairs. "I declare, Natalie must have kept the seamstress busy for months with so many new gowns in her trousseau."

Zina offered a half-hearted smile when Adella looked her way. The girl had been acting odd ever since Jeptha arrived to help bring in Natalie's things. The two had ignored each other, never speaking a word, with Zina giving Moses directions as though Jeptha was not in the room. Something was definitely amiss here, but Adella would wait until they were alone to get to the bottom of it. Knowing the two had secretly been sweet on each other for years, she hoped the young couple would marry now that they both lived at Rose Hill. Adella hadn't mentioned anything to Natalie regarding the matter, but she would as soon as the newlyweds returned. There wasn't any reason why the two slaves shouldn't be allowed to jump the broom.

Glancing around the freshly painted bedroom, Adella smiled with satisfaction. The redecorating had turned out beautifully in spite of Natalie's ever-changing desires. The enormous bed George ordered filled the space, though not so much that it seemed overcrowded. The forest green coverlet matched the drapery, yet the creamy walls kept the room from appearing too dark. A bureau and dressing table with a large mirror sat near the window, with a grand fireplace directly opposite. French doors opened to the adjoining sitting room, and Adella made a mental note to send Joseph into town tomorrow to check on the new wallpaper Natalie ordered.

"This here the last of it, Missy Ellis." Moses' deep voice broke into her thoughts, and she turned to see Jeptha and him carry in another enormous trunk. "It for the sittin' room."

Adella nodded. "Very well. Set it in that room, but we will wait to unpack it after the new wallpaper arrives." She looked to Zina for confirmation of her instructions but found the young woman staring out the window. Was that a tear glistening in her eye?

"If that be all, Missy, I get back to work," Jeptha said when he returned from the sitting room. His gaze strayed to Zina then back.

With a frown, Adella wondered if the couple had quarreled. For a brief moment, she considered ordering them to speak to each other and work out whatever problem they had, but that didn't seem appropriate. While they were indeed slaves of Rose Hill and had to obey her commands, they were also human beings with feelings. They didn't need her meddling in their private business, although she still planned to speak to Zina about Jeptha. If not directly, she could at least steer their conversation in that direction in hopes the young woman would reveal what had her upset and why they weren't speaking.

"That will be all, Jeptha. Thank you for your help." She watched him leave, noticing he didn't walk with his normal springy stride but rather seemed dejected, with his broad shoulders slumped. Most likely from Zina's rebuff, she guessed.

"I takes the wagon on up to the barn now, Missy Ellis, 'less you needs me to he'p with somethin' else." Moses mopped his brow with a square of unhemmed cloth. The big man smiled despite the exertion he'd extended the past hour.

"Thank you. That will be fine. If we have need to move anything heavy, I'll send word to you." He started toward the door when she remembered something. "Moses, before you leave, I want to thank you for your sermon last Sunday. I am looking forward to having you bring a good word to us every week now that you will reside at Rose Hill."

The compliment should have brought a smile, but a hint of sadness crossed his weathered features. "I always happy to talk 'bout Jesus, Missy."

She waited, but he didn't seem inclined to continue. "Are you not pleased to be at Rose Hill?"

He glanced at Zina before dipping his head. "I gonna miss my family, is all."

Shamefully, Adella realized she never once considered the slave's life at the Langford plantation. Moses was simply Natalie's driver and personal errand runner. That he might have a wife and children had never crossed her mind.

"I am sorry, Moses. I … I didn't know you had a family," she said, knowing the words were pathetically inadequate.

A smile softened his face. "Gots me a good woman an' five young uns. The Good Lawd done blessed me mightily since He brought me to the Langfords'. My old mastah tell me the Bible say a man is happy when his quiver is full o' chillens." He grinned. "I a happy man, Missy."

She smiled. "I will speak to Natalie and George about your family when they return. Perhaps it could be arranged for them to come here."

"I shore would 'preciate that, Missy," he said. "I best get on now an' get that wagon to the barn."

"That was real nice of you, Missy." Zina moved toward the nearest trunk after Moses left. She opened it and took out a lovely peach colored gown wrapped in tissue paper. Tossing the paper aside, she shook out the wrinkles on the dress before reaching for the next one. "Moses and Harriet are crazy about each other. She carried on something fierce when we left this morning."

That news greatly disturbed Adella. It wasn't right to tear families apart. Even though the two plantations were less than ten miles from each other, Moses wouldn't be able to spend any time with his wife and children. Being newly in love, she couldn't imagine Seth being taken from her so abruptly, never knowing when she would get to see him again.

"I hope Natalie's father will allow Moses' family to come to Rose Hill. I suppose I need to speak to Papa too, since the decision is really his." She sighed, frustrated by the whole situation. "It isn't right, Zina."

The young woman looked up from her task. "What isn't right, Missy?"

"That you and Moses and Jeptha and Aunt Lu have no say in the decisions that are made about your lives. Moses shouldn't be forced to leave his family just because Natalie is moving to Rose Hill. I imagine you were happy to come since your mother is here, but I'm sure no one asked your opinion, did they?"

Zina shook her head, although she looked a bit uneasy at the turn of conversation. No doubt she'd never had a white person speak to her about slavery in such a manner. Perhaps, Adella thought, it was best to keep her opinions to herself for the time being. Jeptha was the only slave to whom she'd ever spoken so truthfully, and she didn't want Zina repeating something to Natalie, or even to one of the other slaves, thus bringing down trouble if her father or George ever got wind of it. Neither of the men appreciated her sentiments regarding the slaves.

"Well," she surveyed the cluttered room. "I suppose it will take you most of the day to get Natalie's things organized and put away. I'll send Carolina up to assist you."

"Thank you, Missy." Zina smiled. "She's a sweet girl. Mama says she reminds her of me when I was that age."

Adella didn't mention the fact that Zina had been sold to the Langfords by the time she was Carolina's age. Instead, she said, "Yes, Carolina is sweet. And so eager to please."

Zina continued working, and Adella watched, wondering how to broach the subject of Jeptha. Though she felt a twinge of unease, knowing it was really none of her business, she wanted to see the young couple happy. "I assume you will move into your mother's rooms above the kitchen instead of living in the quarter."

"Yes'm." Zina removed a stack of folded lacy pantaloons and carried them to the bureau. "It will be strange not to sleep on a pallet in Miss Natalie's room, though."

Adella chuckled. "I remember the first night Hulda slept away from my room. She said she snuck in and peeked at me just to make sure I was fine. Of course, it was I who insisted I was too old to have my mammy sleeping in the same room anymore. I believe she would still be there, had I not forced her to return to the quarter with her family."

Zina offered a smile and continued working. Adella tapped her fingers, trying to come up with a question or comment that would open the doors to a conversation about Jeptha. Nothing came to mind. Finally, she decided to simply be honest with the young woman.

"I noticed you and Jeptha didn't speak to one another a little while ago." She eyed Zina for a reaction.

For a moment, Zina's hands stilled. "Oh?" She gave a slight shrug. "I guess I was too busy with Miss Natalie's things."

Adella narrowed her eyes. "I don't think that is it. I have known Jeptha my whole life, and I have never seen him act so … down."

Zina met her gaze. "He seemed down to you, Missy?"

"Yes. He kept looking at you, but you never acknowledged him at all." She raised her brow in question, hoping to encourage the other woman to tell her what happened.

Suddenly, Zina burst into tears. "Oh, Missy. I know I shouldn't have, but I hoped when I moved back to Rose Hill, me and Jeptha might ... might ..." Her chin quivered, and she shook her head, sniffling. "But it doesn't matter now. Mama says I just need to get my mind off him and put all my effort into serving Miss Natalie and Master George the best I can."

Adella frowned. "I don't understand. I thought you and Jeptha liked each other? What happened to give you the impression it wouldn't work out now that you're here?"

"Why, because him and Celia are together," Zina exclaimed, misery on her face.

"Celia? And Jeptha?" Adella asked, dumbfounded. "No, you must be mistaken. He would have told me if he was interested in her."

"Master Luther gave them their own cabin down in the quarter, Missy. They living together." More tears pooled in Zina's eyes.

Stunned, Adella sat down on the bed. "You are sure?"

Zina nodded, wiping the trails of wetness from her face. "Celia told Lucy she hoping to be with child soon too."

The air swooshed from Adella's lungs like the time she fell out of a tree Jeptha had dared her to climb. That her friend and companion of all those years would take up with a woman without telling her hurt more than she dared acknowledge. It also answered the question of why he'd been avoiding her lately. And what had Zina said about Jeptha and Celia having a cabin to themselves in the quarter? It was by Papa's orders.

Which meant Seth knew.

"I am sorry, Zina." She felt betrayed by the three most important men in her life. "I had no idea."

A short time later, Adella left the young woman to attend her work. She sent one of the other house servants to locate Carolina and instruct the girl to help Zina. Briefly, she thought about going to the kitchen to see what information she might glean from Aunt Lu about Jeptha, but Celia might have been there. They wouldn't be able to speak freely, even if Aunt Lu was willing to divulge anything, which sometimes she wasn't.

Being in no mood to speak to her father, and with Seth in the fields, that left her little choice. With purposeful strides, Adella left the house and headed to the barn to sort out her troubled thoughts.

CHAPTER EIGHTEEN

Seth continued to take his meals in the kitchen even after Marshall and the other guests departed Rose Hill. Luther hadn't invited him back into the family dining room, and he didn't want to presume to simply arrive at the table without being asked. Although he'd hoped Adella would ask him to join them, she seemed preoccupied and even a little miffed when she came in to speak to Aunt Lu about a supply list. With so many servants about, he couldn't ask her what was wrong. Hopefully, he'd have a chance later in the evening.

"Would you like some mo' dumplin's, Mistah Brantley, suh?"

Hearing the small voice beside him, Seth looked up to find Carolina standing nearby, practically trembling with fear. Her large eyes rounded as she held out a steaming bowl of savory chicken and dumplings. Aunt Lu supervised from her place at the stove, where she patiently waited for a pot of coffee to boil.

"Yes, as a matter of fact, I would. They are delicious. Almost as good as my mama's." He grinned when Aunt Lu looked his way.

"Yo' mama must be a good cook then." Aunt Lu jerked the coffee pot away from the heat just before it bubbled over. "A boy don't grow into a man yo' size with po' cookin'. I should know. I got three boys o' my own."

Seth looked at her with surprise. "I didn't know you had any sons. Are they here at Rose Hill?" He did a mental rundown of the male slaves and couldn't come up with any that might be Aunt Lu's. Though it had taken some time, he'd just about sorted out the slaves by family.

"No, they's all gone ta work on other plantations." A hint of sadness showed behind her eyes.

In other words, Seth thought, *they'd been sold*. At least Zina was back with her.

"How long have you been at Rose Hill, Aunt Lu?" he asked as Carolina dumped a second heaping spoonful of dumplings onto his plate. When he nodded his thanks, the girl scurried away.

Aunt Lu ambled over and poured some of the hot black liquid into his half-full mug. "Massa Luther bought me an' two o' my boys when the youngest be 'bout a year ol'. He be 'bout twenty or so now. Massa Luther an' Miz Martha built this house that year. 'Course, it weren't nothin' as grand as it is now."

"So you have been here about nineteen years."

"Yassuh." She returned to the stove. "I 'spect that about right. I seen lotsa changes 'round here. Some for the good, some not so much. Seen lotsa overseahs come an' go." She looked at him, seeming to measure her next words. "Don't know that I ever likes one as much as I likes you."

Her matter-of-fact words made him smile. "I'll take that as a compliment."

"You should."

He continued eating. Zina entered the kitchen a few minutes later. She greeted him then conferred with her mother about something. He didn't pay attention to their conversation, but a thought did enter his mind as he watched her leave. The same thought he'd had since the first day he saw her.

Zina's skin was so much lighter than Aunt Lu's ebony coloring. He guessed Zina to be about sixteen years of age, which meant she'd been born after Aunt Lu came to Rose Hill. Knowing there was only one logical explanation for the cook's daughter to have skin so light, he grimaced. Her father had to be a white man. Yet Seth couldn't bring himself to believe Luther Ellis had fathered the girl.

Lucy's image floated through his mind.

Was George following in his father's footsteps?

He left the kitchen just as the sun dipped below the horizon, oddly troubled. It wasn't any of his business what the Ellis men did with their slaves. He was simply hired on as the overseer, charged with making sure the slaves did their work and didn't run away. White men had fathered children with black slaves for ages. Why did it suddenly bother Seth now?

Feeling out of sorts, he desperately needed to see Adella and let her sweet spirit soothe his nerves. But he'd have to wait until she and her father finished supper. Hopefully, Luther would retire to the library and leave Adella free to sneak away.

Just the thought of her made him smile. He'd never experienced these feelings for a woman before. Once when he was a new Ranger and full of himself, he'd thought himself in love with the daughter of famed Captain John "Rip" Ford. He'd only seen Fannie on a few occasions, but her golden hair and deep-blue eyes had stolen his heart. Or so he'd thought. Apparently, a number of other Rangers felt the same way. Word soon circulated through the ranks that the young Miss Ford was a bit of a flirt and had half the regiment under her spell. Seth had sworn off women then and focused on his career. That is until it was cut short by a gunshot wound.

Not willing to sit in his cabin and wait for Adella, he decided to check on Freedom. Joseph and Jeptha had worked with the stallion since the day they broke him, but Seth had been too busy to participate. Not to mention his leg wouldn't tolerate another wild ride. According to Joseph, the horse was responding well under Jeptha's patient care. It was a shame Luther or George would be the ones benefiting from the slave's hard work.

Just as he drew near the barn door, an angry shout pierced the air, followed by the screams of a woman. They came from inside the building. He tore open the door and stood still, listening to see which direction he should go. A movement caught his attention. Zina came charging around the corner, her hair in disarray and the front of her dress torn, exposing frilly underthings.

"Oh, Mr. Brantley, he gonna kill him! You gots to stop them!"

"Who, Zina? What are you talking about?"

More angry voices reached him. A man cried out in obvious pain.

"There," she sobbed, pointing in the direction from whence she'd come. "He's gonna kill him. I just know it."

Seth didn't wait to learn who it was she spoke of. The sound of hard blows landing on bodies led him to the far end of the barn where the tack room was located. The door was closed, but he could hear scuffling coming from within. When he yanked the door open, there was Jeptha straddled on top of Monroe's barrel chest, the big man lying flat on his back on the dirt floor. Blood poured from his nose and mouth, and his eyes were rolled back in his head. One arm lay at an abnormal angle.

Jeptha landed another solid strike on the man's jaw, his own blood spilling from his nose and dripping down onto Monroe's shirt. When Jeptha raised his fist for another hit, Seth stepped in and grabbed him by the shirt collar.

"What's going on here?" He yanked the slave to his feet.

Jeptha's breath came in hard gulps as he tried to twist away.

Zina appeared in the doorway, her eyes wild and fearful. She held her torn dress together with both hands.

"Well?" Seth looked between the two. Jeptha's last blow had rendered Monroe unconscious, but his breathing told Seth he was still alive. Although that might not have been the story, had Seth not arrived when he did.

"He done tried to have his way with her." Jeptha wiped the blood from his nose with his shirt sleeve, leaving a smeared swath across his cheek. Already his left eye was beginning to swell closed, revealing Monroe had landed a few blows before Jeptha got the better of him.

Seth looked to Zina for confirmation, although the evidence spoke for itself. "Is that true?"

She nodded, her gaze traveling to Jeptha.

"What were you doing in the barn?" A feeling of dread began

to settle in Seth's gut. Luther Ellis would be livid when he heard about this.

"Ain't her fault. He attacked her, Mistah Brantley," Jeptha interrupted when Zina started to answer.

Seth let loose of Jeptha's collar. "You keep quiet for now. I want to hear what Zina has to say."

When he faced the young woman again, he noted how shaken she appeared. That Monroe tried to rape her was infuriating, but he also knew Luther would want a full accounting of what transpired.

"Why were you down here?" he repeated. "I just saw you in the house a little while ago."

"I …" Her gaze flitted to Jeptha briefly then back. "I came looking for Jeptha. I wanted to speak to him about … something."

Frustration rolled through Seth. "I need you to tell me the whole truth, Zina. Master Luther is going to be furious when he learns his driver was nearly beaten to death after trying to force himself on you. Out with it. Why did you come looking for Jeptha?"

Fresh tears pooled in her eyes and slid down her cheeks. She turned away from the men. "I wanted to find out why he's with Celia. I was going to tell him that … that I wanted to be with him."

A groan came from Jeptha. "Girl, you shoulda stayed away. If I hadn't come in and found you—" His jaw clenched, and he turned to Seth. "She didn't do nothing wrong, Mistah Brantley. That animal," he pointed to Monroe's still body, "he done wrong. He deserves the punishment."

Though Seth agreed with the statement, he knew it wouldn't be that simple. Not when Luther learned what happened. That Jeptha had nearly beaten Monroe to death would not sit well with the plantation owner.

"Master Luther will decide who is punished. Right now, we need to get Monroe to his cabin and have Mammy look at him." He turned to Zina. "Get back to the house," he said, gruffer than he intended. "Find Miss Ellis and tell her everything. Everything." When she departed, crying quietly, he returned his attention to

Jeptha. "Get Joseph and two other men to help you carry Monroe to the quarter. I'll figure out what to tell Master Luther about this mess after Mammy sees him."

Jeptha didn't move.

"Well?"

"Why can't you just let me finish him? He an animal, Mistah Brantley. This ain't the first time he done this. Won't be his last if you let him live. Just walk away, suh. Just walk away."

Seth knew what Jeptha intended to do. While he disliked the big driver with a passion, he couldn't simply let a man be murdered. "I can't let you do that."

"He don't deserve to live."

"That is not for you or me to decide."

"Who then? God? God don't care 'bout us Negroes. We wouldn't be slaves if He did. So what's it matter to Him if one slave take the life of another slave?"

Seth stared at the other man. For one insane moment, he wondered if Jeptha was right. Would God care? Wouldn't they be better off without Monroe?

Reason took over. "Go get Joseph and the others."

Several tense moments ticked by before Jeptha stalked from the barn.

Looking at Monroe, Seth felt no pity. It was probably wrong to feel such, but he almost wished he'd let Jeptha finish the job.

❧　☙

Papa's features grew hard and turned scarlet as he sat behind his desk in the library, listening while Seth recounted the tale of what took place in the barn. It pleased Adella to see that Papa was as angry as she about Monroe's disgusting behavior. She hoped this would be the incident that finally convinced Papa to sell Monroe and get him off Rose Hill land. While she'd never approved of Papa selling off their slaves like stock, she would make an exception for Monroe. His behavior fit that of an animal, so he deserved no more.

Her attention returned to Seth as he described the scene he came upon an hour ago. He and Jeptha stood just inside the library doorway, with Zina standing to the right of where Adella sat on a small sofa near the fireplace. Already a faint bruise was visible on the young woman's cheek. There was no telling what other injuries she might have suffered had Jeptha not intervened. Righteous anger boiled Adella's blood, and she could hardly wait to see Monroe's face when Papa loaded him onto a wagon and sent him to the market in Galveston.

"Mammy set Monroe's broken arm, but he may also have a concussion," Seth said, bringing his somber report to an end. "She volunteered to sit with him through the night and keep watch."

The room grew quiet, with all eyes on Papa, waiting for his response.

"What in blazes was that gal doing in the barn in the first place?" Papa finally bellowed, his angry glare focusing on Zina. "She is a house servant and has no business in the barn or anywhere else."

Zina visibly trembled, but she remained silent, knowing the question was not directed at her but to Seth.

"She needed to speak with Jeptha. When she didn't find him, she attempted to leave. That's when Monroe attacked her." Seth kept his voice even, and his gaze never wavered from Papa, despite the tense atmosphere. Pride welled up in Adella. As formidable as Luther Ellis could be, Seth was not intimidated.

"And Jeptha? What got into you, beating Monroe like you did? You know better than that." Papa glowered at the slave.

Jeptha kept his eyes downcast, but the muscles in his jaw twitched. "It weren't right what he tried to do to her, suh."

"It is not your place to decide what is right on this plantation, boy!" Papa stood abruptly, nearly knocking his chair over. "Fact is, that is Monroe's job. And if he wants to take a little pleasure with a gal, that is not any of your business."

"Papa!" Adella gasped, horrified he would say such a crude, despicable thing.

He shot a glare at her. "Stay out of this, Adella Rose. You have mollycoddled Jeptha 'til he thinks he can do something like this and get away with it. Well, I won't tolerate a slave thinkin' he can take down my driver just because he's the pet of the owner's daughter."

Adella stood, mouth agape. "He is not my pet. He is a human being. A human being with more decency than you, apparently, since he sees the wrong in what that animal Monroe was about to do to Zina."

She'd never spoken to Papa in such a manner. But then she'd never seen such coldness of heart in him before.

Papa shook his head with obvious disgust, then turned to Seth. "Take him to the shed. He can spend the next three weeks wishing he had minded his own business."

Before Adella could protest the unfair punishment, Seth stepped forward.

"I think that is rather harsh, sir, considering it was Monroe who was out of line."

Without warning, Papa swept a stack of papers and books off his desk. A framed picture of Mama near the edge teetered and finally crashed to the floor to join the chaos. Adella stared at the angry man as though he were a stranger.

"I did not ask for your opinion, Brantley!" His enraged voice echoed in the book-lined room. "I gave you an order. Take him to the shed or get off my land!"

For several moments, they all stood in shocked silence. Adella felt close to tears, deeply wounded by Papa's appalling behavior. How glad she was Mama wasn't here to witness it. It would break her heart to know Papa sided with the beast Monroe over Zina's honor. Aunt Lu and Mama had been close as sisters over the years. She'd have never allowed Zina to be treated so deplorably.

"As you wish, sir," Seth said after a long moment, sending a wave of fear speeding through Adella. Did he mean to leave Rose Hill?

He grasped Jeptha by the arm. "Let's go."

They disappeared into the hallway, with Zina hurrying behind, the sound of their footfalls receding quickly.

Fighting to control her emotions, Adella wanted to lash out at Papa and demand he recant his orders to put Jeptha in the shed. To make him spend three weeks in the disgusting shack behind the quarter was unchristian, especially when all he'd done was save a young woman from rape. Knowing Jeptha as she did, he would do it all over again despite the harsh punishment.

Years ago, she'd first learned of the shed when Roland, one of the field workers, spent four weeks in the small enclosure after stealing a slab of bacon. She and Jeptha hid a short distance away the day he was released and watched as the broken man slowly crawled out, shielding his eyes from the bright sunshine. She couldn't believe how different he looked. Gaunt from eating only stale bread twice a day. Hunched over because a grown man couldn't stand upright in the tiny shed. A slight breeze carried his foul stench to where Adella crouched, causing her to wrinkle her nose. When she asked Jeptha about it, he matter-of-factly explained the lack of outhouse privileges for occupants of the shed. After that, Adella avoided going anywhere near the place.

She looked at Papa now. His eyes glazed with anger as he continued to stare at the now empty hallway. When his gaze eventually shifted to her, Adella felt a tremor of fear snake through her. Briefly, she wondered if Mama had ever had to deal with him in this state of mind. If she had, Adella had never been aware of it.

Deciding it was best to remain calm, she settled back down on the edge of the sofa. "I understand you are angry, Papa." She clasped her hands in her lap. "But what Monroe tried to do to Zina is inexcusable. There is also the fact that Zina belongs to Natalie."

"You don't know the first thing about running a plantation this size, Adella Rose, so dispense with your childish 'right and wrong' judgments." Papa yanked his chair back in place and sat down. "Monroe is the best driver I have had in years. Since he took over, we rarely have trouble with the slaves. And when we do, he takes care of it. Jeptha has sufficiently ruined that now. Every slave on the place will have it in their minds that they can best Monroe."

The pronouncement seemed exaggerated, but Adella kept that to herself. "I myself have been uncomfortable when Monroe is around. Now he has attacked a woman who is not even a Rose Hill slave."

"Zina is most assuredly a Rose Hill slave, young lady." A scowl darkened his face. "The moment Natalie became George's wife, her slaves and anything else she owns became George's property."

Adella hadn't considered that. For a moment, alarm swept through her, realizing for the first time that any property she owned would immediately become her husband's upon marriage. Thankfully, she didn't believe Seth would be the kind of husband to lay claim to anything she brought into their marriage, even servants. She had little doubt, however, that Marshall Brevard held the same convictions as her father and brother. Yet another reason to bring an end to their engagement as soon as possible.

She rose from the sofa. "Since I do not believe we will see eye to eye regarding Monroe, I will leave you to your business."

"Just a moment." He picked up a folded sheet of paper from the floor where it had landed when he cleared the desktop in his anger. "Marshall has invited us to Le Beau next week. I have sent an acceptance."

Adella stared at him. "I wish you had consulted me first, Papa. I already told Mr. Brevard I felt it was too soon to make a visit to his plantation. You and he may have been plotting this engagement for some time, but it is all very new to me. I do not appreciate being left out of the decisions regarding my own life."

"The man is your fiancé. I think it high time you see where you will live, don't you?" His tone indicated he thought her nonsensical.

Wishing she could blurt out the truth regarding her plan to marry Seth, Adella carefully worded her response. "I simply need time to adjust to all the changes that are taking place."

"Well," Papa said, tossing the missive to the empty desktop, "I have already sent a letter of acceptance. It would be rude at this point to cancel. We will go as planned. However, in the future, I will make an effort to consider your opinions."

Without another word, Adella spun and exited the room.

CHAPTER NINETEEN

Drawing near the small shack at the edge of the quarter, the stench coming from the low-slung building nearly overwhelmed Adella, but she wouldn't let that prevent her from speaking to Jeptha. He'd been in the tiny, stinking shed two days now. On the morrow, she and Papa would travel to Le Beau, and she had to know how Jeptha was faring before she left. She'd scarcely seen Seth since he removed Jeptha from the library that night, so getting news of Jeptha's condition through him proved fruitless.

Mid-morning sunshine glinted off the tin roofs of the quarter when Adella stopped and glanced behind, making certain no one watched her. Mammy and her herd of little ones were the only slaves in the vicinity, with everyone else off working in the fields or their various jobs throughout the plantation. Bent over a wooden washtub, Mammy hadn't noticed Adella sneak around to the backside of the quarter where the shed was located. Or if she had seen Adella, she hadn't made it known—the old woman's running chatter to the children playing around her never paused.

A mangy dog ambled toward Adella, wagging his tail. He'd probably picked up the scent of the bacon and cheese she'd tucked into the deep pocket in the folds of her skirt. The image of the skeletal Roland emerging from the shed all those years ago was imprinted on her memory. Jeptha was young and strong, but even he needed nourishment if he was going to survive three weeks in the fetid shack.

Nearing the door, she fought the urge to cover her nose. "Jeptha?" she said, keeping her voice low.

Sounds of movement came from inside the shed. "Missy Ellis? That you?"

"Yes." She smiled, relieved to hear his voice, strong as ever. "I've brought you some food."

Silence followed for several moments. "You shouldn't'a done that, Missy. You know the rules. If your pappy finds out you done come down here an' brought food, you'll be in a heap o' trouble."

Adella squared her shoulders. "Papa's rules are inhumane. Forbidding anyone from bringing you extra food is wrong. Two slices of stale bread a day are not enough."

A sigh came from inside the shed. "Ain't gonna argue with you. I starving already, and it's only been two days."

Reaching into her pocket, she took out the napkin-wrapped bacon and hunk of cheese. The dog inched closer, but she shooed him away. Eyeing the padlock on the door, she frowned. "How can I get this to you? I don't have the key to the lock."

"Don't need it. There's a cut-out over yonder, to your right. That's how they get the bread to me."

Adella looked and saw the opening, not much bigger than her hand. She moved to it. Jeptha's face appeared in the hole.

"This how I get me some fresh air, too." He filled his lungs as proof.

"Oh, Jeptha." She passed the food to him. Immediately, he disappeared into the dark interior. "I wish there was something I could do to convince Papa to let you out. It's wrong for you to be in this horrible place when all you did was help Zina."

"How is she?" he asked, his mouth obviously full of food.

Adella didn't want to tell him the truth. That Zina had barely said a word since Seth took Jeptha away. Her downcast face and the slump of her slim shoulders spoke of her grief and guilt. To Jeptha, however, she said, "She is worried about you, I am sure. As are we all."

"No use wastin' your worry on me, Missy. I gonna be fine. Maybe a little hungry an' weak, but I be fine."

The odor drifting from the hole in the wall nearly made her gag. "Is it as awful as it smells?"

Jeptha chuckled without humor. "Worse. If I had me a shovel, I could turn the ground in here an' bury some of this filth. That might help."

Adella shook her head, anger with Papa rising to the surface. "I will never forgive Papa for this."

Voices carried to her. Someone was coming.

"I best go now before someone sees me," she whispered.

Jeptha's face appeared in the small opening again. "Thank you, Missy, for the food."

"I will try to get more to you when we return. Papa has insisted we go to Le Beau for a few days. We're leaving before dawn." She'd thought about enlisting Zina to sneak food to Jeptha, but the risk was too great for the young slave woman. If Adella got caught, she would only earn her father's angry words. If Zina or another slave were found bringing food to the shed, they would face a severe lashing and possibly be taken to the market in Galveston.

Careful to make her way back to the house without being seen, Adella went directly to the kitchen wing. A strong cup of tea was just the thing she needed to calm her nerves. She hadn't realized that sneaking down to the shed had her so on edge. But as she neared the house, her legs turned to jelly, nearly sending her to the ground.

Entering through a back door, Adella bumped headlong into Celia in her haste to find Aunt Lu.

"Celia," she said, grasping the girl by her arms so she wouldn't fall. "I am sorry. I didn't see you."

The young slave nodded and righted herself, keeping her eyes on the ground. "It not yo' fault, Missy. I not lookin' where I goin' is all."

Adella hadn't thought much about the girl since Zina's revelation that Papa had all but ordered Jeptha to take Celia into his cabin. So much had happened since then she'd forgotten about it. Now, however, she studied the slave, wondering if Celia had feelings for Jeptha, and how his confinement might affect her.

"Have you spoken with Jeptha since he was put in the shed?" she asked, hoping to find answers to her questions about why Papa would choose this girl instead of Zina to take up with Jeptha. It made no sense to her why Papa would involve himself in the romantic affairs of the slaves, especially when he clearly had no regard for their welfare.

Celia's amber eyes widened, and she met Adella's gaze for the first time. "No, Missy. We uns ain't 'llowed to have contact wit' da one in da shed. Massa threaten us'n's if we do."

This news did not come as a surprise, given Papa's behavior of late. While she didn't want to divulge her own visit to the shed to the young woman, she felt a bit of empathy, guessing Celia would be worried about Jeptha.

"I am sure Mr. Brantley will make sure Jeptha is given his rations and is as well as possible."

Even to her own ears, the promise sounded empty. How well could one possibly be when held captive in a filthy shed that wasn't fit for an animal?

Annoyance flashed across Celia's face. "My man shouldn'ta done what he did. Should'a minded his own biz'ness, is what he should'a done. Beatin' Monroe was wrong. He lucky that Negro gonna live. Otherwise, Massa Luther sell him, or worse."

Adella frowned, confused by her anger. "What Monroe did was wrong, Celia. Jeptha simply tried to protect Zina. I am sure he would do the same thing for you or any of the women at Rose Hill."

Celia simply shrugged. "All I know is my man ain't gonna be 'round for three weeks. Then when he come out, he be worthless for who knows how long."

The pitiless words spoke for themselves. Celia did not care about Jeptha, not the way Zina did. Adella resolved then and there to do everything in her power to see that Jeptha did not have to live with Celia when he was finally released.

With little to say to her father these days, supper was a quiet affair. Papa's mind seemed elsewhere, plotting and planning her future with Marshall, no doubt. Adella wished they could postpone the trip to Le Beau, but no amount of arguing on her part convinced him to put it off. Indeed, he seemed all the more eager to go, desiring to leave behind the drama of the past few days and relax, he said. Just that afternoon, Adella had attempted to discuss Jeptha's plight with him once again, until he'd lost his temper with her.

"Jeptha will remain in the shed the full three weeks. If you insist on nagging me about it, I will increase his punishment—one day for each time you mention his name."

The unfairness of such a pronouncement still infuriated her, but she'd held her tongue. She didn't want her own stubbornness to cause Jeptha to spend even one extra day in the confines of the shed.

Making her way from the house, Adella headed across the lawn and down the hill to the creek. The early evening air felt warm and sultry against her skin, reminding her that summer's brutal heat was not far off. Toads croaked, and crickets chirped, offering a unique song only they could sing. Glad to be away from the upheaval the upcoming trip put the entire house in, Adella felt a twinge of guilt at leaving Hulda and Carolina busy packing her trunks for the journey. But the truth was she held no opinion on the gowns she should take or whether she had her matching slippers or not. It mattered not what Marshall might think of her appearance. His was not the smile of appreciation she longed for.

Her heart quickened, as did her pace. She hadn't spoken to Seth since the terrible night he escorted Jeptha from the library. With Monroe recovering from his injuries, Seth had no help managing the workers. Here and there throughout the day, she'd caught a glimpse of him, usually as he rode from one field to the next. Knowing she had to see him before she left for Le Beau, she'd trusted Moses to deliver a message to him, asking him to meet her at the creek later that evening. With so much commotion around her, she needed his calming reassurance that everything would be fine once they were married.

Hurrying into the thicket near the water's edge, Adella slowed. A sweeping glance of the area revealed Seth had not arrived yet. The sun edged along the horizon, so it was possible he had not come in from the fields yet. No matter. She would wait all night if she must.

Settling on the soft grass, she leaned back against the trunk of a cypress tree, her eyes closed and her face lifted to the slight breeze. Dreams of happy days with Seth filled her imagination. It seemed only moments passed when a sound nearby startled her. Her eyes flew open, and she found Seth sitting beside her, grinning in the fading light.

"I didn't want to wake you," he said, reaching to tuck a tendril of hair behind her ear from where it had blown across her face. The caress of his fingers sent chills sliding down her spine.

"I must have dozed off." Her gaze hungrily took in his day-old whiskers and the tired lines around his eyes. "Have you eaten?"

He held up two thick slices of bread with a slab of ham sandwiched between. "This was the best Aunt Lu could do in a hurry."

She frowned. "I'm sorry. I should have thought to bring you something."

He shrugged. "I've eaten plenty of simple meals like this. Some days when I was out on the range, I was lucky if I had hardtack and jerky."

She watched as he took big bites of the sandwich. "How have you been? Even though I dislike the man immensely, Papa says Monroe was the best driver he has ever had. I imagine you have had your hands full with him unable to work."

Seth nodded while chewing. He took a long drink of water from the canteen he'd brought with him. "Your father feared we would have trouble from the workers with Monroe gone. I've been running from one end of this plantation to the next to make sure they know nothing has changed. I am still the overseer; they still need to do their jobs."

The question that had niggled her mind ever since they'd declared their love for one another pushed forward. "Seth, after we're married, it is unlikely Papa will keep you on as overseer. Are you certain you can't rejoin the Rangers?"

He swallowed the last bite of his meal and shook his head. "They made it clear my injury would slow me down too much. And to be honest, I think they are right. Being in the saddle much of the day has convinced me I need to find work that isn't done from the backside of a horse."

She bit her lip, wondering for the first time how he planned to make a living once they left Rose Hill. Papa surely wouldn't offer him a dowry, as he'd most likely done for Marshall. What would they live on after they married?

As if reading her mind, Seth reached for her hand. "You don't need to worry," he said, giving her fingers a squeeze. "I have an idea I'm working on. Nothing I want to reveal just yet, but I promise we won't starve."

With his hand still holding hers, their future seemed promising rather than frightening. "I'm not worried. I trust you. You can tell me your ideas when I return from Le Beau."

At the mention of Marshall's plantation, Seth frowned. "I don't like the idea of Brevard still believing he is your fiancé. There is no telling what liberties he might attempt."

His concern brought a smile to her face. Though his jealousies were unfounded, they pleased her nonetheless. "My heart will remain here at Rose Hill, with you. You have nothing to worry over."

"Good." He drew her hand to his lips, where he dropped two warm kisses on her knuckles. "Promise you won't be alone with him. Keep Hulda nearby when your father isn't handy."

"Actually," Adella said, trying to concentrate on the conversation even while he turned her hand over and planted several more kisses on the tender part of her palm. "Carolina will attend me. Hulda doesn't travel well, and I asked Papa—"

She gasped as his lips moved to the sensitive area of her wrist. Tingles ran rampant through her body in the most delicious way, and all she could think about was his warm breath on her skin.

"You asked Papa what?" A mischievous gleam brightened his eyes.

For all the world, she couldn't remember what she was about to say. "I … I don't know."

The deep rumble of laughter in his throat cleared her mind. She jerked her hand away. "You rogue," she said, but the laughter in her own voice wouldn't convince anyone she was angry. "I asked Papa if Carolina could accompany me, hoping to train her to take Hulda's place when the time comes. Surprisingly, he was agreeable."

Seth leaned back on one elbow, the muscles in his arm straining against the fabric of his shirt. He stretched out his bad leg. "I'm glad. Carolina adores you, so you will have no trouble keeping her near."

Adella sighed. "I would rather not go at all. If only we could tell Papa about us now and be done with all this nonsense."

He straightened, his eyes searching her face in the growing darkness. "Soon," he promised, his voice husky.

When his gaze strayed to her lips, Adella couldn't help but moisten them in anticipation. That was all the invitation Seth needed before capturing her mouth in a passionate kiss. Her arms had a mind of their own, and soon her hands were roaming his back, enjoying the feel of the hard muscles she found there. His own hands cupped her face, his long fingers drawing her closer until they were both breathless.

When he pulled away, Adella tried to draw him back, but he held her at arm's length and chuckled. "As much as I would like to continue, my love, we can't. Not yet."

A cool breeze drifted between them and brought her back to her senses. Heat filled her face, and she touched her lips, still burning with his passion. What must he think of her, acting so brazen? Oh, but his kisses ignited something in her she'd never imagined.

The grin on his face revealed his own pleasure. "I think I am going to enjoy being married to you, Missy Ellis."

They stood and slowly made their way back to the house, dark but for a few candles in the parlor window.

"Seth," she said, remembering she needed to speak to him about Jeptha. "I know you have to keep Jeptha in the shed and follow Papa's horrid rules, but will you please make sure he has fresh water and bread each day?" She glanced at him in the darkness and thought she saw him nod.

"I will."

When they reached the front steps, Seth brought her hand to his lips again. "Promise you will come back to me, Adella Rose," he whispered, though she couldn't make out his expression in the dim light of the house.

A shiver of happiness ran its course through her entire body. "I promise."

On quiet feet, Adella entered the house, her heart full with the knowledge she would soon be Seth's wife. She would make the trip to Le Beau to appease her father, but when they returned, she was determined to put an end to the charade.

She loved Seth Brantley.

Nothing her father nor Marshall Brevard could do would change that.

CHAPTER TWENTY

"I said, Adella Rose, I wondered if you might like to have the parlor redone before the wedding."

Marshall Brevard's voice broke into Adella's reverie and dragged her back to the present. Sitting on a blanket in the shade of an enormous oak tree, surrounded by the beautiful grounds of Le Beau, she'd become lost in daydreams of her future with Seth. He'd hinted he had some ideas of where they would live and how he would make a living, and her imagination conjured all manner of delightful possibilities. Truthfully, she'd be happy living in a tiny cabin, as long as Seth was by her side.

Turning, she found Papa and Marshall looking at her from where they sat in wicker chairs. Judging by the frown Papa wore, her woolgathering had not gone unnoticed. "The parlor?" she asked, hoping to convince them she'd been paying attention. What had Marshall said about that room?

"Yes." A patient smile rested on Marshall's narrow face. "It has not been redone since before Helen passed away. I thought you could start with it since it is smaller. Then once we are married, and you are living here at Le Beau, you can take on the larger rooms. I know how women like to redecorate when given the opportunity. Any changes you wish to make are fine with me. No expense is too great to make my wife happy."

Knowing Papa watched her closely, she offered a small smile. "Thank you, Marshall. I will give it some thought."

Stifling a sigh, she turned her gaze back to the small lake in front of them. The strain from the pretense of the past three days was beginning to wear on her. When they had first arrived at Le Beau, she thought she could continue to hold off Marshall by acting the shy maiden. Though he'd been a perfect gentleman in his physical approach to her, his persistent references to their wedding and their life afterward had sufficiently rubbed her nerves raw. She wanted nothing more than to stand and shout that she would never be his wife. Instead, she had to endure his attempts to woo her.

"What do you hear from your friends in Washington about who will be the next President, Marshall?" Papa sipped from the small glass of amber liquid one of the Le Beau servants had poured for him shortly after they'd walked down to the lake. Adella frowned, knowing Mama hadn't liked it when Papa imbibed. He had the tendency to become loud and unpleasant when he drank. "With less than a year before the Democratic convention convenes, I am concerned that we haven't heard any rumblings of a frontrunner. The papers say this could be the most important election since the country was formed."

Marshall offered a grave nod. "I, too, am concerned. As you know, I am on good terms with Senator Ward. I received a note from him a short time ago expressing similar sentiments. The Democrats *must* nominate a man who can silence the northern abolitionists once and for all. Their assiduous calls for the end of slavery simply cannot be tolerated any longer."

"Hear, hear!" Papa lifted his glass in salute before downing the last bit of drink. A young black man dressed in a coat with tails, despite the warm day, stepped forward to take the tumbler. He set it on the tray he held with white-gloved hands. He refilled the empty glass and set it next to Papa on a small table.

"Matthias has it on good authority the Republicans are anxious to elect a man who will make it his priority to end slavery throughout the Union. It matters not to them that the Southern states are dependent on cotton and sugarcane production." Marshall's upper lip lifted in disdain. "Their only concern is for the darkies. We growers who pay their salaries through our taxes are of little importance."

While Adella had heard some discussions between her father and brother regarding northern abolitionists' calls for the end of slavery, she hadn't paid much attention. Of course, she agreed that slaves should be free, but there seemed no possible way for this to happen. Slavery was legal in all the southern states as well as some in the middle of the country. Only in the North were black men and women free to move about and obtain jobs.

But Marshall's comments made her wonder if perhaps freedom for the slaves was indeed possible. "Do you truly believe a new president could change the laws regarding slavery?" She thought of Jeptha, sitting in his own filth inside a shed where he couldn't stand up straight, all because he had defended a helpless woman against an animal of a man.

Marshall turned surprised eyes to her. Papa met her question with a deep scowl.

"If the Republicans are successful in putting their man in the White House next year," Marshall said, "they will have a fight on their hands, to be sure. No Democrat worth his salt will vote to end slavery." He offered a benevolent smile, the kind you would give a child who didn't understand a grownup conversation. "But you needn't worry your pretty head over it, Adella Rose. You will have much more pleasant things to occupy your mind next year. I hope to hear the sound of small feet running about Le Beau soon enough."

Irked by his rebuff of her interest in the subject, she didn't stop to feel mortified that he insinuated marital intimacies in front of her father. Ignoring the comment, she continued the conversation. "If there is no concern that a new president could change things, then why does it matter which side wins the election?"

Before Marshall could answer, Papa slammed his glass down on the table. "Leave politics to the men, Adella Rose. You know little about the issues at hand, and your prattling questions are wearisome. Of course it matters what man is elected. The rights of Texas and every other slaveholding state are at stake." He looked heavenward with a heavy sigh and shake of his head, as though seeking divine help for his addlebrained daughter.

Several tense moments ticked by, with Adella sitting in humiliated silence, before Marshall cleared his throat. "I am sure everything will right itself, my dear. We have God on our side. He won't let the will of the ungodly take away all He has given us."

Her brow raised. "You believe God gave you slaves? What then of the slaves' belief that God will one day set them free?" Involuntarily, she glanced at the young black man who stood nearby yet gave no indication he listened to the conversation.

"Adella!" Papa rose from his seat. With wobbly steps, he stomped toward her. "I told you to stop this nonsense."

She drew back in fear, thankful when Marshall stood and intercepted her father. "See here, Luther," he said, taking Papa by the arm in a respectful yet forceful manner. "I am not offended by Adella's questions. On the contrary, I am pleased to see that my future wife and I will have lively conversations from time to time. There is no harm in her asking questions."

Papa stared at Marshall, clearly taken aback by his response. After several seconds, he huffed. "You will have your hands full with her, Brevard. She has no comprehension of all that goes into the running of a plantation. Her silly ideas ... her befriending the darkies. I am glad to be rid of her." Without a backward glance in Adella's direction, her father stalked off toward the gleaming mansion, up a slight rise from the lake.

Hurt by his disrespectful outburst, she could only hope the liquor provoked him to say such mean things. They'd had their disagreements over the slaves before, but his behavior of late had grown decidedly harsh toward her for no apparent reason.

"I am sorry our discussion ended so poorly." Marshall took a seat on the blanket next to her without asking her permission. He pulled a blade of grass and twirled it in his long fingers. "I am sure your father's intentions toward you are, in his mind, for the best. Southern women, especially, are seen as too delicate to participate in the rigorous and often tempestuous conversations surrounding politics and business and the like." He turned and studied her with a familiarity Adella found uncomfortable. Finally, he smiled. "I am pleased to discover my beautiful rose has a thorn or two. It will serve to keep me on my toes, I think."

The charade became too much for her. She had to bring this farce to an end immediately. "Marshall." She closed her eyes for a long moment. What could she say to lessen the blow? When she opened them again, she found his face very close. "I ... I can't ..."

Before she could utter another word, his mouth descended upon hers. His moist lips moved over hers in such a possessive way, she sat wide-eyed and stunned, unable to think. When he reached to draw her closer, Adella pushed him away, removing herself from his grasp.

"Stop, please," she said, putting distance between them on the blanket. Her gaze darted to the servant behind him, and when Marshall turned to look likewise, she hurriedly wiped his kiss from her mouth.

When his ardent gaze returned to her, he looked pleased. "You mustn't be so timid, Adella Rose. My servants are quite discreet. We are, after all, betrothed."

"That is what I need to speak to you about." She scooted another inch or so away.

Hope shone in his gray eyes. "Are you ready to set a date? Tomorrow isn't soon enough for me, you know."

For a moment, Adella felt a pang of guilt. She should never have gone along with the engagement. Marshall would be hurt when she told him the truth. He deserved a woman who loved him, and who would bear him all those children he longed for. That she was not that woman didn't bother her, but her role in his pain and embarrassment did.

"Marshall." She took a deep breath, and sending a silent prayer heavenward said, "I can't marry you."

He stared at her, confusion replacing the hope she'd seen in his eyes only minutes before. "Of course I didn't mean we would marry tomorrow, Adella Rose. I was jesting. Let us decide together on a date. Say, a month from now. That will give you enough time to have your trousseau made and begin on the changes to the mansion you wish to make and—"

Adella shook her head, silencing him. "No, Marshall. I mean, I can't marry you, ever."

Making a slow study of her face, he narrowed his gaze. "You are quite serious, aren't you?" When she nodded, he turned to the servant. "Leave us." His angry voice startled the young man, who immediately hurried away.

"Please, let me explain," she began, her stomach in knots, but he held up his hand.

"There are things you need to know, Adella Rose, before you make any rash decisions," he said, a deep frown pulling his sandy brows together. "Your father doesn't believe you should know details regarding his business affairs, but suffice it to say agreements have been signed and put into place. Agreements that are irrevocable."

The grave tone in his voice gave her pause. "What kind of agreements? And what has this to do with me? With us?"

"Everything. It has everything to do with you. With us." He stood and offered his hand. "Come. Let us sit and discuss this like the business partners we are."

Adella accepted his assistance and followed him to the chairs he and Papa had occupied a short time before. But his words confused her. "Business partners? Papa and George run the plantation. Papa is correct when he says I know nothing of their business. They don't think I possess the intelligence to understand the things involved with running the plantation."

Once they were settled in the chairs, Marshall leaned back, a peculiar smile on his face. "That is where I disagree with your father and brother. I believe you have plenty of intelligence. In fact, I trust that once I reveal the agreement I have made with your father, you will not only understand but will be in a position of power, should you opt to use it."

He made no sense. Adella had little power over her father and brother, but she remained silent, waiting for him to continue.

"Your father approached me several months ago with a proposition." He turned to look out on the lake. The sun slipped ever lower in the afternoon sky, making the water sparkle like a sea of diamonds.

"A proposition? Do you mean our engagement was his idea, not yours?" Adella asked, surprised by the feeling of disenchantment that news brought. Although she held no romantic thoughts for the man beside her, it wounded her female pride to think he hadn't sought the engagement himself.

Marshall chuckled. "Now, now, don't get ahead of me. The proposition had nothing to do with you. At least, not at first. It seems your father has overextended himself financially. Quite substantially, as it turns out."

Shocked, Adella gaped at him. "Are you certain? How substantial?"

"To the point that no banks will loan him money. He has mortgaged Rose Hill beyond what he can repay." Marshall leveled a serious look at her. "Your father is in financial ruin, Adella Rose. His mismanagement has put the plantation in jeopardy. Bankruptcy was his only option. Or it was until I came to his rescue."

She stared at him, unable to accept what he'd told her. Could it be true? Surely Papa would have told her if he was in such serious trouble. "Does my brother know?"

"Yes." Marshall nodded. "As your father's heir, he had to be included in the agreement."

A sinking feeling began in her gut. "What is the agreement?" she whispered, afraid of what he would tell her.

"I have agreed to a partnership of sorts with your father. A percentage of all profits at Rose Hill will come to me for the next ten years. In exchange, I will carry the bank notes until Luther is able to repay them. With a good harvest the next few seasons, it is very likely he could see himself free of the debts he has incurred within three or four years."

Adella's mind whirled, trying to recall anything her father might have said or done that would've hinted at the terrible predicament he was in. But there was nothing. They lived as they always had, with plenty of food and gowns and luxuries very few people could afford. Father continued to purchase land and slaves as he'd always done. With Mama so ill for two long years and the year of mourning following her passing, Adella admittedly hadn't paid much attention to her father's business dealings. Why should she have? Nothing was amiss, or so it had seemed.

But if what Marshall said was true, then they were indeed in financial ruin. What of the plantation and George's inheritance? How could Papa be so careless in his spending to put all they had in such danger?

Yet the plantation did not belong to the banks. They'd been saved.

Her eyes sought the man next to her. Their rescuer. The agreement surely must have included more than what he'd revealed thus far. "And me? Where do I fit into all of this?" Adella's voice held no emotion. The answer to her question was obvious.

Her father had sold her to the highest bidder.

"Luther needed cash to pay off the additional land he purchased and to buy more slaves to work it. I supplied the revenue … under the condition that you and I marry." He leaned forward to capture her gaze. "But hear me out, Adella Rose. I had not seen you since you were a small child. I had no idea you had grown into such a lovely woman. When I came to Rose Hill to discuss the business agreement with your father and saw you again, I knew I wanted you to be my wife. It had nothing to do with the agreement."

"But Papa paid you a dowry." She grasped at anything to prove his story was not as it seemed.

Marshall shook his head. "I am afraid you are mistaken, my dear. The only dowry I gain in marrying you are the few slaves you will bring with you from Rose Hill once we're wed."

Carolina's sweet face filled her mind. Papa had willingly consented to Adella's training the girl to become her personal maid, all the while knowing she was little more than a bride-price to him.

A wave of nausea swept through her. She stood abruptly. Clutching her stomach, she started for the house. "I must go. I need to be alone. To think."

"Wait, Adella Rose." Marshall hurried to catch up to her as she practically stumbled through the grass. "I know it sounds as though you were bought and paid for, but that doesn't have to prevent us from having a happy life together. I can offer you a lifetime of luxury. Anything you want, it's yours. I know you don't love me, but in time I believe our affection for one another will grow."

With abandon, Adella shook her head, tears streaming down her face. "No, Marshall. It won't. I cannot marry a man I don't love. Not when I love someone else."

The change in his face took only a moment. It went from soft and pleading to one as cold as stone. "You speak of Brantley."

She nodded, suddenly aware that her admission could put her family in great peril. She had no idea what legalities were involved in the agreement between Marshall and her father. What if he took Rose Hill from them in retaliation?

When she started for the house again, he didn't follow.

With a feeling of despair that nearly overwhelmed her, Adella knew, in one way or the other, her life would never be the same.

CHAPTER TWENTY-ONE

A full week had passed since Seth locked Jeptha in the shed. Making his daily trek to it now, he carried fresh water and a small burlap bundle Aunt Lu prepared for the confined man that should contain two slices of stale bread. But one whiff from the package told Seth that wasn't the case, and he couldn't help grinning. There was no mistaking the distinct aroma of bacon wafting up from the rough fabric. Yesterday, it had been roast beef. The day before that, ham.

Shaking his head, Seth knew he should toss the meat to the dogs and reprimand Aunt Lu for breaking the rules, but he couldn't bring himself to say anything, neither in acknowledgment that he knew the meat was there nor in discipline. The fact was he wished he could simply let Jeptha out of the shed, at least until Luther and Adella returned. But there were slaves on the plantation he didn't trust to keep quiet about it—Celia, for one. Despite being Jeptha's woman, she seemed rather put out that he'd gotten himself locked away, especially when she learned his punishment had to do with Zina. When Seth warned her against going near the shed, she informed him she had no intention of visiting Jeptha.

"He got hisse'f thrown in dat nasty place. Now I gets dat ol' bed all to myse'f. He can stay in der as long as Massa want. Don't make no never mind to me."

Seth sighed.

Women. It didn't matter the color of their skin, there just wasn't any way to figure them out. Take Zina, for instance. The day after the incident he'd run across her in the kitchen. The fear that came into her eyes when she saw him still unsettled him. It was as though she expected him to snatch her up and drag her down to the shed, even though she'd been there when he tried to defend Jeptha to Luther.

Following the path that took him past his cabin, he headed toward the far end of the quarter. The sun was yet to make its appearance over the horizon, but there was enough light to observe the slaves' morning activity. Trails of gray smoke billowed up from cook fires, where pots of corn mush were being prepared. From the open door of one crude cabin, a baby squalled. A dog barked nearby. Soon he'd need to blow the ram's horn, summoning everyone to work, but he'd wait until he finished delivering the sparse meal to Jeptha. He also needed to check on Monroe and see how the man's recovery was coming. Seth despised the thought of Mammy having to extend kindness to the vile driver, but the old woman didn't seem to mind. Monroe's wounds were healing, but it would be some time before his arm and ribs mended. One could only hope that time spent with the kind old woman would soften the man's cruel heart.

"Mornin', Mistah Brantley, suh!"

Seth turned to find Oliver hurrying toward him on bare feet. The eager smile on the little boy's face never failed to bring one to his own lips. "Morning, Oliver."

"You's goin' ta see Jeptha?" he asked, eyeing the water and burlap bundle.

"Yes." Seth continued walking. Oliver fell into step beside him, making an effort to match Seth's long stride by taking huge leaps of his own.

Seth grinned and slowed down a bit. "It's gonna be another hot one today. You be sure to have some nice cool creek water in that bucket of yours."

The little boy nodded with enthusiasm. "Yassuh, I sho' will." He reached into one of his pockets and pulled out a round, shiny white rock. He held it on his flattened palm. "Looky heah what I found yest'day, Mistah Brantley. I gettin' water from the creek over by the chu'ch, an' there it be, jest a-shinin'. It pure white, it is. Just like them snowflakes that falls come winter."

Seth observed that it was indeed.

"Mammy say it remind her o' what us'n's heart look like when the Lawd wash it clean. She say he take out all the ugly black sin an' make it all nice an' white, like this here rock." He cocked his head and looked up at Seth. "Is yo' heart already white 'cuz you's a white man, Mistah Brantley?"

The question caught Seth off guard. He felt certain his heart was not white, but confessing such to the boy didn't seem quite appropriate.

Not waiting for an answer, Oliver shook his head. "Naw, I don't think that how it work. Mistah Haley was a white man, but I know fo' sho' his heart weren't white. He meaner than Monroe, an' Mammy say Monroe's heart is blacker than his skin."

Seth certainly wasn't going to argue with that.

"Mammy say I should keep this here rock in my pocket so's it remind me to al'ays do the right thing. Says I don't wanna grow up an' act like Monroe. Says this rock can be my con ... con ..." He looked up at Seth for help.

"Conscience."

Oliver smiled. "Yep. That what Mammy say."

They rounded the edge of the quarter and went toward the shack.

"That there shed sho' do stink," Oliver said, wrinkling his nose as they drew near. He waved at the horde of flies buzzing around the place.

"You best not do anything that will get you put in there." Seth gave the boy a stern look. "It smells even worse inside. Run on back to the cabin now and get ready for the day."

"Yassuh, Mistah Brantley." Oliver skipped away in the direction they'd just come from.

Seth walked over to the hole that had been cut out of the shed's wall. "You awake, Jeptha?"

Several moments passed before a low moan came from the other side of the wood. "Yessuh. I 'wake."

Seth frowned. Jeptha sounded weak. Long days without proper food and exercise were no doubt taking their toll on his body. Despite Aunt Lu's sly attempts to sneak extra food to him, the deprivation was mounting. Added to that were the hot, sultry temperatures of the past few days, which would be even worse sitting in a stinking, windowless shack.

Guilt pricked Seth. As overseer of the plantation, he should have been more aware of Monroe's history of attacking women. Had he known what the man was capable of, Seth wouldn't have allowed him so much freedom, especially after the workday was over. After he'd broken up the fight and locked Jeptha up following their meeting with Luther, the reality of what could have happened slammed him in the gut. Not only would Zina have been violated, but it could have happened to any of the Rose Hill women, including Adella.

Awful scenarios had rolled through his mind that night, keeping him awake nearly until dawn. What if Monroe had found Adella Rose alone in the barn sneaking an apple to Freedom? Luther was a fool for keeping the slave. Monroe should have been sold after the first incident.

Jeptha's grimy face finally appeared in the hole. The whites of his eyes had a yellowish tint to them. "I hopes you got a big ol' side o' beef for me today, Mistah Brantley, suh."

Seth gave a half-hearted chuckle. "I wish I did, Jeptha." He passed the burlap bundle through the hole. "But all I've got is Aunt Lu's stale bread again."

Their eyes met. Seth simply stared back, giving no indication that he knew there was more than stale bread in the wrapping, although he didn't believe for a moment the slave was fooled.

Jeptha gave a nod. "Thank ya, kindly, Mistah Brantley, suh." His face disappeared from the hole.

A silent message of trust passed between them in that moment.

What it meant, Seth had no idea, but somehow he felt exonerated for not keeping Monroe under better supervision.

"When Missy s'posed to get back?" Jeptha's voice came from inside the shed, down low and to Seth's right. He must have been sitting on the ground to eat his meal. Seth couldn't imagine having to spend one hour in this stinking hole, let alone three weeks. He had to admire Jeptha. The man hadn't uttered a complaint the entire seven days he'd been in there.

"I'm not sure." Seth leaned his back against the wall. Truth was, Adella being away at Le Beau was driving him mad. He hated the thought of her anywhere near Brevard. Seth imagined Luther plotting with Brevard to make the marriage happen as quickly as possible. He ran a hand through his hair and let out a frustrated sigh, wishing he hadn't convinced Adella to wait to tell her father about them. They should have declared their love immediately and dealt with Luther's anger, come what may.

"Missy a real smart lady, Mistah Brantley. She ain't gonna do something she don't want to do."

Surprised, Seth turned to look over his shoulder at the hole in the wall. He almost expected to find Jeptha peering at him, reading his very thoughts. But the hole was empty.

"I don't know what you mean." Had Adella confided in the slave? Did he know about their secret plans to marry?

A light chuckle came from inside the shed. "I known Missy nearly my whole life. Funny thing is, if we was the same color, we'd be like brother an' sister. I knows I ain't got no right to such, but I feel kinda protective of her. Don't want her making no big mistake that can't be undone."

"No, we wouldn't want that." Brevard's smug face flashed across Seth's memory. He shook his mind free of it.

Jeptha chuckled again. "I 'spect she'll make the right choice when the time comes. I'll be right happy for her when she does."

Seth grinned. If he didn't know any better, he'd think he'd just gained Jeptha's approval to marry Adella Rose.

❦

Adella sat in Le Beau's beautifully appointed library, her stomach in knots. Papa had summoned her shortly after breakfast, although she had not partaken of that meal in the dining room. Nor had she joined the men for dinner the evening before. After her conversation with Marshall down by the lake, she'd been ill—if not physically, then spiritually and emotionally. Learning that her father had, by all accounts, sold her to Marshall Brevard left her reeling. Clearly, she was no more than property to him, like one of his slaves.

With a nervous glance at Marshall, who stood near the grand fireplace, she wondered how much of their conversation he had divulged to her father. He gave nothing away as they waited for Papa to arrive. He took out his pocket watch once again, glancing between it and the clock on the mantel. After a moment, he opened the glass face of the porcelain timepiece to adjust the hands.

"Ah, I see my daughter has finally allowed us the privilege of her presence," Papa said, entering the room. With a loud bang, he closed the double doors behind him.

Marshall frowned. "I don't think the slamming of doors is quite necessary, Luther. We are all adults here. This matter can easily be resolved without resorting to boorish outbursts."

Adella's brow raised. Never had she heard anyone speak to her father in such a manner. Shifting her gaze to Papa's face, he seemed taken aback as well.

"See here, Brevard—" he began, only to have Marshall interrupt.

"No, Luther. You are the one who needs to see." He glanced at Adella, who was certain her shock was evident on her face. "This whole affair should have been handled with greater care. Had Adella Rose been privy to the agreement months ago, we would not be in the predicament we find ourselves in today."

Papa glared at Marshall. "I have never discussed business with a woman, and I do not intend to start now, daughter or not. Not even my dear departed wife was ever included in business discussions."

"Perhaps she should have been. Mayhap then your finances would not be in the sorry state they are now, hmm?"

Adella gasped. Surely such a rude comment was uncalled for.

Papa's eyes rounded and his fists clenched. "How dare you!"

The meeting had hardly begun, and emotions were already out of control. "Please," she said, her voice trembling. She stood, glancing between the two men. "Can't we discuss this calmly, without insults and angry words?"

Marshall inclined his head. "My apologies, Adella Rose." He glanced at her father. "Luther."

Several ticks of the clock passed before Papa gave a begrudging nod. "Let us resolve the situation and be done with it." He moved to sit at a polished mahogany desk, and his eyes settled on Adella as she returned to her seat. "Marshall tells me you have refused to marry him."

His composure surprised her. She had expected him to bellow threats at the very least. "That is true, Papa," she said, guarded. Something about his calmness set her on edge.

"He also informs me that he has told you the nature of our agreement with regard to my financial situation."

Adella nodded, embarrassed for her father. That he'd mismanaged Rose Hill funds to the point of needing Marshall's help was certainly not something he would wish to review with his daughter.

"Then you understand the dire circumstances that forced me to make decisions involving your engagement and pending marriage." Papa drummed his fingers on the desk, speaking of her future as though it were of no more importance than the purchase of a plot of land.

"Yes." She cast a quick glance at Marshall. He stood with his back to her, looking out a tall window. The edge of the small lake was just visible through the trees, and she couldn't help but remember his expression when she admitted she was in love with Seth.

Papa leaned back in his chair, his eyes narrowing on her. "Let me understand, then. You are fully aware that we could lose Rose Hill if you do not marry Marshall, yet you willingly refuse his offer of marriage."

Adella swallowed the fear rising in her throat. Putting the complicated issue in such blunt terms left her shaken. "Surely there is another way to secure the funds to pay the debts, Papa." She looked again to Marshall, but he continued to stare out the window.

"No, Adella Rose. There isn't. The banks won't lend me any more money." He gave a humorless laugh. "Imagine that. Luther Ellis, owner of the largest plantation in Williamson County, denied a loan at the very bank where I have deposited untold thousands over the years. But can they help a man out when times get hard? No. They have their eye on Rose Hill, you mark my words. And they will get it, too, if you persist with this silly notion of marrying Brantley."

Adella's eyes widened.

"Yes, I know about him." He smirked. "How you think you are in love with him."

"I am, Papa," she said, but he cut her off.

"This is not about love, Adella Rose. It is about your future. It is about George's future. You may not like it, but the fate of Rose Hill is now in your fickle hands." He closed his eyes for a long moment before leveling a stern look at her. "You must marry Marshall, or we will lose the plantation. The home your mother and I built together. I cannot make it any more plain."

She returned his gaze, the gravity of their situation rendering her mute. Since learning of her father's financial disaster the day before, she'd thought of little else. Surely there was a way to raise the necessary funds and pay the debts without sacrificing her dreams of marrying Seth. Yet she had to assume her father had exhausted every avenue to come up with the money to no avail. His pride would have not allowed him to ask for Marshall's assistance if there was any other way.

Swallowing her own pride, she stood and moved to Marshall's side. He turned to her, his face a mask, devoid of emotion. "I am begging you, Marshall. If you care for me at all, continue with the business agreement with Papa, but don't force me to choose between love and my home."

He shook his head. "I am not forcing you to do anything, Adella Rose. I have asked you to be my wife. Despite the events of the past twenty-four hours, I am still willing to marry you. I know we can be happy if you will but allow yourself to see beyond your childish fancies."

Anger welled up inside her. "Why can't you simply do the right thing and help Papa? He is your friend."

"I am a businessman, Adella. I have achieved my wealth by making decisions that benefit me financially. I would be as poor as a pauper if I gave money to everyone who asked."

His blasé remark infuriated her. She was angry with Papa for putting her in this position, but she despised Marshall for making her father look like a beggar. He and her father had a very lucrative business deal from which Marshall would benefit for the next decade. Papa certainly didn't deserve the man's scorn.

She turned back to Papa, determined to find a way out of this for all of them. "Isn't there anyone else who would loan you the money? Surely Mr. Langford would help now that Natalie and George are married."

"I will not have Langford knowing my business," Papa said with a scowl. "I've known the man for two decades. He would have never given his consent to the marriage had he been aware we were on the verge of bankruptcy. George will inherit Langford's holdings someday, but we need the money now."

Adella refused to give up. "Perhaps Seth's father could help. He has been your friend—your *true* friend—for many years. When he was here for the wedding, he gave Seth and me his blessing. I know he would help."

"Daniel knew about you and Brantley?" Papa's scowl deepened.

"Seth spoke to him about us."

"I don't know what lies Brantley told you about his father's finances, but suffice it to say Daniel would not have the kind of money I need to save Rose Hill. Which is yet another reason why you need to abandon this nonsensical idea of marrying Brantley, Adella Rose." He slammed his palm against the desktop. "He has nothing to offer you. No property, no inheritance. Marshall, on the other hand, is willing to give you the world on a gold platter. You are a fool if you can't see the difference."

Her chin rose. "You may see it as foolishness, Papa, but there are more important things in life than money. Seth and I will not have much starting out, but I believe in him. God will provide if we but seek Him."

Papa shook his head in disgust. He looked past her to Marshall, who had turned from the window and now faced Papa. He gave a single nod, which Papa returned. The silent communication was evidently planned. Again, their calm in the face of her refusal unnerved her.

Papa's attention fell back on Adella. "If you continue to spurn Marshall, you will leave me no choice but to take measures I would rather not." Papa leaned back against the leather chair, the wooden frame creaking under his weight in the silent room.

Adella's heart drummed against her ribs. He couldn't force her to marry Marshall, but the look of triumph in his eyes sent a wave of apprehension racing through her veins. "What measures?"

His face hardened. "You leave me no choice. If I am to lose the plantation, I will have no need for workers. Therefore, I will sell the slaves, one by one, starting with Jeptha."

For a moment, Adella couldn't breathe. Surely he didn't mean it.

"He is young and healthy and will fetch a good price at the market in New O'leans. Sugar cane growers are always in need of a strong back." Papa's eyes narrowed on her. "After I sell Jeptha, I will sell Lusanne, then Carolina. Each day that you ignore your responsibilities as my daughter, I will sell off a slave." His brow raised in thought. "Of course, Negroes don't last long in the cane fields. The brutal work breaks them fairly quickly, from what I hear, especially old women and children." He chuckled. "Those cane plantations go through slaves faster than the traders can keep the markets stocked."

Marshall smirked as though Papa had told a joke.

With tears stinging her eyes, Adella stared at Papa. In her heart, she knew he was not making idle threats. He would do exactly as he said. Jeptha, Aunt Lu, and the others could suffer untold misery if she refused to marry Marshall. Though she'd never been to a slave auction, she envisioned the horror of being bought and sold like livestock, not knowing the kind of person who purchased you or how you would be treated. To know that she would be responsible for her friends enduring such an experience when she herself would be safely married to Seth, was something she could not bear.

Defeat came with her next breath, even as Papa's vile threat hung in the air. She sagged with the sudden loss of all her hopes and dreams. She couldn't marry Seth. Not if it meant putting Jeptha and the others in jeopardy. Tears spilled down her cheeks.

"I will have your decision." The gleam in Papa's eyes revealed he already knew her answer.

Forcing the words to her lips, Adella closed her eyes. "I will marry Marshall."

CHAPTER TWENTY-TWO

From the far north section of cotton fields, Seth watched Luther's carriage enter Rose Hill land and travel up the long tree-lined lane to the house. He'd chosen this field to oversee today for the very purpose of knowing the moment the carriage returned from Le Beau. Though the conveyance was little more than a brown spot from his distant vantage point, thus preventing him from making out the occupants through the open windows, relief surged through him.

Adella was home.

More than anything, he wanted to race Chester across the acres of plants that separated him from the woman he loved. It was all he could do to stay put, supervising the daily drudgery of slaves hoeing one row after another, they unaware of the rush of elation that enveloped him. If they noticed their master was home, they didn't make it known. No one stopped to look toward the east but instead continued tilling the dirt, removing tiny weeds that, if left growing, would fast overtake the money-producing cotton.

Seth sat back in the saddle, the tension he'd felt all morning easing from his body. From the moment Adella left with her father to visit Brevard's home, he'd lived for this day. He'd done nothing but think of what he would say to Luther the moment they returned in order to claim Adella for his own. There wasn't anything the older man could say that would keep him from marrying her. He knew Luther would be angry. The possibility of his disowning Adella had crossed Seth's mind more than once. But one would hope Luther's long-standing friendship with Seth's family might soften the blow of her breaking the engagement to Brevard.

With his back to the afternoon sun, he watched the carriage make the final turn in the lane and disappear beyond the trees, taking them on to the house. He would have to wait until after the evening meal before he could see Adella. He had work to do, and she was no doubt tired from the long day of traveling. But the moment they were alone, nothing would stop him from taking her in his arms and holding her the way he'd longed to since the day she left.

Returning his attention to the workers, he touched the scrap of paper folded in his shirt pocket. On it, he'd calculated how much Luther owed him in salary, and although the sum was not much, added to the bit he'd saved from his Ranger days, it would give him and Adella a start. And if what Pa said about their neighbors back home wanting Seth's talents was true, he might be able to increase the savings until they had enough to travel to Oregon.

Oregon.

The very word made him smile.

It would be too late in the season to head west if he needed to work to save more money. With all the mountain ranges they had to cross filling with snow by early fall, it wouldn't be wise to start their journey until next spring. But he guessed it would only be a short nine or so months before he and Adella could pack up their belongings and head off into their new life on the frontier. Until then, he was certain Pa and Ma would welcome them to stay on the farm.

"Mistah Brantley! Mistah Brantley! Hurry!"

Brought out of his reverie by the cry of alarm, he turned in the saddle to find a cluster of slaves some distance away. One of the women—it looked like Oliver's mother, Millie—stood apart, waving frantically at him.

Kicking Chester into motion, he quickly came upon the group.

"Lucy havin' her baby, Mistah Brantley! Right now!" Millie said, pointing to the young woman kneeling on the ground, surrounded by the others.

As though she needed to verify the validity of Millie's words, Lucy doubled over and let out an anguished cry. Her hands gripped her swollen belly, and Seth saw her slight body shudder with pain.

Unsure what to do, he glanced back in the direction of the house. It was too far for the pregnant woman to walk to the quarter, and he couldn't let her deliver the child here in the field, despite knowing that other plantation overseers would do just that. This baby was George's child, after all, whether he acknowledged it or not.

"Help me get her on my horse," he said to several of the men standing nearby.

Screaming in pain, Lucy fought the men as they took her by the arms and hauled her up none too gently. Despite her large belly, the men easily hoisted her into Seth's waiting arms. When she looked at him, he saw terror in her eyes.

"I'm going to take you to Mammy. She'll know what to do."

Whether his words comforted her or not, he couldn't tell. She squeezed her eyes closed and clutched her belly. "Hurry, suh," she breathed.

He didn't need to be told twice. Holding the young woman with one arm, he pushed Chester into a gallop. Not caring that the horse's hooves tore up cotton plants as they sped across one field after another, Seth sent up a silent prayer, asking God to please keep him from dropping the woman in their frantic flight.

It seemed forever, but finally, the quarter came into view. Mammy stood outside, hanging freshly laundered clothes on a line tied between two trees. Several naked youngsters played nearby. She looked up in surprise as Seth charged toward her.

"Mammy, Lucy is having her baby!" he shouted just before he pulled back on the reins. Chester skidded to a stop, sending a cloud of dust into the air.

"Lawd have mercy, I thought you's gonna run me over." Mammy put her hand to her ample breast, her fright evident on her wrinkled face. One of the toddlers began to wail and ran to

Mammy, clinging to her skirt, while the others stared wide-eyed at the big horse. "Why you's comin' in here like da world on fire, Mistah Brantley? Womens been havin' babies since da beginnin' o' time. Ain't nothin' to yell 'bout, scarin' ever'body."

Ignoring the old woman's reprimand, Seth swung out of the saddle. Lucy moaned as he lifted her into his arms. "Where should I put her?"

Mammy looked puzzled. Finally, she motioned to the ground. "You can jest put her down, Mistah Brantley. I take her on in to da cabin."

Nodding, he set the young slave on the ground, but she immediately crumpled into a moaning heap. Alarmed, he looked at Mammy for help, but she waved him off.

"Go on, now, Mistah Brantley. I done delivered dozens a' chillens. Lucy heah ain't nothin' special." She gave him a pointed look. "Neither is her young'un."

With that, Mammy walked over to Lucy, coaxed her to her feet, and disappeared with her into the closest cabin. The gaggle of youngsters stayed outside and continued to stare at Seth.

Unsure what to do next—should he wait to see that Lucy was safely delivered of her child, Luther's grandchild?—Seth glanced at Chester. The horse's sides still heaved from their race to the quarter, and he needed a long drink of water before heading back into the fields. Perhaps by then the baby would have made its appearance. With one last glance toward the closed cabin door, he took hold of the lead and walked the animal toward the barn.

❧ ❧

Adella breathed in the musty scent of manure and hay, listening to the sound of Freedom munching his apple. She and Papa had only been home a few minutes, but she'd needed the solitude of the barn to gather her thoughts before facing anyone. The entire journey home from Le Beau had been filled with Papa's plans for

Rose Hill. He acted as though money were not an issue and spoke more freely than he'd ever done about his ideas to increase the plantation's profits.

"With Marshall as my son-in-law, those bankers will think twice about denying me a loan, you mark my words. We'll be able to plant the acreage we purchased last fall and acquire even more land. 'Course that will mean buying more slaves." He smirked. "I would guess that yellow gal I bought for Jeptha is carrying his seed by now. It would be a shame if she turns out a girl child. I didn't go to all that expense and trouble for another house servant."

The disbelief Adella felt upon hearing his declaration still unnerved her as she remembered the conversation.

"You bought Celia for Jeptha? Just so they would have children?"

Papa nodded. "Yes. That is the reality of owning a plantation the size of Rose Hill. We need strong, capable slaves to work it. It would be cost-effective to raise our own, don't you agree? To get the best product, however, one can't leave them to their own carnal instincts. Making sure Jeptha mated with the right gal was imperative." Seeing her shock, he huffed. "It is high time you started thinking like the wife of a plantation owner instead of some spoiled child who believes the slaves are her friends."

"Some of them are my friends," she'd argued. In fact, she'd wanted to say, some were dearer to her than her own family members. But she'd thought better of blurting out such a thing to her father, when the past two days had clearly proven he cared nothing for her, or anyone else, for that matter.

"Marshall won't tolerate you mollycoddling his slaves the way you have mine. He uses the whip more than we do. As soon as I get rid of Brantley, I will hire a new overseer who is not afraid to discipline. Marshall has someone in mind he'll recommend."

It made sense that Papa wouldn't keep Seth on as overseer, but for some reason, she'd hoped he would be here when she came for visits after she married Marshall. That it would be painful to see him was something she'd accepted, yet that pain would be worth enduring if she could but see him and hear his voice. Now, even that hope had been snatched away by Papa.

Stroking Freedom's silky mane, she couldn't help but smile despite her heartache. "Jeptha has certainly done a good job with you. Remember when you wouldn't let me come near?"

The horse continued to munch, never flinching when she moved her hand to pat his strong neck. He was no longer the skittish creature he'd been when he first came to Rose Hill. With hard work and persistence, Jeptha had managed to break the wild streak in the animal. She'd heard Papa tell Marshall he intended to use Freedom as a stud, hoping to strengthen the bloodline of the plantation's horseflesh for profit.

She heaved a sigh.

No one escaped being exploited by Papa, it seemed. She'd never thought she and a horse would have so much in common, but just as they'd broken Freedom and forced him to do their bidding, Papa had broken her. She'd bowed to his will despite the desperate desire to run away. At least she'd won the battle against him when he and Marshall insisted the wedding take place immediately. With more fortitude than she knew she possessed, she'd steadfastly refused to have her wedding at Le Beau. Finally conceding, Marshall agreed to come to Rose Hill in a week's time. By then she would have her belongings packed, although there would be no time to have her trousseau sewn. No matter. She wasn't the excited bride like Natalie. She'd just as soon wear black the rest of her days since she was indeed in mourning. Mourning the life she would never have with Seth.

Leaning her forehead against the cool wooden stall, she shook off the despair that threatened to overtake her. She needed to focus on the good that would come from her marriage to Marshall, the most important being that Jeptha and the others would be safe. She'd made Papa promise he would never sell them if she went through with this, and he'd given his word. Despite the pain he'd caused her, she believed he would keep his promise. It also brought her a measure of comfort to know her sacrifice would benefit her family for generations to come. Rose Hill would remain theirs, with George inheriting it eventually. To know that his children would one day live on the land she loved helped soften the deep feeling of loss that gripped her heart.

A noise behind her drew her attention. She gasped when she saw him.

"Seth!"

The smile that filled his face brought tears to her eyes. He was so handsome, so dear. How could she face life without him by her side?

"I assume those are tears of happiness at seeing me," he joked.

She could only stare at him. Though she'd rehearsed what she intended to say, words refused to come now.

A slight frown puckered his brow. "You don't look well." He closed the gap between them and touched her cheek. "Adella? What's wrong?"

Involuntarily, she leaned into his hand. "Oh, Seth." Tears spilled onto her cheeks. How could she tell him that everything was wrong?

Concern washed over his features, and he tipped her chin, giving her nowhere else to look but into his hazel eyes. "Tell me what's going on, Adella Rose."

Knowing now was not the time or place to tell him about Papa's financial debacle, the agreement he and Marshall had come to, and Papa's threat to sell the slaves, Adella forced a smile to her trembling lips.

"I am just happy to see you," she said, her voice shaky with emotion.

His thumb caressed her cheek, sending warm tingles up her spine. "I have missed you."

He chuckled. "I have been going mad, imagining all sorts of terrible things. Knowing Brevard would do his best to occupy your attention nearly drove me insane. I almost talked myself into riding to Le Beau a few days ago. If Aunt Lu hadn't sprained her ankle and had the house in an uproar, I would have."

When she didn't smile at his teasing, he grew serious. "Something *is* wrong. I can see it in your eyes. Tell me. Is it Brevard? Did he take advantage of you?" His anger mounted. "I will kill him if he laid a hand on you."

With tears running down her face, Adella shook her head. "No, no, Seth. Nothing like that happened." Closing her eyes, she took a deep breath before meeting his gaze again. "There is so much to tell you, but not here. Not now."

A deep frown settled on his face. "Adella Rose, what is this about? You must tell me."

"I ..." Words failed her. She implored him with her eyes to understand.

"Adella, please." He gripped her arms. "You're scaring me."

With a pang of deep loss, as one letting something of rare beauty escape, she took a step away from him. "I can't marry you, Seth," she whispered, her whole body shaking with emotion.

A horse whinnied from a nearby stall in the stillness of the barn.

Seth stared at her, confusion and hurt shining in his eyes. "What do you mean, you can't marry me? Of course you can, Adella Rose. Whatever your father and Brevard said to convince you otherwise is not the truth. You and I are in love. Your father will understand when we tell him."

Without meeting his gaze, she shook her head. "No, Seth. I have to marry Marshall. We will lose Rose Hill and all the slaves if I don't."

"You aren't making any sense," he said, anger raising his voice. "What do Rose Hill and the slaves have to do with anything? With us? You don't own them. They aren't yours to lose."

"Papa is in terrible financial trouble, Seth." She wrapped her arms around her waist, the ache in her heart making it difficult to breathe. "He and Marshall have come to a business agreement that will allow Papa to keep Rose Hill."

It took a moment, but Seth's face suddenly grew stony. "Let me guess. You are part of that agreement."

Ashamed to admit she'd been used in such a way by her own father, she ducked her head. "Yes."

"I don't believe it." Seth's fists clenched. "They are lying in order to get you to marry that buffoon. I refuse to believe the mighty Luther Ellis is in such financial ruin that only his daughter's marriage can save him. Are you so naïve that you can't see that?"

His accusing tone hurt. "It is true, Seth. I saw the document they both signed, giving Marshall a portion of Rose Hill profits for the next ten years. They're waiting for George to return and sign the papers before everything is finalized."

She watched the play of emotions cross his face. Anger. Disbelief. Frustration.

"Even if that is all true," he said, his voice clipped, his jaw tight, "it doesn't mean you have to marry Brevard. We can work something out to help your father. I won't take a salary, and my father would help, I'm certain."

Hopelessness settled in her heart. "It is not just Rose Hill in jeopardy, Seth." She bit her lip to keep it from trembling. "Papa threatened to sell the slaves if I don't marry Marshall. He will start with Jeptha and then Aunt Lu and Carolina. I … I can't let them go through that. Don't you see? I would be responsible for their misery."

With no warning, Seth jerked his hat from his head and threw it against the stall, startling Freedom. The horse nickered and backed away.

"Don't you see that your father is using the only weapon he has to make you do his bidding?" Seth's irate voice echoed in the cavernous barn. "So you marry Brevard. What's to prevent Luther from selling the slaves afterward? After it is too late for you and me?"

Adella's chin trembled. "He promised," she said, realizing how feeble such a defense sounded in the face of all her father had done.

Seth stared at her as though she were insane. "And you believe him?"

For the first time since she'd agreed to Papa's and Marshall's demands, she began to have doubts. "I don't know what to believe. Papa promised he wouldn't sell them if I marry Marshall, but on the way here he told me terrible things. Did you know he bought Celia to give to Jeptha? He wants her to have babies. Boy babies. So he won't have to buy more slaves."

She expected Seth to appear surprised, but he didn't.

"You knew?"

He nodded. "Yes. He told me after he purchased her what he planned. I have never been opposed to slavery, Adella, but some things just aren't right. Breeding slaves is one of them. Fathering slaves is another."

Adella stilled, shocked at the implications Seth made with that statement. "Are you accusing Papa of … of …?" Heat rushed to her face, and she couldn't utter the awful words.

"I don't know about your father, but I do know for a fact George has fathered at least one child with a slave."

The charge hung in the air between them. It couldn't be true. George was her brother, after all. Mama had raised them to be God-fearing, morally upstanding people. To allege the kind of behavior Seth insinuated was like a slap in Mama's face.

Indignant, Adella lifted her chin. She had to defend her family, even against Seth. "I realize you are angry with Papa, but to accuse George of something so heinous is uncalled for. He is no saint, but I cannot believe he would do what you have accused him of doing. Why, he and Natalie just celebrated their wedding. "

"You want proof?" Seth snatched his hat off the ground. "Fine. I will give you proof."

In the next breath, he took her by the arm and hauled her toward the door.

"You're hurting me, Seth." Tears sprang to her eyes, more from their argument than from the pain. When she tried to get away, his grip only tightened on her arm. "Where are you taking me? Please, Seth. Stop this. You're scaring me."

But he remained mute and continued to lead her down the cart path until they reached the quarter. Passing several cabins, he came to a stop in front of the one where Mammy lived. The door stood open, and two tiny dirt-smudged faces peered out at them. The distinct sound of a newborn baby came from within.

"What are we doing here?" she said, her voice just above a whisper.

Seth finally turned to her. "Giving you proof." His voice, hard and sure, brooked no argument.

With wide eyes, she stared at him. Then, ever so slowly, she turned toward the cabin. The baby's cries had quieted, replaced by the low murmur of Mammy's and another voice in conversation. Propelled by an unseen hand, Adella cautiously made her way into the dimly lit cabin.

Mammy glanced up from her place beside the crude bed, surprise on her face. "Missy, what you's doin' heah?" She shot a look down to the occupant in the rumpled covers.

Lucy lay slightly propped up, with her hair wild and loose from her kerchief, and her gown pulled down to partially expose one breast. Her eyes rounded with fear, and she looked from Mammy to Adella and back. Then she looked down at the tiny babe asleep in her arms. With protective instincts, the new mother clutched the bundle closer to her before returning her wary gaze to Adella.

Time seemed to stand still while Adella fought to take in what she was seeing. Seth's accusation of George fathering a child was ridiculous, yet he'd brought her to this cabin to offer her proof it was true.

Her eyes drifted down from Lucy's golden brown face to the face of her baby.

The infant's skin was nearly as white as her own.

CHAPTER TWENTY-THREE

Seth stood in the doorway to the small cabin. He hated that he'd done this to Adella, but she had to know the truth. She had to know the kind of men her father and brother were. The kind of man Marshall Brevard might be, too. Men who didn't blink when it came to using others for their own gain.

"How can this be?" Adella whispered, her hands pressed against her breast.

"Now, Missy, whatever you thinks goin' on heah, just never you mind it." Mammy came to Adella's side. "You's get on back to da house now. You's all tuckered out, I 'spect." The old woman tried to steer Adella toward the door, but she wouldn't budge.

"No." She moved to the edge of the bed with determined steps. Lucy stared up at her, chin trembling. "Who is the father of your child, Lucy?"

Lucy's eyes darted to Mammy, who shook her head. The young slave woman returned her gaze to Adella. "I dunno, Missy." She cowered against the pillow.

But Adella wasn't fooled. "Yes, you do, Lucy. Tell me the truth. I am not going to hurt you or the baby. Who is the father?"

After a long pause, Lucy's face crumpled. "It yo' brother, Missy. Massa George be da father o' dis little chile."

The room grew still. Only the sound of the baby stirring in Lucy's arms interrupted the silence. Finally, the little one let out a tiny wail.

"Shhh." Lucy jostled the bundle, her fearful eyes going from the child to Adella.

With her back to him, Seth couldn't see Adella's face. But he could imagine the thoughts whirling through her mind. That her own brother had fathered this child meant it was part of her bloodline.

"Is it a boy or a girl?" she finally asked, her voice strained.

"It be a girl, Missy." A faint smile came to Lucy's lips. "I name her Mara. Ol' Moses say it mean bitter." She looked down at the babe, who peacefully slept again. "But I think o' her as bittersweet. Don't much care for da way she come to me, but I gonna love her anyhows."

After a long moment, Adella's tense shoulders sagged. She turned then to look at Seth. When their eyes met in the dim light, he knew she accepted the truth. The child was George's. He offered a small nod, simply as a way of saying he understood her pain.

"May I hold her?" she asked softly when she returned her attention to Lucy.

Hesitating just a moment, Lucy gathered the baby's rough blanket around her and held up the precious bundle.

Taking great care, Adella accepted the babe and nestled it against her breast, staring into the wee face. With her free hand, she wiped a tear that trailed down her own cheek. Seth crossed the space that separated them and put his arm around her waist. She needed his support now more than ever.

"Hello, Mara." She touched the soft skin of the baby's cheek with the tip of her finger. "I'm your Aunt Adella."

Seth tightened his grip on her, knowing how difficult it was for her to admit the truth.

When Adella eventually passed the baby back to Lucy, their eyes met. "I will see that you have extra rations." She turned to Seth. "I don't want Lucy working in the fields any longer. When the baby is old enough to stay with Mammy, Lucy is to be assigned to the weaving house."

Surprised by the authority in her voice, Seth's brow raised. "Yes, ma'am."

His response brought a hint of a smile to her lips. With one last

glance at the sleeping babe, she bid the two slave women good-bye and led the way outside into the fading sunlight. They walked a short distance from the quarter in silence before she came to a stop beneath the branches of a huge oak. Inhaling a deep breath, Adella closed her eyes.

"Are you all right?" Seth worried she might collapse.

When she opened her eyes again, he expected to see tears, but he was wrong.

"Yes, I'm fine. In fact," she said, with a slight laugh, "I am better than fine. For the first time in weeks, I feel like I am in control of my life once again."

Confused but thrilled she wasn't falling apart, Seth smiled. "And when did this come about? Because the last time I looked, you were meeting your niece born to a Rose Hill slave."

She nodded, sobering. "Yes, it is shameful what George has done. I cannot imagine what poor Natalie will do if she ever finds out." A look of resolve replaced the concern in her eyes. "But when I looked into Mara's tiny face, knowing she has Ellis blood flowing through her veins, I realized I could not allow Papa and George to continue using people and ruining lives at their whim. They may own the slaves because manmade laws give them that right, but I know God does not look down on this with favor."

It was all Seth could do to keep from capturing her in his arms right there in broad daylight. "You amaze me, Adella Rose Ellis." He loved her more than ever.

That love was mirrored in her blue eyes when she gazed at him. "Do you forgive me for being weak and letting Papa and Marshall convince me there was no other choice?"

Risking the chance someone might see, Seth caressed her soft cheek. "There is nothing to forgive, my love."

"Let's go tell Papa I won't be marrying Marshall. He won't be pleased, but it cannot be helped." Her brow puckered into a frown. "I fear what he will do, especially to the slaves, but I won't allow him to take away my only chance at happiness with his threats and bullying."

As much as Seth wanted to do that very thing, it didn't seem the best plan. "I don't think we should tell him just yet."

"Why not? I want us to be married right away, Seth."

Her anxiousness warmed his blood, and he ached to plant a kiss on her upturned mouth. "As do I, but we need to think this through."

"Well, we haven't much time." She frowned. "Marshall will arrive a week from tomorrow. We are to be married here at Rose Hill a few days later."

"One week then," he said, his mind already whirling, working to come up with a solution.

"If only there was some way the slaves could get away." She glanced back to the quarter. "They will be the ones Papa will punish when I refuse to marry Marshall."

Knowing she was right, Seth mulled over the problem. He had no doubt Luther would follow through with his threat to sell the slaves, especially the ones favored by his rebellious daughter. Seth had no money to buy the slaves himself, not that Luther would sell them to him anyway. No, in Luther's anger at Adella's betrayal, he would exact as much pain on Jeptha and the others as he possibly could. And that meant taking them to the market and letting fate fall where it may. It was therefore up to Seth to find a way to help the slaves and still whisk Adella away from Rose Hill forever.

An idea began to take root in Seth's mind—a crazy idea, but one that just might work. Reaching for Adella's hand, he kissed her knuckles.

"How would you feel about being married to an outlaw?"

❧ ❧

"Jeptha?"

Seth glanced from side to side, making sure no one watched him sidle up to the stinking shed. The sliver of moon barely put out enough light to see his hand in front of his face, but still, he couldn't take any chances on being caught now that Luther had returned.

"Jeptha!" he said a little louder, although he kept his voice low enough that it wouldn't travel to the quarter nearby. Everyone should be asleep by now, but one could never be sure who might be up and about.

"Mistah Brantley, suh? What you's doin' here in the dark?"

Seth shushed him. "Keep your voice down. We don't want the entire plantation to wake up."

A soft chuckle came from the opposite side of the wall. "I reckon not if it ain't mornin'. Didn't think I'd been asleep that long."

Cool night air made Seth aware he was sweating. Whether from nerves or the coat he'd worn, he wasn't sure. With the back of his hand, he mopped his brow, giving one last look toward the quarter. "I have something for you," he said, reaching into his coat for the large burlap-wrapped bundle he'd tucked there on his way out of the kitchen earlier.

He grinned, trying to imagine what Aunt Lu would say when she discovered the leftover meat pie from dinner was missing. Along with a thick hunk of cheese, some ham, and two of Freedom's apples.

"What you got, Mistah Brantley?" Jeptha said, his voice closer and no longer muffled by the wall. Seth guessed his face was in the hole, but he couldn't see him.

"First, I need you to give me your word you won't tell a soul about this. Not even Celia."

Jeptha snorted. "That gal don't give a lick 'bout me. She done found her a new man, from what I hear."

That bit of news surprised Seth since he hadn't heard about it, but it would certainly work in their favor if Celia were occupied. He briefly wondered who had risked punishment to sneak bits of information to Jeptha. "Good," he said. "But I still need you to give me your word."

"I won't tell no one that you came to see me tonight, not that anybody care."

Putting his trust in the black man didn't come easily to Seth, but he didn't have a choice. "Here. Take this," he said, stuffing the items through the hole.

He felt Jeptha's hands receive the food. "I ... I don't unde'stand, Mistah Brantley. Why you's givin' me all this food? Massa Luther take the whup to my back if he find out I has this."

"He won't find out as long as you don't tell anyone about this." Looking back over his shoulder, Seth lowered his voice even further. "Don't eat it all at once. Your stomach isn't used to getting that much food. It will make you sick, and you'll vomit it up. Eat it nice and slow. We need you to gain your strength."

The other side of the shed was silent for a good long time. Finally, Jeptha said, "We? Who's we?"

Taking a deep breath, praying his trust was not misplaced, he plunged forward. "Missy Ellis is in trouble. Master Luther is forcing her to marry Brevard to save the plantation from financial ruin. He's threatened to sell all the slaves, starting with you, if she doesn't marry him."

He heard Jeptha blow out a breath. "Guess I done for. Why you bring me this here food? So I be nice an' fat when I get to that market down Gav'ston way?"

"No, of course not," Seth said, frustrated the other man would even think that. "Missy Ellis and I plan to run away together and marry. We want to take you with us."

An owl hooted from a nearby tree, but Jeptha remained silent.

"Did you hear what I said? We want you to go with us. Maybe some of the others. You can head down to Mexico or even out West."

"You ain't funnin' with me, are you, Mistah Brantley, suh? So's I'll agree to somethin' then get a whuppin' or somethin' worse for plannin' to escape?"

The other man's suspicion was justified. "No, Jeptha. If Missy

Ellis could come down here, she would tell you this herself. But we only have one week to get everything ready. You won't make it if we don't get some food into you and build up your strength."

"You's serious, ain't you?"

"Completely."

The nightly chorus of crickets, toads, and whippoorwills filled the air while Seth told Jeptha about the plan. "I haven't worked out all the details, but you will need to be ready to travel by next week. Adella and I will take care of gathering provisions. I figure we'll start off together, but we might need to split up eventually, so we'll need to make sure you have enough to get you to Mexico."

Silence came from the shed again. For a moment, Seth wondered if Jeptha had fallen asleep.

"I don't know what to say, Mistah Brantley," he finally said. "I dreamed 'bout going to ol' Mexico ever since a Negro passed through here talkin' 'bout it. Massa Luther sold him right quick so's he wouldn't *infect* the rest of us with his lies, is what Massa Luther say. But I know'd that boy tellin' us the truth. Says we's free in Mexico." He paused. "More than anything, Mistah Brantley," he continued, his voice cracking with emotion. "More than anything, I wants to be free."

Later, when Seth walked away from the shed toward his own cabin, he couldn't help but shake his head at the irony of it all.

A runaway slave desperate for freedom stole his career and nearly ended his life.

Now he desperately wanted to free this slave who had become his friend.

CHAPTER TWENTY-FOUR

Adella paced in front of the parlor window, wringing a lace handkerchief and wondering what Seth had accomplished in the two days since they'd last spoken. He'd planned to tell Jeptha about their scheme and begin gathering the supplies they would need. She'd been poised to do her part as well, but George and Natalie returned home from their honeymoon trip several days earlier than expected, sending the house into an uproar. Natalie, doing her best to fulfill her role as mistress of the manor, had everyone scurrying here, there, and everywhere, changing this or rearranging that. And if she wasn't barking orders at the servants, she monopolized Adella's time by regaling her with tales of the gorgeous hotels and plantations they'd stayed at while traveling.

"Really, Adella Rose, you and Marshall simply must visit the Royal Hotel in New Orleans," Natalie said from her place on the settee, where she thumbed through yet more wallpaper samples. She held one up, tilted her head as though envisioning it on the parlor wall, then tossed it aside. "They have the most stunning chandelier in the foyer, with gas lights, mind you. Senator Slidell and his lovely wife took us to dinner there, twice. George ordered champagne, and the Senator didn't blink an eye. Can you imagine?"

Listening to Natalie prattle on about their trip, knowing George had been fully aware of Papa's financial situation and his plan to marry off Adella in order to save them from bankruptcy, she nearly growled in answer. "Can I imagine George letting someone else pick up the bill for his own extravagance? Why yes, Natalie, dear, I can. My brother has become very adept at using people for his own gain."

Clearly taken aback by her gruff response, Natalie's smooth brow furrowed. "Adella Rose, you haven't been yourself since we returned. Is something troubling you?"

How she longed to blurt out the whole truth. That everything about their lives was a lie. That Papa had sold her to the highest bidder because they were broke—worse than broke. The debts Papa owed seemed insurmountable. Adella honestly didn't know what Papa and George would do when she ran away with Seth. She prayed Marshall would do the honorable thing and continue with the business agreement, but that was out of her hands. She had let them use her long enough. From now on, she was in charge of her own life.

"Natalie, don't you ever get tired of pretending? Pretending that money can buy happiness. Pretending that money will make things all better when in reality it makes things worse?"

Natalie looked confused, blinking several times. "I don't know what you mean, Adella Rose. Surely you don't wish you were poor, like those wretched souls we saw in the slums of New Orleans." The petite blonde shuddered. "Living in hovels, with children as filthy as the dirt. Of course money can't buy happiness, but it certainly makes life easier, don't you agree?"

Adella studied her sister-in-law. She seemed content in her marriage to George, despite the wedding day jitters that nearly caused her to call off the ceremony. Perhaps she did love George or had at least fallen in love with him during their trip. A slight flush filled Adella's cheeks, knowing she and Seth would soon enjoy the intimacies Natalie and George experienced. Things done in the privacy of a marriage chamber were unknown to her, but she couldn't keep the warmth from forming in her belly when she thought of Seth claiming her as his wife.

But what of Lucy?

The young mother's face flashed across her mind, along with the tiny babe who had Ellis blood running through her veins. Would George acknowledge Mara as his child? The possibility of that happening was remote, at best. Though Seth hadn't accused George of fathering other children, it seemed likely his indiscretion with Lucy was not his first. What if he went back to his old ways despite being a married man?

She looked again at Natalie. The girl deserved so much better than what George would give her. Had the circumstances been different, Adella and she might have become true sisters over time. But as things stood, it wasn't likely she'd ever see Natalie again once she and Seth rode away from Rose Hill.

"I hope you will be happy here, Natalie. I truly do."

Natalie glanced up from the colorful squares of paper she'd spread out on the low table in front of her. Her fine brows arched. "Why, thank you, Adella. That means a great deal to me. I know it must be difficult for you to watch me take charge of Rose Hill Manor. But you will soon be busy as mistress of Le Beau. Perhaps you'd like to look through these samples, and we can compare notes on paint colors and fabrics. I understand Marshall wants you to redecorate the entire house. Won't it be so much fun?"

Adella didn't answer. There was nothing left to say.

Later, she made her way to the kitchen wing. The noon meal had been served, and preparations for dinner wouldn't begin for a while. In this brief lull that took place each day, Aunt Lu could often be found alone in her room above the kitchen.

Making certain no one noticed her, Adella ascended the stairs quickly and found the older woman sitting on the edge of the narrow bed with one foot propped up on a low stool.

"Missy," she exclaimed, a smile spreading across her face. "Been a long time since you's come up yonder ta visits me."

Adella grinned, looking about the sparsely furnished room that never changed. "I remember sneaking up here when I broke one of Mama's porcelain vases. You found me curled up asleep under your covers."

With a deep chuckle, Aunt Lu nodded. "I 'member that time, an' lots o' others. I 'member, too, the talks we's had up here after

Miz Martha goes on ta heaven."

Aunt Lu patted the bed beside her. Adella took the offered seat.

"I don't think I would have survived those days without you, Aunt Lu," she said, taking the older woman's work-worn hand in hers. "You are as much family to me as Mama was."

"Aw, that sho' do make my heart warm, Missy." Aunt Lu put her other hand over Adella's.

"How is your ankle?"

"Oh, it be fine. Jes' sore if I stands on it too long."

Knowing she only had a short time to explain the details of the plan to Aunt Lu, Adella took a deep breath. "Aunt Lu, I need you to listen to me." She squeezed the woman's hand. "I can't marry Marshall like Papa wants." Her voice caught in her throat, feeling emotional and shy about revealing her deep feelings for Seth to another living soul. "I love Seth," she whispered.

Aunt Lu's face broke into a smile. "I know'd it. I been watchin' the two o' yous. He loves you too, Missy. I can tell."

Tears sprang to her eyes. "I know he does. We want to be married, but Papa won't allow it. While I was at Le Beau, Papa confessed some terrible things. He is in financial trouble, Aunt Lu. So bad, he could lose Rose Hill. To save it, he made a business agreement with Marshall, but it also involves me. I must marry Marshall."

During the brief telling of the tale, Aunt Lu's eyes grew wider and wider. "Oh, Missy. Don't you know Miz Martha be rollin' in her grave if she know'd what Massa Luther doin'."

"That isn't all, I'm afraid." Adella hated that she had to tell the precious woman the rest of the sordid story. "Papa says if I don't marry Marshall, he will sell all you slaves. First Jeptha, then you, then Carolina. He will start with those I care most about, then each day I refuse to obey him, he will sell another slave until they are all gone."

Tears rolled down her face, staining the blue material of her gown. Shame filled her, even though she had nothing to do with

Papa's despicable threat. But her skin was white, and she was the daughter of a white plantation owner. That in itself made her as guilty as Papa in the slaves' eyes.

"Oh, Missy." Fear and pain filled the deep crevices of Aunt Lu's lined face before she closed her eyes. "Oh, Lawd," she breathed, hanging her head.

"Seth and I want you and Zina to come with us," Adella plunged forward, giving Aunt Lu's hands a little shake to get her attention. "We haven't worked out all the details yet, but we will have to leave within a few days. Marshall arrives Saturday, believing I will marry him a few days later. We have to be gone by then, or Papa will force me into the marriage, I am sure of it."

A confused frown tugged Aunt Lu's brow. "You mean you's gonna buy me from yo' pappy?"

Adella shook her head. "No. He wouldn't sell you to me, even if I had the money. Papa is determined to punish me and anyone I care about if I don't bend to his demands." She held Aunt Lu's gaze. "I want you to run away with us. And Jeptha, if he's willing. Maybe Lucy, too, although I haven't talked to her about it."

Shock came over Aunt Lu's features. "You mean you's talkin' 'bout us'ns runnin' away, like them Negroes we's hear 'bout bein' chased down by them patterollers an' they dogs? Oh, no, Missy. No, no!" She stood, limping on her hurt ankle, and crossed to the single window, shaking her head and muttering, "No, Lawd. No."

"I wouldn't ask you to do something so risky if I didn't believe you were in even greater danger by staying." Adella went to the woman. Aunt Lu's fear-filled eyes met hers. "Papa will sell you, Aunt Lu. He will take you to the market in Galveston because he knows how much I love you."

Her choked words brought tears to Aunt Lu's eyes. "Oh, honey chile, I loves you, too. You like one o' my own, you is. But ... but what you's askin' me ta do ..." She shot a look at the open door to the stairwell then back to Adella. "What you askin' me to do," she repeated in a lowered voice, "it be too dange'ous. And my Zina?

No, no, I cain't lose her. 'Sides, she belong to Miss Natalie, so she be safe."

"Aunt Lu, you know as well as I do any slaves Natalie owned are now owned by George. I wouldn't put it past Papa to convince George to sell Zina as well." She softened her voice. "You may lose her anyway. At least if the two of you go away with us, you'll know where she is and have a chance at a new life together. A life of freedom, if everything works out the way we hope it will."

A tiny spark of interest ignited in Aunt Lu's eyes upon hearing the word *freedom*. "You really think you an' Mistah Brantley can get us'n's outta here safe like? Where we go? We got's no papers or nothin'. Them patterollers go up an' down them roads, lookin' for runaway Negros." She shuddered. "I don't even wants to think 'bout what'll happen if them white men's catch us'n's."

Realizing it would take more solid assurances of their plan to convince Aunt Lu of its validity, she reached out to grasp the woman by the arm. "Please think about it, Aunt Lu. Seth and I don't have all the details worked out yet, but when we do, we will have to move quickly."

A voice from the kitchen below called to Aunt Lu. She cast a fearful look at the door then back to Adella.

"I think on it, Missy," she whispered. "I ask the Lawd what to do. You best be doin' the same."

Adella watched her hurry from the room, realizing that the older woman was right. They desperately needed God's direction if this wild plan was going to work. Kneeling right there at Aunt Lu's bed, Adella poured her heart out to the Lord. Above all, she had to make sure their plan was the right thing to do. Too many lives were at stake for them to fail.

How long she knelt there, Adella didn't know. But when she stood, a faint smile crept to her lips.

She knew exactly what needed to be done.

"I went down to the quarter today to see about Monroe."

Papa made the announcement while the family gathered on the porch after dinner, to escape the stuffy house. The day had been the hottest of the season thus far, but they all knew summers in Texas brought temperatures well over one hundred degrees before it was all said and done.

"How long before he can get back to work?" George asked, sipping from a small glass of amber liquid.

Adella noticed that since he'd returned from his honeymoon trip, her brother partook of the drink more often than he'd done before. Papa, too, imbibed more in recent days. She supposed the strain of their financial situation drove them to it.

"I'll give him a few more days to let his ribs heal, but we'll need him in the fields by next week." He cast a pointed look in her direction. "It seems we will be in need of an overseer soon."

Adella ignored the barb, fearing she might slip and reveal her elation that Seth would no longer be the overseer at Rose Hill. Little did Papa realize she would be gone as well. Would he care?

George chuckled. "I always knew my little sister was gullible, but to actually believe Brantley wanted to marry you for love is preposterous. He was after your money, Adella Rose. Plain and simple."

"As you were after Natalie's?" she said, outraged Papa had apparently revealed her private matter to George and that her brother would use it to poke fun at her.

Hurt filled Natalie's eyes, however, and Adella regretted her outburst.

"I am sorry, Natalie," she hurried to say. "I didn't mean that."

George scoffed. "Yes, you did. I fear you have many hard lessons to learn, little sister, about the decorum expected of a planter's wife. Marshall certainly has his work cut out for him. You can't spew every thought that enters that head of yours. It would do you well to pay close attention to my wife, who is flawless in her role as a planter's wife. Everyone in New Orleans thought so."

Though Adella longed to defend herself, she had already offended Natalie once. She couldn't afford to do so again, so she remained silent.

George tossed the remaining liquid down his throat and stood. "Come, Natalie. Let us retire for the night. I would not want you further insulted by my dear sister."

Natalie stood and followed George inside the house without looking at Adella. Tomorrow, Adella made a mental note, she would need to repair the damage her careless words had done. She truly did like Natalie, as well as feel sorry for her.

Not wishing to linger on the porch with Papa, Adella stood. "I believe I will retire as well."

"Sit down, Adella. I will have a word with you."

Unhappy at being detained, she sat on the edge of the wicker chair and waited. Whatever her father had to say was of little importance at this point, but she would give him the respect due his position as her father.

"I trust you have come to terms with your marriage to Marshall," he said, taking a cigar from his breast pocket. He struck a match on the leg of his chair and lit the end, puffing smoke into the air.

Although she didn't want to lie, she couldn't be honest with him either. "My future is in God's hands," she stated simply, which was absolutely the truth.

Papa gave a humorless laugh. "God himself could not have arranged a better marriage for you. Someday I hope you will have the decency to thank me instead of acting as though I forced you to sell your soul to the Devil."

"The fact that you have sold me at all is what troubles me, Papa. Marriage should not be about money and debts and property. It should be about love and the desire to make a happy life with another person. Marshall is a fine man, no doubt, but I believe he would be far happier with someone other than me. I don't love him, and I suspect I never will."

Squinting through the smoke of his cigar, Papa said, "Your brother is right, you know. As Marshall Brevard's wife, you will need to learn to keep your opinions to yourself. No planter worth his salt wants a wife who can't maintain the proper etiquette demanded of her position. Your mother would be horrified at your behavior tonight."

Adella gasped. "You dare speak of mother's disappointment with me when you are guilty of selling her daughter to the highest bidder because of your own mismanagement of Rose Hill funds."

Before she knew what he was about, Papa stood and slapped her so hard it knocked her from her seat. Sprawled on the porch, Adella stared up in horror, the side of her face throbbing with fire.

"I will not tolerate your disrespect. You know nothing of the business of Rose Hill. Learning a few facts from Marshall does not give you the right to criticize me. The sooner you learn to accept male superiority in business matters, the better it will be for you. Your mother learned that lesson early in our marriage. You will do well to follow in her footsteps."

He left her then, disappearing into the house.

Adella sat where she was, too stunned to move. In all her years, Papa had never struck her. He'd always treated her like a princess, his special girl. Tears welled in her eyes, realizing her father possessed a side she had never known existed until recently.

The sound of heavy footfalls running toward the house brought her face up. She looked out into the darkness. Fear of being assaulted again, this time by an unknown assailant, sent her to her feet. Before she could reach the door, he came into the circle of light cast off from the porch lantern.

"Adella," Seth panted, taking the steps two at a time to reach her side and grimacing when his injured leg landed on the hard wood.

"Oh, Seth," she breathed, falling into his embrace. When she felt his strong arms encircle her, the tears began to fall. She clung to him as though he were a lifeline.

"I saw what he did," Seth said between clenched teeth. "I was watching you, hoping we'd have a chance to talk. I am going in there and giving your father what is due him." He pulled her out of his arms, looking at her face. "Are you all right?"

She shook her head, a sob catching in her throat. "No, but I will be, as soon as you take me away from here."

Cradling her head against his chest, Seth whispered words of love and promise. With his heartbeat beneath her cheek, she pressed ever closer, knowing the steadfastness of the sound matched that of the man who loved her.

When she finally quieted, he stepped away. "I won't allow him to ever touch you again."

With angry strides, Seth moved to the door, but she couldn't let him confront Papa. Not yet. "No, Seth. Wait, please."

"Adella, he struck you. I won't stand by and pretend I didn't witness it."

She heard the frustration in his voice. "He will send you away tonight if you go in there. Or worse. I don't know what Papa is capable of anymore."

Running a hand through his thick hair, Seth glanced between her and the door before he finally acquiesced. "Fine. But if he so much as raises his voice to you, I am taking you out of here. Jeptha and the others will simply have to fend for themselves."

Loving him even more, she laid her hand against the rough stubble on his cheek. "Thank you, Seth," she whispered.

He took her hand and pressed his warm lips to the center of her palm. "I love you, Adella Rose."

A soft gasp came from just inside the open door.

Startled, they both turned to find Natalie staring at them.

CHAPTER TWENTY-FIVE

"Sit still, Missy, an' le'me get this here poultice on that swellin' o' yours."

Seth watched Aunt Lu apply a cloth with a smelly mixture wrapped inside to the red, swollen area of Adella's face. That the place bore the shape of her father's hand nearly undid Seth. It was all he could do to keep from barging into Luther's private chamber and laying the man out flat.

"Do you think Natalie will tell George?" Adella asked, holding the cloth in place while Aunt Lu moved to the stove and prepared a cup of herbal tea for her. When Seth gave her a questioning look, she responded with a slight smile. "It's all right. Aunt Lu knows of our plans and that we want her and Zina to come with us."

From the look Aunt Lu tossed his way, Seth got the impression the woman wasn't too keen on the idea of joining them. He couldn't blame her. All slaves knew severe punishment awaited them if they were caught trying to escape.

Heaving a sigh, he sat on the long bench at the table where the house servants took their meals. The whole affair was getting more complicated by the minute. "I don't think we should wait to find out if Natalie will keep quiet. If she tells George what she saw and heard, you will never get away. After what I saw tonight, I wouldn't put it past Luther to lock you away until Marshall and the preacher arrive."

Adella accepted the cup of tea Aunt Lu handed her. "I am glad Mama never knew how cruel Papa could be. It would break her heart to know he struck me in anger."

An odd expression crossed Aunt Lu's face before she turned away.

"Aunt Lu?" Adella said, tilting her head to look into the other woman's eyes. "You know something. Is it about Mama?"

The servant shook her head. "I jes' thinkin' you's right, is all." She returned to the big stove, keeping her back to them.

Adella set her cup down and followed her. "What is it, Aunt Lu? Please tell me." Her brow rose. "Was Papa cruel to Mama?" she asked, clearly alarmed at such a thought.

"Oh, Missy," Aunt Lu said, upset. "I promised Miz Martha never ta speak on it. An' I hasn't ever tol' nobody."

Seth watched the play of emotions rush across Adella's face as she stared at the other woman. Shock. Disbelief. And finally, resignation. After seeing him strike his own daughter, it wouldn't surprise Seth to learn he'd abused his wife, too. But he hated that Adella had to find out such terrible things about her father. She'd adored him all her life. To discover he wasn't the champion she'd always believed must have been difficult.

"Tell me."

The soft command brought tears to Aunt Lu's eyes, but she nodded. "I had ta doctah Miz Martha lots o' times, Missy. Mostly her bruises be under her clothes, where they's hidden. But sometime she has some on her face, like yourn."

Covering her mouth with her hands, Adella's shoulders shook with silent weeping.

"I sorry, Missy." Aunt Lu took Adella in her arms. They stood holding each other for several minutes before Adella quieted.

"I never knew." Her face revealed her broken heart. "Mama never said a word."

"'Course she didn', chile. He your pappy. Ain't do no good ta tell a chile sech things 'bout their pappy."

When her eyes found his, red-rimmed and full of her father's betrayal, Seth's resolve to take her away from Rose Hill filled every crevice of his being. "I won't leave you in this house with that man another minute." He stood, his mind plotting even as he spoke. "I'll saddle Chester, and we'll leave tonight." With an apologetic glance at Aunt Lu, he said, "I'm sorry, but we can't take any of the slaves with us. Not tonight. I will have to come back for them later."

Adella clung to Aunt Lu's hand. "I can't leave them, Seth. Especially now that I know what Papa's true nature is. He will be furious, and he'll take it out on the people I love."

"I understand that." Seth tempered his frustration as best he could. "But if Natalie is this minute telling George what she saw, we have until morning before your father learns about it. I won't take a chance on him hurting you again, Adella Rose."

Love shone in her eyes. "I will be careful. If I must, I'll fight back. Papa apparently has never had anyone defend themselves against his brutality. He won't expect it."

Despite the gravity of the situation, Seth smiled. "That's my girl."

"So, is we runnin' away or isn't we?" Aunt Lu looked from one to the other.

Adella stared at the woman. "Does that mean you will come with us?" Hope spilled from every word.

With a pat on Adella's cheek, the woman nodded. "If you's brave 'nough ta risk stayin' on account o' me an' the others, Missy, then I 'spect I cain't let you down. It scare me nearly ta death ta even think on it, but if my Zina could be free ..." Tears sprang to her eyes. "Well, it'd be worth it, I tells ya."

While the two women hugged, the full weight of what they hoped to achieve settled on Seth like an anvil. It wasn't just about getting Adella away from her father now. If their plan worked, they would leave the plantation with at least three slaves that didn't belong to either of them. Maybe more. If caught, they could all hang.

"We need to put a plan in place," he said, getting their attention. "There is no time to waste. It will all hinge on Natalie and whether she tells George what she saw tonight. If she does, we have a few hours, at most. If she hasn't said anything come morning, then we may have a couple more days to gather supplies and get organized."

Adella, with her arm around Aunt Lu's shoulders, smiled bravely. "It's going to work, Seth. I know it. Earlier today I asked God to show me the way, and He did."

If there was ever a time when he needed faith, it was now. More than anything, he hoped she was right.

※ ❧

Papa and George exited the dining room when the morning meal was complete, leaving Adella alone with Natalie. Neither had remarked on the bruise to her face, all but ignoring her presence for the most part. That the two men discussed the possible purchase of more land as they exited appalled her. It didn't seem to bother either of them that it would take borrowed money to pursue their gains.

Glancing across the table as soon as the door closed behind them, she nearly sagged with relief seeing Natalie daintily sip tea from her cup, her demeanor calm and poised as usual. Natalie had arrived late to the meal, leaving Adella to wonder if she weren't coming so she wouldn't have to be involved in the scene Papa would surely create, had he been told of what Natalie witnessed on the porch. But it became obvious soon after she arrived that she had not revealed the information about Seth and Adella to her husband. The meal proceeded with little interaction between them, and Papa seemed fully engrossed in his plans to broaden Rose Hill's borders.

After several minutes of silence, Natalie dabbed her rosebud mouth with the corner of her linen napkin, laid it on the table, and looked at Adella for the first time since she'd entered the room.

"I suspect you wish to speak with me in private." Her glance took in Carolina, standing in her usual place in the corner nearest the door to the kitchen wing.

At Adella's nod, Carolina disappeared, leaving them completely alone.

"Natalie," she began, only to be interrupted by Natalie's raised hand.

"Adella Rose, as your sister, I insist you cease whatever it is you're doing with that man and come to your senses. You will be a married woman by week's end, for mercy's sake. What would poor Marshall think if he learned of such escapades days away from your wedding?"

Praying all night for the right words to say to Natalie if given the opportunity, Adella knew she had no choice but to be honest with the woman. Come what may, she owed Natalie the truth.

"Natalie, please hear me out." She stood and walked around the large table, taking the seat next to the other woman. Keeping her voice low, Adella plunged in. "I can't marry Marshall. I love Seth, and he loves me. We want to spend our lives together." When Natalie's eyes rounded, Adella took her hands in hers. "Please don't say anything to George or Papa. They would not understand."

Natalie's brow furrowed. "Adella Rose, you cannot be serious. Mr. Brantley has nothing to offer, whereas Marshall owns one of the largest plantations in Texas. Why, you will be the envy of every woman in the state when you become mistress of Le Beau."

"I know it doesn't make any sense to you," Adella said, the love she had for Seth making her smile. "But I would rather live a simple life as Seth's wife than live a life of luxury with Marshall. I don't love him, and I know I never will."

For several ticks from the clock on the mantel, Natalie stared at Adella. Finally, she narrowed her eyes and drew closer. "I believe you really are serious."

Adella nodded. "Yes."

"What do you intend to tell Marshall? Your father will be furious, you know." Her blue eyes shifted to the bruise on Adella's face.

"Papa will be more than furious, Natalie." All night she'd debated on telling her sister-in-law the particulars of Papa's financial woes, but finally decided it wasn't right to keep Natalie in ignorance. She had as much right to know the seriousness of their plight as Adella. Natalie was, after all, an Ellis now.

"The truth is, Papa and Marshall struck a business deal. It included marriage to me." At Natalie's surprise, she gave a humorless laugh. "Not very romantic, is it? That is not the worst of it, though, Natalie, dear. I am afraid Rose Hill is in financial trouble. Terrible trouble, according to Papa. Because of the direness of the situation, he has signed an agreement with Marshall, giving him a portion of the profits for the next ten years."

Natalie stared back at Adella, her frown deepening. "Does George know about this?"

"I assume so. His signature was required on the paperwork."

Adella prayed she'd made the right decision to reveal all of this to Natalie. Seth hadn't agreed that Natalie know the details, but Adella knew what it was like to be a woman living under the power of men who thought you were too silly to understand business. Her conscience wouldn't leave her sister-in-law to continue on unaware of the circumstances, especially when she would be the only Ellis female left once Adella married Seth.

After a time, Natalie looked out the floor-to-ceiling window to the manicured lawns. "It makes sense now." Her voice held a solemn note Adella had never heard come from the young woman before.

Puzzled, she asked, "What does?"

"George's behavior on our trip." Natalie looked down at her hands in her lap. "He got angry with me several times when I tried to purchase things. Trinkets, mind you. Nothing of great importance or cost. And when I suggested we stay in the Royal Hotel in New Orleans instead of staying with friends, he yelled at me." Her eyes traveled to Adella's bruised face again. "I feared he might strike me."

Her whispered admission sent a new wave of sadness crashing into Adella's heart. "Oh, Natalie." She took the younger woman protectively into her arms. How she longed to tell Natalie what she'd learned the previous night about Papa's violence toward Mama. To warn her that George could well follow in their father's footsteps. But she couldn't betray Aunt Lu's confidence.

When Natalie pulled away, she stood, wiped a lone tear that trailed down her pale cheek, and moved to look out the window. "What do you intend to do about Mr. Brantley?"

Believing she could trust Natalie, Adella joined her. When Natalie's shimmering gaze met hers, Adella looked into the eyes of a friend and sister.

"I intend to marry him."

CHAPTER TWENTY-SIX

From the entrance to the barn, Seth watched Marshall Brevard's carriage draw up to the front of the main house. His liveryman, dressed in a dark coat and crisp white shirt, jumped to the ground and hurried to open the door for his master. Brevard exited the coach, stretching muscles no doubt cramped from the long journey from Le Beau. With the sun setting on the western horizon, Seth couldn't make out the details of the man's face, but he could well imagine the self-satisfied expression he'd wear, gazing at the vastness of Rose Hill, believing its daughter and its resources would be his in a few short days. Mounting the steps, Marshall quickly disappeared through the front door.

"You sho' you want this big ol' hoss shod, Mistah Brantley, suh? Seems a mite soon, him being so new broke an' all."

Seth turned to Moses, who led Freedom in a docile walk. "Yes," he nodded, glancing toward the big animal. "He'll be ready for regular riding soon. We don't want any damage to his hooves."

Though the answer was true enough, Seth felt a bit dishonest. Freedom would indeed be ridden soon. They planned to take him on their flight away from Rose Hill, with Jeptha astride the very animal he'd helped break. While he didn't particularly like the idea of taking a horse that didn't belong to him, Luther had yet to pay him his wages and most certainly wouldn't once he discovered that Seth and Adella had run off together. Suffice it to say, the horse would have to act as payment instead.

"He sho' be a han'some hoss," Moses said, running his hand down the big animal's muscular neck. "Don't 'spect there be too many like him in these parts." He met Seth's gaze evenly. "Reckon if he got away, someone be sho' to recognize him an' bring him on back to Rose Hill."

For a moment, Seth wondered if the big black man was sending him a warning. As though he knew of their plan to escape and take Freedom with them. Adella had sworn Aunt Lu to secrecy, with the exception of letting Zina in on the plot, and the only other person who knew of their plans was Jeptha. Earlier, Moses had delivered a note to Seth from Adella, reassuring him of Natalie's silence after speaking with her that morning, but it hadn't said anything about their plan. And even if it had, Seth was certain Moses couldn't read.

"I gets on shoeing him for you, Mistah Brantley, suh." Moses turned without waiting for Seth to reply to his ponderings and led the animal toward the other side of the barn, where the farrier worked. He whistled a song that Seth recognized as one the slaves sang when they didn't think he was listening:

If I had two wings, bright angels above,
I would fly away to the kingdom, bright angels above.
You gotta escape for your life, bright angels above,
Oh run, run, mourner run, bright angels above.

Still troubled over Moses' strange behavior, Seth mounted Chester and rode out to the fields. If word got out about their plan and circulated through the quarter, they would be in a heap of hurt. Not only was it possible Luther might hear the rumor, but some of the slaves could demand to be taken along with them when they fled. A simple threat to reveal the plot if denied passage could bring calamity before they'd even begun their journey.

How had things become so complicated?

With dusk closing in, the workers gathered their tools and started toward the quarter, backs weary from the long hours of hoeing and bending. Seth rode ahead and met them as they entered, taking his daily headcount. The irony of his own plan to help several slaves escape weighed heavy on his mind. But the fact was, since he'd come to know Jeptha as a human being instead of a slave, as well as Aunt Lu, the idea of slavery didn't sit well with him, as it had all his life. Who gave Luther, or even Seth's own father, the right to own a person? The law said it was legal, but who wrote the law? A white man, giving other white men the right to own someone simply because the color of their skin was dark. Perhaps knowing he'd helped a few slaves gain their freedom would put the memory of the man who shot him to rest once and for all.

Deciding Chester needed a good rubdown, he led the horse into the barn. He was so focused on grooming the animal and going over their plan in his head, he didn't hear Oliver approach until the boy was standing next to him.

"Well, hello," he said, wondering what brought the child to the barn at this late hour. "Shouldn't you be eating your supper and getting ready for bed?"

Oliver nodded but didn't budge.

Seth knelt down so he could see the boy better in the dim lantern light. "Did you need something, Oliver?"

A frown tugged the boy's brow. "Is you leavin' Rose Hill, Mistah Brantley?"

The question rocked Seth. Had someone gotten wind of the escape? "Why would you ask that?"

"I heard Hulda talkin' to Mammy. Says Massa Luther gettin' him a new overseer from Massa Brevard. Says you gots ta leave on account o' you's nicer to us Negroes than ol' Mistah Haley." He cocked his head. "Is dat true?"

Seth sighed with relief. "I'm afraid it is true. At least the part about Master Luther getting a new overseer."

The boy's shoulders slumped. "I don't want you to leave."

Touched that he would even care, Seth chucked Oliver under the chin. "You keep doing a good job, and I'm sure the new overseer will notice."

Oliver shrugged. "Guess so." But his dejected tone said he didn't believe it. He turned to leave, then stopped. Reaching into his pocket, he pulled out the white stone. Examining it for a moment, he suddenly handed it to Seth. "I wants you ta have this here rock,

Mistah Brantley, suh. It remind you o' me. An' God."

Seth stared at the boy, speechless. Finally, he found his voice. "I … I can't take that, Oliver. It's your treasure. You found it."

"Yassuh, but I thinks yous might need it mo' than me." When Seth accepted it, the boy grinned. "'Sides." He pulled out a second white stone from the same pocket. "I finds me 'nother one jes' this mornin'."

Seth laughed. "Then we'll have matching rocks. I sure appreciate you giving it to me, Oliver. I'll keep it always."

Seeming satisfied, Oliver skipped out of the barn. The moment he disappeared, Seth's smile vanished. What would become of the little boy once he and Adella were gone? Would Luther follow through with his threat to sell the slaves, including the children? With a heavy heart, he finished grooming Chester, the white rock tucked safely in his pocket.

Darkness fell long before he returned to his cabin. A glance at the big house revealed lighted windows on every level. The occasional boisterous male laugh or voice carried across the vast lawn, and he envisioned Luther, Marshall, and George celebrating the upcoming business merger. How he wished he could rescue Adella from them that very night, but it made more sense to wait until they were fully prepared.

Entering the pitch-black cabin, Seth closed the door and set the bar across it. He needed to sort through the supplies he'd gathered so far with Aunt Lu's help. It wouldn't do to have someone come looking for him unexpectedly and find the extra rations of dried beef, cornmeal, and hardtack spread out on the small table. Though the fare was sufficient for him and the slaves they'd be taking along, he wondered, not for the first time, if Adella realized all she was giving up. She'd never gone a day without plenty of food, hot water, and clean sheets. How would she fare on the trail, keeping out of sight of main roads, eating off the land for days on end?

Sitting on the edge of the straw-filled mattress, he heaved a sigh. Was it fair of him to take her away from the life she was accustomed to simply because he wanted her for himself? Marshall Brevard could offer her a lifetime of comfort. What could Seth give her? A few coins in his pocket and a promise of hard work. But starting out their marriage on the run, with months of uncertainty ahead, brought doubts and a nagging question.

Was he doing what was best for Adella, or for him?

Later, after he'd hidden the supplies beneath his bed where he stretched out, a soft knock sounded at the door, interrupting the night sounds that lulled him nearly to sleep. Guessing it must be well past midnight, he figured it could only be an emergency or other bad news to disturb him at this hour.

Surprise brought him fully awake when he opened the door to see Adella in the faint light of the moon. "What are you doing here?" He glanced toward the darkened main house, expecting to find Luther or Marshall fast on her trail. "Is something wrong?"

"No," came her soft reply. "I ... I just needed to see you."

He couldn't help but smile. Knowing he shouldn't, considering the complete impropriety of the circumstances, Seth stepped onto the porch and enveloped her in his arms. Immediately, she molded to his body, fitting perfectly, as though they'd been formed together from the beginning of time. He tightened his hold even as the passion that raced through his body told him to back away.

"I've missed you," he whispered into her hair, breathing in the light scent of lavender that stirred his blood even more. "You don't know how many times I have wanted to storm into the house and make certain Brevard was keeping his distance."

Her cheek pressed into his chest. "You don't know how many times I wished you had."

"Has Brevard made advances toward you?" He gently pushed her away so he could see her face.

"No." She shook her head, but there was enough hesitation in her voice that Seth wasn't convinced.

"Wait here." He dashed into the cabin to grab a candle and some matches. When he returned to her side, he grasped her hand.

"Come with me. We'll go to the chapel and talk."

They avoided going directly through the quarter, even though it would have been shorter. When Seth shut the chapel door behind them and lit the candle, the quietness of the place felt strange. Normally the walls practically shook with voices raised in song or shouts of praise.

"Why couldn't we talk in your cabin? No one is awake to know." Her innocent eyes searched his face.

Reaching to tuck a tendril of hair behind her ear, Seth chuckled. "I didn't bring you here because I was afraid someone would see you enter my cabin."

"Why then?"

Her naiveté was beyond charming. "Because, my love," he said, rubbing her cheek with his thumb. "Being alone with you, with my bed mere steps away, would be far too tempting."

Even in the muted candlelight, he saw her face flush. "Oh." Her eyes rounded. "And you believe you can … can behave here?"

His laughter echoed in the empty room. "I would never risk the wrath of God by misbehaving in church."

Grinning, she seemed to relax. "Then let us sit. I want to hear all about the preparations." Taking a seat on the nearest bench, Adella waited for Seth to join her. "Aunt Lu said she gave you some supplies, though she believes we'll need more."

Sobering at the topic, he nodded. "Yes, we will. We should be able to find game along the way, but we can't count on always being able to start a fire. I am certain Brevard and your father will hire men to track us so we will be on the move until we cross the border into Mexico."

"Mexico?" She frowned. "I thought we would go west, toward Oregon."

Seth shook his head. "I've given it a lot of thought and believe the safest place for the slaves is Mexico. Once they are out of danger, then you and I can decide where to go from there." He paused, his earlier question of what was best for Adella surfacing.

"Is something wrong?"

When he met her gaze, the trust he found shining in the blue depths almost pained him. Taking a deep breath, he had to offer her a way out. "Adella, before we go any further, I want you to think about what you will be leaving behind. I can't offer you the life Brevard can—if not Brevard, then someone else more to your liking. I'm sure if your father considered it, he would be able to come up with someone else to help him with the financial problems without forcing you to marry Brevard."

Her eyes filled with tears as he spoke, and her chin trembled. "Are you saying you don't want to take me with you?"

"No." He grasped her hand with both of his. "I am saying if you want to change your mind, I will understand. The life I'm offering you won't be easy. We have hard riding ahead and long days without adequate food or privacy or water to bathe in. Starting out our marriage on the run from your father, helping some of his slaves escape no less … well, I'm not proud of what I'm about to put you through."

Her countenance relaxed then. "You aren't putting me through anything, Seth. I am a willing participant. If I stay, Papa will indeed force me to marry Marshall. He and George have signed the papers, giving Marshall a percentage of Rose Hill's profits. The only remaining detail in their plan is the wedding."

"You are certain?"

"Yes, I am certain. I will be a married woman in a matter of days, and I would much rather be married to the man I love."

The impish grin on her lips was more than he could bear, and he captured her mouth with his in one swift move. Her arms went around his neck, and he pulled her against his chest. The sweetness of her ignited a fire in his belly, and it was all he could do to pull away, breathless, remembering where they were.

Big eyes met his in the flickering candlelight, and he grinned. "I guess I was wrong about misbehaving in church."

She bit her lip. "What will we do about … about a minister?"

Her shyness made her all the more alluring.

"I have thought about that, too." He put a safe distance between them so he wouldn't be tempted to kiss her again. "There's a small town on the border. Last time I went through, a missionary had started a church there. Hopefully, he's still around and can perform our ceremony." He paused, his eyes taking in her beauty, finding it hard to believe she really wanted to marry him. "You will make a lovely bride, you know."

She smiled. "I know I can only bring a few gowns with me, but I would like to wear something special for our wedding."

"Of course." He took her hand. "I wish you could bring them all, but we'll be riding double on Chester until we cross the border. Hopefully we can purchase a wagon and some mules once we get the slaves settled."

Reaching into her pocket, Adella pulled something out. "I brought this." She handed him an expensive looking necklace with sparkling blue stones. "I thought perhaps we could sell it when we needed money."

Surprised, Seth studied the jewels. He determined they were probably sapphires, though he had never seen one in person. "Is this yours?" He didn't want to take anything more from Luther than was absolutely necessary.

"Yes, my mother gave it to me just before she passed away." The sadness in her voice spoke louder than her words. "Mama never really cared for fancy jewels, but Papa gave it to her for Christmas one year. I remember how the color of the stones perfectly matched her eyes."

"Then we can't sell this, Adella. It is too valuable a keepsake." He handed it back to her. "Leave it at Rose Hill with your father, as payment for the horses and food. Maybe one day, after he forgives you, he will return it to its rightful owner."

She clutched the necklace to her heart. "Do you think he will ever forgive us? It wasn't fair of him to use me in his business agreement with Marshall, but he is still my father." A catch in her voice revealed her emotional turmoil at leaving. "I wish he would give us his blessing. Surely a daughter's happiness is more important than money."

Seth knew it wasn't, at least not in the case of Luther Ellis, but he didn't voice his opinion. "I hope one day he will come to see the truth in that. Now we must figure out the best time to leave. Are any guests invited to the wedding?"

Adella shook her head. "Marshall didn't want anyone other than the family to attend."

"Good." Seth's mind whirled with the plan he'd come up with. "That gives us two days to finish preparations with little distraction. On the night before the wedding, my guess is your father and Marshall will be in a celebratory mood. We can only hope they imbibe a bit more than usual, giving us plenty of time to make our escape."

"I would like to take Lucy and the baby with us." Her gaze was pleading but her voice firm.

"Adella." He ran a hand through his hair. "We are already risking more than we should by taking three slaves. We will be riding hard and fast with very little rest. There isn't any way we can take a new mother and an infant. I'm sorry."

Frustration clouded her eyes. "Seth, Mara is George's daughter. She has Ellis blood flowing through her veins. I can't leave her here, knowing Papa plans to sell off the slaves one by one. Even if he knew about Mara, I don't believe it would keep him from taking her to market."

"I understand you care about her." He wished now she had never learned about the baby. "But if we take them, we will jeopardize the safety of everyone else. You know what will happen if we're caught. The slaves will be beaten or even killed, and you and I could face the hangman's noose for helping them escape."

The reality of what faced them, should their plan fail, brought silence inside the chapel. He hated to put it so candidly, but she had to know the danger.

"I know you're right," she finally said, seemingly resigned.

He grasped her hands. "It is not that I want to be right, but we have to face the truth of what we are about to do. I wish we could free them all, but we will have to be satisfied with getting Jeptha, Aunt Lu, and Zina away."

She nodded, though the pain remained in her eyes.

They discussed their plans a while longer, then Seth walked her back to the house, keeping to the shadows of the oaks.

"It will all be over in a few days," he said, his voice low in the darkness. "Then we can start our new life together." His forced cheerfulness didn't bring the smile to her face he'd hoped to see.

"But what will the lives of the slaves be like after they are sold?"

Her solemn question dogged him all the way back to his cabin.

CHAPTER TWENTY-SEVEN

"Ah, there you are, Adella Rose."

Startled by Marshall's voice in the otherwise silent barn, Adella jumped, causing the apple she was about to offer Freedom to drop to the ground and roll out of his reach. Turning, she wondered how Marshall had found her here since he and Papa disappeared into the library shortly after breakfast. George and Natalie had gone to the Langfords' for the day, leaving Adella free to ready her belongings for their journey. She'd come down to the barn in search of a saddlebag but couldn't resist bringing a treat to the magnificent horse.

"Marshall," she said with a nervous smile. "I didn't realize you were looking for me. The library door was closed, so I assumed you and Papa had more business to discuss."

"We did, briefly." He drew up next to her, his eyes taking liberty in their pursuit of her face and then her body. "But I have had enough talk of business. I want to spend time with my bride today. I thought perhaps we could ask the cook to prepare a picnic lunch, and we could go for a ride together." He caressed her cheek. "We have had so little time alone."

A shiver of unease raced through her. Retrieving the apple, more to put distance between them than anything, she forced herself to appear unaffected by his touch. "Oh, Marshall, you know I am far too busy packing to enjoy such frivolity."

He clutched his heart in mock offense. "You wound me, Adella Rose."

Keeping space between them, she smiled. "I am sure Papa would enjoy a ride in the country as you men did before George's wedding. Perhaps you could go hunting. Aunt Lu mentioned how nice it would be to have venison roast for supper."

His brow pulled into a frown. "If I go hunting, it won't be on the whim of a slave. You are far too accommodating of your servants, Adella Rose. After we are married, and you assume your role as mistress of Le Beau, I will expect you to manage the household with a firm hand. I don't believe in coddling the slaves, nor do I believe in befriending them. Is that understood?"

Angry words rushed to her mouth, but she bit them back, knowing there was no point in arguing with the man. She would never be mistress of Le Beau. "I am sorry you feel that way, Marshall," she said instead. "You, of course, are master of your home and may dictate the rules as you please."

"Thank you." He seemed satisfied with her swift compliance. "I have every confidence you will learn quickly. The bad habits you have acquired while growing up with indulgent parents will diminish with proper training."

She stood with her mouth agape at the insult. "Bad habits and indulgent parents?"

"Yes. It is clear to me you have been allowed more freedom than a daughter should be given. The fact that a Negro boy was your closest companion is horrifying at best. I blame your mother, as I am sure your father was far too busy running Rose Hill to be aware of such things. Your mother, however, should have known better."

How dare he!

She clenched her fists to keep from pummeling the infuriating man. "My mother was the dearest woman in the world, Mr. Brevard. Should you ever speak of her again to me, you will do so with the respect due the deceased."

His eyes narrowed. "As you will address me with the respect due your husband."

Never!

She turned her back to him. "I don't believe we will be able to spend the day together. I have quite a list of things I need to get done."

"And yet you found time to come down to the barn to give a horse an apple?"

The hardness in his voice brought her attention back to his face. "I needed something from the barn, for my packing. I thought to bring Free ... the horse a treat. He is such a beauty, I can't resist."

Closing the distance between them in a swift stride, Marshall took Adella in a rough embrace. "My thoughts exactly," he said before forcing his mouth onto hers. The kiss was painful and demanding and held nothing of the sweet passion she felt when Seth kissed her.

Pushing against him, Adella broke free. "How dare you? You have no right to treat me in such a vulgar manner."

"I have every right, Adella Rose." He grabbed her again and brought her hard up against his body. "You are mine, and I have had just about enough of your naïve virginal rebuffs. We will be husband and wife in two days. It is time you understood what that means."

Fearing he intended to assault her there in the barn, Adella struggled to break free. "Let go of me!"

But he was stronger and had her up against the wall, his hands roaming her body, when the sound of someone whistling reached them. Marshall cursed under his breath and released her just as Moses came around the corner, carrying a bucket.

"Oh, Mistah Brevard, Missy Ellis. Didn't know you folks was here. I jest comin' to feed ol' black there an' give him a good brushin'." He moved past them and opened Freedom's stall.

Marshall glared at the black man's back. "Do you have to do that now?"

"Oh, yessuh, Mistah Brevard, suh. Mistah Brantley done tol' me to get on in here an' get this ol' hoss taken care of. Wouldn't want him to find I ain't done it like he asked."

Marshall cursed again. "Come along, Adella Rose." He reached for her hand, but she jerked away. His hard stare bored into her. "I said, come along."

With a step away from him, she shook her head. "No. I am upset, and I want to be alone."

Tension practically sparked the air. With a glance at Moses, who pretended he was engrossed in currying Freedom, Marshall dipped his head, though his tightly clenched jaw revealed his anger. "As you wish. I will see you at the house, where we will continue our discussion."

He took his leave, stalking away without a backward glance. Seth would be furious if he learned what had transpired. She looked over at Moses, who hummed quietly while working a hard-bristled brush along Freedom's flanks.

"I suppose you heard everything." She felt weary from the pretense and uncertainty of the past several weeks. If only she and Seth were headed west to Oregon by now—all these troubles would be behind them.

"Ain't none o' my biz'ness, Missy. I jest comin' ta do my job an' hears some unpleasantness is all."

With a heavy sigh, she nodded. "Thank you, Moses."

He glanced up. "You's welcome." A knowing look shone in his steady gaze.

She walked over to stand on Freedom's other side. The horse's eyes were half closed, as though he enjoyed the grooming immensely. "He certainly is a different horse than when they first brought him in."

Moses chuckled. "I 'spect so, Missy. I heard he 'bout as wild as a hoss can be when they cotched him. But," he paused, glancing at her, "now he gonna fill a pu'pose the Good Lawd knew 'bout fo' he done got cotched. He jes' like the rest of us'n's now."

"How so?" she asked, intrigued.

"God gots a pu'pose for ever'body, I 'spect. Even critters. Sometimes he got to break the wildness outta us 'fore he can use us, though. Sometimes bad things has ta happen in order fo' the good to take place."

"Are you saying bad things can end up being good?"

"Yassum, I 'spect I is."

Skeptical, she said, "I'm not sure I agree with you, Moses. Take slavery, for instance. How can you being a slave end up being good?"

A soft smile filled his face. "'Cuz I a slave, I met my Harriet, an' we's blessed with five chillens. Don't get me wrong, Missy. I not sayin' I like bein' a slave, but I found some happiness in the midst of it."

She thought of Seth. His injury prevented him from returning to the Rangers, but it brought him to Rose Hill. If he hadn't been shot by the runaway slave, he would have never come to work as their overseer, and she would have no choice but to marry Marshall.

"I think I understand what you're saying."

"Ain't al'ays easy to find the good, but it there, if we'uns look hard 'nough."

Leaving the barn a short time later, she had the strangest feeling his words were meant to prepare her for something. With all the uncertainty and danger involved in their plan to leave Rose Hill, she could imagine all kinds of bad things happening. Would God really bring good from it all?

She glanced in the direction of the quarter, knowing she had a difficult decision to make. Her heart told her to take Lucy and the baby with them when they escaped, but Seth had already voiced his opposition to the idea. His reasons made sense, of course. Taking a new mother fresh from childbirth and her infant on a long, arduous journey was beyond foolish. Yet Adella could not shake the certainty she felt that the baby would be in danger if she remained at Rose Hill. She couldn't bear knowing that she'd had the opportunity to save her own niece from a life as a slave and yet did nothing.

Biting her lip, she came to a conclusion. She would speak to Lucy. If the young woman expressed a desire to go with them, then

Seth would simply have to trust her decision.

❧ ❧

Early in the morning on the day of the planned escape, long
before the horizon began to grow light, Seth quietly made his way
to the shed behind the quarter. For the past several days, he'd snuck
food and milk to Jeptha, hoping to get the young slave travel-
ready. They would have no time for rest stops once they left Rose
Hill. His time with the Rangers taught him the first few days were
critical. They had to put many miles between them and Rose Hill,
which would require hours of hard riding, only giving the animals
a short rest from time to time. They would keep that pace until he
was certain they were far enough away to give them a lead, but
even then, the journey to the border would demand everything
they had.

Even before he could make out the silhouette of the shed in the
dark, the foul stench told him he'd arrived.

"Jeptha?" He kept his voice lowered, glancing toward the rows
of cabins to make certain no light shone from a window, indicating
someone was awake this early.

A rustling noise came from inside the shack. "Yassuh," came his
sleepy voice. "I here."

Seth had to grin. Where else would the slave be? "How are you
holding up?"

Jeptha's face appeared in the hole, the whites of his eyes glowing
in the darkness. "I better, thanks to the food you's been bringin'.
Befo', I weak as a newborn kitten, but now I feeling stronger. Been
movin' around in here some, kinda runnin' in the same spot to get
my muscles goin'."

"Good." Seth breathed a sigh of relief. They couldn't afford to
take Jeptha if he were ill or too weak from deprivation. "If all goes
as planned, we'll leave tonight."

Jeptha's eyes widened. "Tonight? Whoo-wee. Jes' the three of us? You, me, and Missy?"

Recalling Jeptha's feelings for Zina, he wasn't sure how the slave would react when he learned Zina and Aunt Lu were also escaping. "Missy has asked Aunt Lu and Zina to come along."

"Is they?" he said after a few moments.

"Yes."

A grin revealed Jeptha's teeth. "That real good news, Mistah Brantley, suh. Real good."

Seth didn't quite agree, mainly because the more people they took, the more danger everyone was in, but he could understand the young man's pleasure. "I've brought you some food and water— some for drinking and some for bathing. There's also a change of clothes. Don't put them on until it gets dark tonight. And keep them off the ground, if you can," he added as an afterthought, knowing the ground inside the shed must be covered in filth.

Jeptha's hand reached through the hole for the food, jars of water, and clothing. "Yassuh, I do that. Got's a couple nails pokin' through the wood up high I can hang 'em on. Sho' will be nice to get outta these here nasty rags."

"Be ready as soon as it gets dark," Seth said, his heart pounding. They were really going to do this thing tonight. It seemed surreal.

"How you gonna get me out of here, if you don't mind my askin'?"

"Master Luther keeps the key to the padlock in a drawer in his study." Seth lowered his voice even further. "Aunt Lu will get it sometime today."

Several seconds passed before Jeptha gave a low whistle. "Sho' makes me nervous, what we's 'bout to do."

Hearing that, Seth felt it only fair to make sure the slave knew all the dangers they faced, in case he wanted to change his mind. "You know if we are caught, they will beat you. You could also hang."

"I knows it, suh," came his quiet reply. "The patterollers killed my pappy when he done tried to run away."

Seth's brow rose in surprise. "I didn't know that. How long ago did that happen?"

"I not more'n a baby at the time. It befo' Massa Luther buy my mama an' me. Mama say our ol' massa sold us on account o' my pappy causin' trouble." He paused. "Guess I followin' in his footsteps. Befo' she die, Mama tells me freedom in my blood. She be right proud if she knew I chasin' it down."

Seth thought of the slave he'd encountered at the border. Like Jeptha's father, that man had risked everything for freedom. Sending up a silent prayer, he hoped the fate of those other men would not be Jeptha's.

Light edged the eastern horizon. The slaves would be up and about soon, and he didn't want to be seen near the shed. The less folks knew about who was involved in the escape, the better.

"Be ready. I don't know when exactly we'll come for you, but once we leave Rose Hill lands, we will need to ride hard and fast."

"Mistah Brantley?" Jeptha's tone was uncertain. "Why you doin' this? You an' Missy could leave here easy 'nough without goin' to all the trouble to take me and them others with you. If we gets caught, you be in jest as much trouble as us'n's."

It was a question Seth had pondered for days. "I guess you could say I have learned some things about myself since coming to Rose Hill that I didn't much like. Hopefully, this is a way to set things right."

Returning to his cabin, the magnitude of what they were about to do weighed heavily on him. What if they were caught? Would they all face the hangman's noose because of him? The lives of four other people depended on his knowledge and expertise. They trusted he could get them safely to Mexico. But what if he made a wrong choice on the trail?

Ramming his hands into his pockets, the cool smoothness of Oliver's stone met his touch. He removed the rock and studied it, remembering what Mammy had told the boy. Could God really make a sinner's heart as white as the stone? Did God even care about his creation? Looking at the world around him, Seth had his doubts.

But what if God did indeed care? What if he actually heard the cry of the helpless, wanting to guide the sinner home?

Grasping the rock in his fist, Seth fell to his knees.

"God in heaven, I need your help."

CHAPTER TWENTY-EIGHT

Adella stood in her dressing gown at her window, gazing out at the new morning. Clear blue sky and birdsong greeted her, as though it were just an ordinary day, rather than the last time she would wake up in her room and look out on Rose Hill land. The scent of Mama's roses wafted upward on a light breeze, bringing tears to her eyes. Oh, how she would miss the vibrant colors and perfume from the dozens of bushes decorating the house's landscape. Leaving them was almost as hard as leaving Mama's grave, which she had visited the day before. Though she knew her mother was long in heaven, it still troubled her to know she might never place flowers beneath the stone marker again.

Had Mama felt this way leaving her home and family back in Virginia when she and Papa set out for Texas? The circumstances had been different, of course. Papa and Daniel Brantley had been invited by Stephen Austin himself—whose father had been friends with Grandfather Ellis years before—to join him and other settlers in the lands newly acquired from Mexico. It must have been frightening for Mama to climb into a covered wagon with her baby boy, heading into territory inhabited by various Indian tribes and very few white people. But she'd followed the man she loved in much the same way Adella would.

An idea sprang to her heart. Mama brought cuttings of rosebushes with them when she and Papa left Virginia. Couldn't she also take one with her when she and Seth left tonight? The very thought lifted her spirits and brought a sense of urgency. As soon as she could, she'd go to the kitchen and ask Aunt Lu for a burlap bag. Surely they could find room for one small plant.

After turning from the window, Adella dressed in the gown she'd specifically chosen for her last day at Rose Hill. The deep coral had been Mama's favorite color, and Papa always commented that Adella reminded him of Mama when she wore it. If nothing else, she wanted her father's last memories of her to be favorable. That he would be furious when he discovered her betrayal, as he would most assuredly view her marriage to Seth, left her heavy with regret.

A soft knock sounded at the door.

"Come in." She gave the room a quick scan to be certain the two valises she'd packed were tucked out of sight beneath the bed. Not even Hulda knew of her plans, despite the older woman's presence in and out of Adella's rooms. Knowing Papa would question the servant after he discovered Adella missing, she didn't want to put her former nurse in jeopardy and force her to lie. Surely Papa wouldn't sell the old woman in his fury.

When the door opened, Adella was surprised to see Natalie enter the room. "Why, Natalie, dear, you're up early." She tried to smile, but apprehension prevented one from forming. They hadn't found another opportunity to discuss Adella's situation after their conversation in the dining room. With Natalie's mother unwell, the young woman felt obligated to attend to Mrs. Langford, which meant spending several days and a night away from Rose Hill.

"I hoped to speak with you before we go downstairs to breakfast." The grave tone in Natalie's voice worried Adella.

"Oh? Come, let us sit." She motioned to the two matching chairs that flanked the ornate fireplace.

Once they were seated, Natalie's expression grew serious. "Adella Rose, your wedding to Marshall is tomorrow. I simply must know what you plan to do. In all honesty, I didn't expect to find you still here when I returned home last evening. In fact, I hoped you would be gone, that is if you insist on continuing with your ridiculous notion to marry Mr. Brantley."

"Is it ridiculous to marry a man I love, Natalie?" she asked, hurt by the other woman's disapproving tone. "I know you had feelings for George before you married, and I hope they have grown since your wedding day. Surely you understand why I must choose to follow my heart."

Natalie's fine brows drew together. "We are not discussing my marriage, Adella Rose. You have put me in a very difficult position. Knowing your intentions regarding Mr. Brantley, as well as knowing the financial predicament of Rose Hill, makes me wonder if telling your father what is going on is for the best."

Adella stared at Natalie with wide eyes, panic racing through her veins at the very thought of Papa learning of their plans. "You can't, Natalie. I took you into my confidence as my sister and friend when I disclosed those details to you."

"I realize that." Natalie seemed to back down for a moment. "But I have had time to think it over since then. What you are doing is not right. Your father made an agreement with Marshall, and you as his daughter must honor it, despite your feelings for Mr. Brantley. I am sure, given time, you will come to care for Marshall. He seems a pleasant man and can offer you far more than a poor overseer ever will."

"I thought you understood. I see I was wrong." Adella stood and walked to the window. Acres of cotton fields stretched over the horizon, with slaves already hard at work ridding the ground of weeds. If Natalie was determined to reveal their plan to Papa, Adella must act quickly and get word to Seth. All their careful plotting would be for naught if they had to flee prematurely. Jeptha and the others would have to be left behind, and she couldn't bear to think of what would happen to them amid Papa's anger.

"I understand you believe you are in love with Mr. Brantley." Natalie lifted her hand to look at the gold band on her finger. "But sometimes we have to put away our girlish notions of what marriage and love are and accept the realities we face as daughters and wives of important men."

Adella shook her head. "I don't want that reality, Natalie. I would rather have the love of a good man and live a humble life than live in a mansion with a man I can barely tolerate. What happiness could there ever be in an existence such as that?"

Unexpected tears sprang to Natalie's eyes, and she turned away.

"Natalie?" Adella hurried over and knelt at her sister-in-law's feet. "What is it? I didn't mean to hurt you, if indeed it was my words that brought these tears."

Waving Adella away, Natalie quickly composed herself. "You should not speak of things you know nothing about, Adella Rose. Many women sacrifice for the good of their families. A loveless marriage is nothing new. My own mother bettered her family by marrying my father, and I—"

She pressed trembling lips together and looked away.

Adella grasped the other woman's hands. "I'm sorry, Natalie," she whispered. "More than anything, I wish happiness for you and George."

"Then marry Marshall." Natalie's words were tinged with anger. "Without Marshall's money, Rose Hill could be lost. Do you want that on your conscience? Your family's heritage gone because you selfishly chose to disobey your father's wishes?"

Adella closed her eyes, the truth of Natalie's words knifing through her heart. The accusing questions were not unfamiliar. She herself had examined her motives for days, knowing if she married Seth, it put the plantation and Papa in a precarious position. Yet she clung to the belief that Marshall would, in the end, do what would benefit him, which was keep to the business agreement.

Resolved, she met Natalie's gaze. "I can't marry Marshall. Seth and I will leave tonight." There was no need to mention the slaves that would accompany them. The less information Natalie possessed regarding the escape, the better. "If you believe it is your duty to inform Papa, then so be it, but it won't change anything. As your sister, however, I am asking you for your silence."

For a long moment, she waited for Natalie to respond.

Finally, the young woman gave a slow nod. "I believe you are making a grave mistake, Adella Rose, but I will keep your secret."

Adella practically wilted with relief. "Thank you, Natalie. I have one last request. Please take charge of Carolina. She is a sweet girl, and I fear what Papa might do after I'm gone." It broke Adella's heart to leave the child behind, but Carolina's mother and siblings belonged to Papa. With Zina gone, Natalie would be in need of a maid.

Natalie frowned, but she nodded. "Very well."

With tears stinging her eyes, Adella embraced her sister-in-law, knowing they would most likely not have another opportunity to say good-bye. "You will be in my prayers. I will write as soon as I can and let you know where we are."

"You had better." Natalie tightened her arms around Adella. When she pulled away, she sniffled. "Here I thought I was finally getting a sister."

"We will always be sisters," Adella said, smiling through her own tears.

After Natalie departed, Adella went to her bureau and retrieved a cameo brooch Natalie had admired on more than one occasion. She would leave it for the young woman with a note expressing her love and gratitude. She also needed to write a note for her father and one for Marshall. The latter would offer her sincere apology for any embarrassment she caused by disappearing the day before their wedding and beg him to please keep his agreement with her father to make Rose Hill solvent again.

With pen and paper, she sat at her desk to compose the most difficult letter of her life.

Dear Papa …

※ ※

Seated at the long servants' table in the kitchen, Seth stared at the lukewarm supper on his plate while Aunt Lu bustled about, casting nervous glances his way. It was imperative he speak with her in private, but Celia continued to mill about, not really accomplishing anything but apparently hoping to look busy. Preparations for the wedding supper were laid out, and Seth had to commend Aunt Lu for thinking of it. Appearing as though nothing were out of the ordinary was essential to the success of their escape.

With nerves on edge, Seth tried to eat, knowing he'd need the nourishment for the long days ahead. But despite the tenderness of the pork roast and seasoned potatoes, he had a hard time swallowing. Tangible fear seemed lodged in his throat now that the hour they'd waited for was upon them.

Finally, after an exasperated sigh, Aunt Lu dismissed the girl. "Ain't nothin' else need doin' in here, Celia. Get on home now. Gots a busy day tomorrow." As soon as Celia disappeared, Aunt Lu's shoulders sagged. "Didn't think we's ever gonna be rid o' dat worthless gal."

"Are you ready?" he asked, keeping his voice low. There was no need to explain what he meant.

She nodded. "Uh-huh. We gots our bundles hid up yonder," she said, pointing to the stairs that led to the room she shared with Zina. "My Zina 'fraid Miss Natalie knows somethin'. She keep lookin' at her strange-like."

"As far as I know, Natalie is only aware that Missy and I will leave tonight. If she has suspicions of anything else, she didn't mention them to Adella."

"May jest be we's on edge, what with all the sneakin' an' secrets."

"And the key?" he asked.

With a cautious glance toward the door, she took a small item out of her apron pocket and handed it to him. "Weren't no problem gettin' it while I dustin' an' straightenin' things. Don't 'spect Massa even miss it, 'cuz I put an ol' key from the cellar lock in the drawer where this un be. Look 'bout the same to me."

Seth grinned. "You are a genius, Aunt Lu."

She smiled. "If that word means I smart, then I reckon I is a gen'us."

"We'll leave as soon as everyone settles in for the night. Meet in the barn, in the tack room. If you get there before me, hide somewhere until I call for you." As he'd done with Jeptha, he wanted to be sure the woman understood the danger of what they were about to do. "You don't have to do this, you know. If we get caught, I won't be able to protect you or Zina. Master Luther will be furious when he discovers you're missing. I have no doubt the patrollers will be on our trail all the way to Mexico."

A grave look shadowed her eyes. "Massa Luther tells Missy he sell me if she don't marry up with Mistah Brevard. I 'spect he'd keep his word after you'uns leave, he be so mad. I seen that man's hatefulness when he angry. Reckon he make sure I sold to some worthless white man to work them fields." She shook her head. "I too old for that, Mistah Brantley, suh. Seems best to take a chance on bein' free an' live out my days in ol' Mexico if that where the Good Lawd wants me."

Seth couldn't argue with her logic. "I will do my best to get you there safely."

A peaceful smile rested on her face. "That's what I prayin' fo'."

After leaving the kitchen, Seth took the path around to the front of the main house. Windows were open to let in the evening breeze, and he heard rumbles of voices from within. Quietly, he gained the porch, hoping to steal a peek into the parlor, where he supposed the group would be gathered for the night.

Keeping hidden behind a large potted plant, Seth saw the backs of George and Marshall seated on the sofa nearest the window. Adella and her father were out of sight, but Luther's laughter at something Marshall said made his presence known. Natalie sat facing the window. When Seth edged closer to try to glimpse Adella, Natalie's brow furrowed, and she leaned forward as though she'd seen him in the darkness.

Jerking back behind the plant, he decided it wouldn't be good to be found on the porch. Luther had already made his dislike of Seth clear. They didn't need an altercation hours before the escape.

Just as he reached the bottom step in his quest to get away, the front door opened. Thinking Adella must have somehow known he was there, he turned.

"Natalie." He was surprised to find the petite blonde coming toward him. A quick glance into the lighted foyer told him she was alone.

"I would like a word with you, *Mr. Brantley*." Her accentuation of his name served as a reminder to address her more formally. She was, after all, married to the son of the plantation owner. Carefully, she descended the stairs, with the muted light from the windows offering the only aid in the otherwise dark night.

"Of course, Mrs. Ellis." He remained where he stood. The farther away from those windows, the better. Especially since he had an idea of what she wanted to discuss.

"I hope you know what you are doing, Mr. Brantley." Her voice was low but her tone hard. "Adella Rose is not thinking with her head, so I have come here to ask you to please reconsider this foolishness. Let her do her duty to her family and marry Marshall."

He'd expected this, but it still rankled. "With all due respect, Mrs. Ellis, Adella has made her choice. If it helps, I want you to know I will do everything in my power to make her happy. Our life won't be easy in the beginning, but I will work hard to provide everything she could ever need or want."

The frown on her dainty brow indicated what she thought of his promises. "So you won't even consider riding away alone tonight? Even if I offered you a substantial payment?"

Seth's eyes widened. "Are you offering me a bribe?"

"Call it what you will. I am simply looking out for the interests of my husband and the future of Rose Hill."

The voices from inside grew louder, followed by laughter.

"I appreciate your loyalty to your family, Mrs. Ellis, but I must decline. I love Adella. You can't put a price on that."

A long moment ticked by before her face softened. "You really do love her, don't you?"

"Yes, I do." He smiled despite the seriousness of the situation. "I don't know why she loves me, but I am going to do my best to deserve it."

She gave a slight nod. "I imagine you will." She cast a glance at the house, and Seth wondered at the longing he read in her eyes. When she looked at him again, she blinked away a sheen of tears. "God go with you, Mr. Brantley. Take care of my Adella Rose."

She turned and hurried up the steps and into the house.

Seth made his way back to his cabin, thankful Natalie was no longer a concern. Her silence was granted, it seemed, as well as her blessing. Though it didn't matter to Seth, he knew Adella would appreciate her sister-in-law's kind words.

If everything else fell into place, they would leave Rose Hill in a matter of hours.

CHAPTER TWENTY-NINE

The clock on the parlor mantel chimed midnight, echoing in the stillness of the house. Adella stood on the upstairs landing, still as a statue, making certain no one stirred below. Earlier, when Papa brought out the liquor decanter, she'd retired to her room. Despite Marshall's pleas for her to stay, she'd declared her need to rest before the morrow, which was true. Her undoing nearly came, however, when she gave Natalie a goodnight hug. The other woman held her tightly, bringing Adella to tears. It was several hours later when the drunken voices finally quieted.

After the timepiece grew silent and all was quiet again, she tiptoed forward, the two valises she carried heavy weights in her hands. Beads of perspiration broke out on her face, both from nerves and from the cloak she wore. Though summer heat currently greeted them each day, she would need the warm garment later; yet she had no room in either case to pack it and was forced to wear it.

Gaining the bottom of the stairs, she moved soundlessly down the hall leading away from the foyer. It seemed wiser to exit the back of the house than go through the front door. Though everyone was asleep, she couldn't help feeling the whole plantation knew of their plans and was prepared to stop them.

Passing by the kitchen wing, Adella peeked through the window, wondering if Aunt Lu and Zina had already made their way to the barn. The three had decided earlier not to meet here but would regroup in the barn with Seth and Jeptha.

And Lucy and Mara.

Adella's stomach fluttered with nervousness. She hadn't yet told Seth the mother and baby were joining them. What if he refused to take them? But her conversation with Lucy repeated in her mind, and she knew she'd made the right decision.

"Oh, Missy," Lucy cried, tears streaming down her face when Adella whispered the invitation to her. "I prayed to the Lawd for a way to get this lil' angel away from here, but ain't no way fo' me ta leave on my own. Yo' brother come down here the night he gets back from his trip. Says he don't want Miss Natalie to ever find out 'bout Mara, so's he gonna have to get rid o' her. I cryin' an' beggin', but he say she cain't stay. Soon as she old 'nough, he gonna take her to the market."

A chill swept Adella at the memory. The callousness of her own brother astonished her, but she also knew he would do exactly what he said. He would sell his own child to cover his sin.

The warm night air nearly suffocated her as she hurried across the yard toward the barn. Seth had warned her to use the smaller back door instead of the larger one, whose hinges groaned fiercely when opened. Stealing into the dark building, she was tempted to light a lantern, but gradually her eyes adjusted to the darkness. Carefully, she made her way to the tack room where they were to meet. Horses stirred in their stalls when she passed. One whinnied. Finally, she arrived at the door and slowly opened it.

Three women crouched together in the shadow of feeble lantern light. A wide sling wrapped around Lucy's shoulder held the baby sleeping peacefully against her chest.

"Missy," Aunt Lu said, sagging with relief. "We uns thought fo' sho' we done got catched befo' we even gets started."

Adella set her bags down and gave each woman a hug. "Have you seen Seth?"

They shook their heads.

"He is probably getting Jeptha. We will wait here for him like he instructed."

But as the minutes ticked by and he didn't arrive, fear started to wear her nerves raw. Finally, unable to bear it a moment longer, she stood. "He should have been here by now. I must find out what's taking so long."

The others nodded, but the faint moonlight coming through the small window reflected their own worry.

Leaving off the cloak, she was again thankful she'd chosen a simple dark blue dress that would blend in with the night shadows. When she arrived at Seth's cabin, Adella called his name with a loud whisper. Her heart pounded as she waited, but there was no response. Fearing something might be wrong, she reached for the latch on the door. Again, she called for him, but the small cabin was empty, save for a few furniture silhouettes.

Uncertain if she should go back to the barn or keep searching, her gaze settled on the dark area behind the quarter. Perhaps Seth was having difficulties getting Jeptha free from the shed. She knew Aunt Lu had given him the key, but maybe the lock wouldn't budge, or some other problem arose. Hurrying in that direction, under the shadow of the great oaks that dotted the property, Adella had almost reached the edge of the quarter when a dark figure leaped out from behind a tree trunk. A scream began in her throat, but a strong hand clamped down on her mouth.

Her heart thundered in her ears. Had Monroe recovered and now lurked in the darkness? Would he do to her what he'd attempted with Zina?

Her knees gave way and blackness claimed her.

❧ ❦

"Adella Rose!"

The urgent whisper, accompanied by a none-too-gentle shake, brought her eyes open. Seth's face loomed above her, and above him loomed starlit sky amid tree branches.

"Thank goodness." He cradled her in his arms. Her cheek rested against his chest, and she felt his rapid heartbeat through the material.

"What—" she began, only to have him put his hand over her

mouth again, this time, more gently.

"Shhh," he whispered.

With his help, she sat up and sent him a questioning gaze. He nodded toward the quarter. Looking in that direction, Adella saw light came from one of the cabin windows. Someone was awake.

"We can't release Jeptha until whoever is awake goes to bed." He spoke against her ear, his warm breath sending tingles down her neck. "I have been watching for the past hour. No one should have a light on. They know it's against the rules. I am tempted to find out who it is, but I would rather not let anyone see me."

"No," Adella agreed. "We can wait. Surely whoever it is will turn in soon."

Seth heaved a sigh. "I hope so. We should have been on the road by now. Are Aunt Lu and Zina in the barn?"

She nodded. "Yes." Knowing now was the time to confess, she took a deep breath. "And Lucy and the baby."

Shock registered on Seth's face. "Adella, I told you we couldn't take them."

"I know." Torn between the need to obey his wishes and the sureness that taking the mother and child was the right thing to do, she'd gone with her gut instincts. "George told Lucy he planned to sell Mara as soon as she was old enough. He doesn't want Natalie to know of his indiscretions."

"That doesn't surprise me." Seth's brow pulled into a frown. "But taking them along puts us all in jeopardy. I don't have enough provisions for her."

"I told Aunt Lu to pack some extra things."

After a moment, he blew out a breath. "We will need a miracle to get to Mexico without being caught."

Grasping his hand, she kissed his knuckles. "Then that is what we will pray for."

❦

They sat in the dark for several minutes before the light in the cabin finally extinguished. Giving whoever had been awake time to settle in before releasing Jeptha, Seth was surprised when the cabin door opened a short time later, and someone exited. A tall form walked past the other cabins, heading in the direction of the main house, directly in front of where Seth and Adella crouched.

He felt her grip his arm. Practically holding his breath, Seth wondered if George was up to his old shenanigans again. But with Lucy hiding in the barn with Aunt Lu and Zina, whose cabin had he been visiting?

The man passed through the shadows beneath the tree, and when pale moonlight touched his face, Adella gasped.

Marshall Brevard slowed and glanced behind him. "Celia?" he hissed. "Is that you following me, girl?" He cursed, moving his head side to side as though trying to see into the darkness.

When no answer came, he waited a few moments longer before continuing on to the house.

Sickened, Seth turned to find Adella's hand over her mouth. He gathered her in his arms and felt her shake with silent sobs. With more gratitude than he could ever express, he thanked God for keeping her from marrying that man. There was not a doubt in his mind Brevard would continue his sordid behavior even with a wife as beautiful as Adella.

After several minutes, Seth moved so he could see her face. He cupped her cheeks with his hands. "You are safe from him," he whispered. "You never have to see him again."

"I know." Tears flooded her eyes.

With one last embrace, Seth helped Adella stand. His leg cramped and ached from crouching so long, and he dreaded how much it would hurt during the long journey ahead. The small bottle of Mammy's ointment he'd packed would have to last him until they reached the border.

"We need to get out of here. I'll get Jeptha. Go back to the barn, and I will meet you and the others there. Chester, Freedom, and another horse are already saddled."

"All right," she said, her voice trembling.

Seth kissed her softly. "It will be over soon."

Nodding, she turned back toward the barn and disappeared into the dark night. On silent feet, Seth made his way to the shed.

"Jeptha?"

Movement sounded right away. "Whoo-wee, Mistah Brantley," he whispered. "I done figured you's gone wit'out me."

Removing the key from his pocket, Seth quickly had the door open. "We had a bit of delay, so we will have to make up time by riding hard." He looked at the slave in the moonlight. "You're sure you're up for this?"

"Yassuh." Jeptha smiled. "I can almost taste freedom."

Seth closed the door and replaced the lock. He noticed Jeptha had the fresh clothes on. "The others are waiting for us in the barn."

Jeptha fell into step beside Seth. "I cleaned up best I could with the water you brung, but I'd like to wash my feet in the trough if that be all right."

Though their voices were barely above a whisper, each word seemed to echo in the still night. Seth put his finger to his lips then pointed to the trough near the barn door, to which Jeptha nodded. Leaving Jeptha to his bath, Seth went inside to prepare the women.

Adella hurried to him when he opened the tack room door. "Is everyone ready?" He glanced at the slave women, taking note the baby slept in some sort of holder Lucy wore around her torso. They could only hope the infant stayed asleep and quiet until they were far away from the plantation. A crying baby would alert the world to their presence.

"We're ready." Adella offered a tremulous smile.

Jeptha entered the small room then. With a little cry, Adella went to him and made to hug him, but he put his hand out to stop her. "I a mess, Missy. Don't want you gettin' my stench on you."

"Nonsense." She ignored his warning and hugged him anyway. When she pulled away, Seth noticed a slight smile on Jeptha's face. "I have something for you." Adella reached into the deep pocket of her skirt, pulled out a folded paper and handed it to him.

"What's this?"

"It is a letter stating you are a free man."

Seth was as surprised as Jeptha appeared. He hadn't known she planned to forge freedom papers, but he had to admit it was a wise move.

Jeptha stared at Adella, wide-eyed. "It be real?"

Adella shook her head. "I wish it were. I wrote it and signed Papa's name." She motioned to the women. "They each have one too. In case we get separated, or something happens, it might fool someone long enough for you to get to the border."

Jeptha stared at the document in his hands for a long moment, then looked at Adella. "Thank you, Missy. Just havin' this piece of paper, though it isn't real, means freedom is real. And it will be mine—ours," he looked at the women, "very soon."

The change in Jeptha's speech was amazing. Listening, Seth would never have believed he wasn't an educated man if he hadn't known better.

Aunt Lu's mouth fell open. "How you learn ta talk like that?"

Jeptha smiled at Adella, who grinned. "I had a good teacher."

"We need to saddle up," Seth said, anxious to be on the road. "Jeptha, you and Zina ride Freedom. Aunt Lu and Lucy will take the mare."

The group sprang into motion. Bags were gathered and tied to saddles, though each slave had only a small bundle. They quietly led the horses out of the barn. When Seth lifted Adella onto Chester's back, she turned to look at him, her eyes wide and luminous.

"No regrets?" he asked softly, knowing this had to be extremely difficult for her. To leave her family home with the possibility of never returning would give anyone doubts.

But the tender smile on her lips reassured him. "No regrets. I am ready to begin our life together."

With a slight squeeze of her hand, he turned to help Aunt Lu and Lucy. Jeptha and Zina were already mounted. It took three attempts to get Aunt Lu into the saddle.

"Oh, Lawsy." Her eyes rounded and her fists clenched around the saddle horn. "I ain't sat a hoss since I's a chile."

Seth chuckled. "This horse is real gentle. You won't have any problems getting her to do what you want."

He turned to help Lucy and realized they had a problem. With Lucy wearing the baby in a sling on her chest, she couldn't sit behind Aunt Lu without squashing the child.

"Can you put the baby on your back?"

"I can try," Lucy said.

Just as she undid the knot at her shoulder and started to carefully twist the wrap without waking the baby, Aunt Lu gasped. Seth looked up at her, but she was staring at something behind him.

When he turned, all his hopes for the future with Adella vanished in an instant.

Marshall Brevard stood in the shadows of the barn, a gun pointed at Seth's head.

CHAPTER THIRTY

"Well, well, what do we have here?"

Adella whirled around in the saddle, shocked to hear Marshall's voice behind her. Terror filled every crevice of her being when she saw his gun trained at Seth.

For just a moment, his gaze flitted to her. "I can't say I am shocked to find my bride running away with her lover, but I am disappointed in you, Adella Rose. You had me fooled. I thought you actually cared about your family and Rose Hill. I see I was wrong."

"I do care," she began, but Seth shook his head.

"You don't need to explain yourself to him, Adella. Your father gave us no other choice."

Marshall laughed without humor. "And stealing his slaves? I suppose he gave you no choice in that either. I had a suspicion something sinister was taking place. It is good I came to check on it."

"I suppose you got that suspicion as you left the quarter a little while ago."

Surprise washed across Marshall's face for a brief moment at Seth's words before he sneered. "You see, that is your problem, Brantley. You don't mind your own business. Helping slaves escape isn't exactly saintly behavior, now is it?"

"These folks are leaving of their own accord." Seth stood his ground despite the danger. Adella sent a silent prayer heavenward that Marshall would not accidentally fire the gun in his anger.

After a moment, Marshall smiled. "I will enjoy watching you hang, Brantley. You have been a thorn in my side long enough. And just so you know, despite Adella's poor decision tonight, I will still take her as my wife. She is young and foolish, and I can forgive her that. She will thank me, too. No other man would have her once it is found out she was caught running away with the overseer."

Humiliation burned in Adella at his insinuation. "Seth and I are to be married, Marshall. There is nothing improper here except yours and Papa's plans to force me into marriage with you."

He looked at her, and the smile vanished. "I went to your room tonight to leave a present on your bureau so you would find it first thing on our wedding day. When I saw your bed empty, I knew you had run off with him. Get down from that horse, Adella Rose." The hard command echoed in the stillness of the barn behind him. "This nonsense has gone on long enough. You and I will be married as soon as this man's dead body is cut from the hangman's noose."

"No, Marshall." She lifted her chin. "Seth and I are leaving, and there isn't anything you can do about it." She hoped her false bravado fooled him. Inside she was quaking.

"Oh, I think there is plenty I can do, Adella Rose." He cocked the gun and leveled his aim at Seth. "Say good-bye to your lover, dear wife."

"No!" She threw her leg over the saddle and slid to the ground. "Stop this, Marshall."

He grinned, apparently satisfied with her terror. "Step over here now like a good little wife," he said, motioning to his side.

Fear paralyzed her. Seth's very life depended on her next action. She looked at him with indecision.

"Stay where you are, Adella." Seth's eyes implored her to trust him. "He won't shoot me. He may not be much of a gentleman, but he's no murderer."

"You are a fool if you believe I won't shoot you, Brantley. I will be a hero, simply shooting a thief as he tried to make off with stolen property." Marshall looked at Adella again, his full attention on her. "If you don't come here right now, I will blow his head off."

In a flash, Seth leaped forward, knocking Marshall backward. He stumbled but caught himself before falling.

"Why you—"

The gun fired at the same moment a dark figure behind Marshall hit him over the head with something metal. He crashed to the ground, the gun clattering away.

Lucy's baby began to cry, awakened by the commotion.

A dog barked somewhere in the quarter as Moses stepped out of the shadows, a shovel in his hand. "Guess he be out fo' a while," he said matter-of-factly, looking down on Marshall.

Adella rushed to Seth. "Are you hit?" She ran her hands over his arms and chest, praying she didn't find a bullet hole. She'd never been so frightened in all her life.

"No." He looked down at his body as though he expected to see blood. "I'm fine. He missed me." He glanced at the big black man standing over Marshall's body. "Thank you, Moses."

"Oh, Lawsy!" Aunt Lu shrieked, her attention focused below her.

Lucy sat on the ground beside the horse.

Even in the faint moonlight, the red stain spreading across the sling was unmistakable.

❦

Seth knelt beside the young mother, trying to figure out if it was her or the whimpering baby who'd been struck by the stray bullet.

"Oh, Mistah Brantley." Lucy's expression was one of sheer pain, answering his question. "I hurt. I hurt bad."

Adella dropped to her knees beside him. "Let me take the baby so you can see where Lucy's injured," she said, lifting the tiny girl out of the lopsided sling. The baby, her skin almost as white as Adella's hands, quieted.

Removing the swath of fabric, Seth immediately knew it was

as bad as Lucy declared. The bullet hit her just under her breast on her right side. Blood poured from the hole in her dress. With no exit wound on her back, it meant the bullet was still lodged inside. During his Ranger days, Seth had seen enough gunshot wounds to know the chances of Lucy surviving were slim.

His eyes met Adella's. She looked back at him with fear shining through her tears.

"It bad, ain't it, Mistah Brantley?" Lucy's weak voice dragged his attention back to her.

What could he tell the young woman but the truth?

"I'm afraid it is."

She closed her eyes and grimaced. "I knows it. I can feel it." When she nearly toppled over, Seth gently laid her on the ground with the wadded up sling under her head.

Just then a loud voice came from the direction of the big house. Was that George?

"You folks need to get on outta here." Moses knelt beside them. "I takes care o' her."

"We can't leave without her and the baby, Seth," Adella said, her panicked gaze searching his face. She clutched the infant closer. "You know what George will do."

"Lucy is badly injured, Adella. She would never survive the journey." He glanced at Moses. "Take her to my cabin and get Mammy."

The big man nodded. As he reached to gather the wounded woman in his massive arms, Lucy roused. Her gaze sought Adella.

"You takes her wit' you, Missy," she said, pain-filled eyes pleading. "Takes my Mara wit' you."

"I ... I can't," Adella said, clearly shocked by the request. She looked at the baby and back to Lucy.

"Yassum, yous can. She be yo' blood. If yous leave her, she be sold." Tears streamed down Lucy's face, and she grimaced in agony. "I not gonna make it, Missy. Ain't no one ta protect my girl after I gone, 'cept you."

Adella looked down at the baby, her chest heaving.

Another shout sounded up the hill. Seth recognized George's voice, though he couldn't make out the words.

"We have to go." Seth helped Adella to her feet. When her fearful eyes met his, he read her anguish. Taking the baby put them all in greater danger, yet leaving the child to suffer Luther's wrath or George's apathy was beyond cruel. With a glance at the baby's peaceful face, he knew they had to take her. "Hopefully, we can find homesteads along the way where we can buy milk."

Adella released a sob, whether from relief or not, he didn't know. With Moses cradling the injured woman, Adella held up Mara so Lucy could kiss her baby good-bye. Aunt Lu and Zina cried quietly as they watched.

"Tells her 'bout me someday," Lucy whispered, her voice weakening. "Say her mama love her an' wan' her to have a happy life."

"I will," Adella choked.

Seth gently took Adella by the elbow. "We need to go."

With a nod, she allowed him to lead her back to Chester. Taking the tiny bundle from her, Seth waited while Adella mounted. He passed the baby up to her, the responsibility he'd just taken on weighing heavily.

He walked back to Moses. "I hate to involve you in this—"

"I already involved, suh," the big man said, full of confidence.

"Yes, I suppose you are."

"I know you's doin' the right thing, so I glad to he'p." He glanced at Marshall's still form. "What should I do wit' Mistah Brevard there?"

Seth took the key to the shed from his pocket and tucked it in the big man's hand. "This is the key to the shed. I will let you decide what you are willing to do."

"I be prayin' for you all," Moses said. "The Lawd go wit' you."

Seth mounted Chester with Adella and the baby in front of him. The gravity of their situation prevented him from fully enjoying the moment he'd anticipated almost since the day he arrived at Rose Hill and saw Adella standing on the porch, barefoot with her hair tumbling loose. Though he held her in his arms now, with the promise of her becoming his wife soon, the very real danger they faced in the coming days kept his elation at bay.

He looked over at Jeptha astride Freedom, with Zina seated behind. Determination shone on the black man's face. "We're ready, Mr. Brantley."

Their bravery and trust humbled him. *Lord, let me be worthy of it*, he breathed.

With tangible fear in his gut, he nudged Chester forward, the odds of making it safely to the border beyond impossible.

CHAPTER THIRTY-ONE

B one-weary.

That was the only way to describe how Adella felt sitting near the small campfire three nights later. True to his word, Seth pushed them hard once they left Rose Hill land, riding through the night and most of the next day before they stopped to rest. Though the shortest route to the border would have been south, through Austin and San Antonio, Seth felt they would draw far too much attention if they went that direction. Instead, he'd taken them west into the hill country, where disappearing in the thick cedar and mesquite trees and rolling landscape would give them protection as they traveled. The riding was more difficult, often taking them up steep, rocky hills, and on more than one occasion, Adella wondered if they were lost, only to have Seth point out a landmark he recognized from his Ranger days. Once he felt they were out of danger from the patrollers, he'd turn them south toward Mexico.

Her eyelids felt heavy as she watched Jeptha kneel across from her, turning the spit and sending juices from a rabbit down on the hot coals where they sizzled and popped. Not even the delicious aroma of cooking meat roused her, exhaustion filling every crevice of her sore, battered body. Aunt Lu and Zina apparently weren't affected by the promise of food either, because they were stretched out beneath a cedar tree, sound asleep, with baby Mara wedged between them. Seth had gone on a scouting mission and would be back within the hour, hopefully with a full canteen of fresh milk from a nearby farmer. She hoped he didn't plan on making them travel through the night again. It had taken all her strength the last hour of their journey to keep from falling off the horse in a dead sleep.

Jeptha whistled a low tune as he worked to arrange the spit so the meat wouldn't burn. He seemed more invigorated than ever.

"Aren't you exhausted?" she asked, the effort to speak taking far more energy than it should.

He glanced up. "I tired, for sure. But," he paused, a smile lifting one side of his mouth.

"But what?"

He gave a shrug. "I don't expect you to understand this, Missy, but the closer I get to real freedom, the stronger I feel," he tapped his chest, "in here."

"I do understand," she said, her eyes growing misty. "I have known you all my life, and this is what I have always dreamed for you. It only makes me sad that once we reach Mexico, we'll have to leave you there. I may never see you again." A sob caught in her throat.

Jeptha shook his head. "Naw, Missy. You ain't never gonna be rid of me. Not for good, leastwise." Glancing around them, an expression of peace settled on his face. "I ain't never been away from Rose Hill. Had me no idea there was pretty country like this in Texas. I figured it was all cotton and corn fields."

Adella knew he was changing the subject and went along. Better to leave the emotional good-byes for later. "The farthest I have traveled is to Austin, and that was ages ago when Mama was still with us." She let out a wistful sigh. Mama had been on her mind often the past three days. She wondered what her mother would think of what she'd done. Would she see it as a betrayal of the family she had cared so much about, or would she understand Adella's need to start a life of her own with a man she loved?

They sat quietly for several minutes. The fire popped and crackled. Cicadas buzzed in the trees, drowning out any birdsong.

"Do you suppose your pappy will sell all them slaves like he say?" Concern shone in Jeptha's eyes when he looked at her.

"I don't know." Adella had asked herself the same question over and over since leaving. "I hope not, but Papa would have been furious when he discovered I was gone. If he does anything rash, it will be my fault."

"Ain't your fault." Jeptha frowned at her. "Massa Luther makes his own decisions, Missy. You may not be one of his slaves, but he treated you like his property just the same. If you'd stayed and married Mr. Brevard, you would've been trading one master for another." He nodded in the direction where Seth had ridden off. "That there Mr. Brantley ain't like them. He may not be like them white folks up north that think we Negros should be free, but he don't got the hatred in him that some whites do."

Adella remained silent, knowing Seth still struggled with a mixture of feelings regarding the runaway slave who shot him—especially now that he himself was involved in helping four slaves escape.

Within the hour, Seth returned. Adella breathed a sigh of relief seeing Chester break through the trees. It made her nervous when Seth rode off alone, searching for provisions and scouting their route for the next day. She rose on stiff legs to greet him, her backside nearly numb from long hours in the saddle.

His tired smile met hers. "There are some German immigrants living a few miles from here." He removed a bulging burlap sack from his saddle. "When I asked about buying some milk, they insisted on giving me bread, sausage, and potatoes as well."

She took the sack from him, peeking in it as though treasures were inside. "Fresh bread." She breathed in the wonderful aroma. "I didn't realize how much I missed Aunt Lu's bread until this very moment."

"Guess I gonna have ta bake some soon as we gets settled." Aunt Lu rose from her slumber and slowly ambled toward them. Apparently, her muscles were as sore as Adella's, for she limped along with stiff movements. She took the bag from Adella. "If y'all wants, I can fry up some o' these taters."

After the past few days of beans and hard biscuits, their little meal that night would be a feast.

Mara began to fuss then. When Adella reached for the canteen of milk still hanging from the saddle horn, Seth caressed her cheek.

"Mara is a lucky little girl to have you for an aunt. You are going to be a wonderful mother someday." The timbre of his voice was low and warm.

"I hope so." She longed for their wild journey to be over so she could become Seth's wife, fully and completely. His eyes told her he felt the same.

After changing Mara's soiled cloth, Adella sat down to feed the baby. Aunt Lu had come up with the method of using one of Adella's handkerchiefs rolled up and wedged into the canteen opening, allowing the milk to soak in. It took a bit of coaxing for Mara to accept it that first day, but she'd become accustomed to the contraption and eagerly filled her tummy with fresh cow's milk. So far she hadn't suffered any problems, which Aunt Lu had warned might happen with the sudden switch from her mother's milk.

Looking into the baby's deep blue eyes, Adella couldn't help but wonder at the love she had already for the tiny girl. Knowing George would have sold the baby, Adella felt nothing but gratitude that they'd been able to whisk her away. Her only regret was knowing Lucy would not be there to raise her daughter as a free woman.

After their delicious supper, while Aunt Lu cleaned things up and Adella and Seth checked the animals, Jeptha and Zina took a short walk. Always staying within sight of the camp, Adella couldn't help but glance their direction every so often, wondering at the seemingly serious discussion.

"What do you suppose they're talking about?" she asked Seth while he curried Freedom. The horses had worked very hard and deserved a little pampering.

Seth glanced over his shoulder at the couple and shrugged. "I imagine they have a lot of sorting out to do. What they'll do when they get to Mexico, where they'll go. I'll offer as much advice as I can, but ultimately, it will be up to them to find their way."

Biting her bottom lip, Adella sighed. "I hope we've done the right thing, bringing them with us." When Seth didn't reply right away, Adella frowned. "Do you wish we hadn't brought them?"

He seemed to think over the question, his hands stilling while he stared off into the night. "I'm not sure. I don't begrudge them their desire for freedom. I can't imagine being owned by someone, with no choice in the matter." His eyes met hers. "But I have broken the law by helping them escape. It used to be my job to hunt down people like us and bring them to justice. At least, the justice prescribed by the law." He ran the curry brush over Freedom's neck. "Part of me knows what we've done is right and good, but the other part isn't so sure."

Adella knew he'd done everything for her, despite his great struggle with it. Placing her hand on his arm, he looked at her. "Thank you, Seth." She hoped her eyes spoke everything her heart couldn't put into words.

He nodded.

A few moments later, Jeptha and Zina made their way over.

"Missy Ellis. Mr. Brantley. We has something we want to say." Jeptha gained their full attention with his serious tone. Glancing at Zina, she gave him a shy smile. He took her hand in his and pulled her closer to his side. "Me and Zina want to get married as soon as we reach Mexico. Seems a good way to start our lives as free Negroes. We ain't asking your permission, being as we're free now." He looked over at Zina, who had love and pride shining in her eyes as she nodded, then back to Seth and Adella. "But we'd be honored if you'd give us your blessing."

"Of course you have our blessing." Adella hurried forward to embrace first Jeptha, then Zina. Tears of happiness rolled down her cheeks, and she laughed. "I have been trying to get you two together for a while now."

Aunt Lu came over then, wiping tears from her face. "I gettin' me another son, Missy. An' this time I ain't gots ta worry none 'bout him bein' sold away."

Adella gathered the precious woman into an embrace, praying all the years of pain and heartache she'd suffered at the hands of Adella's own father would be replaced tenfold with long years of peace and joy—and freedom.

※ ☙

As the eastern horizon filled with rose-colored hues, Seth knew he should wake the others and get the group moving again. They'd been on the trail a little more than a week now with no sign of the search party Seth felt certain Luther Ellis had trailing them. But just because they hadn't seen anyone didn't mean they were safe. Not until they crossed the Rio Grande would Seth feel he could let his guard down.

Yet he stayed where he was, sitting on a boulder just up the rocky hill from where they'd made camp, massaging his painful leg. The vast Texas landscape spread out for miles around him, silhouettes of trees and cacti becoming sharper in the lightening sky. In a short time, the sun would peek over the edge of the world, bringing a new day and all the promise that held. He'd loved mornings like this when he was a Ranger. He'd loved waking up surrounded by God's creation, knowing he was doing exactly what he'd been purposed to do.

The thought did not bring a smile.

Where was that purpose now?

It seemed the farther they rode away from Rose Hill, the guiltier he felt. Leaving with Adella was one thing, but to take four slaves that didn't belong to him weighed heavily on his mind. That he'd come to believe slavery wasn't the moral institution he'd always been taught it was didn't matter. The law was on Luther Ellis's side, and Seth had willingly broken it by helping Jeptha and the others escape. The fact that Adella intended to bring Mara to Oregon with them meant they would continue to be lawbreakers indefinitely. Yet how could he refuse her own flesh and blood, a tiny, helpless baby?

He looked south, toward the Mexican border.

The slaves' new lives awaited them there. He'd been honest when he told Adella he didn't begrudge them their freedom. He was happy for Jeptha and Zina, with their dreams of marriage and raising a family. It was the same dream he and Adella had. *Dreams like that should be for all*, he decided, *not just those with white skin*.

He let out a frustrated sigh.

If he really believed that, then why did he still struggle with guilt? Why did he wonder if they should turn around and face the punishment they deserved for helping slaves escape?

Adella must have sensed his inner battle. She hadn't pressed him but cast worried glances in his direction as they rode mile after mile in silence. Her firm confidence that what they'd done was right and good made his doubts that much more noticeable. And unbearable. He'd grown more withdrawn, to the point he hadn't spoken much to anyone in two days. Jeptha had noticed, as had Aunt Lu. But they'd left him alone, their years as slaves no doubt reminding them a white man's business didn't bear meddling.

"Morning."

Seth turned to find Jeptha standing halfway up the hill. "Morning." He rose from his seat. "I was just coming to wake everyone. Looks like it's going to be another hot one. Best get some miles in before the heat gets too bad."

Jeptha nodded but didn't move toward camp. His brow furrowed, and he worked the twig he'd stuck in the corner of his mouth.

"I can tell you have something you want to say," Seth said after a few beats.

"Yes, sir, I do." He closed the distance between them, tossing the twig to the ground. "Fact is, sir, I gets me the feeling you're wishing you hadn't taken on this here journey, helping us get to ol' Mexico."

Seth's brow raised at the candid statement. It was as though Jeptha had read his very thoughts. Thinking of the black man as an equal rather than a subservient slave would take some getting used to. With that being the case, Seth figured Jeptha deserved the same type of candidness. "You're right. I am. I have never broken the law before, and I'm finding it doesn't sit well with me to do so now."

Several silent moments ticked by.

"You thinking you'll turn us in?" Worry slowed Jeptha's words.

Seth shook his head. "No." He knew his answer was true despite his inner struggle. "The price of clearing my guilty conscience is too great. You and Zina and Aunt Lu—and even little Mara—all deserve freedom."

Jeptha visibly relaxed. "I'm glad to hear that, Mr. Brantley."

"But it doesn't change the fact that what I've done is wrong."

"In whose eyes?" Jeptha's gaze pierced him. "The white man says he can own us Negroes, but did anyone ask us? Did Massa Luther ask me if I wanted to belong to him? To slave hour after hour, day after day, for his gain? Just because I born with black skin don't give no one the right to *own* me like I some kind of animal. Don't matter what the *law* say. It matter what I say, and I say freedom is meant for everyone, not just white folks."

The impassioned speech hit Seth in the gut. To hear a slave demand freedom should have frightened him, but instead, it broke something inside, down deep in his soul.

Suddenly, the memory of the man who shot him filled his mind. Seth had hunted him down like an animal. He'd had no intention of treating the man like a human being. The law was on Seth's side, and he'd prided himself on carrying it out. But what of the man who simply yearned for freedom? Who'd risked everything—like Jeptha and the others were doing now—to grasp what Seth and every other white person took for granted?

He looked at Jeptha, but it was really the dead runaway lying on the ground at the Mexican border that he saw. A man he hadn't known, and would never know, but who'd impacted his life in the most profound way imaginable. Seth had believed the man ruined his life.

How wrong he'd been.

"I'm sorry," he rasped, the knot of hatred he'd carried in his heart for over a year unraveling and flowing out of him like water from a spring. "I'm sorry for what I did to you."

Jeptha nodded, seeming to sense a deeper meaning in the words. "I 'spect we all has things we need to ask forgiveness for. Things we's ashamed of. Don't matter what color of skin covers your bones. Least that's what Mammy always said."

Seth appreciated his understanding. Maybe someday he'd tell Jeptha about the man at the border. A man, like Jeptha's father, who'd died chasing after freedom. He sent a silent plea heavenward, praying Jeptha would not end up like them.

They made their way down the hill and back to camp where the women were busy rolling blankets and preparing a light meal before they resumed the long journey. Together, Jeptha and Seth moved toward the horses to get them saddled. After several minutes, Jeptha glanced at Seth, a puzzled look on his face.

"Guess your leg is feeling better this morning," he said.

Seth paused, confused. "Not really. Why?"

Jeptha nodded toward Seth's leg. "You ain't limping."

Looking down at his leg, Seth realized the constant pain wasn't there. He rubbed his thigh. The muscles weren't tender the way they'd been for over a year. Sitting in the saddle the past week had brought untold misery, and Seth knew his limp had been more pronounced. Adella had worried over him just last night, voicing her concern that he needed to take a day to rest his leg.

Baffled, he walked away from Chester, turned, and came back. No limp. No pain. Nothing but two normal functioning legs.

"I don't know what to make of it." He looked at Jeptha, who clearly seemed as bewildered as Seth. "I could barely get up that hill a little while ago. Now ..." He stared at his leg. "It doesn't hurt at all."

Jeptha shrugged and went back to work, but Seth stood staring at the place up the rise where he and Jeptha had talked. He remembered that the throbbing pain in his leg was present while he watched the sunrise. It was present when Jeptha asked if Seth planned to turn them in. But he couldn't remember feeling the pain when they returned to camp.

It struck him then what had happened.

The pain disappeared the moment he forgave the slave who had shot him.

CHAPTER THIRTY-TWO

The Rio Grande lay before them, brown and murky and beautiful. Oh, so beautiful. Against so many odds, they'd made it safely into Mexico.

Three weeks, Seth thought. Three long, exhausting weeks had passed since the night they rode away from Rose Hill. Patrols had dogged them the entire way, coming far too close on more than one occasion. Ironically, it had been his experience as a Texas Ranger that saved them. Knowing the trails and roads to stay off, and locating sympathetic Tejanos who offered them shelter and food, he'd kept the little group traveling west and then south. Finding enough milk for Mara was a challenge, and once when the canteen they'd filled at the last homestead ran empty, a Cherokee woman living with her white husband and young child offered to nurse the baby. Every step of the way, it seemed that God was looking after them, and he couldn't help but think the prayers of Moses and Aunt Lu were somehow reaching heaven.

Adella came up beside him, cradling a wide-eyed Mara. She smiled. "The reverend is here."

Seth glanced behind her to their camp in the cottonwoods lining the river. Jeptha and Zina stood talking to a tall, thin man. Aunt Lu stirred a pot of beans over an open fire. Their little family, as they'd taken to referring to themselves over the past weeks, were safe. They'd crossed the river at dusk yesterday, just down from Fort Duncan. The town of Eagle Pass, where Reverend Peterson had traveled from, lay upstream. Earlier that morning, Seth had ridden in for supplies and stopped by the mission he remembered from his Ranger days. The preacher was happy to cross the river and perform two wedding ceremonies.

Seth put his arm around Adella's waist and drew her close. "I was just thinking how amazing it is that we're here. All of us."

"Yes." Adella leaned her head against his shoulder. "I thought all was lost several times." She pulled away to look him in the eyes. "But you kept us safe, Seth. None of us could have made it without you."

Knowing this beautiful woman would be his wife within the hour stirred Seth's blood. He smoothed her soft cheek with his thumb. "No regrets?"

"None. I pray Papa will forgive me someday, but my future is with you."

Together they walked back to camp. While the women talked with the reverend, Jeptha approached Seth.

"I want to thank you for what you done for us, Mr. Brantley. I can't hardly believe it, but here I stand ... a free man." He shook his head, getting his emotions under control. "I dreamed about this day for so long." With a laugh, he added, "But I sho' didn't have no white man in my dreams."

Seth smiled. It felt good knowing he'd helped Jeptha and the others escape bondage. It felt good down deep, to that place where he'd made peace with the man who shot him. And with God.

He extended his hand to Jeptha. "I'm proud to call you friend. If all goes well, I plan to start a horse farm in Oregon. If you ever want a job breaking horses, you've got one with me."

Jeptha looked at the offered hand then met Seth's gaze. He grinned and grasped Seth's hand. "Thank you. I just might do that."

They made their way over to the women. Seth came alongside Adella, who looked beautiful in the rose-colored gown she'd brought along especially for their wedding ceremony.

"Are you ready to become Mrs. Brantley?" he whispered close to her ear.

The love and hope that shone from her eyes when she looked

at him warmed him down to his dusty boots. "I have been ready since the day you rode into Rose Hill, looking far more handsome than any man should."

He raised his brow. "Oh, you have, have you?" He planted a kiss on the end of her nose then cocked his head to look down at her feet. "There's just one thing I need to check before the ceremony."

"What?" she asked, clearly puzzled.

"Just making sure my bride is wearing her shoes."

Acknowledgments

Two dear people who made this book possible will never see its publication. Long before I was born, my parents, Albert and Ann Chaparro, loved Jesus and they loved books. I am eternally grateful they passed both loves on to me. Thank you, Mom and Daddy. I know you'd be proud of your baby girl. If heaven has a library, I'll know where to find you when I get there.

To my husband Brian, I would not want to take this journey without you. Thank you for always believing in me. Thank you for being my chauffeur and for patiently touring old plantations, farms, forts, museums, and antique stores. Adventure awaits, my love.

To Taylor and Austin, although the publication of a book is an exciting achievement, you, my sons, are my greatest accomplishment. God has amazing plans and purposes for each of you, and I'm so honored to be your mom.

Thank you to my agent, Les Stobbe, the champion of new authors. Your wisdom and experience are surpassed only by your deep faith in God.

To my editor, Kathy Davis, thank you for believing in this book and for making my first journey into the world of book publishing a delightful experience. Thank you to Eddie Jones, publisher, for giving me this opportunity. Many thanks to all the staff at LPC who worked on this book in various ways. I am blessed to be part of the LPC family.

Thank you to Paula Bicknell, the best critique and prayer partner a girl could ask for. You challenge me to be a better writer. I'm so tickled we are on this journey together.

To my fellow authors at American Christian Fiction Writers, thank you for your friendships, your knowledge and the willingness to share it at conferences, and for the amazing examples of what it means to be a writer for the Kingdom.

To all my friends and family who have asked about my writing over the years, encouraged me to keep going, and waited patiently for my first book, thank you! I hope you enjoy this book enough to ask about the sequel.

Although I used many resources in my research, one book in particular deserves a shout out. *I Was Born in Slavery: Personal Accounts of Slavery in Texas*, edited by Andrew Waters, provided priceless true narratives of former Texas slaves. Reading their own words, and hearing their voices in my mind, served to remind me how important it is to tell the story of Texas slaves with as much accuracy as possible. I named many characters after actual slaves to honor their memory.

Above all, thank you to my Savior, Jesus Christ, for loving me enough to carry my sins to the cross. To Him be all the glory.